THE SCHOLAR OF EXTORTION

The Scholar of Extortion

REG GADNEY

faber and faber

First published in 2003
by Faber and Faber Limited
3 Queen Square London WC1N 3AU

Typeset by Faber and Faber
Printed in England by Clays Ltd, St Ives plc

A CIP record for this book
is available from the British Library

ISBN 0–571–22076–2 (cased)
ISBN 0–571–21783–4 (paperback)

2 4 6 8 10 9 7 5 3 1

For Fay with love

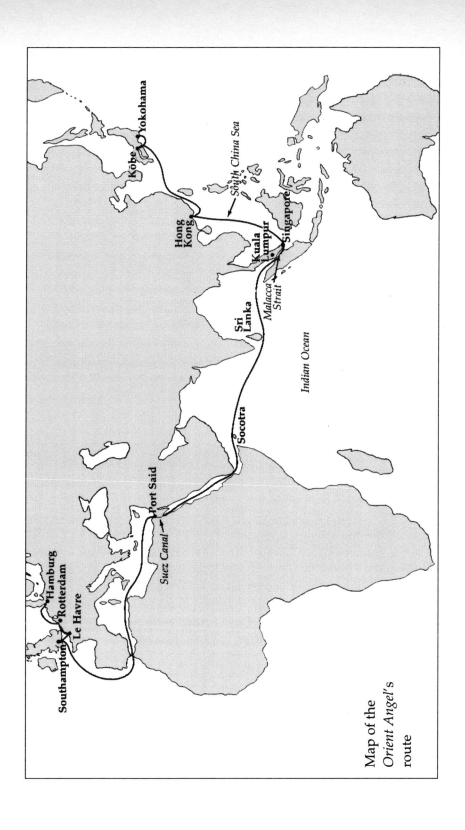

Map of the
Orient Angel's
route

Study as though the time were short, as one who fears to lose.
CONFUCIUS

I once acted for the defence of a spy whose trial at the Old Bailey was mostly held *in camera*. Matters of national security were involved. As it turned out the jury found the man guilty and he was sent to prison for a long stretch. After the man had been sentenced the judge requested that I, as counsel for the defence, along with counsel for the prosecution visit him in his room. There, we were introduced to an officer from the security service. The man from the security service explained that he was required to let us read what he called the Damage Report, a document of the utmost secrecy. He was required to show it to us no matter what the outcome of the trial might have been. The Damage Report was the precise and detailed outline of the damage the prisoner had done to national security. It made for rather chilling reading and, to some considerable degree, alleviated the initial disappointment I felt when the jury returned its verdict.

GEORGE CARMAN QC
TO THE AUTHOR
9 APRIL 2000

ONE

The Winter

STATEMENT OF WITNESS

[Criminal Justice Act 1967, s.9]

Statement of: Alan Rosslyn
Age of Witness: over 21
Occupation: Private Investigator
Address: Basement Flat,
                    195 Claverton Street,
                    London SW1

This statement consisting of 2 pages signed by me is true to
the best of my knowledge and belief and I make it knowing that
if it is tendered in evidence, I shall be liable to prosecution
if I wilfully state anything which I know to be false.

Of the major criminals I've encountered, I believe
the international maritime terrorist Klaas-Pieter
Terajima to be the most dangerous. He's a psychotic
murderer.
     You could say that our paths crossed because of
my close friendship with Inspector Winston Lim of
the Hong Kong Police. Or on a personal level
because I subsequently fell in love with Winston's
adopted daughter Mei.
     I first visited Hong Kong when I was a special
investigations officer with HM Customs & Excise.
That was when I first met the Lim family. It was
some time later, after I had left Customs & Excise
and became a private investigator, that I went to
Hong Kong for the funeral of Winston's wife,
Kitty.
     I remember that it was at Kitty's funeral that I
made this solemn promise to Winston Lim. If anything untoward happened to him I promised to keep

3

watch over Mei. 'Until hell freezes?' he said. I
told him: Yes. I owed him my life. It has always
seemed to me the very least I could have done for
him.

Signed: *Alan Rosslyn*

Signature witnessed by: Chief Superintendent Ronald Costley

Signed: *Ron Costley*

Signature witnessed by: WPC Michelle Seifert

Signed: *Michelle Seifert*

TROPICAL CYCLONE WARNING

AT 11.18 GMT, TYPHOON YANYAN WITH CENTRAL PRESSURE 970 HECTOPASCALS CENTRED WITHIN 60 NAUTICAL MILES OF ONE THREE POINT SIX DEGREES NORTH, ONE ZERO NINE POINT TWO DEGREES EAST AND IS FORECAST TO MOVE WEST AT ABOUT 8 KNOTS FOR THE NEXT 24 HOURS. MAXIMUM WINDS NEAR THE CENTRE ARE ESTIMATED TO BE 65 KNOTS.

The veteran Hong Kong police inspector Winston Lim steadied himself against the turbulence of Typhoon Yanyan. The storm was buffeting the Jetstream-41 aircraft with dreadful force. Peering down at the fury of the South China Sea, Winston watched the wind driving white streams of spray from the summits of the waves. Sheer and almost vertical, the waves rose up to heights of fifty, even sixty, feet and then toppled down into measureless black hollows.

'Okay?' Winston said to Xiao Qingze, the frightened young police officer seated next to him in the aisle seat.

Xiao was struggling to open a can of cold green tea. 'Yes, sir.'

'When we feel happy, Xiao – what do we tell each other?'

'We feel happy, sir.'

Green tea dribbled from Xiao's shaking lips. He looked miserable.

'Here,' said Winston. 'Take my hand. You're safe.'

Xiao held Winston's hand tight. 'I'm sorry, sir.'

'Feeling the fear's nothing to be ashamed of,' said Winston. 'Think of the poor bastards down there.'

Neither Winston nor Xiao, the young police officer on temporary secondment from Beijing and visiting observer of Winston's investigations into maritime terrorism, could make out any sign of the vessel reported to be in distress, the Chinese cargo ship MV *Xiang Chuan*.

'*Xiang Chuan*'s down there somewhere,' Winston said.

'I'd like to think you're right, inspector,' said Xiao. 'If *Xiang Chuan* has sunk,' he added, 'there's not a chance in hell of any of her crew surviving that.'

'I know,' said Winston.

'Sir?' Xiao said.

'I said, "I know" and don't piss your pants.'

'Yes, sir.' He withdrew his hand from Winston's.

'You mean no,' said Winston. 'Think of the typhoon as a cobra. The genus *Naja*. Rats attract it. Swallows them whole. The venom acts rapidly on the nervous system. Imagine it in bed with you at home. It raises the head. Spits the toxins. You freeze in fear. You should've dodged. If you didn't, then – *zip-eee-dee-do-dah*. She has you. Blinds you with its poison. Maritime terrorists are like cobras too. Don't feel the fear, Xiao. Feel it and you're gone.'

Xiao offered no comment and Winston continued to stare at the violence of the sea a few hundred feet below. *There's not a chance in hell of any of her crew surviving that.* The less experienced police officer Xiao was probably right. But Winston wanted to prove him wrong.

'We don't even know how many crew are aboard,' said Xiao.

'I know,' said Winston. 'I know.'

'You know?' Xiao said. 'You didn't say.'

'I said I don't know how many crew are on board,' Winston said more loudly than he intended.

'You have to be sure of that, sir,' said Xiao.

'Don't you panic. I heard you, sonny. I heard you.'

Winston had a fair idea of how many desperate men must be down there fighting for survival. He was not about to speculate or engage Xiao further.

It was not that he disliked Xiao, just that sometimes he found him tiresome. There was something knowing about him. A know-all, an ambitious young man, Xiao was pushy, too deferential. Too pleased, not only with his own abilities, but because he knew that Beijing now had the upper hand when it came to law enforcement policy. Too much control and interference by the party. And Xiao knew that Winston knew. Still, Winston quite liked him. You couldn't deny his dedication. In Xiao's shoes and at his age, he must have been similar.

True, Winston had wearied of Xiao remarking upon what he already knew. Xiao was the sort of young police officer who always seemed to repeat what you said as if he were taking down evidence in support of his own reputation and career and status. Presumably, Xiao thought that such repetitions elevated him to the status of expert. If Winston had him in his department, he would by now have taught the young man the lessons in humility that even some veteran police officers never seem to learn. To be fair, Xiao was honest, keen, fit and probably much more intelligent than he seemed on first acquaintance. Moreover, as the Commissioner had said, it was a feather in the cap of the Hong Kong police service that Beijing had specifically named Winston as the officer they wanted Xiao to shadow.

Winston was Number One Enemy of the maritime terrorists in South East Asia. He had spent a decade at war with the most violent of the seagoing criminals. By day he hunted them by land and sea. By night he pored over the statements of supergrasses. He had succeeded in bringing at least a dozen of the most dangerous maritime terrorists to justice.

Winston thought briefly of his best friend and colleague, Steve Kwok. He wished Steve were here with him. It was with Kwok that he reviewed the best secret information about the enemy. They acted fast, always knowing that the information they gleaned soon dated. Steve shared Winston's dedication to the work; like Winston, he seemed to have inexhaustible reserves of energy. They shared a code of unspoken phrases and subtle voice inflections. Their dialogues were intellectual exercises. They paralleled the way in which Winston and Steve dealt with their supergrasses. Pragmatists, their approach had nothing to do with ideological abstraction. Their social lives were limited. They were always careful to avoid discussing cases in restaurants or hotels. It was all too easy inadvertently to let slip names and places. They also avoided discussing personal matters. Unreconstructed, as some might say, they left family matters to their wives. The arrests and the prosecutions had continued until, without warning, progress was halted.

Steve had been taken, literally off the street in Hong Kong, and tortured by the nameless head of a maritime terrorist syndicate. The same day, masked men confronted Steve's wife Catherine on her doorstep. They took a blowtorch to her face. Now terribly disfigured, it was a miracle that she had survived and that the doctors had saved her sight. The injuries to Steve's feet had been so severe that the doctors had no alternative. They amputated both feet.

Winston was shaken to the core. *Poor Steve. Poor Catherine. Poor all of us.*

We don't even know how many crew are aboard.

What Xiao had said about MV *Xiang Chuan* was true. Ever since the duty officers at the Maritime Rescue Co-ordination Centre had responded to the distress call, they had tried – and failed – to establish the number of crew aboard. What Xiao did not know, however, was that Winston was convinced there were maritime terrorists aboard the vessel and that Winston wanted to nail them.

'There's even confusion about the ownership of the vessel,' said Xiao. He took a sudden breath as the aircraft jumped, juddered and tilted like a child's toy kite. He felt as if he'd been punched in the solar plexus.

'Yes,' said Winston, 'there's always confusion in these sorts of operation. It's not like it is in story books, sonny. Remember, Xiao, the manuals may tell you that effective police work is neat and tidy. Take it from me, it isn't. You have to expect the unexpected. Only, please – don't piss your pants.'

Winston sensed Xiao's acute lack of comfort. Years back he would probably have felt the same.

Xiao squeezed his bladder muscles. But the lurching of the plane defeated his efforts to control the gush. Xiao felt the flow of warm urine seeping into the fabric of the seat.

Winston glanced at Xiao, who was now struggling against the turbulence to make a note of Winston's remarks. He wrote slowly, like a schoolboy, with the cheap police issue ballpoint pen held in his left hand like a stage dagger. Winston pitied Xiao his unnecessary diligence. Unusually for a police officer, Winston rarely took notes. Whether the solution to a crime in the line of duty required theoretical or practical expertise, Winston was very rarely proved wrong. He trusted intuition, memory and know-how, and when it came to using force – he relied on his formidable reserves of physical strength and fitness.

He glanced at his waterproof watch and calculated the time since the MRCC had ordered the Jetstream to its present whereabouts. By now it had flown to a position some four hundred or so nautical miles south east of Hong Kong.

'Have we wet ourselves, sonny?'

'No, sir.'

'Promise me?'

'Yes, sir.'

'It's the tea,' Winston advised him. 'Green tea is a diuretic.'

'Sir?'

'You drink too much green tea, sonny boy.'

How long was it since the crew of the Jetstream had fixed the location of the distress signal by electronic means? Thirty minutes? Maybe longer. The pilot, co-pilot, crew and Winston should have seen something by now. That's if there was something down there to see.

The cloud base lowered. The monstrous waves and the winds were so powerful they contributed to what was called an IRM or Increased Risk Mission. In layman's terms, an IRM is a mission that will find no survivors. Even so, as it had been ordered, the Jetstream searched the raging ocean at the lowest altitude the storm clouds allowed.

Winston finally saw something unusual in the cauldron below.

'Look, Xiao, down there. At five o'clock. Look. See?'

'What is it?' said Xiao.

'What do you think it is?' Winston asked.

'You tell me,' said Xiao.

'It's a strobe light,' Winston said.

'A flashing strobe light, sir.'

'Yes,' said Winston. 'That's what strobe lights do. They flash.'

'They flash,' said Xiao.

'Yes, Xiao,' said Winston. 'They flash.' He wanted to tell Xiao he sounded like a parrot, but the voice of the pilot in his headphones prevented him from doing so.

He was about to tell the pilot what he thought must be the position of the labouring ship when the co-pilot's voice sounded in Winston's headphones. The co-pilot said, 'We can't identify the vessel, sir.'

'Let's try again,' said Winston.

'We're getting low on fuel.'

Winston got the message. Low on fuel. In other words, it's no more use. We have to head for home. 'Drop a marker buoy,' he said. 'Do what you have to do.'

'What does he have to do?' asked Xiao.

'Later, sonny. Later, please –'

9

The radio marker buoy was dropped into the ocean and, changing course, the Jetstream headed back to Hong Kong International Airport.

'Are you a really happy cop?' said Winston.

'Yes, sir,' said Xiao. 'Are you?'

'Sometimes.'

2

It was not unusual for Winston Lim to be aboard any of the Government Flying Service fixed wing aeroplanes on such a mission above the South China Sea. The planes often operated far out to sea in support of the Narcotics Bureau, searching for or tracking suspected drug-smuggling trawlers. These operations resulted in either deterring trawlers from reaching Hong Kong or facilitating arrests and seizures of illicit cargo. Winston had co-ordinated more operations like these than he cared to remember. He had an impressive record of success.

He made regular use of the Government Flying Service aircraft to monitor the movement of illegal immigrants or those engaged in maritime terrorism, the modern and more terrible equivalent of maritime piracy. He flew on such missions either in one of the Sikorsky H-60 helicopters or in one of the Jetstreams, which were capable of operating farther out to sea.

Unusual circumstances surrounded the search for the MV *Xiang Chuan*. Circumstances and details that, on this occasion, Winston had kept to himself.

It had been ostensibly to go on a search and rescue mission that, late in the afternoon, Winston accompanied by Xiao had boarded the Jetstream in the security restricted area of Hong Kong International Airport.

There was, so Winston had been told by a reliable informant, a fair chance that members of a maritime terrorist cell were among the crew of the MV *Xiang Chuan*.

The cell had used the vessel before, one of several small ships its members used for clandestine travel between mainland China and Hong Kong. With members of the cell apparently aboard, according to his source, the MV *Xiang Chuan* had even been seen in the Malacca Strait and Indonesian waters. Winston regarded them as personal enemies. His personal targets. The arrest of these maritime terrorists would represent a pinnacle of achievement in his already distinguished career.

The operation to find MV *Xiang Chuan* had been a combined search, rescue and, into the bargain, arrest operation. The triple combination also represented something of a first for Winston. He was determined it would be successful. But even he knew that the major obstacle facing him was the natural one: Typhoon Yanyan. Now it forced him home.

3

The plane landed with a thud on the reserved runway at Chek Lap Kok, Hong Kong's international airport. The turbines roared in reverse and slowed the ground speed.

'Home again, sonny,' said Winston, hiding his disappointment.

'Home, sir,' said Xiao.

'Except for us there's no such thing as home. Home is where we are right now, praise be. Where we are right now. Look at those lights. Ever since I was a boy I've loved them.'

Xiao made a note. He hoped the inspector would fail to see the damp patch he'd left on the seat. It was his bad luck to have been given the aisle seat. He would have to get out first and Winston Lim would see the traces of his incontinence.

When they left the plane, Winston glanced at the wet patch and said nothing about it. Xiao understood why so many people had great affection for Winston Lim.

4

Next morning, the Jetstream returned to the previous location with neither Winston nor Xiao aboard.

Winston had been summoned to lecture to students taking a course in maritime terrorism at the Police Training School at Wong Chuk Hang in Aberdeen. The course was the pet project of the Commissioner of Police. Winston's request that it be postponed was declined. Perhaps, he reckoned, the Commissioner was thinking of Beijing and the presence of government officials, selected foreign diplomats and local journalists.

The Commissioner said, 'You mustn't disappoint our invitees, and especially the students.'

'But sir –'

'You're our man, inspector. There's no but about it. Do it.'

The Commissioner could tell that Winston wanted to be elsewhere.

The notice on the door to the lecture hall said:

For the benefit of his audience in the lecture hall, Winston had pinned some enlarged text on the display board beside the lectern:

PIRACY CONSISTS OF ANY OF THE FOLLOWING ACTS

a) any illegal acts of violence or detention, or any act of depredation, committed for private ends by the crew or the passengers of a private ship or a private aircraft, and directed

  (i) on the high seas, against another ship or aircraft, against persons or property on board such ship or aircraft;
  (ii) against a ship, aircraft, persons or property in a place outside the jurisdiction of any State;

b) any act of voluntary participation in the operation of a ship or an aircraft with knowledge of facts making it a pirate ship or aircraft;

c) any act of inciting or of intentionally facilitating an act described in subparagraphs (a) or (b)

ARTICLE 101
PROVISIONS OF UNITED NATIONS CONVENTION
ON THE LAW OF THE SEA
TO BE TREATED AS PART OF THE LAW OF NATIONS

* * *

Winston held his audience rapt. His reputation as a hands-on police officer went before him. As a lecturer, he was popular because he treated the students as his equals – which, of course, they knew they weren't. He adopted an anecdotal style and throughout his talk he tested the audience with questions and answers.

'Attacks by maritime terrorists against major commercial ships have increased during the last year. By how much? Anyone?'

'They've doubled,' said a young woman in the front row.

'No,' said Winston. 'They've almost *trebled* to three hundred a year. During last year alone, almost a hundred merchant marine crew members have been brutally murdered in South East Asian waters. The new international maritime crime syndicates ensure that their people are well armed, well equipped and highly professional practitioners of the mercenary's skills. They're violent high seas terrorists. They take no prisoners. We aren't talking about pirates. That's what governments and insurers call these criminals because they want to play down the threats. We're talking about MTs. Maritime terrorists. Sometimes they are politically motivated. Sometimes they are financed and given succour by highly organised and streamlined networks of global commercial conglomerates.'

The editor of the Hong Kong based newsletter *Maritime Confidential* was on his feet.

'George Tsang. *Maritime Confidential*. I have a question. Which conglomerates are you thinking of?'

Winston was not about to name them, even for his sightless friend Tsang.

'Such people should know better, George,' said Winston. 'But some people never learn. They take risks. They don't heed the consequences. Money dictates what they do. Let's take two examples.'

A colour transparency of *Manju Alpha*, a new ship of ten thousand tonnes deadweight was projected on to the screen.

'*Manju Alpha* fell victim to a surprise attack by twenty armed men shortly after she had left Kuala Tanjung in Indonesia. She was carrying a cargo of aluminium ingots worth twenty million US dollars. She'd been bound for Kobe in Japan. The masked raiders threatened the Mexican captain and his crew with extreme violence. The master, with a machete at his throat, had no alternative but to tell his twenty-four Japanese and Filipino crew members to surrender. Bound hand and foot, the crew were gagged, blindfolded and dumped into rubber inflatable boats. They were left to drift for two weeks, until a Thai fishing vessel finally rescued them. The Thais found them starving, dehydrated, near death. And what happened? Nothing.'

Now he saw the man from the Australian High Commission on his feet.

'Dr Burnal Graer. Australian High Commission.'

Winston had no time for Graer, whose personal predilections had attracted the attentions of South East Asia undercover officers monitoring the tourist sex trade.

'Can you throw any light on the mystery of where *Manju Alpha* ended up?' asked Dr Graer.

What, for reasons of political sensitivity, Winston could not say in so many words was that he suspected the hijacked ship and cargo had made its way to mainland China. The network of minor ports, combined with the corruption endemic among the Chinese customs hierarchy, has created the world's most thriving market for stolen cargoes.

'We cannot be sure,' said Winston.

'Can you tell us what happened to the master?' Graer asked.

It was rumoured that Graer had been an acquaintance of the man.

'Eventually,' Winston replied, 'a charge of smuggling drugs was brought against him. Then it was dropped and he was released. The raiders were repatriated to Indonesia.'

Here again, Winston omitted to say that there were indications of a high degree of organisation and a suspicion that the Chinese authorities had colluded in the attack. The Chinese maintained they had insufficient evidence to prosecute the raiders. Winston had little doubt that criminal western interests controlling maritime terrorist groups were behind the attacks.

Winston continued, 'A spate of bloody attacks ensued throughout the region. Take the *Vanonlan Deng*. Does anyone recognise the name?'

No one recognised it.

The image of *Vanonlan Deng* was projected on the screen.

'She was seized just outside the waters of Hong Kong. Her twenty-four crew members were shot and dumped at sea, and a dozen of the bodies were eventually retrieved in the nets of Fujianese fishermen.'

Once again, what Winston could not say was that the Chinese announced they had apprehended the mastermind behind this and other attacks. The Chinese never named him.

'That the *Vanonlan Deng* was never found points up the ease with which sea raiders can hide a ship's whereabouts. They had simply painted out the ship's name. They changed the registration papers in Belize or Honduras or Panama. And, as far as we know, they docked the renamed *Vanonlan Deng* in Zhangjiagang. A ship's paperwork is easy to forge. The cargo had already, quite legitimately, changed hands several times in transit. Innumerable copies had changed hands between shipping agents, consignees, stevedores, owners and customs officials.'

Here there was a break for questions from his audience. Winston took a question from a woman student. 'Was the stolen cargo traced?'

'No, it wasn't.'

Winston refrained from saying that, with the rule of law either weak or non-existent on the southern Chinese coastline, the stolen cargoes easily found their way to corporations who asked no questions about such very low-priced commodities. Then again, some of the cargoes were chemical substances of the greatest value and affordable only by nation states.

An American woman announced herself as Birgit Swann. Winston knew her to be a CIA officer. She was a friend of Graer's and not a woman Winston trusted.

Swann asked, 'Surely there's been an increase in security provisions about such ships?'

'I can only tell you', Winston said, 'that the world's shipping lines are ignoring security aboard their ships to an extent that's as dangerous as it's irresponsible. The reasons for this are easily explained. For a start, no single international agency co-ordinates the patterns of major maritime crime. We are talking in billions of US dollars. Nation states and law enforcement agencies remain extraordinarily indifferent to mayhem at sea. When it comes to maritime crime, few police forces show any genuine inclination to co-operate with those of other countries.'

'With the exception of Hong Kong?' the American woman said.

'I like to think so,' said Winston. 'Most frequently, shipping lines show a deep reluctance to report crimes at sea that might destroy the confidence of clients. Investigations take time, time is money, and with competition increasing at a pace among international traders, such investigations damage profit margins. The British are particularly adept at issuing official statistics that cover up the seriousness of the problem. Meanwhile, for maritime terrorists, it's oceans wide.'

A man who, by way of introducing himself, said '*Chinese People's Daily*', asked, 'Can you give us an example of the most dangerous areas?'

'Yes, I can indeed,' said Winston. 'With the sole exception of the Dover Strait, the Malacca Strait is the world's busiest and most congested commercial shipping lane. Some six hundred ships a day pass through it. The variety of cargoes includes toxic chemicals, radioactive substances and crude oil. Whether anyone likes it or not, Japan alone reprocesses over ninety per cent of its nuclear material in Europe. Shipment of this material is through the Malacca Strait.'

A map of South East Asia was projected on to the screen.

Pointing at the map, Winston continued, 'Five hundred or so miles in length, the Malacca Strait is the longest strait in the world used by international maritime commercial interests. It effectively links the Indian Ocean with the China Sea. It's the shortest route for ships trading between the Middle East and Asian countries. As you'll appreciate, the waterway connects the territorial waters of Indonesia, Malaysia and Thailand to the shorter Singapore Strait at the southern end. The strait varies from two hundred miles to eleven miles in width and from seventy to less than ten metres in depth. Any questions?'

From the back of the lecture hall, a young woman said, 'Why can't the littoral states – Singapore, Malaysia and Indonesia – agree on a better system of security?'

'Would you give your name, please?' Winston said.

'Mei Lim, sir.'

'A very good question, Mei Lim.'

Mei Lim was his daughter and Winston had not expected her to be here.

'First, consider these crucial facts. Sea traffic in the Malacca Strait comprises thousands upon thousands of small craft. Fishing vessels. Tankers and bulk carriers. Tankers with deep draughts. There are container ships with greater capabilities of speed. Gas, chemical and petroleum tankers travel between the major refineries of South East Asia. Barges and passenger ferries.

'Second, the littoral states can't even agree to spendUS$30 million to build what's really a marine electronic highway, embracing charts with real time updating and identification of the sort you have in the world-wide aviation industry. They argue that ships from almost every seagoing nation in the world use the Strait. So why shouldn't everyone else pay? Confusion reigns. The Japanese have made the only really valuable contribution to navigational aids. When it comes to funding the war against maritime terrorism, the issue of national sovereignty raises its cobra-like head. The littoral states don't want to pay out the money at the time, as they don't want to yield control of what's a major strategic waterway. Each year many billions of US dollars worth of goods and services are transported through the Strait of Malacca and the related shipping routes of the Strait of Makasar, Lombok and the South China Sea. Does that answer your question, Miss Lim?'

'Very thoroughly,' said Mei. 'Thank you, sir.'

'How long does a vessel take to transit the strait southbound to Singapore?' Winston asked her.

'Two days and nights,' Mei said.

'Correct. So let's take an interesting example. A ship entering the Malacca Strait from Sumatra. During the first day she'll approach One Fathom Bank with some two hundred miles of the most treacherous seaway of the Strait ahead. I don't have to tell you that masters and watch keepers are under very considerable stress indeed. Skilled watch keeping is required to navigate the Strait, including general surveillance of the ship. The bridge watch should consist of at least one officer qualified to take charge of a navigational watch and at least one qualified or experienced seaman. Qualified deck officers should permit the master to take rests from regular watches. For deep draught vessels navigation must be precise. Why?'

George Tsang answered, 'Such vessels require staging in order to meet the tidal window at a specified time over areas of critical depths.'

'Why?'

'Transits must be timed to pass such controlling areas not more than thirty minutes either side of high water –'

'Okay, that's fine, George –'

Winston paused. He had noticed a woman clerk approaching the lectern. 'Excuse me a moment, ladies and gentlemen –' Winston said.

The woman clerk whispered to him. 'There's an urgent call for you, sir.'

'Who is it?'

'Maritime Rescue Co-ordination Centre.'

'Give me one more minute –

'Given the density of traffic congestion,' Winston continued. 'Given the cross traffic, fishing vessels and innumerable local craft in narrow channels at One Fathom Bank, Port Dickson, Philip Channel and Middle Channel in the area of Horsburgh Lighthouse, we are presented with a very dangerous situation. So, you see, the maritime terrorists have a great natural advantage. I regret I must end here . . . Finally, remember, we're fighting a war against unseen enemies. Some of the most shadowy and violent individuals are engaged twenty-four hours a day in organised murder, theft, violence, coercion and extortion. They have the upper hand. For how long they will continue to maintain their supremacy is a matter for conjecture. We are short of resources. Short of manpower. Above all, we are short of counter-intelligence. As for my colleagues, they share with me an absolute determination to fight and win.

There was applause as he left the podium. The lights were raised, Winston caught Mei's eye and they smiled at each other. She was young and very pretty. Some of the students who had no idea who Mei was gave Winston knowing looks.

Outside the lecture hall he followed the clerk to the nearest telephone.

6

The officer of the Maritime Rescue Co-ordination Centre was on the line.

'The pilot of the Jetstream has spotted a capsized lifeboat, survival dinghies and life jackets floating on the waves. There are no signs of survivors. There are additional rescue services committed to the search, including a Philippine military plane. The nearby Chinese vessel, *Yuqihai*, has picked up several members of the missing crew of the Cuban freighter *Cajio Atlantico*. Another vessel has sent out an SOS signal within range of Hong Kong. There's a chance the mayday could be from the *Xiang Chuan*.'

'Has her identity been confirmed?'

'No.'

It struck Winston as suspicious that, the vessel having sent out a mayday, its identity was as yet unknown.

'I want a car to take Xiao and me to the airport. I want it now.'

7

TROPICAL CYCLONE WARNING

YANYAN. ALL POINTS THREAT. UNUSUAL MOTION
NOTED ALONG FORECAST TRACK.

Later that afternoon, with Typhoon Yanyan still raging across
the South China Sea, the Government Flying Service ordered the
dispatch of a Sikorsky H-60 helicopter to join the search of the area
where the *Xiang Chuan* was now thought to be. The report said that
the *Beijing Handong*, a Chinese heavylift cargo carrier, was now in the
area. She was laden with oilfield equipment. She too had taken a
severe pounding in the storm.

The Sikorsky was scheduled to depart within the hour and the
flying conditions were appalling.

Summoned by telephone, the rescue team assembled at the Hong
Kong International Airport along with Winston and Xiao. They gathered in the briefing room, where the pilot, co-pilot and crew chief were
discussing the weather conditions and studying aeronautical charts.

Three rescue swimmers arrived. They were carrying survival
equipment: Fontel Marine neoprene orange hooded survival suits,
and support vests containing Solas grade red hand flares, Pains
Wessex fifteen-minute smoke signal canisters, radios, compasses and
knives.

Winston Lim, a powerful swimmer in his own right, was carrying
similar equipment in a canvas sports bag. Whereas the other rescue
swimmers carried one knife each, Winston carried a hidden close-
combat blade. The blade was strapped out of sight just above his
left ankle.

The rescue swimmers were imposing men. Like Winston, trained
by the military in the skills of what the Americans call pararescue

jumpers, they were in a state of permanent readiness and peak physical condition. They were capable of parachuting into the ocean by day or night with rubber inflatable boats and diving gear. They called the mountainous seas Our Pool. Now they were going to pay Our Pool a visit.

After Winston had introduced Xiao, the pilots, crew chief and rescue swimmers left the building. A police jeep ferried them the short distance to the Sikorsky's parking bay in the area reserved for the Government Flying Service at the perimeter of the airport.

The rescue mission was rated an IRM. Plans had been put in place to keep a tanker plane on stand-by. If necessary, it could refuel the Sikorsky in mid-air, a very dangerous operation in storm conditions.

8

The twenty metre long Sikorsky H-60 is a large and impressive helicopter with a range of six hundred kilometres. It's capable of maximum speeds of two hundred and sixty five kilometres per hour in normal weather.

There was the obvious problem that the storm conditions were still extreme. The air turbulence alone was enough, in normal circumstances, to prohibit the flight of the Sikorsky into the centre of the storm, and there was the ominous meteorological warning. 'Unusual motion and storm force increases' had been noted along the forecast track.

The pilots, crew chief and rescue swimmers boarded the helicopter. Winston and Xiao boarded it after the others and found their way to their seats. The doors and sliding doors on the port side were closed and fastened and the fastenings rechecked.

Winston settled back in his seat. Once it was permitted, he would change into the Fontel Marine survival suit. As a precaution against dehydration he began to drink from a water canister. He was certain that his targets, the cell of maritime terrorists, were aboard either the *Xiang Chuan* or the *Beijing Handong*. He felt the familiar acidic combination of fear and expectancy churning in his gut.

9

Darkness was falling when the Sikorsky reached the rescue zone, within minutes of the time of arrival predicted by the pilot.

'Oh no,' said Xiao. 'Look at that –'

He was alerting Winston to what they had already seen below: fuming spray and the foaming white water illuminated by the circle of the powerful floodlights situated beneath the helicopter.

White waves cascaded like landslides over precipices. The winds were so powerful that they made the helicopter jump, and it seemed as if it might even tip and tilt out of control, to be snatched by a wave into the ocean.

Somewhere above the Sikorsky a Jetstream joined the search.

Winston spoke over the intercom to rescue swimmer 1. 'Fast rope down?'

'Maybe not,' said rescue swimmer 1.

'Nothing there,' said rescue swimmer 2.

'Not yet,' said 1.

'There,' said Winston. 'See?'

The floodlights had picked out the labouring *Xiang Chuan* a thousand to eight hundred feet below. She presented a piteous sight. There was no conceivable way any of the rescue swimmers could land on board the vessel.

The only hope for rescuing the survivors was if they were swimming in the water. No one could land on the ship's deck to rescue them in this. In these weather conditions, no one needed to be reminded that survival, let alone rescue – even in the water – would be virtually impossible. Everyone knew it. The view was confirmed by the crew chief: 'We can't lift them from the ocean.'

True. The rescue cables would tighten, loosen, tangle and even decapitate a man if they caught around his neck.

The pilot radioed the Jetstream to signal to the *Xiang Chuan* that rescue was impossible.

The Jetstream came back with the news that there were still four men on board.

The voices over the intercom ran over and into each other.

'We can't get them.'

'You don't *want* to go?'

'We *do* want to go. But we *can't* go.'

'You don't want to lower the basket?'

'It won't work.'

Winston interrupted: 'There's an emergency beacon.'

'You want to take a closer look?'

'No. No. No signs of survivors in the water.'

'There's fresh green dye in the water.'

'No one there.'

Now the pilot received additional reports. A Hong Kong navy jet carrying thermal imaging devices was somewhere near.

'No chance in hell of rescuing anyone.'

Everyone knew. Winston reckoned there might be one lucky chance.

'Who wants to collect the dead?'

No one. No one did – except Winston. For whatever reasons, Winston entertained, almost to the point of obsession, the idea that his targets were down there, and he wanted them alive.

'Can we expand the search area?' That was Winston.

'For a limited period only.' That was the pilot.

Winston drew on his Fontel Marine survival suit. Xiao followed his example. The pilot lowered the Sikorsky as close to the surface of the raging ocean as he dared. Dead or alive, there was perhaps a chance of spotting someone.

Soon after the decision to widen the search area had been made, the pilot heard something on the radio. A signal – weak, but nonetheless a signal. Stronger. Weaker. In and out of hearing.

Over the intercom, the pilot's voice said, 'A life raft. Someone alive aboard. Being carried fast by the waves.'

'Oil slicks,' said the co-pilot. 'And a life raft.'

'Signs the life raft has been deployed.'

'No survivors.'

'That's it,' said the pilot.

'No,' said Winston. 'Wait. See?'

'Sure. She's a Chinese vessel.'

'The *Beijing Handong*.'

'Another life raft.'

'Any sign of the *Xiang Chuan*?'

'Zero.'

'There are survivors aboard –' The remainder of the pilot's words were lost in a rush of deafening static.

It could have been 'Oil.'

Perhaps it was the co-pilot speaking: 'Pressure gauge.'

Winston recognised that something was going very wrong. Acid had risen from his stomach into his saliva. It felt like bleach working on his gums.

10

Smoke poured into the cabin. The stench of it was bitter in the nostrils. Choking, temporarily blinded, Winston reached for the oxygen mask. With that, the lights went out. In the darkness Winston heard the noise of Xiao throwing up.

The pilot was transmitting MAYDAY. As best he could, he was giving the location and said he was going to ditch.

Winston felt the helicopter dip and drop. *The pilot's going to make a controlled ditch. Approaching the heaving surface of the ocean into the wind. A ditch into hell.*

Winston knew the routine. *Level altitude at three hundred feet a minute descent. The chances of survival? Zero. Rescue? Zero. I have no night vision. Where's the life raft.*

He released his safety harness, took a deep inhalation of oxygen, held it in his lungs, then he pushed past the retching Xiao in the direction of the open jump doors. As he went for the exit he tugged hard at Xiao's sleeve. Twice he pulled, urging Xiao to follow. Unfastening his safety harness, Xiao threw up again.

Winston made out the rescue swimmers and the main life raft, silhouetted against the light of the white ocean. *I pray the pilot's signalled the* Beijing Handong. *Lord have mercy. But how far below is the raging sea? Hard to guess within a hundred feet.*

He heard the failing strength of turbines. The hover became a drop. Its force drove the oxygen from his lungs.

He saw a gloved hand yank down the door release lever. Took a deep breath and jumped.

In mid-air a deafening whistle filled his ears. His body gathered speed. He somersaulted. He found himself falling in a foetal position. Twisting himself, he managed to get his feet beneath him.

White spray clawed at his cheeks and eyes. Then the white turned black.

Winston had a hard physique. His hair was cut short. The skin next to his eyes was creased with smile lines. He was rarely heard to raise his voice in anger and he showed disapproval with a wordless stare.

A widower, he had kept work and his private life in separate compartments. He kept fit by playing regular badminton at the police club and by swimming. Anything he had to prove he proved to himself away from others. If he had a professional fault, it was perhaps a reluctance to share criminal intelligence unless he was convinced of its efficacy. His obsessions were threefold. His work, his investigation of maritime terrorism and his love for his daughter Mei. Mei who, after graduating in law, had decided to follow in her father's footsteps and join the police. If Winston was proud of his adopted daughter's intention, he never said. He would only say he wanted her to follow her own instincts. He didn't want to influence her – other than to help her overcome the problems that face most twenty-year-old Hong Kong Chinese women in the twenty-first century, of which Mei had overcome her fair share.

11

He plummeted into the raging ocean at forty-five miles per hour.

The impact of the collision smashed several of his ribs and two bones in his lower left arm. It tore ligaments in his right ankle and began massive internal haemorrhaging in his lower stomach.

He saw the whiteness of the water through a red veil. The only thing that seemed to promise hope was the blurred shape of the life raft careering sideways down the waves as if propelled on the rolling crest of an avalanche.

The shape of Xiao in his Fontel Marine survival suit was visible. A strobe light was flashing. Clutching the edge of the raft, Xiao was screaming, 'SWIM, SWIM!'

Xiao watched Winston swimming for his life. Finally, with his assistance, Winston began to haul himself aboard. They were drifting dangerously close to the rolling and pitching hull of the *Beijing Handong*. The waves were sideswiping them from all directions. Neither Winston nor Xiao could have seen the curling wave behind them that snatched the life raft and flipped it over like a toy. The raft seemed to surf away from them down the waves, forwards, sideways, then backwards, until it vanished altogether in the darkness.

From somewhere aboard the *Beijing Handong*, a flare was fired. It blazed overhead like an arc light. There was more shouting from the deck above. Whoever was shouting must have seen that Xiao had disappeared beneath the surface. But Winston could just be seen, flailing about in the water.

Perhaps he had realised that the *Beijing Handong* was listing heavily. What he could not have known was that extensive flooding had occurred in the ship's cargo hold. *Beijing Handong* was as good as lost.

She was filling rapidly, and the master had realised the time was fast approaching when he would have to issue the order to abandon ship. He had also signalled the *Xiang Chuan*, which was approaching the disaster area.

Guided by the flare, the eight thousand tonne *Beijing Handong* tilted, plunged and rose again. The heavylifters, her twin one hundred and fifty tonne cranes, seemed top heavy as if they were conspiring to drag the ship beneath the roaring surface of the ocean.

The *Beijing Handong* drifted nearer and nearer to Winston. By now, he in turn had been carried closer to Xiao, who had once more surfaced. More flares shot into the night air. A cargo net was thrown overboard by the crew, who were time and again punched by the waves crashing across the sloping decks.

With an agonising struggle, Winston succeeded in heaving himself into the net. With his one good arm, he tried to pull Xiao in after him. Retching, Xiao fought against the weight of the seawater. Winston held him. Xiao held Winston's arm and managed to flop into the cargo net.

They were like giant fishes rising to the deck. The net was swinging from side to side. Their bruised fingers snagged the cords. The waves hammered and banged them repeatedly against the side of the steel hull.

Xiao believed that Winston had lost consciousness and might fall out of the net altogether. Then he saw Winston retch again. He grabbed and clutched at Winston's clothes and in so doing Xiao felt himself slipping sideways and downwards.

Within feet of the hull he slipped back into the sea, holding on to the net for dear life. The howling storm drowned the screams from above.

The crew on deck had seen two more swimmers in the sea within feet of the hull. They were drifting towards the stern and the ship's fourteen-foot propeller blades, churning the water and threatening to slice them like a giant butcher's cutter.

More flares shot skyward. They illuminated the swimmers' progress. One of the swimmers could be seen. He was floundering, panic-stricken. The other was trying and failing to support him. A few yards from the raft, the combination of a colossal rising wave and the heaving of the crew on deck raised the net with Winston in it, with Xiao holding slippery cords and what little he could grasp of the net.

By the time the net reached the edge of the pitching deck, both the other swimmers had vanished beneath the waves.

Hands reached out. They held on to Winston and Xiao until a final pull brought them toppling over the rail. At first sight, Winston looked to be at death's door. His mouth was stretched wide open, his teeth bared, gasping and twitching like a dying fish.

It was Xiao who seemed the more likely to survive.

There were a few shouts of apparent disagreement. Distorted by the force of the wind, the volume of the shouting rose. The voices were yelling about the Sikorsky. It had disappeared.

Could anyone see the pilots, crew chief or rescue swimmers?

Winston and Xiao, the only survivors, were carried as fast as possible towards the stern and the single lifeboat.

12

The *Beijing Handong*'s free-fall enclosed lifeboat was readied for evacuation at the head of the steep ramp over the transom. Once launched, it would splash down into the raging sea well clear of the sinking ship. A conventional lifeboat fitted high above the side of the ship would have proved no use. The *Xiang Chuan* stood by ready to take aboard the survivors.

With the fourteen crew, Winston and Xiao securely strapped in, the streamlined lifeboat struck the sea and headed on a course in the direction of the flares exploding in the sky above the *Xiang Chuan*.

Forty minutes later, as one by one the survivors were hauled aboard the *Xiang Chuan*, the *Beijing Handong*'s bow lifted. Stern first, she sank, leaving a vast and churning pool of oil.

13

Winston was stretchered below to the temporary sick bay.

His Fontel Maritime survival suit had already been slit open.

The ship's first aid man immediately set to work. He could see bones in Winston's right leg were severely fractured. Winston's chest and lungs were heaving abnormally.

The first aid man suspected that Winston was also suffering internal bleeding. The severe damage to his lungs seemed to be consistent with injuries by battering and pressure and God knows what besides. Assisted by the crew member acting as orderly, the first aid man made Winston as comfortable as possible. Given the rolling and tossing of the ship, it was far from easy.

Xiao lay on a makeshift examination table near Winston. Exhausted, he was drifting in and out of consciousness.

'How is he?' Xiao asked feebly.

The first aid man was evasive. 'It's a matter of getting him to shore as soon as possible.'

The orderly asked Xiao if he was comfortable and Xiao mouthed Yes.

'Try and rest,' the orderly told him. The orderly smiled and left Xiao alone.

Xiao's mind was confused. He thought he heard a whispered conversation between the first aid man and the orderly. The first aid man's presence was required elsewhere to see to a member of the crew who had injured both legs and was in great pain. Xiao thought he heard the first aid man tell the orderly to keep watch on the two patients. Or was he telling the orderly to assist him? The brief discussion, a disagreement of some sort, ended. The outcome was that the first aid man and the orderly left Winston and Xiao alone in the sick bay in a hurry.

14

Xiao's vision was blurred. He thought he saw the arrival of another of the ship's crew. The man in the all-weather protection suit had the hood fastened beneath his eyes across the face.

He saw him lean over Winston. He was tearing open some protective packaging.

Xiao tried to speak, but nausea overcame him.

Whoever it was who had entered the sick bay now removed the identification tag that dangled from a chain around Winston's bruised and swollen neck. The ID tag read 'Winston Lim'. Attached to the chain were two small gold crucifixes and two silver hearts. One of the silver hearts was engraved 'Mei', the other 'Kitty'. Opening the hood of his all-weather protection suit, the man removed the chain, slipped it over his head and tucked it inside the collar. He noticed Winston carried a hidden close-combat blade. The blade was strapped out of sight just above his left ankle and he left it there.

Even the inexperienced eye could see the signs of the multiple injuries Winston had sustained. Who would tell exactly how the injuries were sustained or the treatment applied? The ship's first aid man would later testify to the quantity of the painkilling drug he had administered. There would be several minor, conflicting and some-what inconclusive views about the treatment. But the inventory of drugs and medications remaining could be checked against the emergency supplies that been administered. No one would doubt, particularly in the conditions of the raging tropical storm, that the ship's first aid man had done all he could.

Xiao tried and failed to focus his eyes. The man in the all-weather protection suit seemed to be producing a small phial and a syringe.

The quantity of diamorphine in the phial was enough, once injected into the bloodstream, to cause Winston to die quickly without pain.

The man felt for a suitable vein in Winston's lower left arm, inserted the needle and squeezed.

Xiao's lips were cracked. The saliva in his mouth was dry. Losing consciousness he croaked, 'What's happening?'

Wearing Winston's ID tag, and the gold crucifixes and silver hearts on the fine chains around his neck, the man with the syringe had already made his exit.

TWO

Man never shows what is in his heart
unless mourning one near he loves.
TZU-KUNG

15

South China Morning Post

AFTERMATH OF RESCUE TRAGEDY
BEIJING DETECTIVE PRAISES HERO LIM

Before departing Hong Kong for Beijing,
Xiao Qingze said: "I owe my life to the
heroism of Winston Lim. Truly one of
Asia's finest."

Hongkong Daily

**INSPECTOR WINSTON LIM PRAISED
IN WAKE OF TYPHOON DISASTER**

Xiang Chuan's first aid man said:
"Winston Lim died with dignity,
in peace and without pain. It was
a hero's death."

STATEMENT OF WITNESS

[Criminal Justice Act 1967, s.9]

Statement of:	Alan Rosslyn
Age of Witness:	over 21
Occupation:	Private Investigator
Address:	Basement Flat,
	195 Claverton Street,
	London SW1

This statement consisting of 2 pages signed by me is true to the best of my knowledge and belief and I make it knowing that if it is tendered in evidence, I shall be liable to prosecution if I wilfully state anything which I know to be false.

Mei asked me to deliver the eulogy to Winston. The funeral service was held at St Stephen's, the Anglican chapel in the grounds of St Stephen's College on Tung Tau Wan Road in Stanley, on the south side of Hong Kong Island. The chapel was built as a memorial to those who died there in World War Two when St Stephen's College formed part of the Stanley Internment Camp. Winston lost several relatives in the hellhole.

In recent years, accompanied by his wife Kitty, St Stephen's was Winston's regular place of worship. It seemed only yesterday I stood beside him at Kitty's funeral in St Stephen's. It was hard to believe that, after so short an interval, Winston too had gone to his Maker.

I met Mei Lim in the foyer of my hotel. Winston's only surviving relative; she drove me to St Stephen's Chapel. It was a day I wish we'd all been spared.

I had carefully rehearsed my eulogy to Winston.
According to Mei, others would apparently speak of
Winston's distinguished career.

My task was to speak about Winston Lim, the man.
The man, moreover, who had saved my life. The man
for whom I had the greatest respect, admiration
and affection

Signed: *Alan Rooslyn*

Signature witnessed by: Chief Superintendent Ronald Costley

Signed: *Ron Costley*

Signature witnessed by: WPC Michelle Seifert

Signed: *Michelle Seifert*

Light rain across Hong Kong
Scattered clouds
Temperature 54° F / 12° C
Humidity 77%

The funeral of Winston Lim brought many of the wise and the good from across South East Asia to Stanley, on the south side of Hong Kong Island.

The story of the heroic rescue attempt and the circumstances of his death had already featured prominently in the newspapers of South East Asia. It was therefore no surprise to Rosslyn that a crowd of onlookers had gathered outside St Stephen's Chapel, which was packed with mourners. Among them, Rosslyn recognised some officers of the Hong Kong Customs service he had collaborated with in his days as an undercover investigator for HM Customs & Excise.

There were other faces he remembered less well from service duty in the past. Other men and women he had probably encountered in the line of South East Asia duty. Their careers and lives had taken different turns – like Rosslyn's, who was now an investigator in the private sector of criminal investigation. He had taken leave from Milo Associates of London to fly to Hong Kong to be present at Winston's funeral at the request of Winston's daughter Mei.

The scent of white lilies filled St Stephen's. Uniformed duty officers of the Hong Kong Police hovered around the entrance. Winston had many friends among the officers of the law enforcement agencies in Hong Kong and throughout Malaysia and Singapore. Rosslyn noticed that some of the local police officers were armed. Perhaps they too were numbered among Winston's friends and admirers. Like Steve Kwok, the wheelchair-bound Hong Kong police inspector who shook Rosslyn's hand.

Rosslyn was shocked to see Steve Kwok in a wheelchair. Rosslyn had no idea he had been disabled and wondered what had happened to Kwok, who had been Winston's closest colleague and was apparently now taking over Winston's investigations.

'Good to see you, Steve.'

'I wish it were in other circumstances.'

'Me too.'

'You going to call on me tomorrow at headquarters – at the Crime Wing?'

'I look forward to it,' said Rosslyn.

Various people handed their business cards to Mei, who entered the church on Rosslyn's arm. She accepted each one with a silent nod of thanks and slipped them into her black handbag. Winston had been admired and respected. There were also reporters from the press, the radio and TV.

Two priests, one Chinese and one British, took the service and there were eulogies from two former colleagues of Winston's, who spoke movingly about him. It was the British priest who bowed to Mei and Rosslyn in the front row, indicating that this was the moment for Rosslyn to speak.

Rosslyn stood at the head of the aisle, a tall, dark figure of authority and kindliness. He was perhaps a little too lean for his considerable height.

He addressed the congregation without looking at his notes.

'You have heard others speak this morning of Winston's distinguished career. Of his courage. His honesty. His gentleness. He was a police officer who thought of his duty as service to others. He once told me that the idea of a police force was anathema to him. He believed in police service, not force. With hindsight, the manner of his going, in making a desperate attempt to save the lives of others, has about it a strange sense of the inevitable.

'All of us here today profoundly wish it had been otherwise. And it is too short a time, much too short a time, since many of us here today were present with him, and with Mei, when we paid our last respects to Kitty, his wife and Mei's mother.

'Winston was a gregarious character. He loved stories. He loved children and they loved him, especially perhaps the dexterity he demonstrated when he did conjuring tricks for them. Sleight of hand was one of his many talents. He was without sentimentality and he had no time for anyone who paid him those fulsome compliments he so often and so rightly deserved. He also respected the rights of friends and colleagues to take risks, most of all when such risks were undertaken to assist others frequently weaker or less fortunate than himself.

'Many were the times when he took operational risks without endangering the lives of others. I have reason to owe a lasting debt of gratitude to Winston for those several occasions when we worked together on dangerous operations here in Asia and back in Europe. Once, with great calm, he risked his life to ensure my safety. It was during a seize and search operation near Hung Hom Ferry Pier, when I was attacked by an informer I should have known better than to trust. It was Winston who calmly talked the man into surrendering his loaded gun. Had it not been for Winston's powers of persuasion, I would not be here today. I have little doubt there are others here today who could tell a similar story. I owe him my life.

'Winston and I undertook several investigations together. Over the years, in the area of maritime terrorism, these have expanded and have become more complex. Many such investigations remain incomplete. We have a duty to honour Winston and see that they are completed.

'I know too of his familial loyalty. To Kitty. To Mei. He adored them both. And he was certainly mindful to wish that those of us who loved him should show that love to Mei. That, indeed, we will do.

'He wore his beliefs lightly, without pomposity or self-righteousness, and showed a gentle tolerance towards those who, without sharing in his beliefs, sought to challenge his Christianity.

'His life was perhaps a sort of journey. A journey to the paradise he believed in. It is therefore appropriate that Mei has chosen the final hymn, the hymn we know as Bunyan's "Who would true valour see". And there are other words of Bunyan's that seem appropriate to Winston's going:

I am going to my Father's, and although with great difficulty I have got hither, yet now I do not repent me of all the trouble I have been at to arrive where I am. My sword I give to him that shall succeed me in my pilgrimage, and my courage and skill to him that can get it. My marks and scars I carry with me, to be a witness for me, that I have fought his battles, who now will be my rewarder.

When the day that he must go hence was come, many accompanied him to the riverside, into which as he went, he said, Death, where is thy sting? And as he went down deeper, he said, Grave, where is thy victory? So he passed over, and all the trumpets sounded for him on the other side.'

The congregation was silent. Returning to his pew, Rosslyn glanced at Mei, seeking some look of recognition that his eulogy had been appropriate.

Instead of catching his eye, she turned her face aside, and as the choir and congregation began to sing *Who would true valour see,* Rosslyn saw her small frame convulse with sobs. He took her hand. Mei held his hand so tightly that he felt her fingernails might penetrate his skin. She leaned her face closer to his and he felt her tears on his cheeks.

18

There was a muted atmosphere at the luncheon afterwards at the restaurant Tables 88. Serving east-meets-west cuisine, the restaurant is appropriately situated in the Old Stanley Police Station. Tables 88 had been Winston's favourite and there must have been almost sixty people present, who were provided with seven courses.

Struggling to regain her composure, Mei acknowledged the condolences. Sometimes in Cantonese. Sometimes in English. Her black silk overcoat was creased and there was an aura of vulnerability and frailty about her diminutive figure. Rosslyn sat next to her during the lunch. He noticed that several times she accepted cups of weak tea only to set them down on the table without drinking. She ate almost nothing. The conversation was stilted and polite. There was no sign of Steve Kwok.

Most of the guests left as soon as lunch was over. A few lingered on, talking quietly among themselves. Among them, in dark glasses and carrying a white cane, was a Chinese in a blue linen suit. He approached Rosslyn and introduced himself.

'The name's Tsang. George Tsang,' he said, 'Thank you for your eloquent address. I also owe my life to Winston. He was a wonderful and very brave man. I publish a monthly private newsletter. *Maritime Confidential*. Subscription only. For the shipping business. If I can be of help to you on the inside track, let me know. One habit of omission I acquired in London is that I don't carry a business card, but you'll find my phone number in the book.'

'I'll make a point of calling you.'

'Good,' said Tsang. 'I'd like you to meet my wife Diane. Alas, she's had to stay at home with our several cats. She was a cousin and close friend to Kitty. Kitty's confidante in times of trouble.' He offered his hand to Rosslyn. 'Remember the name: George Tsang.'

Of the others who made themselves known to Rosslyn, there was a couple who fulsome in their praise of his address.

'You must have done that kind of thing before,' said the large Australian who introduced himself as 'Dr Burnal Graer, Australian High Commission'. The Australian wore an ill-fitting ginger toupee, and Rosslyn could see wisps of red hair where the toupee joined the florid temples. Graer was smoking a small cigar. 'Staying on the island long?' he asked.

'A few days,' said Rosslyn.

Graer stepped aside with a theatrical bow. 'May I introduce my companion, Birgit Swann. Birgits from the American Consulate General's office.'

Before Rosslyn could tell her how he was, Graer interrupted loudly: 'Birgit's in the Legal Office. US of A.'

'Any time we can be of help, call us,' Swann volunteered. 'Our house is your house.'

Before Rosslyn could thank her, Graer said, 'You should do that thing. Birgit does great Chiu Chow cuisine. Swatow food.' He gripped Rosslyn's arm tightly. 'Seriously, if we can be of any help, mate – with, say, that incomplete investigation of yours – you only have to lift the phone. Fax. E-mail. Whatever. For good old Winston's sake. Here –'

He handed Rosslyn his business card. Rosslyn read:

Dr BURNAL GRAER PhD
Visa Officer

23/F Harbour Centre
25 Harbour Road, Wan Chai
Hong Kong
People's Republic of China

Telephone: 852 2827 8881 Fax: 852 2585 4457
E-mail address: graeracghkadm@netvigator.com

'That's me,' Graer said. 'Never fear, Graer is here. No problem if it's South East Asian territory.'

'It could be.'

'Then let's lunch when next you're on my patch,' said Graer. 'And by the way, that poetry was great. Really. I mean that thing. Good. A favourite of my mother's, Milton.'

'Bunyan,' the American woman said.

'That's who I said – Bunyan,' Graer said. He hurriedly lit a fresh cigar. The confidential smile had vanished. 'Tell me what really happened. The truth. Hidden agenda. Winston was a hard man. You think it was an accident?'

'Yes. It was an accident.'

'Could have been avoided, couldn't it?' said Graer. 'There must be a hidden scenario. At the end of the day, you knew Winston pretty well?'

'Yes.'

'Me too,' said Graer, staring hard across the room at Mei. 'And look at her. He loved her so much. Can't beat that set-up. Father and daughter. The girl's sweet. Looks young enough to be a schoolgirl. It's so bloody sad.'

'I know.'

'Tell me,' said Graer. 'What about the other chappie in the sea – the man from Beijing?'

'I dare say he's back there by now.'

'Who was he?' said Graer.

'A police officer who'd been seconded as some kind of observer to shadow Winston's work routine.'

'*Shadow*?' said the American.

'Yes,' said Rosslyn. 'A shadow. To gain from Winston's experience of maritime terrorism investigations.'

'I'd be interested to have the Chink's account of things,' said Graer.

'It won't bring Winston back,' said Rosslyn.

'Bloody right,' said Graer. 'But you know what I mean?'

'Perhaps,' said Rosslyn.

'Do we know anything about the ship's medic who was with him when he died?'

'No,' said Rosslyn. 'Should we?'

Graer shrugged. Beads of sweat had formed where the ginger toupee joined his forehead. 'If you come across him, let us know. We'd like a chance to have a little talk with him.'

'About what?'

The American woman said, 'All kinds of people had a way of – shall we say – of entering Winston's domain. People at the edge of things.'

'What's your interest in him?' asked Rosslyn.

Graer was looking uncomfortable. 'What Winston knew.' The smile on Graer's watery lips was fixed. His eyes were working the room for signs of anyone else he could buttonhole among the departing guests.

'Excuse me,' said Rosslyn. 'Do you know where the men's room is?'

Dr Graer pointed to the exit with the small cigar held between his thumb and forefinger. 'Take a left, mate.' Cigar ash fell to the floor. 'Follow the pictures of the little boy with his legs apart.'

'Good to have met you,' said Rosslyn.

'You too,' said Graer.

Rosslyn reckoned he might have made an enemy of the egregious Dr Burnal Graer and his American friend Birgit Swann. Ignoring Graer's directions to the men's room, he began to search for Mei to tell her he would keep his appointment with her later that evening. It was not going to be the happiest of occasions.

19

Mei's sparse apartment in Chung Hom Kok is where, apart from her two Siamese cats, she lives alone. The potted plants on the window sill beneath the bamboo blind are in need of care. A pale blue sheet of cotton covers the steel rail of clothes, mostly white, which stands beside the window. A white silk dressing gown hangs from the hook on the door. Next to the door is a large mirror. In one alcove is the tiny space serving as a kitchen. In the second alcove there is a small sofa bed covered with a black silk quilt. Apart from Natsume Soseki's *Botchan* and the *Mini Rough Guide to Beijing* on a folding table, there are no books. The volume of the CD player is on low –

> Probe me with your love
> Kiss me with your snake tongue
> Probe me with your love
> I don't care how long you take
> So long as we've begun.

The Siamese cats are cross-eyed. The eyes are blue; their hair is blackish, sleek and short.

Rosslyn was seated at the only table, in the centre of the room.

'Would you care for whisky?' Mei asked. 'This was Dad's. Glenfiddich.'

'A small glass,' Rosslyn said. Whisky was not a drink he liked much.

He toyed with his glass and watched her doing likewise. 'Your father would've wanted me to ask you,' he said. 'About you, Mei.'

She turned her eyes away. 'Ask me.'

'I loved him very much,' Rosslyn said. Love suddenly seemed too strong a word.

'He told me,' she said. 'What is there left to talk about?'

'We can talk about your future. But if you don't want to, I'll understand. If you have any problems, if there's anything I can do –'

'I – only have to say –'

'Yes?'

'You know something, I don't want to stay on here any more –'

'Don't you have friends here?' he asked.

'I have Kasuko, who lives upstairs. She's a poet, Japanese. She's blind. That's how she was born. Her grandmother survived Hiroshima. Kasuko's mother was born blind. I guess it's hereditary. And I have Botch and Chan. The cats. Aren't they beautiful? Then I suppose there are people who want to be my friends. Funny, isn't it? When you lose a loved one . . . how many people suddenly want to be your friend.'

'Like who else?'

'You, Mr Rosslyn.'

He wanted to tell her what Winston had said. *Promise me to keep watch over Mei – until hell freezes?*

'You know, Mr Rosslyn,' she said, 'you're the third person who's asked me today if I have friends. They volunteered to help me. That Australian diplomat for one, Graer. I heard he's a sex tourist when he goes on leave.'

'I met him after the lunch at Tables 88,' said Rosslyn. 'Along with his American friend.'

'She's another strange one. What did they ask you?'

'What I knew of the young police officer from Beijing who was with your father. Xiao.'

'What did you tell them?' she asked.

'Nothing. I don't know anything about him.'

'Did they mention anyone else to you?'

'Yes, as a matter of fact, they did,' said Rosslyn. 'They asked me about the ship's first aid man. The man who tried to save your father's life.'

'You know anything about him?'

'No.'

'There are rumours', she said 'that Dad's death wasn't natural.'

'Where did you hear that?' he asked.

The cats climbed into her lap and she held them close.

'The rumours?' she said. 'There's talk that he was set up. What could have been more perfect than his being engaged on some search and rescue mission only for him to have found himself staring into the eyes of his assassin? It's so beautifully logical. So Chinese, Mr Rosslyn. Dad loved the stories of Dashiell Hammett. He liked Hammett's idea of red harvests. People talk; I wouldn't dirty your hands with red harvests, Mr Rosslyn. My father moved among professional criminals. He was familiar with reprisals and vengeance and instruments of death. But it's no use speculating on matters of which very little is known. Dad hated gossip. His obligation was to get the truth and nothing but the truth. Has no one told you why my father was on that mission? To interrogate suspects among the crew of *Xiang Chuan*. My father could achieve miracles, Mr Rosslyn. But calming a typhoon was probably something even he couldn't achieve. Have you spoken to the owners of *Xiang Chuan*?'

'No. Do you want me to?'

'About what?' she asked sharply.

'About exactly how your father died,' said Rosslyn. 'I mean, if you have even a shadow of doubt about it, I should ask.'

'Forget it. There's nothing you can do.'

'What about Steve Kwok?' said Rosslyn. 'What happened to him?'

'He was brutally assaulted. He lost his feet. His wife was disfigured. Like my father, Steve Kwok knows some dangerous people. And, if you don't mind, I'd rather not talk about them or Steve. Not now. You go home to London and leave things be. We must let my father's soul live on, don't you feel, in peace.'

Avoiding each other's gaze, they sat in silence. Rosslyn was the first to break it.

'I do know that your father will have left a great deal of business unfinished.'

'He always kept it to himself. In his head. It will have died with him, I think. We never discussed his work. Unfinished business – another way of saying the future. That's what the future is, Mr Rosslyn. Unfinished business. Most of us very wisely keep it to ourselves, don't we?'

Which was what, Rosslyn felt, she intended to do.

The doorbell sounded and she left Rosslyn seated at the table to listen to the voice over the speaker. The man's voice said something in English that Rosslyn couldn't quite catch.

'I have to leave now,' she said.

'Before you go, let me tell you that I'll think carefully about what you've told me. I want you to be sure to tell me if there's anything I can do to help you. Believe me. I promised as much to Winston.'

'And did he make you promise "until hell freezes" – was that the phrase he used?'

'Yes, actually it was.'

'Dear Dad,' she said. 'He used to promise things and whenever he intended to break a promise that's what he said. "I promise you this. I promise you that. Until hell freezes."' She was looking at her face in the mirror by the door. 'I guess I've inherited that from him. When I was in trouble that's what I'd say. I have to go.'

The bell sounded with greater insistence. Rosslyn imagined the caller was a late night date.

'You should remember, Mr Rosslyn,' Mei continued. 'Remember what the Chinese say about the dead. "The dead do not tell the truth." Tell me, are you going to speak to the Commissioner of Police before you leave for London?'

'I can if you want me to. About what?'

'About my application to join the Hong Kong Police,' she said.

'Is that what you want me to do for you?'

'Yes. You can have a word with him in my support. Hong Kong hasn't changed. It's still a matter of who you know if you want to get places. I know the Chief of Police was very impressed by your address in St Stephen's.'

'How do you know that?'

'His wife told me.'

'Okay. I'll see what I can do for you.'

'I'd appreciate it if you'd help me. Call me from London when you get back. Tell me what he says.' She was rummaging in a ceramic jar, tearing some pack or other open. In the reflection of the wall mirror he saw her slip whatever it was she had removed into her coat pocket. 'Can I trust you?' she asked.

'Try me.'

'Prove it by staying here for five minutes after I've left. Then let yourself out. The door locks itself. Just make sure it's shut tight.' She went to the window and raised the bamboo blind. The cats had curled up on her bed. 'Good-night, cats,' she said. 'Sweet dreams. See you in the morning.'

'Help yourself to the whisky,' she said. 'And thank you again for all you said about Dad. I very much appreciate it. What you said – it

55

was so nice.' She turned off all the lights except a small reading light above the sofa bed. Opening the door, she said, 'And I also appreciate what you didn't say.'

She left before he could ask her what she meant.

Whisky glass in hand, he looked at the CDs next to the Bose. Four CDs by Snakeskin, including *The Best of Snakeskin*, featuring 'Probe Me':

> Probe me with your love
> Kiss me with your snake tongue
> Probe me with your love
> I don't care how long you take
> So long as we've begun.

He lifted the lid of the ceramic jar. Inside was a selection of condom packs.

Drinking down the remains of the whisky in his glass, he went to the speakerphone beside the door and lifted it.

There was the clatter of footsteps echoing on the concrete floor of the entrance hall, the sound of the entrance door's hinges whining and then, above the noises of the street, he heard the sound of laughter. Mei's laughter.

Then her voice. 'Sorry to have kept you waiting. I had a visitor.'

Then a man said, 'Does he know anything?'

'No,' said Mei. 'He's just some dumb-fuck British gumshoe.'

Slamming the door shut, Rosslyn left the apartment and took the stairs two by two to the ground floor. He pushed through the exit into the crowded street. As he expected, there was no sign of either Mei or this lover of hers who also had the idea he was some dumb-fuck British gumshoe. He remembered he had left the CD playing. Too bad. It could go on playing all night for the benefit of Mei's cats, Botch and Chan.

20

The Crime Wing of Hong Kong police headquarters is at Caine House on Arsenal Street in Wan Chai.

Next morning, Rosslyn was subjected to a thorough body search on his arrival there. A woman police officer took a note of his date and place of birth. Explaining that the Crime Wing was on Red Alert, she took his photograph and fingerprints. Another police officer led him to a waiting room.

While Rosslyn waited for his appointment with Inspector Stephen Kwok, he entertained misgivings about Mei. She had been less than frank. Yet he had no regrets about having lied to her about trusting him, and it was first for Winston's sake, second for Mei's, that he had telephoned Hong Kong police headquarters to seek the appointment with the Commissioner to recommend Mei. The Hong Kong Police were among the world's most professional. They would make up their own minds about Mei's suitability. It would not, he felt, have much if anything to do with the dumb-fuck British gumshoe.

Rosslyn had been put through to one of the Commissioner's assistants. The officer was courteous. Rosslyn explained he had an appointment with Inspector Kwok in the Crime Wing later that morning. He added that he would like to pay his respects to the Commissioner. The clerk took Rosslyn's details and, having said that he could speak over the telephone in confidence, promised to pass on a message to the Commissioner immediately. The clerk called back shortly, as he had promised, and said the Commissioner would see him before his meeting with Kwok in one hour's time.

He was kept waiting for almost another hour before a civilian clerk told him, with 'much regret', that the Commissioner was unable to see him that day. Instead, the Commissioner had suggested Rosslyn might care to talk to the Deputy Commissioner who headed

C Department, the Director of Personnel and Training. Rosslyn was shown into the DC's office.

The Deputy Commissioner, in uniform and shirtsleeves, listened to Rosslyn's explanation of his visit. The DC, a friend of Winston's, had been at the funeral and congratulated Rosslyn on his address.

Rosslyn spoke about Mei and said that he would be happy to recommend her as a police trainee.

'How well do you actually know her?' the DC asked.

'I can hardly say I know her well.'

'She's a very beautiful young woman,' the DC said. He smiled and turned to his desktop computer screen. 'I see that we've already interviewed her. Further, she passed the physical fitness test at our police training school. She attended the selection board. A superintendent and two inspectors chaired the interview. They put questions in Cantonese to her. She seemed self-confident. Showed ability in communication skills and analytical thought and a determination to serve the community. It was a wide-ranging interview, including general knowledge of police and current affairs and common sense. She did well.'

He tapped the keyboard.

'We've taken it further. Our vetting unit has carried out integrity checking. She passed her medical examination. Hold on while I see if I can find anything else to tell you.'

The DC stared in silence at the screen.

Rosslyn walked to the window and looked out across the compound.

A team of builders was at work on the conversion of a long and low building resembling an air raid shelter. Wearing identical brown uniforms, white hard hats and eye and mouth masks, they were putting the finishing touches to arc light installations and an ugly looking stretch of razor wire at the top of the high surrounding walls.

'Admiring Beijing's latest handiwork?' the DC said from his desk. 'What's it for?'

'Beijing's version of an HSU. High Security Unit. One of the Security Ministry's pet projects. They've spent millions on it. It has its own court, cells, medical centre and interrogation rooms. It's not a place you'd want to visit.' He paused. 'Let's see, on a happier note. Let me explain to you. The recruitment process normally extends over a period of fourteen weeks. This depends on the flow, the number of applicants.'

He talked without looking at Rosslyn and peered at the computer screen.

'Once the recruitment and vetting processes have been completed, she receives a letter telling her of the result of her application. Whether or not she can proceed to appointment as police constable. Okay. I can tell you that she'll be told there are vacancies in the police force. So officers of the Recruitment Group will notify her by letter or telephone to come and collect the appointment letter. The letter will outline her entry salary scale. Terms of appointment and the date she will join the police training school.' Again there was a pause. 'But there's a problem.'

He shut down his computer. 'There's not a great deal we can do about this one. It'll be up to the Commissioner to decide. I have to say that Mei's height is one hundred and fifty centimetres. That's two centimetres short of the minimum to qualify for training as a woman police constable. Physically she's very strong. A martial arts practitioner. Beautiful and very bright. Has working Russian. Fluent Bahasa Melayu, the Malaysian language. Mandarin, of course. Cantonese and Hokkien. But she's very small.'

'What's the chance that the Commissioner will waive the rule?'

'I can't predict,' the DC said. 'I suppose she could apply for some civilian appointment.'

'A civilian appointment – Winston Lim's daughter?'

'Even Winston's daughter,' the DC said. 'If I were you, I wouldn't raise her expectations. You understand that everything I've told you is very strictly confidential.' He got up from behind his desk. 'Had the Commissioner not told me to be completely open with you, Mr Rosslyn, we wouldn't have had this meeting in the first place.'

'I appreciate your help.'

The DC showed Rosslyn to the door and called for the clerk in the outer office to escort him to the Crime Wing.

'I'm sorry the news isn't happier, Mr Rosslyn. You could say that she's fallen at the last hurdle. I hope I haven't delayed your meeting with Stephen Kwok. A fine man. One of our very finest, that's Steve.'

21

Like Rosslyn, Steve Kwok had been a close friend of Winston's. The three of them had first teamed up three years before at the Transnational Police Conference at the Hong Kong Convention and Exhibition Centre. Money laundering investigations were the interests they had in common: 'Freeze & Seize – International Co-operation in Confiscation and Partnerships with the Private Sector'.

They greeted each other warmly. Kwok steered his wheelchair to the open office door and told his assistant to take his calls. Nudging the door shut, he offered Rosslyn tea and English shortbread.

'You remember how you introduced Winston and me to short-bread? They were good days. It seems a long time ago.'

'Steve, I'm sorry to find you like this.'

Kwok smiled, as if to say okay. 'I'm all in one piece, other than I have no feet. But that can be fixed. Thanks to the miracles of modern medicine I'm getting new ones fitted.'

'What happened, Steve?'

'There was an assault. I'm lucky it's only my feet I lost. And Catherine, you remember my wife? She got hurt badly too. She was lucky not to have lost her sight. It could have been far worse. But, sadly, Catherine's face will never really be the same.'

'I'm very sorry, Steve. Who did it?'

'We never found him.'

'You reckon you will?'

'Who knows, Alan? Who knows? We get by. Yes. We get by. I want to talk about you. Tell me what's happening with this South East Asian tour of yours? Winston mentioned something about it. Or is it too secret for me to help?'

'No, it's simple. I have to review security on ships insured by the United Kingdom office of Ocean World Insurance in Southampton. One in particular, the *Orient Angel*. She's owned by Svenske-

Britannia and British registered. I'm joining her in KL for the journey to Singapore.'

'It's covert?'

'Yes,' said Rosslyn. 'I'll be travelling as an insurance inspector.'

'Did Winston name the ship?'

'No. All I know is that he'd been pursuing some major syndicate for several months. He had asked me to check some people for him in London. Import-export people. In the event, I don't think that anything I gave him proved significant.'

'I have to admit that Winston often kept his cards close to his chest,' said Kwok. 'Even with me.'

'Before he died,' Rosslyn said, 'didn't he tell you who he was looking for – didn't he name names?'

Kwok turned his head to his left and gazed upwards. Rosslyn followed Kwok's eyes to the lens of a small CCTV camera. 'Get the message?' Kwok said. 'Tell me, how do you reckon Mei's taking it?'

'I saw her last night,' said Rosslyn. And while he explained what Kwok knew anyway – that father and daughter had been close – he saw Kwok with his back to the CCTV lens, writing something on a scrap of paper. Then he took his wallet from his rear trouser pocket, deftly removed one of his business cards, and palmed it to Rosslyn with the scrap of paper.

'Catherine and I don't see too much of Mei,' Kwok said. 'She has a very active social life.'

'She's never married?'

'No,' Kwok said with a knowing smile. 'Are you interested?'

'Not in the way you're thinking, Steve.'

'Few men wouldn't be.'

'I don't doubt it. Even the DC mentioned she was beautiful.'

'I'm not sure,' said Kwok, 'but I reckon there's Thai and maybe even some Japanese blood in Mei's veins.'

'Does Mei know who her real mother and father were?'

'I don't know. I think if she knew, then Winston would have mentioned it. But he never did. Not to us. Remind me. Where is it you're staying?'

'The Novotel Century.'

'Good. There's a family matter I'd like you to know about before you leave Hong Kong. There's no reason why you shouldn't be told. I'm taking early retirement.'

'When?'

'Effectively from the end of next week.'

'Is this a sudden decision?'

'Not really. I want a change of life style. And these injuries. They're the writing on the wall. And there's Catherine's condition. You've met Catherine, my wife?'

'We've never actually met.'

'She's originally from New Zealand. There's nothing much to keep me here in Hong Kong any more. We're getting out. There's the family farm. So New Zealand, here we come. You been there?'

'No,' said Rosslyn. 'I hear it's a great place.'

'It is,' said Kwok. 'Winston always wanted to visit us there. Some things are left undone. There it is. It's sad.'

Once inside the taxi bound for his hotel in Wan Chai, Rosslyn read what Kwok had written on the scrap of paper:

Lobby Lounge, your hotel 6 pm

22

Rosslyn's hotel was the twenty-three storey Novotel Century in Wan Chai.

It was at seven that evening, an hour after the appointed time of his meeting with Steve Kwok, that the neatly dressed, fair-haired woman wearing dark glasses approached Rosslyn's table in the crowded, air conditioned lobby lounge.

'Alan Rosslyn?' she asked.

'Yes,' Rosslyn said, getting to his feet.

The plastic surgery had achieved little in the way of disguising the burns she had suffered to her face.

'I'm Catherine Kwok.'

'Good to meet you,' he said, pulling up a chair for her.

'Sorry I'm so late,' she said, looking around nervously. 'I'm afraid Steve can't join us.'

'I'm sorry,' Rosslyn said. 'Care for a drink?'

'If you don't mind, no,' she said. 'Alcohol doesn't agree with the medication.'

'Something else. Tea?'

'No thanks.'

'You'll have a seat?'

'No thanks,' she said calmly. 'I wonder, would you mind walking with me? I find this place too hot.' Hard to believe. The air conditioning was chill. 'It's a five-minute walk to the Convention and Exhibition Centre. Via the covered walkway.' She paused a moment. 'Count to ten and glance at the two men in suits at the corner of the bar.'

Rosslyn left some dollars on the table for his vodka and lime. 'Lead the way,' he told her, and then looked back quickly at the two men. He saw them watching his departure with Catherine in the mirror behind the counter. One of them had his right hand cupped over an earpiece.

Catherine walked in the direction of the exit to the covered walk-way. Then she turned down a short corridor to the lifts.

'Take me to your room,' she said. They managed to squeeze into a lift packed with Chinese businessmen as its doors were closing. The button for floor fifteen was illuminated.

At the fourteenth floor, after the last of the Chinese had got out of the lift, Rosslyn pressed the button for the floor above. Catherine followed him to his room at the end of the empty corridor.

They were both familiar with counter-surveillance. In case the room was bugged, Rosslyn turned on the TV. Their conversation would be lost in the noise of CNN. Rosslyn asked, 'Who are those men at the bar?'

'Twenty-four-hour surveillance,' she said. 'They're armed and they're not on our side – or yours, for that matter. Here, this is from Steve.' She handed him a white envelope. 'Read what's inside carefully. I can't leave it with you.'

Rosslyn opened the envelope.

There were several pages inside it. Most of the text had been type-written on an old-fashioned machine, presumably so that no record would be left on his computer. Judging by the smudges it had been a hurried job.

Rosslyn read what Kwok had written.

23

Winston was closing in on a man called Klaas-Pieter
Terajima. This is all we have on him. Memorise this
document. Then return it to Catherine.

KLAAS-PIETER TERAJIMA

Aliases: Mathias Utagawa. Henrick Shintara.
        Dr Dehaan Sakamoto. Dr Hung. Pastor Pang.
        Pastor Mogens Leung.

Date of Birth:	August 31, 1970
Place of Birth:	Holland
Height:	approx. 1.62 m
Complexion:	Olive
Hair:	Black
Eyes:	Brown
Weight:	approx. 110 pounds
Sex:	Male
Build:	Small
Race:	Chinese/Caucasian
Occupation(s):	Merchant seaman, qualified helicopter pilot, pharmacist, anaesthetist and physician
Nationality:	Japanese/Dutch
Remarks:	Manicured nails. Left-handed. Chews Swedish snuff. Speaks fluent English, Dutch, Japanese, Mandarin, and German.

Terajima is controller of Chinese syndicates known as
Malacca Cartel (MC), SnakeSkin (SS) or Black Shoe (BS).

He was being investigated by Winston in connection
with major maritime terrorism, importation of

explosives, extortion, importation of large
quantities of weapons, violence, bank robberies;
unlawful flight to avoid prosecution; armed robbery;
theft from intercontinental shipment; murders of
Chinese, Malaysian, British and European nationals
worldwide; conspiracy to murder such nationals; maritime terrorist attacks on commercial ships in South
East Asia.

He has taken innumerable hostages at gun- and knife-
point, handcuffed and bound them, and injected them
with unknown substances in order severely to disable
them.

Has high-ranking government and party contacts in
Beijing.

He is believed to have undergone training in
Guangzhon Military Area with Rapid Response Unit.

ZHENTUNG BROTHERS: Anthony, Foster, and Hastings

The ZHENTUNG BROTHERS have joint stakes in the
Zhentung Corporation with business centres in China,
Europe and United States, total worth in excess of
US$25 billion. The businesses are mainly concerned
with Shipping, Oil, Armaments, Pharmaceuticals,
Chemicals and Global Finance.

The Zhentung Foundation run by Anthony Zhentung is a
substantial supporter of the UK Conservative and New
Labour parties, and the Republican Party in the USA.
It also makes large charitable donations through the
Zhentung Foundation in the USA and UK.

Many of their assets are invisible. Their fortunes
listed as property of the House of Zhentung. They
are suspected of financing major maritime terrorist
and extortion syndicates throughout South East Asia
and South America.

Two years ago Anthony Zhentung was granted British
citizenship by the UK Home Office. Citizenship was
refused to Foster and Hastings Zhentung.

It was during this period that there was a split in the relationship between the brothers. Effectively, the triumvirate broke up. The Stockholm law firm of Palmen negotiated the split.

It is believed that, in return for immunity from prosecution in UK and US courts, Anthony Zhentung was prepared to give evidence against his brothers. The reasons for Anthony Zhentung's change of heart are not known, though his Swedish lawyers may very well know them. The Swedish lawyers refused to co-operate with representatives of the Hong Kong Police.

Mentions of Anthony Zhentung in the world media are extremely rare. This in spite of the fact that he socialises with UK politicians, the Queen and Prince of Wales, and the US President. All three Zhentung brothers have attended fund-raising events at which the Prime Minister and Foreign Secretary were present. Meanwhile, Foster and Hastings Zhentung pursue their business worldwide but without reference to or co-operation with Anthony Zhentung. Anthony Zhentung is in effect marginalised. He apparently lives in fear of retribution.

A few months ago, Winston filed an 86-page affidavit at the appropriate Hong Kong Court in secret session with witness statements and additional documents of evidence. No action was taken.

A freelance maritime journalist in Stockholm, Karl Erik Thurdin, claimed that US$50 million worth of kickbacks had been distributed to court. A spokeswoman for the Zhentungs let it be known that the allegations were part of a treasonable conspiracy against the family. There was a perfunctory inquiry in the UK. The findings remain secret.

Foster and Hastings Zhentung are believed to run secret coded accounts in the names of Zego and Landex and UK Verno Associates. Geneva and Luxembourg banks have frozen twenty-five bank accounts. The banks blocked investigations.

Both Foster and Hastings Zhentung have sworn affidavits that they have no connection with arms dealing.

It was Winston's belief that successful pursuit of Foster and Hastings Zhentung would cause devastating political embarrassment in China, the UK, USA and Europe. He still had hopes that Anthony Zhentung would eventually supply the evidence required to secure the prosecution of his brothers.

You should secretly maintain your watch on Anthony Zhentung, but keep your distance. Keep in touch. Let me know of any useful facts.

It was Winston who stood up to the authorities, whose opposition to the pursuit of the Zhentungs'/Terajima's major international terrorism and extortion rackets was as persistent as it was secretive and threatening. With Winston's death, the war is all but lost.

As one of Winston's greatest friends and most admired colleagues, Alan, you should take precautions to ensure your personal safety. Let me tell you that Winston was aware of your connection with Anthony Zhentung. He had been waiting for the right moment to involve you.

As a matter of extreme urgency you should consider distancing yourself from connection with these people. Keep in your mind that Klaas-Pieter Terajima is Controller of Security Operations for Foster and Hastings Zhentung.

24

After he had memorised the key points he handed the notes back to Catherine.

'Do you know anything more about this?' he asked her.

'No. But tell me,' she said, 'about your firm's professional connection with the Zhentung brothers?'

'The firm I work for, Milo Associates, supervises their personal security in London. No more. No less.'

'And you look', she said, 'as though you don't know about them.'

'I know about their legitimate business interests, their domestic routines when they're in London. They claim that there are plenty of people who wish to see harm done to them.'

'They're right.'

'That could well be so. But personal security and protection, that's as far as our involvement goes. I have to say that I can't understand why Winston never said anything to me about any of this. Can you think why that might be?'

'Maybe he was going to tell you,' she said. 'Maybe he wasn't ready to tell you. Who knows? Who can tell? None of us could have fore-seen what happened out there at sea. Not even Winston. He took one risk too many. But then that was Winston. He took calculated risks. And he got his last calculations wrong.'

'And this man called Terajima?' Rosslyn asked.

'You've never heard of him?'

'No,' said Rosslyn.

'Klaas-Pieter Terajima may not be his real name.'

'But he was aboard the *Xiang Chuan*. And he reckoned Winston was looking for him. I know it's only supposition –'

'It is,' Catherine said. 'I know what you're thinking. He could have killed him. As you say, that's only supposition.'

'Say someone had the motive, the opportunity and the means to kill Winston,' Rosslyn said. 'That's to say if Winston died from some cause or causes other than the injuries he sustained –'

'There's no proof of that,' she said. 'The first aid man's report on the cause of death was accepted. You've heard from someone else that Winston may have been murdered?'

'Not in so many words,' said Rosslyn. 'Mei has misgivings. So too, it seems, does Dr Graer, the intelligence officer at the Australian Consulate, and his American friend, his counterpart, who has to be CIA. Mei told me that Graer is, as she put it, weird.'

'So is Swann. They get up people's noses. Graer is said to have some nasty sexual predilections. Did they tell you anything?'

'It was what they didn't say that seemed, well, odd to me. But tell me, how much, if anything, do you think Mei knows about her father's work?'

'Probably more than she told you,' said Catherine. 'You should know that Mei isn't a woman who lets sleeping dogs lie.'

'She wants to join the Hong Kong Police to chase the dogs?'

'Steve can't really fathom why she wants to join. A young and pretty woman of her abilities. She should find herself a better life.'

'Just wants to follow in her father's footsteps?'

'Which makes no real sense to me,' said Catherine. 'I mean, who knows whether she might be one of Terajima's next victims?'

'Has Steve warned her about him?'

'Yes,' she said. 'She says she has no quarrel with Steve's enemies.'

'Maybe she's right.'

'Maybe she's wrong. You know why Steve wants you to know all this? Because if something else happens to him, he believes you can instigate the pursuit of Terajima. Then there are the Zhentungs. Look, we can get them if you help. These people stop at nothing. Nothing. You see if they don't strike again. And how many more people will die? You look at me. Look at me. See what they did. You've seen what they did to Steve. You didn't see me at Winston's funeral. Know why? Because when I see people, when I feel people staring at me, I see my reflection in the mirrors of their eyes. That's what Terajima did. We got too close to the fire. He's the flame. Get too near to it and you get burned.'

They sat in silence for a while. Catherine was on the verge of tears and Rosslyn reached out to touch her hand. Finally, he said, 'I'd like to see Steve again.'

'He can't see you again here in Hong Kong,' Catherine said. 'It's too dangerous for all of us.'

'Tell me why.'

'Believe me.'

'I believe you,' said Rosslyn. 'We could arrange a covert rendez-vous anyway, they're not about to attack me.'

'Oh really, really,' she said. 'You were the friend of Winston. You're the friend of Steve. Me too. And there's Mei. Listen to me, maybe you should never have come to Hong Kong. Maybe you should never have spoken up for Winston in the way you did. Don't imagine, for one moment, that Winston's enemies will not have heard of what you said. And now you're implicated with Mei, with Steve, with me. I do not see how you can turn aside. Or if you walk away, well, as the man says, "If you're not with us, you're against us."'

'Believe me, Catherine,' said Rosslyn, 'I am not going to walk away. For a start, we can meet when I'm in KL at the end of the month. I told Steve. I'll be reviewing security on a ship called *Orient Angel*. I'm joining her in KL for the journey to Singapore. You tell him to contact me there. At the end of the month.'

'We'll be in New Zealand.'

'Then I think you should tell Steve to find time to meet me in KL.' He gave her back the papers.

'You have to have eyes in the back of your head,' she said. 'You have to remember what the maritime terrorists have done to crews. Steve and me. We're the lucky ones. The not-so-walking wounded. Others fared far less well. You should see the photos of the corpses. The castrated. Castrated. How? And you know how. With someone's fingernails.'

'That's what forensic said?'

'Surgical incision with sharpened fingernails. Long and pointed fingernails like a ladyboy's. And the others. You want to know?'

'Tell me.'

'They were left hanging upside down, bleeding, from deck rails. Bleeding alive. Bleeding till they died. That's what they tell me. They bled to death like animals in an abattoir. It gives the killers pleasure to watch. Others, the survivors, they were so severely traumatised they went out of their minds altogether.'

'And you think we can find these people?'

'Terajima? He'll find you. He'll find Steve. He'll find me. But finding

71

him, that's another matter. You're looking for a needle in a haystack. You're looking at Mathias Utagawa. Henrick Shintara. Dr Dehaan Sakamoto. Dr Hung. Pastor Pang. Pastor Mogens Leung. The whole list. Are they one person or several?' She folded the papers into the white envelope. 'You know why Steve's leaving the police? It's not because of his disability. No.'

'He told me something about it. About New Zealand. The farm.'

She shook her head. 'He won't have told you that it's because the guilt has got to him. It's destroyed his will to go on. Guilt because of what Terajima did to me. And Steve and Winston got to them too late. Far too late. No, Steve is certain he's failed himself and failed me. That's what I think.'

'You mustn't think like that, Catherine.'

'That's what the therapists tell me. They know bullshit. And some of those crews. They died in coffins. They'd been fastened into cheap coffins while they were still alive. The coffins had spy holes drilled through the tops so Terajima could stare at them. Eyeball to lousy eyeball. Just imagine how they died.'

'Are you sure of this?'

'It doesn't matter what I'm sure of. That's what the survivors said and Winston never doubted them. Others may have done. But Winston knew the truth of it.'

'What have the law enforcement agencies achieved?'

'*Achieved*? Oh, they've *achieved* a terrific lot. They've saved their fat butts. You know why the police here, the CIA and the Australians closed the investigation? Because they were scared shitless that Winston and Steve would discredit the whole lot of them and that the scandal would cause irreparable damage. No matter about the dead and missing. The disappeared. The maimed. Look, life's cheap, isn't it? Everyone's lives are increasingly cheap, believe you me. The favoured thing to do with life is take it. That way profit lies. That's Terajima. Dr Profit. And the most successful butcher is always the one who loves blood. Ask your butcher when you get home.'

She broke off, exhausted, and for a while turned to gaze in silence at the television.

'I give you my word,' Rosslyn said, 'I'll take a long and careful look at things when I'm back in London. Then we can consider everything when Steve and I meet in KL. Give me your number in New Zealand.'

She handed him a printed card. 'You can reach us at my mother's place. If we're not there, she'll tell you where to get hold of us.'

'And in between times?'

She stared at him without blinking. 'The friends of Winston's are the enemies of Terajima and the Zhentungs.'

'I believe you, Catherine.'

'That's the price of friendship with Winston. The price of what Winston said he wanted of you. To watch over Mei. He will have said something like "You promise me until hell freezes." Did he say that?'

'In so many words, yes. Near enough. I promised to keep watch over Mei.'

'That would be so much easier', she said, 'if Winston were alive. But he isn't. And you could say that we're all of us left alone staring death in the face.'

She turned her head sideways, showing him the full extent of the brutal facial scars. 'You wouldn't want that to happen to Mei.'

'No, Catherine, of course I wouldn't. And I don't want it to happen to you. Or any human being. Never ever again.'

Smiling wanly at him, she said, 'We have so much to do. I hope you have a safe journey home to London.'

'Thanks,' said Rosslyn. 'My best to Steve. You two take care of each other.'

Immediately Catherine left, Rosslyn wrote down everything he had managed to commit to memory. Writing as fast as possible, he noted the main points in his self-invented shorthand.

It was not a perfect reproduction of what he had read. But it made for chilling reading.

25

During the flight to Heathrow the following day Steve's words echoed in his mind.

As one of Winston's greatest friends and most admired colleagues, Alan, you should take precautions to ensure your personal safety. Let me tell you that Winston was aware of your connection with Anthony Zhentung. He had been waiting for the right moment to involve you.

As a matter of extreme urgency you should consider distancing yourself from connection with these people. Keep in your mind that Klaas-Pieter Terajima is Controller of Security Operations for Foster and Hastings Zhentung.

This was the introduction to his adversary. The question that kept on repeating itself in Rosslyn's mind was *Where is he?*

Xiong di bu he ying guo tie.
Quarrelling brothers are harder than iron.
CHINESE PROVERB

26

Klaas-Pieter Terajima loved the view of Beijing framed by the window of his small room. The play of the morning sun across the snow. Shafts of sunlight glowing gold. Shadows of blue, violet and pink. The view afforded him an acute sense of aesthetic pleasure. Beijing might be in the grip of winter, but the city, in spite of its modernistic ugliness, had what he considered to be a peculiar and eternal beauty.

The room was in the university area of north west Beijing, where his neighbours knew him as Pastor Leung. Most considered him to be austere, even ascetic. Others found him affable and courteous. Local wisdom had it that he was a scholar. Terajima had confided in an acupuncturist prone to gossiping that his life's work was a new translation of the *Analects* of Confucius and the provision of a critical commentary upon the philosophy of the Master. The acupuncturist, a widow on the lookout for new romance, hinted that the Pastor had taken a vow of chastity. That, at any rate, was how she had explained away the scholar's rejection of her advances.

Disciplined work, courtesy, delicacy of manner, the brisk solitary walks he was seen to take several times a day: reports of such matters satisfied the curiosity of the local community. More importantly, he was also said to have *guanxi* or useful personal connections with the authorities. His neighbours might otherwise have been suspicious of the officials and occasional foreigners who visited his small office – like the man he was waiting for today. Some of the foreigners were said to be South African and Australian, even Dutch. It was said the Pastor could speak Dutch, a most unfamiliar tongue.

Of course he could. There was something, well, unique about him. The origins of his uniqueness were to be found in his family upbringing in Amsterdam and The Hague. His father had been Chinese and his mother, Kasuko Terajima, part Dutch and part Japanese. Klaas-Pieter's dentists frequently commented upon this racial combination.

As a child he had suffered at the hands of orthodontists. The problem was that the physical form of his mouth's interior was essentially Japanese. It was round and small. But his teeth were Caucasian and large, too large for the mouth, and his second teeth caused havoc with his jaw. His parents, bourgeois and conservative, had spent many pounds on surgeons' fees in London. The ministrations of the surgeons did nothing to alleviate the child's continual headaches. He had rarely been without swabs between his gums soaked in some newfangled painkiller.

The boy was given to violent outbursts, which greatly disturbed his father, a Lutheran theologian. The solitary Klaas-Pieter haunted the canalsides of Amsterdam and made friends among the sex workers, who petted him and early in life – some might say too early – satisfied his precocious sexuality, regularly allowing him, unseen by clients, to watch them in pursuit of their profession.

'Career choices', as his father called them, were endlessly discussed. The teenage Klaas-Pieter wanted to be a doctor, a gynaecologist. He vastly impressed his teachers with his encyclopaedic knowledge of anatomy and neurology. The mysteries of pain particularly enchanted him. At some stage, he rejected his medical studies and joined the merchant marine in Bremerhaven. He experimented with drugs during the periods of rest and recreation he took in South East Asia.

Finally, he jumped ship and began trading in gemstones, drugs, transportable antiquities lifted from temples. He lived according to what he called one-word maxims. Calculation. Observation. Organisation. Control. As to death, he said, 'I laugh at it. And death smiles back.'

It is hard to say when he first acquired his fascination with Confucius and the *Analects*. But Confucian thought seemed to offer him a diversion from pragmatism. It seemed to satisfy his driven mind. This, combined with an extraordinarily receptive memory, his energy, his scrupulous attention to his own security and his inside knowledge of the workings of police forces on several continents, caused him to lead what he called the 'professional life'. Professional in the sense that he earned money in vast sums and studied the best methods available to protect it in European banks, whose rules of secrecy he so greatly admired.

He felt he had much in common with the neat little men and women he dealt with in Luxembourg, whether at the Vansburgische

Landesbank, Notherfurland Kommunalbank or Langeller Meridion-ale Direktbank. They took their commission for diverting his cash flow into Middle East asset management syndicates and American property investment portfolios. He handled the officials with the similar arrogance he showed towards those who commissioned him to plan extortion strategies and to execute murder, robbery and the illicit transportation of arms. It was, of course, inevitable that the pursuit of maritime terrorism, his milch cow – not a phrase he employed, or probably even understood – had attracted him.

Maritime crime, or what he described to the bank officials as MS&R (Maritime Survey and Recovery), suited his temperament to a tee. It was quick to carry out. It was virtually impossible for the booty to be traced. He was demonstrably well suited to dealing with many nationalities. He spoke their languages. Understood their cultures. He was, as he put it, a citizen of the world, without national or racial prejudice. How could any police force in the world, bogged down in traditional local customs, old-world laws and failing systems of criminal justice, hope to catch up with him? Such systems were pathologically committed to power, to lumbering, predictable and failing systems of democracy. The concepts of democracy and citi-zenship with which his father had tried to imbue young Klaas-Pieter had quite simply evaporated.

This sums up something of the man who was enjoying his breakfast of fresh greens inside an omelette wrapped in a pancake, accompanied by a bowl of green tea, *jianbing guozi*. One of the unsung geniuses in the fight against humanity. *Huo xi fuo suo yi. Fu xi huo suo fu.* ('Good fortune lies within bad. Bad fortune lurks within good.')

Terajima considered his successful killing of Winston Lim. He had waited with great patience for Lim's dour obsession to get the better of him: to strike at the moment his opponent was off balance, for the most perfect of unexpected moments. And what a stupid risk Lim had taken with Typhoon Yanyan! The man had shown no respect for nature. Terajima prided himself upon having read his adversary's mind with accuracy. It had sometimes disturbed him that Lim must have understood him just as he had understood Lim. Now his was the victory and the pleasure. He understood Lim and the meaning of the survival of the fittest. *Lim, as they say, is history.*

Of course, as Mother Terajima used to say in her dreadful Chinese: *Qi gai wu zhong, lan han zi cheng* – roughly speaking, 'if you become a lazy beggar it's no one's fault but your own.' Naturally, he would have preferred Lim's ending to have been, as he phrased it to himself, *more Terajima-friendly*, more terrible. Mother would have agreed that he only had himself to blame. There had really been no alternative other than to dispatch his adversary with the lethal injection of diamorphine. Terajima was disappointed that his victim had finally drifted towards his Maker riding high and painlessly on clouds of diamorphine. He would have preferred for Lim to have died fully conscious of his pain.

There had also been another matter that Terajima found mildly irritating. Consulting the website of the *South China Daily News,* he learned that the journalist who had reported the death of Winston Lim had misquoted the ship's doctor. The man should have been even more fulsome still in his praise of Lim. The Master said, 'Listen much, keep silent when in doubt, and always take heed of the tongue; thou wilt make few mistakes.'

No matter. There was the encrypted e-mail of congratulation from Geneva to his bank in Beijing. Declaring themselves well pleased, Foster and Hastings Zhentung had given the green light for the second phase of Operation Global White Out. Unconstrained by the rules of international humanitarian law, Terajima relished his responsibility for its deadly completion. Employing whatever means of extortion, coercion or terror, Operation Global White Out was the wholesale elimination of the intelligence sources aligned against the Zhentung brothers in Europe and South East Asia.

The sun warmed the softness of his skin and fuelled the sources of his inner energies. The sunny disposition brings good fortune. Mother Terajima had once told him as a child, 'There is truth in scraps of wisdom to be found in fortune cookies. Joy too.' But not quite as much joy as he found in the scrap of paper he had discovered waiting him for him in his office mailbox on the evening he returned from Hong Kong. The scrap of paper with the coded message that two million US dollars had been paid into his Vansburgische Landesbank account in Luxembourg. He inserted a tab of Swedish snuff between his lower lip and gum and felt the familiar pleasant rush of adrenaline.

Shortly after Terajima had cleared the remains of breakfast from the table, his visitor arrived. The visitor was Marcel. Marcel was his operational name.

27

He was prematurely grey and overweight. Claiming to be a lawyer qualified in what he called diplomatic law, Marcel was the half-brother of a gemstone dealer in the Philippines.

On edge and sweating, Marcel lit up one of the cigarettes he chain-smoked. It amused Terajima that he made Marcel apprehensive. This morning, as usual, Marcel's apprehension made him aggressive. Marcel liked attempting to score points against Terajima. He was unable to resist asserting himself. The attempts were consistently unsuccessful. Terajima had sometimes wondered why Marcel even bothered to assert himself at all. Let alone so poorly mimicking the South African accent to disguise his real one.

Marcel said, 'The typhoon was fortunate for you.'

'"The smile of the storm offers the best means of execution."'

'I have no time for bloody riddles.'

'I know you are a hunted man,' said Terajima, enjoying Marcel's role of *idiot savant*. '"The wise servant should heed my words."'

'That's as bloody may be,' Marcel said. 'Our friends must be pleased with your score.'

'They are not my friends, neither are they yours. You are the servant-supplier and I am the technician. What happened in the South China Sea is only one small part of our work.'

'It was bloody incredible.'

'I have no belief in the incredible.'

'So what is this business you have in Malaysia now?'

'It's best for you that you don't know,' said Terajima.

'But if you need equipment –'

'– your job is to supply it.'

'Maybe I could offer advice.'

'Don't waste your breath. The only person who offers me advice that I take is me.'

Marcel stared at Terajima. He was unable to disguise the fear and hate he felt. He wiped the sweat from his forehead and Terajima smiled at him, tilting his head with a look of condescension. Not that the Zhentungs themselves had chosen this man Marcel as one of the go-between suppliers of lethal ordnance, guns, explosives and drugs. Oh no. The selection of Marcel had been Terajima's business. Appointments were his choice alone. He loved to exercise the power of patronage. The power to appoint. To sack. To induce expectation and excitement and then remove it with thrilling suddenness.

He had made it his business to look into Marcel's primary cover, his brother's gemstone businesses in Manila. He had even bought some junk from the store of pug-face's brother under an assumed identity. Ostensibly the gemstone dealership was legitimate – or as legitimate as any foreign gem dealer's business is in the Philippines. And the brother had a useful sideline. He also brokered used cargo ships, motor yachts and powerboats. The purchase of the MV *Xiang Chuan* had gone through Marcel's brother's books. His brother had built up well-greased mechanisms to make contacts with suppliers in Malaysia and Indonesia. The sweating Marcel was discreet and careful. But his sexual proclivities, his seedy interest in under-age Asian youth of both genders, might one day prove his undoing. So far it was a wonder he had stayed out of jail. Terajima despised pug-face's predilections.

'Marcel, relax.' Terajima gave his visitor a smile. 'This is the list. Your brother will purchase a high-powered V-shape monohull powerboat in Malacca. Equipped with tanks carrying enough gasoline to cross the Malacca Strait and return. You will purchase it under the name of your brother's business in Manila. The man who will take delivery will contact you. You will deal with him. You will come to me for settlement of your brother's account.'

'It will be expensive.'

'So may your mistakes be.'

'When do you want this powerboat?"

'Have your brother get it now.'

'If there are problems?'

'There will be no problems, Marcel. We don't deal with the weak, who have problems, do we? We deal with the strong, who create solutions.'

'I like to think so,' said Marcel. 'What's the name of the man who'll contact me?'

'Never mind his name,' Terajima said. 'He'll call you at your place of work.'

'Remember I am a government employee.'

'Of course. It's very useful cover, Marcel. Our friend will call you and say he is in business with Tzu-kung.'

'Who's he when he's at home?'

Terajima slowly turned his chair towards the window. 'Code-named after the disciple of Confucius.'

'Ah, yes,' said Marcel. 'I understand.'

Marcel didn't understand. There was a great deal the sweating Marcel didn't understand about the clammy darkness Pastor Leung inspired. With the relief of a man escaping the clutches of a phantom, he left the room without another word.

Terajima was glad to be rid of Marcel's necessary presence.

28

He gazed at the several nail files arranged among the sharpened coloured pencils in the wooden box. Next to the box were CDs and the miniature CD player. It was playing *The Best of Snakeskin* and his favourite track.

> Probe me with your love
> Kiss me with your snake tongue
> Probe me with your love
> I don't care how long you take
> So long as we've begun.

Such sweet memories of nakedness inside the white silk dressing gown.

He took out a nail file and walked to the calendar on the wall. Tapping out the rhythm of 'Probe Me', he sang in a falsetto whisper 'I don't care how long you take.'

Filing his fingernails, he made a mental list of dates and key requirements.

Lifejackets with body armour encased in a high tensile polymer fabric.
Automatic assault rifles.
Sub-machine guns.
Handguns.
Portable canisters of Xeona nerve gas.
Lightweight shoulder-fired anti-aircraft missiles AM-1 LSFMAAMs.
PETN high explosive (pentaerythritol tetranitrate).
TATP (triacetone triperoxide).
Plasticiser.
Fuses.
Detonation cord.

He licked the fine white nail dust from his fingertips. It was time to make the visits of the day.

29

First. To the hairdresser who attended mainly to the Chaoyang Theatre acrobats at the gymnasium where he worked out.

Second. To collect cash from the Bank of China at 410 Fuchengmen Nei Dajie.

Third. To the store in Jianguomen Dajie for the clothes he required. The selection of new clothing was determined by the *People's Daily* forecast for Malaysia.

Mostly Cloudy 89 F 31 C Humidity: 78 Wind: N / 7mph / 11kph Visibility: fair. Dewpoint: 72 F / 22 C.

He selected clothing suitable for jungle and swampland. Work wear for the night at sea in the Malacca Strait.

From Jianguomen Dajie he made his way to the intersection of Xi Chang'an Jie with Xidan Bei Dajie. Here, in the Telecom Office he used a card phone to put through the call to Malacca.

When the man's voice answered in Mandarin, the Pastor said, 'Snake.'

The other man said, 'Skin.'

'Ni hao?' ('How are you?')

'Wo hen hao.' ('I'm fine.)

'What is the status of recruits?'

'Green. I have the full crew.'

'The RV will be the Batu Pahat Rest House.'

'Okay.'

'Xiexie.' ('Thank you.')

'Bukeqi.' ('You're welcome.')

His next call was to London.

'Suzuki Freewind 650,' Terajima said.

'Suzuki Freewind 650,' the voice from London repeated.

'Ni hao?' ('How are you?')

'*Wo hen hao.*' ('I'm fine.')

The voice told him there was a seat booked for him aboard the Malaysian Airlines flight to Kuala Lumpur.

The time of his Kuala Lumpur meeting the following day with Foster and Hastings Zhentung was confirmed. Just over fifteen miles from the centre of the city and conveniently close to the airport, the location was the Pan Pacific Glenmarie Resort.

'*Xiexie.*' ('Thank you.')

'*Bukeqi.*' ('You're welcome.')

Finally, he headed for Andung Lu and the enormous swimming pool. The pool is of Olympic dimensions. Here, with relentless perseverance, he would swim for almost three hours until his limbs ached and his lungs grew weary. He found something especially appealing about the pain of swimming to the limits of endurance. Stroke after stroke, until you reach a state of semi-consciousness. Swimming in the murky waters of the tropics held the greatest appeal of all for him. *Shui zhi qing ze wu yu*, as Mother Terajima had taught him – 'You won't find fish in clear water.'

It was a delightful way of passing the day in Beijing and he cast his mind ahead to Malaysia.

There were two parcels to be collected from his *poste restante*. He looked forward to reading the contents of the first parcel, offprints he had ordered from UCLA and Columbia: 'The Elusive Distinction between Bribery and Extortion' from the *UCLA Law Review*, and 'Unravelling the Paradox of Blackmail' from the *Columbia Law Review*. The second parcel contained the excellent *Maritime Terror* by Gray, Monday and Stubblefield.

Such were the studies that would comprise his in-flight reading aboard the flight to Kuala Lumpur.

30

The following day the chauffeur-driven limousine with darkened windows collected Terajima from the main terminal building of Kuala Lumpur International Airport south of Sepang.

The limousine swept along the North South Central Link and North Klang Valley expressways in the direction of the city. It turned off towards Subang Jaya and Jalan Glenmarie for the Pan Pacific Glenmarie, the three hundred and fifty acre luxury hotel resort with landscape gardens and golf courses where Terajima would be the guest of the Zhentungs.

There was a message waiting for him in his Pacific Wing de luxe suite. A ribbon of purple artificial silk nylon attached it to the spray of orchids on the marble table in the centre of the main room.

> Greetings
> Please join us for dinner in the
> Cenderawasih restaurant at 10
>
> F&H Zhentung

It was while he was swimming in the hotel pool that something struck him as odd about the dinner invitation. There was no mention of Anthony Zhentung.

31

At ten o'clock, the *maitre d'hôtel* escorted him to the Zhentung brothers' table in the Cenderawasih. The restaurant was packed with Japanese golfers from Tokyo wearing the blazers of the Kazusa Monarch Country Club.

When Terajima reached the Zhentungs' table he found the brothers in animated conversation with a Japanese. The brothers wore tailored black silk suits similar to Terajima's. Their table was by the windows, with the view of the sweeping gardens, artificial lake and fountains in the foreground and the manicured golf course beyond.

'Foreign people welcome,' the Japanese was saying. 'Kazusa Monarch Country Club was designed by Jack Nicklaus. Membership twenty seven million yen. *Gorofu* perfect. Three million entrance fee. Very exclusive. Could be Hawaii or California. No *Macdonurondos*. Ninety minutes only from downtown Tokyo.'

Terajima looked across the restaurant. He reckoned the three men at the table near the main entrance were Americans. Nearer he saw a man seated alone. Probably Chinese, he wore a lightweight blue linen suit. What intrigued Terajima was that the man was wearing dark glasses and that there was a white cane beside his chair. He had an earpiece connected to the miniature CD player on his table.

'*Gorofu* course seven thousand and twenty yards long,' the Japanese explained. 'Best in Japan. Featured on worldwide BBC *Terri-Bee*. Pool bar and mah-jong room. Japanese chef serves French food. Play at Monarch with me next time instead of Sakawa Royal Golf Club?'

The Zhentungs politely accepted the Japanese's business card and told him they looked forward to renewing their acquaintance with him when next they visited Tokyo. The Japanese bowed and returned to his table.

'Welcome to KL,' said Foster Zhentung. 'I hope our Japanese friend's presence didn't bore you. He's among the three wealthiest

Japanese ship owners. A golf freak.' Foster Zhentung smiled. 'We're very satisfied with your result,' he said. He beckoned to the waiter to pour the wine.

'I am satisfied,' said Terajima.

'I can imagine,' Foster Zhentung said.

They raised their glasses and made a silent toast.

Terajima doubted that either of the Zhentungs could imagine quite how satisfied he really was. How is Anthony?' he asked.

'He's fine, just fine. Otherwise detained.' It seemed they had no wish to discuss their absent brother. 'The completion of the first stage of Operation Global White Out gives us more freedom to manoeuvre,' he announced. 'Not that it has removed other serious obstacles. There remain those in London, in Hong Kong and elsewhere. There's much unfinished business for you to finish. Tell us, are you contented with the fees paid to date?'

'To date, yes. But if this unfinished business means higher risks, greater complexity –'

'You mean if the locations are in London and the Malacca Strait?'

'Yes. I have my own security to maintain. You understand that it's expensive.'

'If you need us to invest in that, then now is your chance to say so,' Foster Zhentung said. 'What's your major area of concern?'

'Elements in the Hong Kong police who may seek revenge.'

'Revenge for the death of Lim?'

'You mean for the death of Lim and other reasons.'

'Do these "other reasons" affect our interests?' asked Hastings Zhentung.

'I've no immediate way of knowing,' said Terajima. 'People will be making enquiries.'

'And it's your job – shall we say, it's also in your interests – not so much to limit damage as to prevent any damage taking place.'

'I understand that,' said Terajima. 'We have much in common. I too am looking to my future.'

'Which lies with us,' said Foster Zhentung. He glanced at his brother, Hastings.

Hastings gave a slight nod, which seemed to Terajima to be a sign of agreement. 'You have, of course, a general understanding of our international commercial interests? There are those who wish to hinder them. Indeed, there are those who perhaps wish to see them stopped entirely. They will go to any lengths to oppose us. In the past, before your day, there were people who tried to do so. Linked to government agencies seeking to put an end to maritime terrorism. It is only natural that we make it very clear that the effort isn't worth it. You know such people?'

'Sure – the owners of the *Manju Alpha* after she left Kuala Tanjung. You netted fifty million US dollars. There was the renamed *Vanonlan Deng*. It ended up in Zhangjiagang. Major arms consignments. Diamonds. Who knows how many million dollars in six different currencies? And there are others.'

'And you got your ten per cent.'

'I got my ten per cent.'

'Paid into your Luxembourg accounts.'

'Sure.'

'We have to remember how close Lim got. Lim's gone. But there's Kwok.'

'I've broken Kwok. He suffered the penalty for assisting Lim. You know what I achieved in respect of Kwok, to say nothing of his wife. I burned most of her face off. If there are others, I can do the same to them.'

'Some people are very closely protected.'

The three men sat in silence while the waiters brought steamed crabs and jellied pork to the table. The wine waiter refilled the men's glasses and opened a second bottle.

Terajima deftly dismembered his crab. After he had sucked the flesh from the largest claw, he said, 'No one can protect themselves if violence is well planned.'

'Don't forget it,' said Foster Zhentung.

'Do I make mistakes? I never enter the yellow box unless I have three exits.'

'But there is always the risk of betrayal.'

'Sure. I take precautions against that.'

Foster Zhentung stared at the view of the floodlit lake and dancing fountains.

'We have one major immediate target,' Hastings Zhentung said. 'Highly protected.'

'This is the London operation? I have already ordered the *matériel* to do the job.'

'You will be seeing to it yourself?'

'With a professional associate in London who will work under my supervision.'

'But you – *you* will not see to it *personally*?'

'It involves explosives. It's too dangerous for me to do personally in London. I don't wish to excite the interest of British anti-terrorist squads. I need a cut-off. Someone known only to me. He gets paid cash. One hell of a lot of cash. I provide him with the get-out and escape route. I never see him again. He never sees me.'

'What if he is apprehended and he talks?'

'It will be impossible,' said Terajima.

'What makes you so sure?'

'Because once he satisfactorily completes the job of killing your chosen target, I will kill him.'

'*You* will?'

'Me *personally*. I will kill him.'

'And if the body is found? If his identity is traced, say, traced back to you?'

'It won't be. I have prepared the necessary arrangements.'

'What are they?'

'Arrangements for incineration. In the interests of prudence, efficiency and time I will burn him alive. It will, of course, be expensive.'

'Supposing the figure is acceptable to us,' said Hastings Zhentung, 'what guarantee will you give against failure – say, failure arising from unforeseen problems?'

'You may wish to, but I can't afford to consider failure. None of us can afford failure. Unless you are careless, even in the smallest degree, and allow someone prior knowledge of my work. No, I do not deal in problems. I am not an idealist. I am a pragmatist. I deal in solutions.'

'Very well,' said Hastings Zhentung. 'Do you have any questions you want to put to us?'

'Yes. The targets. Who is the first?'

Hastings Zhentung dipped his hands in the finger bowl. 'You have no great need at present to be concerned. Suffice it to say that we have been betrayed. Betrayed in a way that could lead to our exposure. That is what we believe. A close partner has confided in a lawyer.' He wiped his lips and pointed teeth on his table napkin. 'The lawyer fortunately presents us with no difficulty. We have bought his silence. He's formidably compromised. He won't deal against us.

Our partner is unaware of this. For the time being, at any rate. However, we can't be sure when our partner will take things further. He represents a very dangerous risk to us. He will be your target in London.'

'Who is he?'

'We will give you the details you need once the contract is agreed between us tomorrow morning.'

'What is the second target?'

'It's still more complex,' said Foster Zhentung.

All three men exchanged glances. The Zhentungs' eyes were inscrutable. So too was the look Terajima gave them.

The Japanese golfer was approaching the table and the Zhentungs got to their feet.

'I don't wish to talk to this man any more.'

'I don't wish to talk to him at all,' said Terajima.

The three men edged between the tables for the exit. Terajima looked hard at the face of the blind man listening to music. The face seemed familiar to him. He couldn't quite place it and headed for the Spa where he had booked an appointment with the manicurist.

32

The torrential storm broke the following morning at eight o'clock

Foster Zhentung telephoned Terajima to say he and Hastings would meet him in the hotel's main lounge, the Glen.

The windows afforded panoramic views of the rain across the golf course. The restaurant was once more packed with Japanese in blazers.

The Zhentungs and Terajima sat close together near the windows, well away from the throng of Japanese.

The meeting over coffee was brief.

Foster Zhentung said, 'You noticed the absence of our brother, Anthony?'

'Yes.'

'You are familiar with his duplex apartment in London by the river?'

'We've met there many times.'

'We want it *damaged*.'

'*Damaged*?'

'Yes. It is by way of a warning to him.'

'Have you already warned him?'

'Yes, we have. And he hasn't taken it. Such damage will continue until such times as he comes to heel.'

'It could be dangerous,' said Terajima.

'That's a matter you will have to overcome.'

'It will be very expensive for you,' said Terajima.

'We can discuss finance shortly,' said Foster Zhentung.

Terajima was toying with the two small gold crucifixes and silver hearts attached to the gold chain around his right wrist. The manicurist who had attended to his nails the previous night had noticed them around Terajima's neck and she had said it would bring luck if Terajima wore them on his right wrist.

'Anthony's the partner you were talking about last night over dinner?' Terajima said.

'Yes.'

'You said he had talked to his lawyer.'

'Yes. He won't cause us any further problems.'

Terajima looked doubtful. 'You're sure of that?'

'Quite sure. Yes.'

'Tell me,' said Terajima, 'what sort of security is there at your brother's place?'

'Conventional. A man called Rosslyn supervises it. Alan Rosslyn, who's a partner in a firm of private investigators, Douglas Milo Associates. The firm has an association with a London lawyer called Victor Michaelson. Michaelson is on friendly terms with Anthony.'

'This man Ross–'

'Rosslyn.'

'Rosslyn. Is he some sort of permanent fixture at your brother's place?'

'No. Anthony only calls upon him for what you might call special needs. If, say, Anthony has some figure of importance visiting him. Otherwise, there is Anthony's staff. Drivers and bodyguards. Some of them are armed.'

'With what?'

'Heckler & Koch MP5 sub-machine guns.'

'You're talking very serious weapons.'

'That's why we advised you to employ explosives. Serious explosives.'

'They are serious.'

'Such as what?'

'Technically, a mixture of PETN, pentaerythritol tetranitrate, and TATP, triacetone triperoxide. That will do the job for you.'

'That's good,' said Foster Zhentung. 'Similarly, there's the matter of Malacca. This time you will be looking at a container ship. The target is the eighty thousand tonne Svenske-Britannia *Orient Angel*. British registered. Anthony owns Svenske-Britannia. *Orient Angel* is what he calls the pearl of his fleet. You will be given the ship's sailing schedule and so forth by an American associate we employ, a former CIA officer. Your rendezvous with her will be in Batu Pahat at the junction of the roads to Ayer Hitam and Kukup.'

'I choose my own RVs.'

'On this occasion we can trust our American friend to have got it right.'

'Her life won't be worth living if she gets things wrong.'

'I think you'll find she is aware of that,' said Foster Zhentung. '*Orient Angel* is your target. One thing remains for me to make very clear to you – you and your associates will take no prisoners.'

Terajima smiled. 'What makes you think I might?'

'We won't allow that to cross our minds,' said Foster Zhentung. 'Now, your fee. What do you have in mind?'

Terajima always preferred the other side to open the bidding. 'You say.'

Foster Zhentung demurred with a silent grin.

'Shoot,' said Terajima.

'Given that I assume we are talking seven figures –'

'I haven't mentioned figures,' said Terajima.

'It isn't your style to do so,' said Foster Zhentung.

'Yours neither.'

Foster Zhentung sat back in his chair and took a pocket calculator from his inside jacket pocket. He tapped in a figure and handed the calculator to Terajima.

Terajima read: **2 0 0 0 0 0 0**

'UK sterling?'

'UK sterling.'

Terajima shook his head. 'Don't even think about it.'

'You are a very hard man, Terajima-san,' said Hastings Zhentung quietly.

'That's why you pay me. Listen, Zhentung, you couldn't find anyone better than me. No one more reliable. No one who sees into the future like I do. One day, who knows, if your luck runs out, I may have to find another partner like you. It takes time to choose the right partner in life. I guess that's what I've learned from you. So if my luck runs out, what do I face? I'll tell you. I face either a firing squad or the electric chair. Or when I hit, say, fifty and I retire, I will need a pension fund.'

'You already have very considerable funds in Luxembourg.'

'That's my business,' said Terajima.

'Very well,' said Zhentung. 'Show me your sum.'

Terajima took some time to tap the figures into the calculator. He could afford to take his time. He knew and they knew that together they had passed the point of no return. It was a matter of mutual need.

He handed the calculator back to Foster Zhentung. 'There you have it.'

Zhentung read: **6000000**

Zhentung's face was expressionless. 'Final bid,' he said, tapping in: **5500000**. He handed the calculator back to Terajima.

They stared at each other. Eyeball to eyeball. Neither blinked.

'UK sterling. Electronic transfer into my account in Luxembourg now.'

'They're six and a half hours behind us.'

'My bank's always open,' said Terajima. 'Use your mobile phone.'

'Very well,' said Foster Zhentung.

While Foster Zhentung called Terajima's bank, the Vansburgische Landesbank in Luxembourg, Hastings Zhentung spoke up for the second time.

'I have been admiring your wrist chains,' he said almost inaudibly. 'I have often wondered about your personal relationships.'

'Well you may,' said Terajima blankly.

'Who is Kitty?' Hastings Zhentung asked.

'She's dead.'

'And Mei?'

'A girl I know.'

Hastings Zhentung noticed Terajima's expression change momentarily.

A girl I know. There was no hiding it. He could tell that Terajima knew her well.

'You have a soft spot for this Mei?' Hastings Zhentung asked.

'You were the one who said I was a very hard man,' said Terajima.

'The mention of her name brings a soft look to your eyes.'

Terajima shook his head.

'I hope I haven't caused you any offence.'

'I never take offence,' said Terajima. 'I give it. Life is so much easier that way, don't you think?'

Foster Zhentung had finished the business with the Vansburgische Landesbank. He was holding out his mobile phone for Terajima to use it. 'You can confirm the deal is done yourself.'

Terajima got to his feet and walked away from the table, listening to what the Vansburgische Landesbank had to tell him.

As he listened intently, his eyes wandered among the throng in the Glen lounge. He had a sense of *déjà vu*. Across the room, by the exit, was the figure he remembered having seen seated alone the night before in the Cenderawasih restaurant. He wondered what

96

the blind man was doing in a golf club.

'All done,' Terajima said to Foster Zhentung. 'I leave for London this afternoon. Tell me, *apropos* of nothing, do blind people play golf?'

'Why do you ask?' said Foster Zhentung.

'That guy over there, see? He's blind.'

'Then it's just as well he can see nothing of our deliberations,' said Foster Zhentung.

Terajima slowly shook his head in silence. Toying with the silver hearts, one engraved with 'Mei' and the other with 'Kitty', on the chain around his wrist, he turned towards the exit.

33

More contemplative than his brother Foster, the solemn Hastings Zhentung gazed at the rain with a troubled look. He was searching his memory. The ways of Terajima had often reminded him of a maze to which only Terajima knew the solution. There was a darkness in his soul best left unexplored. The man's passion, obsession and egotism sometimes bordered on the demonic. But you had to keep a sense of proportion. The man achieved results. Now he realised that he had, almost inadvertently, thrown some light into the shadows of Terajima's secret life, and it had raised a gnawing and unexpected suspicion he sought to allay. For safety's sake, he could not remain indifferent to it.

'Tell me, Foster, did you notice anything about his appearance? Did you notice his wrist jewellery?'

'The chains around his wrist?'

'Yes. Did you notice what was engraved on the nameplates? The women's names. Kitty. Mei. Kitty was Winston Lim's widow. Mei their daughter. When you were on the telephone to Luxembourg, I asked him about Mei. Asked him if she was his girl. I could tell from his expression that she is. Winston Lim's daughter.'

'It concerns you?' Foster Zhentung asked.

'Yes, it does. The look I saw in Terajima's eyes concerns me. I think it spells a certain sort of danger. We would be better off without her.'

'Then have someone run a check on her. Offer Victor Michaelson more money. Tell him to speak to his diplomat friends. I want no stone left unturned.'

34

STATEMENT OF WITNESS

[Criminal Justice Act 1967, s.9]

Statement of:	Alan Rosslyn
Age of Witness:	Over 21
Occupation:	Private Investigator
Address:	Basement Flat,
	195 Claverton Street,
	London SW1

This statement consisting of 3 pages signed by me is true to
the best of my knowledge and belief and I make it knowing that
if it is tendered in evidence, I shall be liable to prosecution
if I wilfully state anything which I know to be false.

To keep watch over Mei. I was determined to keep
the promise to Winston.
   But she was not answering her telephone in person.
Neither was she replying to the messages I'd left
on her answering machine. I felt I should have
said to the Deputy Commissioner at Police
Headquarters that to reject her application to
join the Hong Kong Police on the basis that she
wasn't tall enough seemed lame. Anyway, wouldn't
an officer with Winston's experience have realised
that this would prove a stumbling block or, had he
lived, would he have found a way of getting round
the problem? I decided to put this to Steve Kwok
when we meet in Kuala Lumpur.
   There had to be an easy way to help Mei. And
there had to be some way of keeping in regular
contact with her. So why didn't she return my
calls? Had she left Hong Kong? Temporarily, even
for good? Given what Catherine Kwok had said,

leaving Hong Kong might be a very wise course of
action for Mei to have taken. And what the Kwoks
said now clarified for me something about Mei's
reactions when I had visited her in her apartment.
Her obfuscation. Her edginess. Even the odd business of what I had heard over the entryphone. That
I'm some dumb-fuck British gumshoe. I've met with
similar reactions in the past when facing someone,
one to one, who was profoundly frightened.
Aggression. Hostility. Defensiveness. I thought
she must be haunted by fear. Like the Kwoks. To
put it bluntly, Mei and the Kwoks believed they
knew too much for their own comfort.

Now, the same seemed to apply to me. We were all
possessors of the Unholy Grail.

Then there was Dr Graer and his American friend.
What business was it of them to seek to help Mei?
They're foreign diplomats and if they'd been
Winston's close friends they would surely have
demonstrated it more than they had done at the
funeral.

What weighed most heavily on my mind were the
facts of what Steve and Catherine had told me. The
contents of the short description of Terajima. The
connection with the Zhentungs. Why the apparent
passivity of the Hong Kong Police in not pursuing
Terajima? Why wasn't Terajima on the Hong Kong
Police's Most Wanted list? If he were an American
he'd have been on the FBI's. Or was the content of
the papers Catherine showed me part of some deception that is finally beyond all of us to unravel?
The connection with the Zhentungs. That's what might
have turned out to be the easiest one to discover.

At this point I reckoned I could wash my hands
of all of them. I could carry on with my life. I
could even find some other line of business in the
world of private investigation.

I could have been sleeping with a quiet mind.

And if there was one iota of suspicion, any
evidence, however small, about the circumstances
of Winston's death I was certain that Mei would
seek to discover it. For my part, it could be said
that, in memory of Winston, to keep watch over Mei
was to search out the truth surrounding the
circumstances of his death.

But there remained my promise to him.

I would, as I have said, keep it. I had the motive to keep it. Unfortunately, right then, I had neither the means nor opportunity to do so.

As Winston once said, Yuan jia lo zai. Bu shi yuan jia bu ju tou — 'The road of enemies is narrow; they will surely meet.' One can't avoid one's enemy. Enemies and lovers are destined to meet.

Signed: *Alan Rooslyn*

Signature witnessed by: Chief Superintendent Ronald Costley

Signed: *Ron Costley*

Signature witnessed by: WPC Michelle Seifert

Signed: *Michelle Seifert*

35

Seated at the kitchen table in his Claverton Street basement flat, Rosslyn had telephoned Mei each day since his return from Hong Kong. There had been no answer.

The CD he had bought at the Hong Kong International Airport was on repeat:

> Probe me with your love
> Kiss me with your snake tounge
> Probe me with your love
> I don't care how long you take.

He had finished reading the week's issues of *Lloyd's List*. His body was still refusing to adjust itself to London time. He kept the central heating system on continually. The old gas-fired boiler was fighting a losing battle against the London cold. He looked forward to returning to the warmth of the Far East for his journey aboard the *Orient Angel*. He had confirmed the arrangements with Ocean World Insurance of Southampton. The weather forecast for Malaysia was for hot weather tempered by sea breezes that would alleviate the humidity in the Malacca Strait. Perhaps his return would allow him the chance to meet up with Mei again. She was rarely away from his dreams. Equally, they were haunted by what Steve and Catherine Kwok had revealed to him in Hong Kong and the scars of the terrible violence that had been administered to them.

He was also preoccupied with how little he knew about the client of Milo Associates, Anthony Zhentung. He blamed himself for not knowing about what was apparently the true nature of the brothers' legitimate businesses, to say nothing of the violent methods of the Malacca Cartel, Snake Skin and Black Shoe, names that were equally unfamiliar to him.

Indeed, if what the Kwoks had said about the Zhentungs was true, there would be those who might justifiably claim that Milo Associates was at best incompetent, even negligent, or at worst, guilty of conspiracy to protect international criminals and God knows what other very serious charges. It seemed, in all respects, that little could be more culpable than that Milo Associates was engaged upon the protection of such people.

For the time being, though, all he had were the notes he had made of the report Catherine had shown him. He didn't even have a word for word copy of it. Just what he had written down in his private shorthand. It added up to hearsay and, from the point of view of the Hong Kong Police or any other law enforcement agency, it had been shown to him illicitly. Not much use in court.

36

Next morning he took his preferred route to the London office of Milo Associates in Marylebone Passage.

From Claverton Street he walked to Victoria Station to take the bus. Snow and the threat of rail strikes seemed to have persuaded many Londoners to take the day off and stay at home. The cold wind in Pimlico stung his eyes. The local newsagent was even running a line in electric heaters. Now a painted notice in large white letters across the window said:

HEATERS SOLD OUT – SORRY.

It was at Victoria, as he was boarding the bus, that he saw the thin man wearing glasses. The slight oriental figure smoking a cigarette at the bus stop was reading *Lloyd's List*, the international shipping newspaper.

37

In Marylebone Passage the fleeting shapes of sleek rats scurrying in the gutters reminded him that the office cleaner Josie, moonlighting from the Fo Guang Temple in Margaret Street, should already have been and gone. She should also have supervised the visit from the people contracted to combat the infestation of rodents. As Josie puts it, 'You're never less than ten feet from a London rat.'

With the undercover man's lifetime habits of suspicion, he looked back along the street. It was empty except for the man he had seen at Victoria studying *Lloyd's List*, who noticed Rosslyn's glance and turned suddenly on his heel.

To the left of the door, which was reinforced with steel, the plaque said simply 'Milo Associates'. It gave no further indication that Milo Associates was the private investigations firm in which Rosslyn was a partner. He released each of the three door locks in turn. Once he was inside, with the door closed, he tapped in the code on the security alarm control box to neutralise it.

The morning mail and a hefty pile of newspapers were on the shelf above the radiator in the gloomy entrance hall. Beside the doormat, there were small cardboard cartons bearing the warning: RODENT BAIT DO NOT TOUCH. HARMFUL KEEP ANIMALS AND CHILDREN AWAY.

Their presence suggested Josie had definitely been and gone and that the rodent exterminators from Enviro Vermin Control Limited had performed their tasks. He gathered up the bundle of mail, circulars and newspapers and climbed the narrow staircase to the first floor.

The office smelt of the pungent cleaning liquid Josie preferred. Rosslyn noticed the rodent person had left their small red and white cardboard cartons by the skirting boards near the radiators. They had also stuffed wire wool in the gaps between the skirting and the floorboards. As Josie would say, 'A good job jobbed.'

He set about reading the usual sort of letters, bills, e-mails and faxes. Most of them were addressed either to Milo Associates or to Duggie Milo personally.

In his thirties – much the same age as Rosslyn – the languid Milo was at the end of a troubled marriage. Presently on leave, he preferred to be on hand for the sake of his two young children.

So it fell to Rosslyn, not Milo, to take on the commission and profitable Far East business of inspecting the security of the *Orient Angel*. He had familiarised himself with the basic practices of inter-national maritime commerce and would be advising Ocean World Insurance of Southampton on standards of shipping security. In the old days, Rosslyn would have discussed the commission with Winston. Not now.

He telephoned Mei in Hong Kong. No matter the time difference. Again, there was no answer.

He was making himself a mug of coffee when the doorbell rang. He only received visitors by appointment. He glanced at his desk diary. Only two appointments were listed:

10.00 Finance & General Purpose Meeting. Victor Michaelson
12.30 Customs & Excise Investigations Division/Lunch

The face on the screen of the small TV entryphone was the face of the man he had seen carrying the *Lloyd's List*. The voice said, 'Mr Rosslyn. I'm a friend of Steve Kwok's. My name's Zhu Jianxing.'

38

Politely decling Rosslyn's offer of coffee, Zhu would obviously have preferred to be elsewhere. He wore a cheap blue scarf and a coat frayed at the sleeves. Rosslyn watched him shifting uneasily from foot to foot.

Zhu would obviously have preferred to be elsewhere. He politely declined Rosslyn's offer of coffee. He said he preferred to stand. Rosslyn watched him shifting uneasily from foot to foot. He wore a cheap blue scarf and a black flat cap. His coat was frayed at the collar.

'May I smoke?' Zhu said.

'Go ahead.'

'Steve has asked me to deliver this to you,' Zhu said, lighting his cigarette. He spoke fast and with a slight lisp. He took an envelope from his coat pocket. 'Do you have a safe here?' he asked.

Rosslyn pointed to the door of the combination safe.

'You have sole access to it?' Zhu asked.

'Along with my partner.'

'Can you change the combination so you are the only one who can use it?'

'I could,' said Rosslyn. 'Why?'

Zhu coughed. He seemed apologetic. 'This is for your emergency use. For your eyes only.'

'What is it?'

'A passport with a People's Republic diplomatic visa and your photograph. A quantity of US and Hong Kong dollars and Chinese currency. You will be taking a risk. We have no alternative.'

'Mr Zhu,' said Rosslyn. 'What are you trying to tell me?'

Zhu looked around the office. 'Do you have recorders hidden here, Mr Rosslyn?'

'I do not.'

'What is that then?' He was staring at one of the small cardboard

cartons bearing the warning: RODENT BAIT DO NOT TOUCH. HARMFUL
KEEP ANIMALS AND CHILDREN AWAY.

'For killing rats.'

'I hope you're telling me the truth.'

'That's for you to judge. What is this emergency?'

'Klaas-Pieter Terajima is arriving in London today. There are those
of your friends who fear for your safety. I am merely taking the
precaution of assisting you.' He opened the envelope. 'Of providing
you with a passport. It's a precautionary measure. Here –'

Rosslyn opened the People's Republic passport and looked at the
diplomatic visa. 'How did you get my photograph?'

'It was taken when you visited Hong Kong police headquarters.'

'Right,' said Rosslyn. 'So it was. But Hong Kong? The place of birth
is wrong. And I'm not a government official.'

'They are Li Kim's details.'

'And I'm British. Not Chinese.'

'The passport says you're British. The visa is granted to those
classified as known and vetted friends of the People's Republic. I
have arranged this personally. It's cleared with Beijing. The Ministry of
State Security.' He produced his business card and handed it to
Rosslyn. 'Here –'

Rosslyn read:

ZHU JIANXING
Assistant Defence Attaché

Embassy of the People's Republic of China
49–51 Portland Place
London W1N 4JL
Telephone: 0207 299 4049

'Look at me,' Zhu said. 'Trust me. Trust your friends, even if they
are unseen. My mother taught me that *Jiu rou peng you hao zhao,
huan nan zhi jiao nan feng* – "You will easily find friends to come to
your party. In times of trouble it's difficult to find friends to help
you." If Klaas-Pieter Terajima is in London, your safety will be

threatened. You've seen what retribution Terajima administers.'

Rosslyn had seen. Steve's missing feet. Catherine's disfigured face.

'Make your journey to South East Asia. You are inspecting some ship, right?'

'Yes.'

'Best you go ahead with it,' said Zhu. 'Meanwhile, remember that Terajima does not always work alone. He has his associates here in London. He has murdered most of those who have done his work. None of his people is indispensable to him to ensure silence. No. They are all disposable. But he keeps them in separate compartments, flattered and seduced by the fees he pays. Fortunately, not all murderers are successful all of the time. But Klaas-Pieter Terajima is successful most of the time. London is not the safe city it once was, is it? Neither is Beijing. Unless you have *guanxi*, or useful personal connections with the authorities.' He smiled. 'You, Mr Rosslyn, you perhaps have the good fortune to have *guanxi*. Sadly, Winston Lim – not enough.'

'Are you trying to tell me –?'

'Winston Lim was murdered?' said Zhu.

'Where's the evidence?'

'There's no hard evidence. Let's agree we have good reason to want to see the end of Klaas-Pieter Terajima. None of us wants to see Terajima get to Mei Lim. We don't want Terajima to get too close to you. So regard the passport and the funds as precautions. Make sure your air tickets to KL are first class. And, of course, that the ticket is open. How confidential are your dealings with Ocean World Insurance?'

'Completely. They do what I say.'

'Good,' said Zhu. 'In the meantime, live your life normally. Don't contact me at the embassy, please. There will be no need for us to meet again.'

'What do you want me to do with the money?'

'Use it to buy people.'

'If I don't "buy people"?'

'Treat it as the gift of the People's Republic. Let us say I am buying you.'

'Buying me for what?'

'Silence. Your silence on the subject of this meeting. It has never taken place. Agreed?'

'That's a pity,' said Rosslyn. 'I was hoping you could recommend me a really good Chinese restaurant.'

'Alas, we can't meet again,' Zhu said with an uncomfortable smile. 'But try the China House in Glentworth Street.'

'Is that your favourite?'

'A junior minister in your Ministry of Defence introduced me to it,' said Zhu. 'It is a comfortable walk from the embassy and here too. They know me there.'

Rosslyn placed the envelope inside the safe and altered the combination code.

'You have never met me in your life,' said Zhu. 'Just as I have never met you. Some alliances, Mr Rosslyn, are best kept secret.'

Rosslyn watched his departure on the entryphone's small TV screen. He had second thoughts about the security of the combination safe. Instead of using the safe to store the passport and money, he used two of the larger boxes marked with the warning: RODENT BAIT DO NOT TOUCH. HARMFUL KEEP ANIMALS AND CHILDREN AWAY.

Do they know Zhu at the Chinese embassy and the China House?

39

A few minutes remained until the others arrived for the start of the Finance and General Purposes meeting at ten.

Rosslyn put through a call to the embassy of the People's Republic of China in Portland Square. 'May I speak to the Assistant Defence Attaché's office, please?'

'Who shall I say is calling?' asked the telephonist.

'China House. The manager.'

He was kept waiting a short while before the man came on the line. 'This is the office of the Defence Attaché. May I help you?'

'If you would be so kind, sir,' said Rosslyn. 'We have a reservation for tonight in the name of Assistant Defence Attaché Zhu. I just want to confirm it's okay.'

'There must be some mistake. Mr Zhu left for Beijing this morning.'

'So he won't be needing his reservation, sir?'

'I am afraid I cannot help you further.'

The telephone line went dead. Zhu had passed a basic test of authenticity.

40

Victor Michaelson, non-executive chairman of Milo Associates, arrived half an hour before the ten a.m. start of the Finance and General Purposes meeting. Michaelson was Duggie Milo's friend and his appointment as chairman had been Milo's idea.

It was customary for Michaelson to look through the company files before these monthly meetings in order, as he put it, 'to bring myself up to speed'.

Rosslyn took Michaelson's silk scarf and cashmere overcoat and hung them next to the door to the lavatory on what was known as the Chairman's Peg. Above the peg was the notice:

FOR THE SOLE USE OF VICTOR MICHAELSON CBE

Rosslyn made Michaelson a mug of coffee and left him to read through the files in silence.

Eminence grise was the role Duggie Milo had devised for the distinguished lawyer.

Rosslyn thought he might take Victor Michaelson into his confidence. *Tell him the contents of the envelope Catherine Kwok had shown him. Tell him about the visit from Zhu.* He was in two minds.

Victor knew more about the Zhentungs than most. He might be more than interested to know what Winston and the Kwoks had to say about them. He thought hard about Victor. He had to be very sure of him. And he wasn't. Victor was Duggie territory, not his.

He thought about confiding in Duggie. He decided against that too.

Suppose that Duggie had come to him with the information? Duggie would play it by the book and say it would be for the best to pass it straight to MI6 or MI5. The whole thing would go round in one big circle and end up back again in Hong Kong.

He very nearly persuaded himself to take Victor to one side and seek his advice. True, Victor loved money. He loved it with a strange and cold desperation. There was something in Victor's background that finally decided him to say nothing – something he found it hard to put his finger on precisely. Apart from greed and self-importance.

Victor Michaelson, the only child of Russian parents who had settled in Manchester during the pre-war years, had been born Viktor Vyacheslav Mikhail in Armenia, of which he remembered nothing.

Like his father, the teenage Viktor disavowed his mother's religious beliefs. But when his father suddenly left home for another woman, the young Viktor eagerly embraced 'conversion' by a popular American evangelist, who had attracted many thousands of the fervent and susceptible to a Manchester football stadium. Young Viktor took matters further still.

Shortly after his fifteenth birthday the young Viktor was accepted as a 'noviciate' at the school of the religious order of St Errol in Borrowdale. His mother raised the fees by taking in lodgers. She was delighted with Viktor's devotion to St Errol, even though, like most people, she may not have been entirely sure who St Errol was. A short time before the school was closed down by the education authorities, Viktor told his mother he was leaving the place because he 'liked women'. Who these women were, the mother had no idea. It seemed a frightful waste of Viktor's intelligence.

It had been young Viktor's good fortune that his devoted mother answered an advertisement in the *Manchester Evening News* placed by a retired Methodist minister in Leeds offering lodging and tuition. Once more, Viktor's mother scraped together the wherewithal and the minister got Viktor a place at Leeds Grammar School. The boy shone academically and won a minor scholarship to Oxford.

Some time during his time at Oxford, Viktor Vyacheslav Mikhail changed his name by deed poll to Victor Archibald Michaelson. He also achieved a first in law at Wadham. By the time he left Oxford, he had replaced the accents of Manchester, Leeds and Russia with a clenched-teeth upper class drawl in the manner of a male member of the royal family.

The tall and suave Victor sported pin-stripe suits, waistcoats and not infrequently a bow tie. Converting to Catholicism, he was regularly to be seen at mass in the Brompton Oratory and lunch at the Travellers' in Pall Mall. Soon enough, he was called to the Bar.

Naturally aggressive, with sparkling eyes and an attentive ear for the bogus and the self-made in general, he enjoyed destroying witnesses. He was, in essence, an intellectual bully. He was admired and feared. Mostly feared.

His record in the High Court was impressive. He successfully defended a spy for the then Soviet Union, famously reducing a senior woman officer of the Secret Intelligence Service to tears as she blurted out the story of her own deception. She was later prosecuted and jailed.

As the result of a trial held *in camera*, a leading solicitor instructed him to defend an Italian science teacher, a former prisoner of war, against a charge of conspiracy to murder the teacher's headmaster. Heard at the Old Bailey, it was a notorious case to do with arcane sexual practices involving small, and even miniature, dogs. Michael-son's observation, 'Had I been able to call the dogs, this trial would have been over days ago,' made headlines on page three of the *Daily Telegraph*. The Canine Charmer was what a tabloid newspaper dubbed Michaelson. And the Canine Charmer was photographed at Battersea Dogs' Home surrounded by unwanted poodles in fur collars. After winning the case, he never looked back.

Then, acting with others for the family of God's banker, Roberto Calvi, he contributed to the overturning of the verdict of suicide. A second inquest was opened, but the Calvi murder remained a mystery.

Some time later, he was invited to become a Supreme Court judge in Sydney. The appointment would have meant a considerable diminution of his earnings. With his track record, Michaelson was by now assured of substantial riches at home. He declined the Sydney invitation and promptly accepted another. Perhaps as a result of his exposing the woman officer of SIS, he was invited to advise the intelligence services and readily accepted. Now, even after his retirement, he was still advising both MI6 and MI5. And he continued to do so at the time he accepted Douglas Milo's invitation to get involved with Milo Associates.

Michaelson enjoyed the gamesmanship and politics and secrecy of private investigation. He also enjoyed his involvement, in a paternal sort of way, with the personal lives of Milo and Rosslyn. He liked, as he said, to keep things *en famille*. He was also presently advising Milo on his divorce. There were also the perks Victor enjoyed.

For example, always with discretion, he would call upon the firm to obtain some intelligence on a subject, so he could compare and contrast it with the contents of some report from the police or one or other of the intelligence services he represented. Michaelson liked, as

he put it, 'to take possession of the higher ground and to have his own take on sources.'

He had supported Milo Associates by introducing Milo and Rosslyn to a firm of the more reliable type of city bankers and also to his own accountants, whose respective representatives, Celia Dupleix and Bruce Wetzel, would be attending this morning's Finance and General Purposes meeting.

Dupleix habitually flexed her muscles at such meetings, presumably with a view to advancing her position in the bank. She had recently been proving awkward. Business had been good for the past quarter. But, according to Dupleix's view, not quite good enough. An extension to the Milo Associates overdraft facility was needed. And, even with Michaelson's support, the chances of getting it this morning were fifty-fifty. Wetzel, the accountant, did her bidding. It was essential for the security of the firm's financial future that Rosslyn take on the commission in South East Asia.

41

The Finance and General Purposes meeting began promptly at ten.

Victor Michaelson took the chair, seated next to Rosslyn. There were apologies from Milo. Over biscuits and coffee, Celia Dupleix and Bruce Wetzel faced Rosslyn and Michaelson across the table.

'Alan, bring us up to date,' Michaelson said.

'There's a batch of possible UK operations,' said Rosslyn. 'Local commercial matters (LCMs). The assessment of future commissions for law firms involving discreet investigations or other commissions for commercial firms burdened by problems of counterfeiting, copyright infringement and commercial espionage. And there are prospective local domestic matters (LDMs), such as the provision of personal protection for high-profile leaders of industry, celebrities plagued by stalkers or the international elderly rich scared of kidnap.'

'Alan,' asked Dupleix, 'how long will you be in the Far East?' A blonde in her thirties, Dupleix was dressed in black.

'No more than ten days at the most,' said Rosslyn.

'It's a good earner,' said Michaelson.

'It is?' said Dupleix.

'My effective cover for the Far East tour,' Rosslyn said, 'is as inspector from the United Kingdom office of Ocean World Insurance in Southampton.'

Michaelson interrupted: 'We prefer to keep our role as commissioned freelance agents secret.'

'My idea,' said Rosslyn. 'I stand to gain a greater degree of trust from the shipping company personnel if I'm considered a regular Ocean World Insurance inspector.'

'Correct,' said Michaelson. 'To all intents and purposes, the firm's engaged upon the routine review of security arrangements aboard several merchant ships operating in the Far East.'

'Wouldn't the job be equally well performed', said Dupleix, 'by one

or more loss adjusters from Ocean World Insurance – personnel selected by the insurance writer to look into policyholders' insurance claims and see to the fairness of the settlements?'

'It might be,' said Rosslyn. 'But they want us to do the work.' He turned through the pages of a folder marked 'Ocean World Insurance'. 'It's a highly profitable exercise. Take a look.' He edged the folder towards Dupleix.

Rosslyn noticed Dupleix turn to the page headed 'Fees Account'.

'A fine pay day,' said Michaelson. 'What my chambers used to call doggie food.'

'Moves us forward faster than the projected forecast,' added Wetzel.

'But there's still a substantial overdraft facility,' Dupleix said quietly. She turned to a sheaf of her own notes. 'Wouldn't it be helpful to reduce rental and rates and so forth? Could you run the firm from home?'

'Clients prefer the chance', said Rosslyn, 'to meet us here or on neutral ground.'

'Couldn't you meet them at their own offices?' Dupleix persisted.

'Sometimes that can be insecure,' said Michaelson. 'Rivalry from colleagues. Leaky infrastructures. Prying eyes.'

'We have a problem,' said Dupleix. 'Not that I specifically have a problem. My superiors do.'

'I propose that we discuss it together, Celia,' interrupted Michaelson. 'There's always the highly profitable business of VIP protection that can tide us over.'

'VIP protection?' said Dupleix. 'Like what type?'

'Anthony Zhentung,' said Michaelson. 'That's a very nice earner. Am I right, Alan?'

'Yes,' said Rosslyn, knowing that, at Michaelson's request, it was being done for nothing.

'Let's see if we can come to some satisfactory arrangement,' said Dupleix.

'If there are any problems,' said Michaelson, 'let me know. Don't hesitate to call me. Lunch at Claridge's, perhaps?'

After some polite chatter Dupleix and Wetzel left.

It was as simple as that. Michaelson had got his way.

42

In Marylebone Passage, Rosslyn told Michaelson that he was grateful to him for his support.

Michaelson smiled. 'Anthony Zhentung likes the idea that he merits private protection. It flatters his ego. By the way, what's really at the heart of your operation in the Far East? Perhaps some of Anthony's people could open doors?'

'*Orient Angel* is sailing from Kuala Lumpur to Kobe in Japan. It's her security I'm looking at for the insurers. Security. Prevention and deterrence of attack.'

'You and I should have a word before you go,' said Michaelson. 'What about some lunch at my club?'

'Thanks. But another day perhaps,' said Rosslyn. 'Do you mind? I have a meeting in the Strand with some man from Customs who has problems.'

'Alan, old man, you don't say. You're beginning to remind me of me.'

43

While Rosslyn took the underground in the direction of the Strand, the British Airways 747 lowered through the mid-morning sky to the runway cleared of snow for its landing. Terajima, modestly dressed as the quiet Dr Hung, was among the first of the passengers to be invited to disembark. Waiting for his one small case in the baggage hall, he made a call on his mobile telephone.

'The purchase is complete?' said Terajima.

'Complete.'

'Alert?'

'Green for go. I will be waiting for you.'

'The motorcyclist is ready?'

'Yes.

'*Xiexie.*' ('Thank you.')

'*Bukeqi.*' ('You're welcome.')

Inserting a tab of snuff into his mouth between his lower lip and gums, Terajima collected his small case from the luggage carousel and headed for the customs check and exit.

He had a rendezvous with a supplier of high explosives in the suburb of Hatton not far from Hounslow and Heathrow. They would be meeting at the entrance to River Crane Causeway Watermeadows, where willow and alders have recently been replanted and dead woodpiles constructed for the benefit of invertebrates and fungi. Kingfishers have been seen there. Tonight the visitors would have no interest in conservation.

44

STATEMENT OF WITNESS

[Criminal Justice Act 1967, s.9]

Statement of:	Alan Rosslyn
Age of Witness:	Over 21
Occupation:	Private Investigator
Address:	Basement Flat,
	195 Claverton Street,
	London SW1

This statement consisting of 2 pages signed by me is true to
the best of my knowledge and belief and I make it knowing that
if it is tendered in evidence, I shall be liable to prosecution
if I wilfully state anything which I know to be false.

I served in the Investigations Division with how
many trainee undercover officers?

But which was the one who has recently been
found dead from gunshot wounds at his home near
Windsor?

The officer's death, apparently a suicide, had
been linked to a vague and suspicious smell of
corruption in Customs.

I could imagine the sort of pressure being
applied to disguise the stink. The Crown
Prosecution Service people would be sniffing around
like pigs in a trough. Customs & Excise would be
resisting their attention like old maids.

And this C & E officer who wanted to see me would
want me to swear an affidavit that the dead officer
was an honourable, straight and loyal officer who's
fallen victim to the stress. All of which I would
have difficulty in substantiating because of the
interval of time that's passed since I last served

with the dead man. That was yesterday. And I only
had the faintest memory of him.
  God knows what the misery could have been that
persuaded the poor bastard to blow his brains out.

Signed: *Alan Rooslyn*

Signature witnessed by: Chief Superintendent Ronald Costley

Signed: *Ron Costley*

Signature witnessed by: WPC Michelle Seifert

Signed: *Michelle Seifert*

45

Rosslyn was seated next to Chapman, the undercover Customs officer, who had shown up punctually in the wine bar off the Strand. A woman he introduced as Elizabeth Henderson accompanied Chapman. Chapman introduced her as 'a colleague'.

In a dark suit, looking like a praying mantis, Henderson mostly remained silent, like an observer, while Chapman took an age to get to the point. She set her mobile phone on the table and fiddled with wooden toothpicks, digging them into her yellow teeth, which were in orthodontic braces, and then examining whatever food remnants she had excavated. It was not an attractive sight.

'You know, Alan, how after long periods of great stress,' Chapman said, 'like undercover police officers or officers of the security services, undercover duty men can change quite suddenly and dramatically.'

'I know.'

'All too often, too late, we crack, and at the end of the day, the bottom line is that others are left to collect up the bits and limit the damage.'

'I was spared that, thank the Lord.'

'Of course you were, Alan,' said Chapman. 'Most of the weaker brethren do have skeletons in the cupboard. The majority of the skeletons rattle harmlessly and can be ignored. Rattle, rattle. Occasionally an officer will go off the wall. Off his trolley. Might even betray the Service. Such betrayals might or might not become public knowledge. Tragedy, courtroom drama and hefty prison sentence follow.'

As if Rosslyn needed telling. But that was how Chapman droned on over drinks and sandwiches in the wine bar off the Strand.

Finally Chapman said, 'It was only that, if you could think of anything from way back that might throw some light on the Windsor thing.'

'It's a long time since I knew the man,' said Rosslyn. 'And I don't really remember him.'

'I understand,' said Chapman, 'Before my time too.'

'I can't help,' said Rosslyn.

Then Elizabeth Henderson withdrew a toothpick from the gap between her yellow front teeth and chimed in: 'Tell me about Milo Associates.' It struck Rosslyn as an unnecessary question. Surely Chapman would have explained the firm to her already.

'What's it got to do with the dead man?'

'I simply asked about Milo Associates,' she said.

'What do you want to know?' said Rosslyn.

'One or two things about your work for some of your clients.'

'Which clients?'

'For example, the Zhentung brothers.'

Rosslyn stiffened. 'We don't breach client confidentiality.'

'This is official, Mr Rosslyn,' said Henderson.

'So you say. Then put it in writing to us. I've no comment to make.'

'If you won't co-operate, then would you object if we had a word with Milo?' she asked.

'Not at all. But he's on leave. Anyway, he'll refer you back to me.'

'Then do I speak to Victor Michaelson?' Henderson persisted.

'You can talk to whoever you want,' said Rosslyn. 'Victor will also refer you back to me.'

'You see,' said Henderson, 'we think you should tread warily.'

'You do?'

'*We* do.'

'Who's *we*?'

'SIS,' she said. 'The Foreign Service is a wide umbrella.'

'So you say,' said Rosslyn.

'That's why I asked you to meet us,' said Chapman, the man from Customs. 'For Elizabeth's benefit.'

'There are rumours in the air,' said Henderson.

'What's new?' said Rosslyn.

'Things aren't what they seem,' said Henderson.

'Now that is something I can believe,' said Rosslyn, whose look did little to disguise his dislike of the Secret Intelligence Service.

'I thought you would have guessed already,' said Chapman. 'I mean, at the end of the day, that's why we're here.'

'Maybe I have,' said Rosslyn. 'I didn't think it was for some sandwiches. You tell me. What's under investigation then?'

'Bank accounts,' said Henderson.

'Whose bank accounts?' asked Rosslyn.

'Black market industrial concerns.'

'Like whose?' said Rosslyn. 'What bank accounts? What black market?'

'In bomb-grade fissile material. Thermonuclear device components. Highly enriched uranium mostly. They're being ferried from Colombia by commercial shipping under the guise of aircraft parts. Some of it's been enriched to ninety per cent. That's a higher percentage standard than the Russians use in nuclear submarines and icebreakers. But someone has to hold the capital investment and act as conduit. You should understand. Use your imagination. In addition, key miniature components for new ICBMs. American components for the fifteen thousand kilometre range MV-54 and twenty-five thousand kilometre range MV-65. Others for the submarine ballistic missile, the BX-70, the naval version of the MV-54, with components of ground positioning systems. They were on the way to Penang. We are talking deep water. Just be sure you can swim in it. And that you know when and where the water's shark infested.'

'What's your source?'

'Let's say the Atomic Energy Agency in Vienna for a start.'

'Fissile material's no use unless you have sophisticated detonation technology.'

'You don't have to tell me that,' said Henderson. 'Tell me about your recent trip to Hong Kong.'

'I was at a funeral. Winston Lim's.'

'*Inspector* Winston Lim's?' said Henderson, with a grinning display of metal and mouldy teeth.

'And you introduced yourself to Dr Graer and a friend of ours and his, an American legal attaché?'

'They introduced themselves to me.'

'What information did they pass to you?'

'They didn't pass any information to me,' said Rosslyn.

'I said *what did they pass to you*, Mr Rosslyn?'

'They passed the time of day.'

Henderson gave a short hiss and bared the dental braces like a cat. 'The Hong Kong Police were interested in your visit.'

'Winston Lim was my friend.'

'They were about to pin something on him, weren't they?'

'First I've heard of it.'

'He was showing a great deal of interest in the Zhentungs, wasn't he?'

'He never told me,' said Rosslyn.

'He didn't – you're quite sure?'

'Why would I lie to you?' said Rosslyn.

'I didn't say you were lying to me. But I think you might be.'

'Then think on,' said Rosslyn.

'Perhaps he might have been set up,' she said calmly. 'You think Winston Lim might have been set up? I know the Hong Kong Police.'

'You may indeed know the Hong Kong Police. I knew Winston Lim and you didn't. Winston had a totally clean record. He was honest. He was loyal. I find it offensive to his memory that you should imply otherwise.'

'But his family life –'

'I know nothing about it.'

'Is that true, Mr Rosslyn? I gather you visited his daughter Mei.'

That hit home. 'I don't like the line you're taking, Ms Henderson. If you think that my interest in Mei –'

'I wasn't *suggesting* – you *and* Mei –'

'Don't even try.'

'But Milo Associates,' she said, failing to disguise another sneer. 'Milo Associates. You don't ask questions, and you take on clients without knowing the full background.'

'We are looking after their personal protection,' said Rosslyn. 'As for Victor Michaelson, he works for you people.'

She leaned across the table. He could smell the staleness on her breath.

'Let me at least *try* to treat you as adult, Mr Rosslyn – encourage me if you can. A man with your experience should know that we employ all sorts and all kinds of people. Maybe even the Winston Lims of this world. Maybe even the Stephen Kwoks. Let me tell you something. I have to say this to you. Times have changed, Mr Rosslyn. They are changing far faster than people like you in the private sector can ever dream of knowing. That's why we're looking at your firm. Including you. We're looking at everyone.'

Rosslyn had paled. He was having difficulty in restraining his temper with the woman.

'You look at everyone,' he said.

'Fucking right,' she interrupted.

'You *look* and what do you *see*? You *see* nothing and no one.'

'Your firm could be in trouble,' she said. 'You're working for the Zhentungs.'

'Get it straight – we are working for Anthony Zhentung on Victor Michaelson's recommendation.'

'Victor's history, Mr Rosslyn. His generation is not yours. Not mine. But the Zhentungs could be of interest to us, and if you were to be more obliging and less downright hostile towards me –'

'– Don't be so accusatory, Ms Henderson. We're not in a law court or a police interrogation room. If you have a complaint, then address it to the firm, in writing. You have our address. Or do what any citizen is entitled to and go to the police. I can just see their faces when you stroll up to the duty desk. And I have to tell you that if this line of questioning has anything to do with the Zhentungs, then you'd better talk to them.'

'We didn't say it was anything to do with the Zhentungs,' said Henderson.

'You've mentioned them,' said Rosslyn. 'Christ, when you people even mention the time of day, the rest of us know there's something wrong with it.'

'Oh, Alan, come on,' said Chapman, assuming the air of peace-maker. 'All we're saying is that we'd appreciate it if you could let us know anything useful straight off.'

'It's in the national interest,' said Henderson.

'I wouldn't think you people would be interested if it wasn't,' said Rosslyn.

He had no idea what the pair were driving at. He had already begun to dislike Henderson intensely, and she seemed to realise it.

'Let this be a warning,' she said. 'A red alert warning.'

He watched her reach into her open leather shoulder bag. It was on the floor between her legs. She was feeling for something, and Rosslyn reckoned that she was turning off a tape recorder, a listening device or something similar.

'If you'll forgive me,' she said, taking up her mobile phone. 'I have to get back to the office. Thank you so much,' she said.

'If I can be of help,' Chapman offered, 'do say.'

'You have my number,' Henderson said.

'I have your number,' said Rosslyn.

'How well do you know the Zhentungs?' she said with a hollow smile.

'My business with clients is never personal,' said Rosslyn.

She exchanged glances with Chapman. 'It's been a very useful meeting,' she said. Then she stared at Rosslyn. 'You're full of shit, *Mister* Rosslyn.'

'Watch your language, *Miss* Henderson.' He looked instead at Chapman. 'I'm sorry I couldn't be of more help about that poor bastard who topped himself.'

'None of us can be of any help to him now,' said Chapman. 'But do let me know if anything springs to mind. You know, Alan, in the midnight hour. That sort of thing.'

'He can't help you with the dead,' said Henderson, with the air of someone who's just thought of something profound without knowing what it means. 'Only with the living,' she added.

'Like all the rest of what you've been saying,' Rosslyn said, 'I have no idea what the hell you're talking about.'

Henderson helped herself to a small handful of the toothpicks from the jar on the table and dropped them into her bag. 'I never said you were a liar, Mr Rosslyn. Don't tempt me to do so now.'

'Temptation is your game' said Rosslyn.

'Ex*cuse* me?' said Henderson. 'I don't get your drift –'

'Think about it,' said Rosslyn.

As a parting gesture she put her face very close to his and bared her teeth. She was pale with rage.

'Don't you ever again criticise my language in front of another government servant. Understand?'

Rosslyn kept his lips shut.

'Do you understand?' she said. 'You are one of those pious chauvinist misogynist yobs who will not permit women to use Anglo-Saxon words. So shove your shitty piety up yours.'

Rosslyn smiled quietly. 'Thanks for the advice. I mean that. I'll be sure to follow it. Let's ask Chapman here to shove it up your cunt.'

She inclined her head towards the exit for Chapman's benefit and the pair of them left without another word.

Rosslyn felt he had failed some kind of test. That at least Henderson – if that was her real name – had decided he'd be of little use to her. There was, he felt, something out of order about the pair. He couldn't put his finger on it at once, but he made a mental note to run a check on them. Henderson was desperate for information. Too desperate. Maybe too ambitious. She reminded him of the banker Dupleix. And there was that mention of the Zhentungs. He was relieved that he had trusted his instinct to keep the information he had learned from the Kwoks to himself, to say nothing to Victor or to Duggie Milo.

A young and attractive Chinese woman was seated alone at the next table reading *Time* magazine.

He watched her draw on her fur coat and leave the smoky warmth of the wine bar for the snow falling across the Strand. Darkness had fallen. The snow flakes sparkled white, yellow and pink in the lights. Hurrying pedestrians shielded their faces against the cold. The young Chinese woman reminded him of Mei.

46

From his flat in Claverton Street he put through another telephone call to Mei's number in Hong Kong.

There was no answer.

47

The tide was low and the river a shade of steel when the figure walked waist-deep into the foul water beneath the river wall.

On granite piers, the wrought iron arches of Blackfriars Bridge, the nearest Thames crossing, loomed out of the snowy darkness behind him.

Ahead stood the Millennium Bridge, the three hundred and thirty metre concrete and steel pedestrian bridge linking the City of London at Wren's St Paul's Cathedral with Herzog and de Meuron's Tate Modern Gallery at Bankside. Beyond the Millennium Bridge were the steel arches, granite cutwaters and piers of Southwark Bridge standing almost hidden in the yellowish mist.

Few Londoners give even a passing thought to the network of 'thrown dead water' pipes once used by the London Hydraulic Power Company. The network of LHPC pipes once linked all four points of the London compass. They still cross beneath the Thames at several points, including Southwark Bridge. Look carefully, and your eyes will see the LHPC initials on the manhole covers, the entrance to the pipes, some of which fell into disuse less than forty years ago. Beneath the manhole covers lie the conduits of cast iron.

The entrance to the pipes that travel beneath Hopton Street is found with little difficulty. It was the Hopton Street entrance that Terajima entered just after six o'clock that evening.

Dressed in an adapted Fontel Marine survival suit, with portable breathing apparatus fastened to his back, he crawled in the southerly direction. The beam from the torch strapped around his head lit the way ahead. It illuminated the filthy hanging plant growths and the scuttling rats he had for brief company. He took with him a lightweight carrier on small wheels loaded with waterproof packages containing high explosives and electrical devices to detonate them later in the evening.

Reaching his destination, he secured the lethal assembly beneath a disused grill, close enough to the surface so that the whole lot could be detonated by high-powered remote control signal. The business of detonation would of course be carried out by his associate, the leather-clad motorcyclist riding the Suzuki Freewind 650.

Terajima would be far from the scene.

48

Cai duo bu lu, yi gao bu xian;
Ai lu ai xian, bi you feng xian.

Don't show off your wealth or talents;
Those who do show off court danger.

CHINESE PROVERB

That same evening Rosslyn joined the throng of guests at the reception in the Zhentung duplex.

The duplex crowned the twenty-first storey of the grandiose office and residential riverside development. It was a fortress within a fortress. Floor to ceiling windows of bullet-proof sheer glass allowed the guests to admire the three hundred and sixty degree view of the City of London in the snow, the towers, city churches and the Thames. The townscape of towers and houses to the south east stretched to the dark blue and white horizon. Fashioned by an ennobled architect, like Anthony Zhentung a man who left school with three O levels at sixteen and the precocious ability to read a balance sheet, the duplex was, as Zhentung put it, the honeypot that attracted social mudflies.

The most senior of Anthony Zhentung's senior personal assistants, Paige Holmes-Williams, formerly a member of staff at Buckingham Palace, had provided Rosslyn with the list of invitees. It included the Deputy Prime Minister, three minor members of the Cabinet, the Lord Chancellor, the Chinese and Israeli ambassadors and the editors of the *Daily Telegraph, The Times, Sunday Times, Observer* and *Guardian*. Most, though not all, had been the recipients of Zhentung's hospitality and favours. Only a word in the ear and Zhentung would instruct his bankers to consider donations to national art galleries, theatres, conservation projects and political parties. The world of the Zhen-tungs was both exclusive and inclusive.

The plainclothes men with responsibility for the protection of the Deputy Prime Minister stayed close to their charge. Likewise, the grim security men accompanying the Israeli ambassador stood with their backs to the windows looking on.

Anthony Zhentung, a small man in his late forties with pomad-ed hair, wore a tailored suit, the badge of the Légion d'Honneur in his lapel and shoes of highly polished snakeskin with gold buckles.

'There you see St Paul's,' Zhentung told the visitors, many of whom were viewing these London landmarks for the first time. 'The Palace of Westminster. The Royal National Theatre. The Millennium Bridge. The Bankside Tate, formerly the Bankside Power Station. The NatWest tower. Tower Bridge.'

For the benefit of the visiting ministers of the governments of Japan and Korea, Jun'ichiro Shirakawa and Kang Han-kyu, Zhentung added: 'London is the city of Zhentung of Riverside. And I also own some acres of God's sky. Let me explain. Come.'

Led by Zhentung and including Rosslyn, the procession of guests made its way to the roof terrace. Here, dining platforms constructed of wood and marble had been built to the level of the balustrade. Zhentung's ten-year-old twin daughters wearing party frocks joined him with their Filipino nanny.

Then, for the delight of his guests, unprompted, and with a whisper of intimacy, Anthony Zhentung intoned a verse from Francis Thompson's poem 'The Kingdom of God':

> The angels keep their ancient places;
> Turn but a stone, and start a wing!
> 'Tis ye, 'tis your estranged faces,
> That miss the many-splendoured thing.

With glasses of champagne in hand, some of the guests called out, 'Bravo. Encore.'

His twin daughters joined in the applause.

Anthony Zhentung was more than happy to oblige with:

> Yea, in the night, my Soul, my daughter,
> Cry, clinging Heaven by the hems;

> And lo, Christ walking on the water
> Not of Gennesareth, but Thames.

Zhentung bowed with a look of modesty and applauded himself in the manner of a winner at a show business awards ceremony. He bowed again, and led his guests like hapless tourists towards the dim light of the passage to the main riverside salon.

They passed by the erotic Chinese paintings of the K'ang-hsi period lining the passage walls to where the marble plaque above the plate-glass doors of the main salon announced 'The Salon of the Kingdom of Heaven'.

Once through the doors, Zhentung pointed out the drawings by Seurat, Van Gogh and Toulouse-Lautrec and the pastels by Degas. Here, in The Salon of the Kingdom of Heaven, Rosslyn found Victor Michaelson pressed up against the wall in hushed conversation with Paige Holmes-Williams. Michaelson turned aside to Rosslyn.

'Alan – someone's here who's very keen to say hello to you. An American. Birgit Swann. An attractive blonde. Says you two met in Hong Kong. Should we know her? Who *exactly* is she?'

'An American legal attaché,' said Rosslyn. 'Most likely CIA.'

'Could be useful. Better make your mark.' Michaelson smiled as if he were about to make a dirty joke. 'She's with a senior man from the American embassy. She seems terribly keen to renew your acquaintance. She actually asked me to join her for dinner, which I can't. Very decent of her. I took the liberty of saying you might be up for it. Dorchester Grill. I wouldn't say no to that, Alan. You should go.'

'I have to stay here.'

'No need to stay here,' said Michaelson. 'The place is crawling with the Protection Squad, the Israelis. God alone knows who else besides. Don't you worry about staying. I'll have a word with Anthony. Take up the American's invitation. Do as I say. Enjoy yourself.'

'Don't worry about us,' said Paige Holmes-Williams. 'We're as safe as houses here.'

'I'll look out for her,' said Rosslyn.

'I rather think –' Michaelson leaned close to Rosslyn's ear. 'She's got the hots for you, boy.'

'Thanks for the warning, Victor.'

'If I were your age –'

'I believe you, Victor. I want to take a look at the rest of the art here.'

In an even lower voice, Michaelson said, 'They're terribly good fakes. The real ones are in a Geneva bank vault. Just in case there's some sort of fire, flood or act of God. As a former Customs investigations officer, I'd have thought you'd have spotted that already.'

Rosslyn joined the guests in the centre of the salon. The *pièce de resistance* was the glass case adapted to display the fourteenth-century preliminary paintings for the National Gallery's Wilton Diptych and a manuscript.

Zhentung was approaching the climax of the tour. He pointed to the bureau table and display unit.

'Said by Christie's to have belonged to Marie Antoinette. Now converted into a modern fireproof display cabinet. Here you see 'The Kingdom of God' in its original autograph manuscript state by the poet Francis Thompson. One is obliged, don't you feel, to give credence to the poet's imagination. D'you agree?'

Everyone agreed. Fuelled by the champagne, the braying of the guests rose. Rosslyn watched Zhentung relishing the displays of subservience and fawning approval. It was hard to square the image of him with what he had learned from Winston thanks to Steve Kwok.

'Hi, Alan,' said the woman's voice next to him. 'Birgit.' Swann was standing with an American. 'Great to see you. Let me introduce you to Minister-Counsellor Fordice Janklow.'

Rosslyn shook the diplomat's hand.

Janklow said, 'We're hoping you may be able to make up the numbers at a dinner I've arranged at the Dorchester.'

'I'd really enjoy that, Alan,' said Swann. 'Can you make up our table?'

'I'd like to,' said Rosslyn. 'Thank you.'

'Great,' said Swann.

'We're entertaining some big hitters,' said Janklow. 'Visiting ministers of the governments of Japan and Korea, Jun'ichiro Shirakawa and Kang Han-kyu. They prefer to dine earlier than we do. We should leave soon. We have cars. Join us.'

'I'll get my coat,' said Rosslyn.

Whereas Victor thought the dinner could prove 'generally useful', Rosslyn thought that the dinner invitation might offer him an opportunity to question Swann. Say about Anthony Zhentung. Winston. About Mei even.

49

Some time between eight-thirty and nine, the last remaining guests thanked Anthony Zhentung and bade him farewell.

VIPs, men of vague diplomatic status and several of Anthony Zhentung's faceless business associates in dark suits headed for the lifts. They made their exits, bound for their chauffeur-driven cars parked the length of Hopton Street in the falling snow. CCTV cameras above the exit doors of heavy steel monitored their progress.

Shortly after nine-fifteen, Anthony Zhentung said good-night to his twin daughters and left the duplex. Holmes-Williams and Malaysian bodyguards accompanied him. His staff carried mobile telephones and miniature Nokimoto metal detectors. Anthony Zhentung and his acolytes took the grander of the two lifts to the lower basement garage. The muzak in the lift was an endless tape of Tchaikovsky's *Variations on a Rococo Theme* for cello and orchestra.

Anthony Zhentung was bound for a late dinner with the president of a German media empire and a royal courtier, a family friend of Paige Holmes-Williams. The others had already left for the private dining club in Chelsea. The royal courtier, Anthony Zhentung's guest of honour that evening, had the ear of the Prince of Wales. Charles was delighted to have received the donations to The Prince's Trust from the Zhentung Foundation. Zhentung was going to hand out still more.

Anthony Zhentung was in an expectant mood. According to the reliable Paige Holmes-Williams, the royal courtier had said that the Prince's private secretary was hinting that Anthony Zhentung was in line for a peerage.

'That'll make you Lord Zhentung,' Holmes-Williams teased. 'What *will* we call you – Lord or Baron?'

'Anthony will do,' said Anthony Zhentung, the muscles tightening his lips into a mirthless grin.

50

While Anthony Zhentung prepared to leave the duplex, Rosslyn was travelling across London with Swann in the chauffeur-driven car provided by the embassy. The car was following another taking Fordice Janklow, the Korean and the Japanese to the Dorchester in Park Lane. Rosslyn and Swann sat together on the back seat.

'I hear you're going back east,' she said. 'To finish the incomplete operation of yours – Winston's unfinished business.'

'No,' said Rosslyn, 'it's a routine job. Nothing to do with Winston. A maritime security review for an insurance company. Client confidential.'

'You must call on me when you're there,' she said. They were crossing the river at Blackfriars. 'Did you see Mei Lim before you left Hong Kong?'

'Yes, I did.'

'Have you heard from her recently?'

'No. She's sort of gone to ground.'

'I'll call my people and we'll find out how and where she is. Mei's so gorgeous. Some of those oriental women are so lucky. Beautiful. Looking after her must be one of the more pleasant jobs you have going.'

'It's personal rather than professional.'

'Talking of which, our friend Burnal says to give you his regards. Dr Burnal Graer, you recall him?'

'Your Aussie friend?'

'We do a lot of business together.'

'How come you were at Anthony Zhentung's?'

'Fordice Janklow's an old friend of Anthony's. You must know Anthony and his brothers pretty well by now.'

'Not really,' said Rosslyn. 'Anthony's a friend of Victor Michaelson, who has close ties with my firm, Milo Associates.'

'Small world. Do you know the other brothers?'

'No. They're pretty reclusive.'

'But you're in charge of Zhentung security?'

'That's right,' said Rosslyn. 'Anthony's personal security.'

'It doesn't touch on his business operations?'

'No.'

'Or the other brothers' businesses,' she said. 'You know about them?'

'No,' said Rosslyn. 'Do you?'

'Only that there's a rumour around of a split between them. Some major falling out. I thought you might know. Given that you're in charge of Anthony Zhentung's security.'

'As I say, it doesn't extend to knowledge of his business life,' said Rosslyn. 'As to his personal life, I didn't even know he had children until tonight.'

'He keeps that side of his life a secret,' said Swann. 'He doesn't in so many words have a wife. She was in the process of divorcing him when she died. It was a nasty business. Anthony had married the sister of Hastings Zhentung's wife. It's a serious family bust-up. You can imagine. You really don't know much about Foster and Hastings or their associates and staff?'

'I'd be happy to tell you if I did,' Rosslyn lied. 'What's your interest in them?'

'Our interest is in what Winston Lim knew. What he took with him to his grave.'

'Haven't you approached the Hong Kong Police?'

'They haven't anything to tell us.'

'What about talking to Steve Kwok?'

'He won't say anything. You have to remember that Beijing has a big input into Hong Kong law enforcement. That might explain the blanket silence.'

'What is it you're looking for?' Rosslyn asked.

'Intelligence in general. Relating to financing of major maritime terrorist and extortion syndicates back home in the States and throughout South East Asia. That was Winston's special territory. We think he must have confided in you.'

'I can't help you.'

The car was turning into the forecourt of the Dorchester Hotel.

'We'll avoid the subject over dinner. What with the Korean and Japanese being guests. We can talk another time.'

138

Swann thanked the driver and asked him to wait for her.

A liveried doorman escorted Rosslyn and Swann into the hotel.

They crossed the foyer and headed for the Grill, where Janklow was already waiting for them at his favoured table with his Japanese and Korean guests.

51

When Anthony Zhentung stepped out of the lift into the basement garage, the uniformed Malaysian driver greeted him with hands clasped in a gesture of supplication. The engine of the custom-built and armoured Mercedes was running. The Malaysian driver reported on his mobile telephone to the concierge that the departure of the boss was imminent.

The concierge who took the call in the foyer was seated at the desk next to his colleague, the former Special Air Service non-commissioned officer. The two men were monitoring the departure of the Mercedes on one of several CCTV screens fixed to the wall just above the desk. The former SAS man was normally on duty in the temporary cubicle of wood and plastic situated at the garage's exit to Hopton Street. The cubicle had been removed to allow construction workers to carry out emergency repairs to the underground sewer pipes that passed beneath the concrete flooring of the garages.

The former SAS man left the foyer and let himself out of the building through a side door to walk the few metres along the temporary wooden gangway on the Hopton Street pavement to the garage exit. Here, when the moment was right, he was supposed to give the driver of the Mercedes the all clear: the signal for the driver to pull out into the street.

Once the bodyguards had used the metal detectors to search underneath the armour-plated car for hidden explosive devices, the final all clear was given for the departure.

It was Anthony Zhentung who took the wheel of the Mercedes. This departure from standard security procedures was perhaps a minor gesture of freedom in a life of restrictions, albeit self-imposed. Paige Holmes-Williams climbed in beside Zhentung in the front passenger seat. Both of them fastened their safety belts.

The driver got into the back seat next to the bodyguard, who discreetly held in readiness his Heckler & Koch MP5 sub-machine gun.

Pre-eminent of its kind, the Heckler & Koch is rarely supplied to civilians. If and when it is, the manufacturers make modifications to the weapon so that, in case of trouble with armed criminals and terrorists, law enforcement users keep the upper hand. Anthony Zhentung's personal bodyguard carried the military and police version. It was a lethal weapon.

The Mercedes left the lower basement garage. Zhentung drove up the ramp, through the upper garage and emerged into the falling snow.

52

As the armour-plated Mercedes came into view across Hopton Street, the leather-clad motorcyclist, face hidden by a black visor and helmet, started the Suzuki Freewind 650 and rode slowly a few metres further down the street.

In the rear view mirror, the motorcyclist saw the former SAS man give a casual wave to Anthony Zhentung at the wheel of the Mercedes: the indication that the way was clear for the car to pull out into the street. Accelerating slowly, it lumbered on to the temporary steel ramp covering the repair work to the sewerage pipe.

At the same time, the motorcyclist triggered the remote control.

Like the epicentre of an earthquake, beneath the steel ramp and the Mercedes, the explosion tore the ground wide open.

53

STATEMENT OF WITNESS

[Criminal Justice Act 1967, s.9]

Statement of:	Mo Kelly Mills
Age of Witness:	Over 21
Occupation:	C.E.O.
Address:	Masons Yard,
	High Street,
	Wimbledon Village,
	London SW19 5BY

This statement consisting of 2 pages signed by me is true to the best of my knowledge and belief and I make it knowing that if it is tendered in evidence, I shall be liable to prosecution if I wilfully state anything which I know to be false.

All hell erupted. An enormous sheet of yellow and white flame shot across the road. The noise was indescribable. A thick and fierce cloud of black and blue smoke followed it. It was like the apocalypse.

There was no screaming. Just a complete, surreal silence. There were horrible fumes from burning plaster, plastic and melting metal. It was an unforgettable and very sour stench. Later I realised the stench was of burning blood and flesh.

I saw some children running round in circles, their hair on fire, like wild animals.

There were more people lying on the pavement, covered in a layer of shattered glass and debris.

I think one was a woman, her face masked with blood, with one leg blown off. The leg was intact and lay a few feet distant from her body. I think, at the time, she was still alive. Her male

companion was lying with his eyes open. He lay
there very still. Terrible.

   Still, there was this eerie silence. Thinking
about it after, I reckoned it couldn't have been
silence. I had been deafened by the blast.

   What I saw was terrifying. A gigantic cloud of
smoke was rising from the building. The whole
thing was on fire. The cloud was blue and black and
was shutting out the sky. Even the snow had turned
red and black. I though the building might collapse
at any moment.

   I never want to see anything like that again.
Never.

Signed: *Mo Kelly Mills*

Signature witnessed by: Chief Superintendent Ronald Costley

Signed: *Ron Costley*

Signature witnessed by: WPC Michelle Seifert

Signed: *Michelle Seifert*

54

The motorcyclist was bound for west London – the M4 motorway and on to the suburb of Hatton, north east of Heathrow's Terminal 4.

It would be near Hatton, at the Faggs Road rendezvous, that the paymaster would hand over the final cash instalment of the fee in euros.

55

Two men in dark suits entered the Dorchester Grill in single file. Circling the centre table, which supported a giant vase of pussy-willow branches and white lilies, they passed the waiters carving roast joints on the stately silver-covered trolley and headed straight for the table where Rosslyn and Janklow's other guests were studying the menus.

Rosslyn was surprised by the man's voice saying, 'Excuse me, Mr Rosslyn. Could we have a word with you in private, sir?'

'What about?'

'Just a brief word, sir.'

'Can I help?' Janklow put in. 'Mr Rosslyn is my guest. My name's Fordice Janklow. United States embassy.'

The larger of the two men in suits showed Janklow his ID. 'I'm sorry to interrupt your dinner, sir. We need to talk to Mr Rosslyn in confidence.'

The man showed his ID to Rosslyn.

Rosslyn got to his feet. 'My apologies,' he said to Janklow.

'It won't take long,' the police officer said for Janklow's benefit.

'I hope you're right,' said Janklow.

'See you later?' said Swann.

'Fine,' said Rosslyn. 'I'm sorry about this. You carry on with dinner.'

'If you'd follow us, sir,' said the police officer.

56

At the snowbound outskirts of Heathrow, beyond the deserted junction of Faggs Road and The Causeway, the motorcyclist turned off the road. Overhead a Boeing 747 lowered, its jet engines screaming. Even in the falling snow, the stench of aviation fuel hung in the darkness. Ice covered the surface of the adjacent reservoir, bordered by scrub and willow trees.

He manoeuvred the motorbike along a narrow track, finally pulling up in front of a set of steel security gates. The warehouses adjoined wasteland that was due for commercial development in the near future. Here he used a pair of heavy-duty cutters to slice through the chains that secured the gates. The road to the warehouses lay ahead.

Still on schedule, the motorcyclist killed the engine and dismounted to walk the short way through the snow to the entrance of the farthest warehouse. Its steel door, with paint-sprayed graffiti scrawled across it, was heavily padlocked. The motorcyclist cut through the chain to release the padlock and opened the high door.

According to prior arrangement, the paymaster would be waiting here alone with the fee in cash.

The plan was that the paymaster would then see to the removal of the Suzuki's registration plate along with the engine serial number and later the dumping of the machine in the nearby River Crane, which flows beneath The Causeway. The ice might be a problem and he would have to find a way to smash a hole in it. That was the paymaster's problem, not the motorcyclist's. The paymaster would then provide the motorcyclist with the euros, a sober suit and the small white transit van. Ahead of him lay the drive to Dover, through the Channel Tunnel, across France and the onward journey to Spain, where he would stay with long-standing criminal associates nominally in the time-share holiday homes business near Malaga.

The motorcyclist wheeled the Suzuki inside the warehouse. The dark and silent interior was warm and reeked of gasoline. Walking a short distance forward across the wet and slippery floor, he paused and waited.

The paymaster was supposed to be waiting inside the warehouse. There was no sign of him. Strange. Always on time for appointments, there was an admirable and almost military professionalism about the way he conducted his business.

Why isn't he here by now?

The motorcyclist decided to cross the floor of the warehouse to the vehicle entrance at the far side. This would be the door through which the paymaster would drive the transit van.

By now, the paymaster was more than six minutes late.

The police. The police are on to him.

What's this delay about?

57

'What the hell is this about?' Rosslyn asked the two police officers.

'You'll see.'

He was seated between the two plainclothes men in the back of the unmarked car. There was a third officer in the front passenger seat. The fourth was the driver. From the urgency of the messages over the radio, Rosslyn could tell there had been an incident south of the river. A bomb blast of substantial proportions.

The route the driver was taking suggested they were approaching Paddington and sure enough the car pulled up at Paddington Green police station.

'Get out. *Move it, Rosslyn.*'

No more Mister.

58

The motorcyclist was still waiting in the warehouse near Heathrow.

He wedged the earpiece of a small radio in his ear and tuned the frequency to a news bulletin that was carrying details of the inferno beside the Thames.

'Earlier this evening,' the newsman said, 'the Deputy Prime Minister and several members of the Cabinet had attended a reception given by Anthony Zhentung at his home on the South Bank.'

Police and emergency services were there in force. There were mentions of police cordons and roadblocks in place at sensitive locations across London that suspected terrorists might target for attack.

The mention of the roadblocks concerned him. If the paymaster kept him waiting for more than another fifteen minutes, then to avoid motorway police roadblocks or temporary checkpoints to the south and east, he would have to be on his way. *What if they close the Channel Tunnel?* And there was the falling snow that would create still more delays. He anxiously retraced his footsteps.

The sweetness of the gasoline fumes was nauseating. He reckoned that somewhere in the warehouse there must be some kind of leaking fuel tank. After a few brief minutes of more silence, he heard the noise of footsteps.

It was the rattle of the chain and the clank of what could have been the padlock against the steel door followed by a moaning sound. He stood very still. There was nothing to be seen.

Maybe it's the wind.

A low hiss seemed to start. The *tttsss* of breath through clenched teeth. The noxious stench was like gas. Someone was there. If this was the paymaster, he would have said something by now. Or if it was a security guard, the man would have spoken or shone a torch. He resisted the overwhelming temptation to light his cigarette lighter and look around, or to say, 'Who are you?' He was reaching towards it, arm outstretched, when he saw the glow. He turned suddenly. The glow erupted and became a wall of flame.

59

Two uniformed police officers escorted Rosslyn to the basement of Paddington Green police station.

'I want to call my lawyer,' Rosslyn said.

'Sorry?'

'I said I want to speak to my lawyer.'

'Does he want to speak to you then?' the police officer said mechanically.

'You heard what I said.'

'Did I?'

The door was thrown open.

Beyond the table and two chairs in the centre of the airless, windowless room Rosslyn saw Elizabeth Henderson. She was standing at the far side of the room beneath the lens of a video camera. A telephone had been placed on the table. Judging from the wire across the floor it looked to be a temporary arrangement.

'Sit down,' she said.

Rosslyn stared at her.

'I said sit down.'

'No thanks.'

'As you wish,' she said.

She turned to the police officers. 'Thank you. You can go now.' Then for the benefit of the video recording system, she said, 'Paddington Green police station, Interview Room. Present Elizabeth Henderson. Foreign and Commonwealth Office. Alan Rosslyn. No solicitor present.' She added the time and date.

'I suppose you are aware', she began, with the prosecutor's tone, 'that along with several other people, Anthony Zhentung was killed an hour or two ago as he was leaving his residence in Hopton Street.' Pausing, she searched Rosslyn's face for a reaction. Finding none, she continued, 'I'd like you to tell me if you know anything about it.'

'No comment.'

'I'm right in thinking you are responsible, on a private basis, for Mr Zhentung's security?'

'No comment.'

'May I take that as a yes?'

Rosslyn remained silent.

'If you don't wish to say anything, so be it. But I hardly need tell you that successful prosecution of you will carry with it a sentence of forty years at least.'

Rosslyn gave her a blank stare.

'But we can, as it were, come to an agreement. Reach an accommodation, say, or call it what you like. Mind you, you'll know that I personally don't have search and arrest powers.'

'No one's said anything about arrest.'

Henderson showed the braces and her yellowish teeth. 'Oh, at last. *He speaks.* I thought you'd lost the gift.'

'I am not under arrest,' Rosslyn said slowly. 'Meanwhile, if you need reminding of my rights, I am entitled to speak to my lawyer.'

'I suppose that will be Victor Michaelson?'

'Yes. Victor Michaelson.'

'If you prove co-operative, anything can be arranged, believe me.'

'In that case, Henderson, let's continue this little conversation in more civilised surroundings.'

'This isn't a *conversation*, Rosslyn.'

'What is it, then?'

'An interrogation.'

'Then I can guess your line of questioning. I don't believe that Anthony Zhentung is dead.'

'Then try telephoning him.' She lifted the telephone. 'Here – go ahead, call him.'

Rosslyn shook his head. 'It's Victor Michaelson I'm going to speak to.'

'No. Call a friend at Scotland Yard and see if what I'm saying isn't true. The bomb could have killed many more people. Including the Deputy Prime Minister, the Israeli ambassador and others. And you, Rosslyn, sit here, not believing me, saying nothing, being unhelpful and being antagonistic. It won't look too good in court, will it?'

Rosslyn remained silent.

'It won't look good in court, Rosslyn, will it?' she said.

Rosslyn looked at her blankly.

153

'Even a moron will fathom that you abandoned your duty deliberately. *Deliberately*. Deliberately so that the bomber would have a free run. And where were *you*? With friends at dinner at the Dorchester.'

'It was Victor's idea that I go. You've spoken to him?'

'Of course I have. Who do you think I am? Go on. Abuse me with your patronising silence. I'm telling you – you're about to find out that you are in the deepest shit you've ever been in.'

'Except that I will nail you, Ms Henderson, on a charge of wasting police time. Of interrogating me without explanation or any reason. You talk of patronising silence. You're the one who's patronising. The shoe's on your little foot.'

'There you go again.'

'Then tell me what this is about.'

She sat down at the table and looked into his eyes without blinking. 'You had a visit from a Chinese registered diplomat?'

'No comment.'

She produced what looked like a prepared questionnaire and set it in front of her like a schoolmistress facing a recalcitrant pupil.

'A man called Zhu Jianxing. Assistant Defence Attaché at the Chinese embassy.'

'Really?'

'Zhu's a spy.'

'You don't say.'

'What was it about, Rosslyn?'

'You tell me. You must have bugged my office.'

'We don't have your place under audio surveillance.'

'Pull the other one, Henderson.'

'You have Victor Michaelson to thank for that. But Zhu was seen entering your office building.'

'I get all sorts of visitors,' said Rosslyn. 'If you have a problem with our Chinese friend, then speak to him yourself.'

'He's in Beijing.'

'Then, Ms Henderson, there's no way he can have called at my office, is there?'

'You can trust us to get evidence correct.'

'I don't trust you.'

'But we want to *trust* you, Mr Rosslyn.'

'I don't *trust* you, Ms Henderson. Trust doesn't enter into this.

Only the truth. And you have a duty to let me out of this piss-hole and get on with your life. Like I intend to get on with mine.'

'Beforehand, I'm going to put a few facts to you. Perhaps you'd tell me if I have them right.'

'You're wasting police time –'

'You started working for the Zhentungs six months ago?'

'I can't remember.'

She marked what Rosslyn had assumed was a pre-prepared questionnaire. 'We can check with Victor Michaelson,' she suggested.

Rosslyn hesitated. 'You can do what you like.'

'You are responsible for Anthony Zhentung's personal protection.'

'So you say.'

'Over a period of some years, you enjoyed the confidence and trust of Winston Lim.'

'He's dead.'

'And you continue to enjoy the confidence and trust of Steve Kwok and his wife Catherine?'

Rosslyn said nothing.

After a moment, Henderson continued: 'You are familiar with the South East Asian criminal syndicates variously known as the Malacca Cartel, Snake Skin or Black Shoe.'

'No.'

'You are familiar with a man called Klaas-Pieter Terajima.'

'Who?'

'A man called Klaas-Pieter Terajima.'

'Is he a friend of yours too, Ms Henderson?'

'I'm asking you if he's one of yours.'

'So you are. So you are.'

'You are aware that Winston Lim had been investigating bank accounts in Luxembourg and Geneva. Bank accounts holding monies on behalf of black market industrial concerns.'

'Like what bank accounts? What black market?'

'In bomb-grade fissile material. You're aware that it has to do with thermonuclear device components. Use your imagination. We are talking deep water. Just be sure you can swim in it. And that you know when and where the water's shark infested.'

'That's word for word what you told me before. You know how much it means to me?'

'Just answer me – yes or no.'

'You want to know how much it means to me?'

'If there's something you want to discuss that I haven't mentioned, then with the greatest respect, you can have the manners to wait until I've finished.'

'No,' said Rosslyn. 'Let's get it over with now.'

'Very well then. How much does it mean to you, Mr Rosslyn?'

'Bugger all.'

'That's not entirely helpful.'

'It's not supposed to be.'

'You know Dr Burnal Graer?'

'Ask him.'

'You know Birgit Swann?'

'While you're at it, ask her too. Call the US embassy.'

'Very well then.' She gave him a look of feigned disappointment. 'I want to return to Winston Lim. Did he ever seek favours from you?'

'Now that's something I can help you with, Ms Henderson. Yes, he did. He asked me once, if ever the need arose, to keep a watch on his daughter, Mei Lim. And that, Ms Henderson, is a personal matter.'

'I'm not concerned with his daughter.'

'That's just one more difference between us. One more nail in the coffin of the failing relationship between you and me. I am concerned with his daughter's security.'

She looked at him with contempt. 'I hope you do a better job protecting her than you've done with Anthony Zhentung.'

'That's a very stupid remark and you know it.'

She folded the questionnaire and laid her hands on it.

'That's it, Ms Henderson?'

'Everything you have told me is true?' she said.

'I haven't told you anything.'

'I think', she said, 'Victor Michaelson will be here by now. I have a deal to put to you.'

'I don't do deals.'

'Well, let's see what Victor has to say, shall we?'

A moment later, Victor Michaelson was shown into the airless room.

60

Michaelson looked crestfallen. 'Alan, old boy, I'm awfully sorry about this.' He turned to Henderson. 'I assume you've told him what's happened?'

Henderson nodded.

'And his daughters?' asked Rosslyn.

'Dead too, I hate to say.'

Puffing up her cheeks, Henderson said nothing.

'I'm very sorry, Alan,' said Michaelson.

'So am I, Victor,' said Rosslyn. 'So am I. I'd like to know right off why I'm here.'

Michaelson assumed an expression of regret. Whether it was genuine not, Rosslyn was unable to tell. 'There's a view that you know very much more about events than might be, let us say, comfortable for you.'

'Is that what you think, Victor?'

'One's caught somewhere between Scylla and Charybdis. You have to appreciate the sensitivity of the position. As it is, a number of people have been murdered. It's a terrible tragedy. Absolutely devastating. The Zhentungs are my friends. God knows, it's one that could've been so very much worse. With the loss of the Lord knows how many distinguished people.'

'I explained that to Mr Rosslyn,' said Henderson, as if she was pleased with the duty she had performed.

'You gather?' Michaelson said to Rosslyn with a smile.

'Gather what?'

'You gather the extreme awkwardness of the situation,' said Michaelson. 'The police and security services are on red alert. You of all people will appreciate that they desperately need to build a picture of all those involved with the outrage. You are in the perfect position to help them –'

Henderson interrupted: 'I don't think Mr Rosslyn fully appreciates the seriousness –'

'Allow me, if I may, Ms Henderson,' said Michaelson, with a look of admonition. 'Let me explain, please –'

'Let me, Victor,' Rosslyn countered. 'I have been brought here under a police escort to be interrogated by Ms Henderson. Where are the charges? What's the explanation? Am I under arrest? I'm being detained against my will and against my rights. This is totally out of order and you know it, Victor.'

'It's perfectly reasonable in the circumstances,' said Michaelson.

'Victor,' said Rosslyn, 'it *is* unreasonable. That I had anything, *anything* at all, to do with what I've been told has happened to Zhentung is a massive fabrication. Ms Henderson here hasn't told me exactly what happened between the time I left Zhentung's place and now. But I can tell you that every possible arrangement was in place to cover Zhentung's personal security. He will have had his own people there, licensed to be armed. They've all been trained in detecting explosives, for assessing any suspicious actions on the part of strangers. I don't have to continue. The security of that place was one hundred per cent effective.'

'Except, the very painful fact we have to face is this – Anthony Zhentung and others have been blown to kingdom come,' said Michaelson.

'And you, Mr Rosslyn,' said Henderson, 'you are in the best possible position to give the police and security services the most valuable of all initial leads.'

'For Christ's sake,' said Rosslyn, 'I wasn't even there. And all you've done is to bring me here and interrogate me as if I'm some sort of suspect. Jesus Christ, Henderson, surely it's not beyond your wit and imagination to see that banging me up like some pissing terrorist isn't going to help you, or me, or even Victor here. What is it – you want to make me a scapegoat? I have told you, I wasn't even there. Do you get it?'

'Yes, I do indeed get it, Mr Rosslyn,' Henderson said. 'It's precisely the point I've been at pains to explain to you *ad nauseam*, which for reasons best know to yourself you obstinately refuse to recognise. You won't co-operate with me. You won't listen to my questions.' There was a short silence. 'Tell me,' she said with what passed for a kindly look, 'is there anyone you would talk to?'

Rosslyn shrugged.

'Alan,' said Michaelson, 'has Elizabeth here suggested to you that some sort of initial, informal, off-the-record deal might be struck?'

'I don't do deals.'

'So you keep on saying,' said Henderson.

'Oh, one can understand what you must be feeling,' said Michaelson. 'Pretty bloody, I dare say.'

'Not pretty bloody. Bloody angry.'

'Of course,' Michaelson said, with what seemed to be understanding. 'But let me put the nature of what's been proposed to you. *Pro tem.* We have what used to be called a cooling-off period. We gather our thoughts together. Do things in the civilised manner. You get my drift, Alan. That's the neatness of our little deal. Not a deal, if you will allow, rather a civilised arrangement. When push comes to shove, we're all on the same side, old boy.'

'Which is what?'

'Let me finish,' said Michaelson. 'You'll leave here with me and return to my flat in Portman Square. I've arranged for my housekeeper to make up a spare room for you. You get a good night's rest away from the glare of any publicity that might arise. Unwanted attention from journalists and so forth. My place is secure. We will be in what one can best describe as no man's land.'

'We've seen to that,' said Henderson.

'I bet you have,' said Rosslyn.

'You get my drift, Alan,' said Michaelson. 'Are you game for it?'

'If you say so, Victor.'

'And the added bonus is that you and I talk things over in a relaxed fashion. Best of all, immunity from prosecution is on the table. The *quid pro quo* is that we postpone your commission for Ocean Insurance and so on.'

'We'll see,' said Rosslyn. 'Does Duggie know about it?'

'About our arrangement?' said Michaelson. 'Oh yes. Indeed he does. I called him. He's in Hawaii. New place. New girl. He thinks it's all very much for the best. For Milo Associates. For you. For me, even. What do you reckon?'

'I reckon there's no alternative,' said Rosslyn.

Henderson sighed. 'Good. Everything's in place. We can leave.'

Michaelson gave a little wave with his right hand. It was a gesture that reminded Rosslyn of an army officer's casual salute. As if

Michaelson were saying, 'Carry on, chaps.' Something like that.

'I hope, Rosslyn,' said Henderson, 'that you were not too offended by my approach.'

'You people are trained to be shits,' said Rosslyn. 'You qualify.'

Before Henderson could reply, the police officers opened the door and stood aside for Michaelson to lead the way to no man's land.

61

By the time Rosslyn and Michaelson left Paddington Green police station in Michaelson's chauffeur-driven car, Terajima had cut some twenty minutes off his schedule on his way from the inferno to Heathrow.

There was no need to slide the unwanted Suzuki into the murky waters of the River Crane. The fire had disposed of it instead. He had had plenty of time in which to dress in the overalls emblazoned with the logo of the British Airports Authority and then to affix the transfer of the BAA logo to the van's sides.

Then, at the wheel of the transit van, he took a circuitous route along South West Road to the junction with Bath Road, at which point the inferno in the warehouse reached its zenith. He inserted a new tab of snuff beneath his upper lip and gums. The substance produced the familiar rush.

He turned left beneath Northern Perimeter Road into the tunnel, joining the slow-moving traffic to the Heathrow terminals.

Once in the BAA car park, he parked the transit van neatly in the ranks of others marked BAA.

The grey suitcase he took with him contained changes of clothing, mostly of Italian manufacture, and toiletries that were French.

In the left-hand side pocket of his jacket he carried a British passport in the name of Dr Hung, dealer in antiquities, whose business was registered in Guernsey.

The snakeskin wallet in his inside jacket pocket contained NatWest and Amex credit cards. Various other cards identified Dr Hung as a Friend of the Royal Academy, British Museum and Tate Gallery, and his Sotheby's card, decorated with an image of Venice by Canaletto, said: PLEASE PRESENT THIS CARD WHEN REGISTERING FOR A PADDLE OR TAKING ADVANTAGE OF ANY BENEFITS TO WHICH IT ENTITLES YOU.

With an affected limp, Terajima walked slowly past the BAA car park guard, who scarcely gave the disabled worker a second glance, and headed for the entrance to the terminal. Once inside, Terajima made his way to the nearest Toilet for the Disabled.

Locked inside the toilet, he stepped out of the BAA overall and folded it into an unmarked white plastic bag. He rolled up his sleeves and wedged the bag hard into the toilet bowl. Then he squatted down and emptied his bowels. Without pulling the flush, he lowered the seat, washed his hands, straightened his dark grey suit, and let himself out of the toilet to join his fellow travellers.

62

When the man called Dr Hung was heading for the check-in desk, teams of London fire officers had already been fighting for several hours to extinguish the inferno beside the Thames.

Hampered by the threat of the building's imminent collapse, it took careful probing in the steaming slush and twisted debris before the firemen found the charred remains of those thought to be Anthony Zhentung, his twin daughters, their nanny, Paige Holmes-Williams and their fellow victims.

The Scotland Yard spokesman told journalists that the police were pursuing their enquiries and continuing their investigations.

Meanwhile, the police imposed a temporary curfew in the immediate area of the catastrophe. Their efforts did little to ease the shock by the local residents, who preferred to believe that they lived in one of the safest enclaves in the world.

The Metropolitan Police had already initiated a murder hunt across Europe, assisted by the French and Italians. They had also laid plans for a reconstruction of the crime and called upon the services of a team of anti-terrorism experts.

Initially, the murders were likened to that of Alfred Herrhausen.

It has to be admitted that most people had forgotten the name of Herrhausen, chairman of Deutsche Bank, who had been blown up in his car in Frankfurt more than a decade before. But unlike Alfred Herrhausen, Anthony Zhentung was not a public figure. Other than a few biographical details rehashed from newspaper cuttings libraries and the public record of his international dealings in the financial press, little of Zhentung's private life was public knowledge. He was said to have been amused by the jealousy of his competitors, who marvelled at the loyalty he inspired in clients. And the Zhentung Foundation had, of course, donated substantial sums of money to The Prince's Trust. No one was sure how much exactly. The point of interest was more that the Prince of Wales had declared himself to be 'personally terribly grateful'.

Mostly, it was the violent manner in which Anthony Zhentung had met his death and the unexplained motive for the murderous blast that first concentrated the attention of news agencies worldwide.

'It was an act of cowardly terrorism,' the police spokesman said at a second press conference. In the interests of the TV networks, it had been convened in front of the police cordons surrounding the devastated building.

Looking strained and weary, the spokesman continued:

'There are at least ten persons dead, maybe more. The damage to property is estimated at many millions. We have no idea who perpetrated this foul and despicable act. But the public may be sure, no expense or effort will be spared in order to bring the perpetrators to justice.'

Then came news of the inferno in the Heathrow area, the second that night.

The Director of Criminal Intelligence said the police had no idea whether or not the two incidents were in some way related.

Once again, like a mantra, the police spokesman reiterated the promise to spare no effort or expense to bring the perpetrators of the crime to justice.

This time he added, 'The public must be vigilant. We cannot guarantee that these people will not act again.'

'Our first thoughts', the Metropolitan Police Director of Criminal Intelligence told journalists, 'must be with the relatives and friends of Anthony Zhentung, along with those of the members of his staff who died. You have to realise that if the device had exploded one hour earlier during the reception, it would have resulted in an even greater tragedy. You may be sure that no efforts are being spared to bring those responsible for these murders to justice.'

63

The first-class ticket Dr Hung presented at the check-in desk showed his flight plan to Amsterdam and onwards to the Far East and Kuala Lumpur.

'Yes,' Terajima told the check-in clerk. 'Yes.' He had indeed packed his own luggage and it contained no electrical equipment. The check-in clerk wore small gold rings in both ears. He gave Dr Hung a smile that suggested he found the face of the dealer in antiquities interesting. Dr Hung thanked the clerk with what seemed to be oriental courtesy and solicitude.

The X-ray security scanner sounded no alert when he walked slowly beneath its arch.

The security woman asked him to step to one side and to raise his arms sideways so that she could frisk him. Then she asked him if she might see his wallet. She felt it carefully. Then she asked him to open it for her. He did as she requested.

She examined the credit cards, the small toothbrush, the safety razor and the cardboard nail file.

'That's fine, Dr Hung,' she said. 'Have a good flight.'

'Why, thank you,' said Terajima as the woman turned to face the next in line.

It was not until he reached the lounge reserved for first-class passengers that he learned of the security alert that spelled trouble. Outbound flights had been indefinitely postponed.

64

Not only did it dawn on Rosslyn that Michaelson's chauffeur was heading for somewhere other than Michaelson's address in Portman Square, but he soon realised that they were heading south of the river.

Rosslyn remained silent. Michaelson muttered something long-winded about the snow and ice 'and the predictability of the British absence of effective measures to clear the streets'.

Perhaps Michaelson sensed Rosslyn's unease. 'Oh, by the way, Alan,' he explained, 'it's part of our arrangement that we talk to one of the anti-terrorist officers at the scene. A man called Costley would like a word with you.'

'I don't think I'll be able to help him much.'

'I dare say', said Michaelson, 'that he'll the judge of that.'

65

Smoke shrouded the London apartment building where Zhentung and the others had died.

Michaelson's chauffeur parked the car a quarter of a mile from the shell of the building and they walked through the snow to the police cordon. A few floral bouquets had already been placed against the walls on the other side of the street. Rosslyn was taken aback by the extent of the devastation in Hopton Street.

Ron Costley introduced himself. He wore a thick blue coat, a woollen scarf and heavy shoes. He was carrying a small pair of high-powered binoculars. The name was familiar to Rosslyn. So was the thin and pockmarked face. But he was unsure where he had previously encountered Ron Costley.

'The building is in serious danger of collapse. It could prove perilously unsafe if you didn't know exactly where to walk.' Costley turned to Michaelson. 'If you don't mind, sir, I'd like to talk to Mr Rosslyn on his own. If you wouldn't mind waiting for a few moments. I won't take long.'

Michaelson said he'd wait in his car.

Showing his ID to one of the police officers on duty in Hopton Street, Costley led Rosslyn towards what had been the entrance to the basement garage. There they stood in silence for a few moments, staring at the bomb crater.

'Let's go inside the building opposite,' Costley said. 'Follow me. Mind your step. We can get a good view from the top of the building. Or rather a view of what little there's left.'

They climbed the stairs of the fire well to the door that led out on to the roof. Costley had the air of the police officer who had seen it all before. Rosslyn followed him to the edge of the parapet.

From there, with the steaming devastation illuminated by arc lights on cranes, Rosslyn made out what had been the entrance to the

Zhentung duplex. With the aid of Costley's binoculars, it was possible to see where the passage had led to what had been the grand salon. Where there had been windows there were open spaces to the sky and, just visible in the snow, the views of St Paul's, Millennium Bridge, Bankside Tate, NatWest tower and Tower Bridge.

Rosslyn asked Costley if the Bomb Data Centre had reached any preliminary conclusions.

'We're using a newly installed system of collation,' Costley said. 'We've logged on details of every explosion and major incident world-wide. The Defence Research Agency at Woolwich has begun analysis of the findings. Bomb fragments. Potentially useful information.'

Rosslyn could tell that Costley wanted to get him on his side. He would let Rosslyn ask questions first. Rosslyn was familiar with the tactic. Costley needed to gain his trust.

'What about the explosives and components?' Rosslyn asked.

'They'll be kept at the Bomb Data Centre. They'll do the usual. Compare and contrast the elements of the explosion with every major incident that's taken place world-wide during the last five years. It takes time. I suppose you're familiar with the procedures, Mr Rosslyn. I've been told you've dealt with similar situations. When you were in Customs.'

'I suppose it's still about the same as it was in my day,' said Rosslyn. 'Was there any kind of preliminary warning?'

'No warning. None,' said Costley. 'Let me tell you what we've done and then I'd like to ask you some questions. Is that okay with you?'

'Fine,' said Rosslyn. 'Then what happened?'

'Pretty smartly after we learned the bomb had exploded, we dispatched the S013 duty officer here. The whole area was sealed off. The duty officer assembled the first witnesses and questioned them. After the fires died down, as soon as the site was safe enough, S013 officers began to sift through the wreckage for pieces of the bomb. For traces of whatever container had been used. They searched the wreckage of the car Zhentung died in. The Mercedes. A number of fragments of the bomb casing were retrieved from the bodywork's remains.'

'How much explosive was used?' Rosslyn asked

'A lot. Possibly PETN – pentaerythritol tetranitrate – and TATP – triacetone triperoxide. There's what you'd expect of plasticiser, fuses and detonation cord. Judging from what we've managed to retrieve so far, we're looking at a remote control device. It has to have been triggered by someone who was in the vicinity at the time at a safe distance from the blast.'

'Didn't you get any leads from the first witnesses?'

'None.'

'Who spoke to the press and media?' Rosslyn asked.

'We briefed a senior colleague. We've made the usual general appeal for witnesses, for anyone who saw anything suspicious and the rest of it. We'll make another appeal in three days' time. So far, we have bugger all to go on. It's impossible to be specific about suspects.'

'You haven't got any?'

'None.'

'No idea as to whether it was the work of a particular terrorist organisation?'

'No. Not so far.'

'Or a particular individual?'

'No. Special Branch, MI6, MI5 and even Customs have formed a liaison committee to pool and co-ordinate intelligence.'

'They've moved fast.'

'They were straight on to it.'

'Who's the chairman?'

'From SIS.'

'You know his name?'

'A woman. Elizabeth Henderson.'

'*Her*?'

'You know her?'

'I do.'

'She's the one chairing the committee,' said Costley. 'They'll be looking at connections between an arson attack near Heathrow that took place an hour or so after all of this happened. Do you know about that too?'

'No.'

'A warehouse has been burned out. It's too near Heathrow for comfort.'

'I don't know anything about it.'

'We don't know anything either. Not yet. Take a long look at things over there,' Costley said. 'We want you to help us.'

Rosslyn looked at the remains in silence. Some of the building seemed to have survived. The walls of the passage leading to the main riverside salon were scorched. The erotic Chinese paintings on silk of the K'ang-hsi period looked as though they'd melted in the charred frames. Above the plate-glass doors to the main salon the plaque announcing 'The Salon of the Kingdom of Heaven' had split in several places. The drawings by Seurat, Van Gogh and Toulouse-Lautrec were only identifiable by what looked like the remains of the brass plaques that had been screwed into the walls beneath them. The fourteenth-century preliminary paintings for the National Gallery's Wilton Diptych must have been completely destroyed.

'The art's gone,' said Rosslyn.

'Fortunately, the real ones are in a Swiss bank,' said Costley.

Standing lop-sided at a forty-five degree angle in the centre of the salon, the Marie Antoinette bureau converted into a modern fireproof display cabinet had been burned and charred. Though the fireproof glass of the case was heavily stained with smoke, Rosslyn could see that the contents had survived.

'Someone's been tampering with the cover to that display case.'

'The fire officers will have needed to see what it contained,' said Costley defensively.

'I could have told them. It's some literary manuscript.'

'Zhentung's lawyers have already been on to us about the thing,' said Costley.

'They must be in some kind of hurry. They've been in touch so soon?'

'I wondered why the hurry, too. It seems Zhentung's will stipulates that those papers should be placed in his coffin. The lawyers wanted to know if the papers survived.'

'Have they?'

'Yes. They're in Zhentung's safe in the apartment. Not in Geneva with the other stuff. They're in the safe. It's fireproof. We took the safe away.'

'Who exactly told you about the contents of the will?'

'Zhentung's personal lawyer called the investigation team. A woman called Palmen in Stockholm.'

'Who spoke to her?'

'Someone on the investigation team. We told her the thing could be collected later. When, we can't say.'

'How much do you know about Anthony Zhentung?' said Rosslyn.

'That's what I want to ask you,' said Costley.

He listened to what Rosslyn had to say, from the time Milo Associates had agreed to take on Zhentung's personal protection, from the day they had started to inspect the duplex apartment, the building and Zhentung's usual movements about London to the vetting of his bodyguards and servants, right up to the reception a few hours before.

'You reckon the security was one hundred per cent?'

'One hundred per cent,' said Rosslyn.

He told Costley about his interrogation by Henderson at Paddington Green police station, about her groundless accusations, about the 'deal' whereby Rosslyn would be questioned by Michaelson and housed at Michaelson's flat.

Costley considered what Rosslyn had told him in silence.

'In my experience, it would be better if you were allowed to carry on as normally as possible.'

'I'll buy that.'

'You see,' said Costley, 'I go back quite a long way. You could say we both do. I really think it'll be best if you and I keep in touch. Shall we say – that we keep you on the outside of things?'

'What about Henderson's committee?'

'The usual talking shop. Oh, I suppose they'll want to interview you at some stage. You can handle that.'

'What makes you so sure this is for the best?'

'Because I like to expect the unexpected,' said Costley. 'Do you have a good memory?'

'Yes.'

'But not, I fancy, quite as good as mine?'

Rosslyn didn't understand. He decided to keep his silence and followed Costley to the other side of the roof, where there was a view of Hopton Street below and Michaelson's car.

'In a minute I'll try to get Michaelson off your back,' Costley said.

'And Henderson?'

'Her too,' Costley said. 'She may be more difficult. We'll see what we can do.'

'Tell me what your move's about.' Rosslyn asked. 'Do you know something about the Zhentungs I don't, is that it?'

'What do I know about them? Same as anyone else. Only what I've read in the papers. We asked the Swedish lawyer if she could offer us anything of use. She said she couldn't. It seems most of their business records are in all sorts and kinds of different places. We asked her whether she could give us access to any of Zhentung's private papers that might be relevant. She said they were in storage. Well, she would, wouldn't she? She said something about there being nothing in the papers that would assist the investigation.'

'Do you believe that?' said Rosslyn.

'I've no reason not to,' said Costley. 'Do you?'

Rosslyn shrugged.

'Let's deal with Henderson,' Costley said. He tapped a number into his mobile telephone.

'Mr Michaelson? Costley. I've had a very useful interview with Mr Rosslyn. He's given me some highly valuable information –'

I haven't told him anything.

'We're going to be continuing this interview a while longer. I've spoken to my superiors at the Yard and there's really no need for Mr Rosslyn to be given protection of the kind Ms Henderson had in mind.' Costley was listening to Michaelson's comments.

'Yes,' Costley continued, 'I've spoken to Ms Henderson's senior –'

– Which is untrue.

'Oh yes, I will make arrangements for Mr Rosslyn's safety. Of course.' A pause. 'There's no need for Mr Rosslyn to stay at your place. We'll have the officers stand down. Thank you. Not at all. Good-night.'

Costley turned off his mobile telephone and slipped it into his coat pocket. 'Your memory's failed you, Rosslyn. We've met before. You don't remember – Winston Lim?'

'Tell me.'

'Winston and Steve Kwok have their friends in the Met. Good men. You don't remember – our delegation three years ago at the Transnational Police Conference in Hong Kong. Money laundering investigations is what we've got in common: 'Freeze & Seize – International Co-operation in Confiscation and Partnerships with the Private Sector'. All that.'

'Now I have it,' said Rosslyn. 'You were there?'

'I was,' said Costley. 'You see what I'm working towards? I was a friend of Winston's. More especially, I know more about Steve Kwok than he knows himself. You know the rule. Touch a police officer and you're dead meat. And you've seen what was done to Steve.'

'You know what Steve told me?'

'I know. And I'm moving on it. First, I'm getting you the hell out of here on the first flight to Kuala Lumpur. We have a window of twelve hours to get you out. We can reduce the scale of alert at Heathrow and get clearance for your flight. We can get ahead of Henderson. We already have. You've met with Zhu Jianxing?'

Rosslyn nodded.

'We've co-funded the operation. That, Mr Rosslyn, you didn't hear from me. You use that passport. Get it tonight and get yourself to Heathrow.'

'What happens if Henderson's people make a move?'

'I'll deal with that if and when I need to.'

'And you, aren't you on the line?'

'I can handle that. There's an assistant commissioner who's a member of my Masonic lodge. If you were on the square as well, it might have helped. That's as may be. You're not. It isn't safe for you to know any more than this.'

'Why not?'

'In case the other side get to you first,' said Costley. 'I wouldn't even fancy my own chances under interrogation by the People's Republic. I wouldn't fancy anyone's. And whatever the outcome, if they get you – you won't get out alive.'

They made their way back across the roof to the entrance to the fire well.

'I have an unmarked car on stand-by to drive you to Marylebone Passage,' Costley said. 'If you're followed there, the driver knows what to do about it. The car will take you on to Heathrow.'

'I'll need to collect some clothes from my place.'

'I've thought of that,' Costley said. 'I took the liberty of having someone pack a case for you.'

'You broke into my flat?'

'Not me personally,' said Costley. 'That's not my line. I had someone see to it who breaks in and enters without leaving a trace. Don't worry. You'd never know. Won't even have disturbed a fly. You'll find you have everything you need for South East Asia.'

'And when I get there?'

'You take on the commission for Ocean Insurance just as though nothing's changed. What's the ship called? *Orient* –?'

'*Orient Angel*.'

'Right,' said Costley. 'You have to understand that there's no alternative. You follow me?'

'Yes,' said Rosslyn. 'One personal thing. Winston's daughter, Mei Lim. I think she should be kept clear of this.'

Costley shook his head. 'Unfortunately, Mei Lim is up to her neck in this. There's no keeping her clear of it now.'

Rosslyn hesitated. 'But in the run of things,' he said. 'The normal run –'

'Nothing's normal,' Costley interrupted. 'Nothing's normal. I don't need to tell you that, do I? You think about the contents of Steve's briefing. If you think that's normal, I'm the Pope. The law of this game is survival. Taking out the enemy before they take you out. Winston was fighting a war. We've joined it. We can't get out of it. Listen, I'm not idealistic about it. Sod the preachers. We are fighting rats with rats. Only thing is that the other rats breed a bloody sight faster than we do. They're bigger. They're nastier. You and I, Rosslyn. We're little people, get it? Think ahead. One day in the future you'll be making a statement to me. Maybe under caution. You know the drill. Get my drift?'

Rosslyn got it.

'Let's find the car,' Costley said. 'We're in luck with the weather. At least the bloody snow's stopped. From now on you're on your own.'

66

STATEMENT OF WITNESS

[Criminal Justice Act 1967, s.9]

Statement of:	Alan Rosslyn
Age of Witness:	Over 21
Occupation:	Private Investigator
Address:	Basement Flat,
	195 Claverton Street,
	London SW1

This statement consisting of 3 pages signed by me is true to
the best of my knowledge and belief and I make it knowing that
if it is tendered in evidence, I shall be liable to prosecution
if I wilfully state anything which I know to be false.

I was driven in the unmarked car to Marylebone
Passage.
   The driver parked near the Fo Guang Temple in
Margaret Street and kept the engine running over.
We agreed to stay in communication by mobile
telephone. I would give her a running commentary,
which then went roughly like this:
   'Marylebone Passage. There's no sign the outer
door locks have been tampered with. The lights are
on in the stairwell. I have deactivated the alarm
system. The office is freezing cold. The blinds
are drawn. I've collected what I need in here.
I'm reactivating the alarm system. The lights are
off. The place stinks of dead vermin. I'm now
returning. I can see no signs that I'm being
watched or followed.'
   The first stage had gone off perfectly.
   When we reached Heathrow the driver parked
outside Terminal 3. She told me my suitcase was

in the boot. She wished me good luck and a safe
journey.

I checked in and the desk clerk explained that I
probably hadn't heard that all flights from
Heathrow, Gatwick, Luton, Stansted and City
Airport had been temporarily suspended. Even the
Channel Tunnel was closed.

My passport was examined.

'Did you pack your luggage yourself?'

'Yes,' I lied.

'Has anyone given you anything to take?'

'No,' I lied.

And so on through security to the First Class
Lounge with my new identity.

I expected it to be packed out and it was. Full
of Chinese. Malaysians. Singaporeans. Some Germans
were barking into mobile telephones, and a few
British businessmen and women were crouching over
laptops. There were women with sleeping children.
A quartet of Hasidic Jews.

I poured myself a cup of black coffee from the
thermos at the refreshment counter. All the seats
in the lounge were occupied, so I found a free
table to perch on. The Chinese on the sofa
opposite was asleep. Arms folded, he was cradling
a briefcase in his arms.

I passed the time watching Sky TV News. The
commentator said, 'Across several continents,
delegated officers of the secret services, police,
investigative journalists, lawyers and insurance
executives are searching for those responsible for
the London killings. No reason for the atrocities
has yet been established and no responsibility has
been claimed.'

The label on the briefcase clutched by the
sleeping Chinese said DR HUNG.

The name seemed familiar. Though I couldn't
quite place it. There must be more than tens of
millions of Hungs in China. Who knows? Perhaps the
name belonged to another Hong Kong Police officer I
had encountered at the Transnational Police
Conference, when I had enjoyed the company of
Winston and Steve Kwok.

Before boarding the plane, I made yet another

call to Mei. No reply. I had to face it. It was
most likely she didn't want to speak to me.

Signed: *Alan Rosslyn*

Signature witnessed by: Chief Superintendent Ronald Costley

Signed: *Ron Costley*

Signature witnessed by: WPC Michelle Seifert

Signed: *Michelle Seifert*

67

Europe prepared for the new day while Terajima attended to the fingernails of his right hand with the slim and pointed cardboard nail file.

He accepted the offer of a hot face towel from the steward, but courteously declined the offer of a glass of champagne. With a fixed smile, he ordered the vegetarian breakfast and then concentrated on the filing of the nails of his left hand. Once he had finished, he cleaned the file with care. He prided himself upon the proven razor sharpness of the file: sharp as a surgeon's scalpel.

The vegetarian meal arrived and he savoured it as much as the prospect of the comfort of the flight ahead. He deserved this luxury. The London visit had been a consummate success. Its sole purpose had been the murder of Anthony Zhentung and the obliteration of his London property. The job had been well done – mission completed with military professionalism. *Money to the bank in Luxembourg. More money than little people would ever dare to dream about.*

Rosslyn declined the offer of breakfast, a variety of fruit juices and champagne. Instead he wrapped himself in a blanket. He thought briefly of Mei and finally fell asleep.

Terajima studied the in-flight magazine. He loved maps. *Maps are true.* It offered a rather good world map. He studied it and calculated that it was a distance of some six thousand miles through several time zones to the coast of the Malacca Strait, the seething commercial waterway between Malaysia and Sumatra.

He adjusted his seat for comfort and arranged the blanket around his legs and body. Before closing his eyes, he unfastened the button of his shirt cuff and withdrew the ID tag that read 'Winston Lim'. Attached to the chain were the two small gold crucifixes and two silver hearts. One of the silver hearts was engraved with 'Mei', the other with 'Kitty'. He opened the fastener of the heart marked Mei. Inside were threaded strands of her dark hair, and he lifted them to his nostrils to inhale her body scent.

THREE

It was something to have at least the choice of nightmares.
CONRAD

68

>> CHINESE TYCOON ANTHONY ZHENTUNG DIES IN BOMB BLAST

London (Reuters) – Billionaire tycoon Anthony Zhentung died Wednesday night in a massive bomb blast that destroyed his Thames-side apartment, killing his twin daughters and eight members of his staff. London anti-terrorist squad believe bomb was detonated by remote control device. Police and security services received no prior warning of the attack. "We believe these cowardly murders may be the work of an international terrorist syndicate," British Home Secretary told Reuters. Neither of Zhentung's brothers, Foster and Hastings, was present. Separated from Anthony Zhentung, his wife Lily is believed to be in hiding with their son.

69

It was poignant that George Tsang had never been able to see the photograph of Winston Lim on the wall of the Hong Kong office of *Maritime Confidential*. Tsang's office is on the ground floor of a ramshackle house on Li Yuen Street East. The entrance is off a narrow alleyway behind a stall selling counterfeit watches and designer accessories.

For the benefit of Steve Kwok, Tsang played back the tapes of the conversations he had recorded between Terajima and the Zhentungs at the Pan Pacific Glenmarie.

Had Kwok not been visiting New Zealand, he would have heard the tapes before. Tsang had called him to suggest that he return to Hong Kong to listen to them in person. Tsang was worried on several scores. Kwok must hear the evidence for himself. He had urged Kwok to take the next flight back to Hong Kong. Kwok had agreed without hesitation.

With intense concentration, Kwok listened to the tapes that Tsang had made.

'Incontrovertible evidence,' said Tsang.

'Yes, it is,' said Kwok. 'I wonder, George, if you were I – what would you do right now with it?'

'Consider the alternative options.'

'Which in your opinion are what?'

'One,' said Tsang. 'You can send the tapes to London. Then they'll have what adds up to Terajima's confession that he murdered or conspired to murder Winston. Similarly, London can arrest Terajima and the Zhentungs for conspiracy to murder Anthony Zhentung, his daughters and the other victims. You can have a copy of the tapes forwarded to the police in Beijing, Malaysia, Sumatra and Indonesia. Spread the contents wide. Make the point that Terajima is acting on behalf of the Zhentungs, who are engaged in sponsoring maritime terrorism. The evidence is all there, Steve. It's Terajima who took the *Manju Alpha* after she left Kuala Tanjung. You also have the evidence that he's going to launch an armed attack on the *Orient Angel* in the Malacca Strait. The ship that Rosslyn's boarding tonight.'

'Tonight?'

'I have the schedule, Steve.'

'Okay, we can prevent him boarding. You know where he is right now?'

'In KL at the Hotel Puduraya.'

Kwok shifted uneasily in his wheelchair. 'I don't want anyone's suspicions raised. The best person to help will be a colleague at police headquarters in KL. We won't approach the *Orient Angel*. I don't want the ship's officers or crew to be any the wiser. What's your other option – option two?'

'Lie low here in Hong Kong and right out of sight of Terajima. Protect both Catherine and yourself. You two can stay with me. Terajima has no idea who I am or where I can be found.'

'I wouldn't be too sure of it, George. He must have clocked you at the Pan Pacific Glenmarie. One day he'll come for us.'

'If he does, then it's too late to do anything about it. I checked in under an assumed name. I also took the precaution of asking the manager to make sure I was told if anyone enquired about me. No one did.'

'As far as you know.'

'As far as I know.'

'Option two. What's the other alternative?'

'Leave matters be. Let Rosslyn board the *Orient Angel*. He's a man after Winston's heart and mind. He can handle the situation like a professional. Take the chance he will.'

'I wouldn't fancy anyone's chances against Terajima.'

'I don't have to tell you that you're the best judge of that, Steve,' said Tsang. 'Now you tell me what *you* would do.'

'Put it like this. What I want is what Winston wanted. I want Terajima caught red-handed and alive. The Zhentungs can be left to stew for the time being. Leave them to the British. Say we warn Rosslyn? Say he doesn't make the voyage? If Terajima's intelligence sources are as good as we've always thought they are, then he may well abort the attack on *Orient Angel* and vanish into thin air. You know that's always been the problem in the past. Not knowing where he is. Not knowing where or when he's going to strike next. Winston said he could feel it in his bones. But Winston can't help us any more. Terajima keeps his sources as secret as you do, George. Like you, he'd be out of business if he didn't. I mean, you don't even tell me your sources, do you? Like, for example, how you knew that Terajima would be at the Pan Pacific Glenmarie. It's not as if he's some sort of golfing freak. Or are you going to tell me something new, that Terajima's a golfing freak?'

'You're thinking that we wait?'

'Maybe. Maybe. And right now – you say Rosslyn's at the Hotel Puduraya. We'll call him there. Where's Mei?'

'I don't know. She's not at her apartment. She hasn't been taking calls for some days. And that brings me to something else I need to tell you, Steve. You have no idea of the extent of the danger that's facing Rosslyn. Mei too. I'm afraid you're not going to like this. Something Diane told me the day I called you in New Zealand, which happened to be our wedding anniversary. I have to say it was one hell of a day to tell me. You need to know this, Steve. It has to do with Winston's Kitty. You know that Diane was her confidante.'

'Try me.'

'I'll start with Mei. You know that she was their adopted daughter?'

'Sure.'

'That she had a major problem as a teenager with drugs.'

'I know,' said Kwok. 'She beat that one.'

'She did. She mixed in some pretty nasty circles. Maritime people. Harbour low life throughout the region. Ran up every kind of debt with all kinds of scum.'

'Winston never told me details.'

'He kept them to himself. He handled Mei pretty much on his own. Kitty, well, she found it too hard to face. She confided in Diane about it all. And did you know that Mei had an abortion?'

'That I didn't know. Did Winston find out?'

'He found out. How, I don't know. Somehow he found out. It really hurt him. Maybe it was a physician who told him. Diane doesn't know, I don't know. But there was serious gynaecological damage and infection. Winston was reduced to raiding some drugs squat on his own thinking he could find out who the father could have been. He didn't find out. Instead, he took Mei home forcibly. He had her checked into a clinic for treatment. Slowly she mended and put the past behind her. In the intervening period – we're talking years rather than months – people she had run up debts with made demands. Five or six thousand US dollars here. Maybe more elsewhere. The circle of low life had a way of closing in. It was as if she couldn't shake off the past. I've no idea how much or what exactly Mei confided in her Dad. Diane doesn't know either. But it seems true enough that, at some point, Mei talked at length to Winston and she grassed up two men. People from the merchant marine who sidelined in minor raids on shipping. To start with, the men didn't of course know she'd grassed. And Winston, instead of telling her to have nothing more to do with them, told her to meet them on some clandestine basis. The encounters took place here. In Stanley. Kowloon. All over. Also in Batu Pahat and Malacca. Maybe you can guess what happened next?'

Kwok was silent.

'She disappeared. For several months or so. Winston and Kitty were beside themselves with worry. How could they know where she was or what could've happened to her? Winston was on the verge of making a clean breast of the whole business to the Commissioner.'

'Because he'd involved family?'

'Right. And he had. He'd used Mei. He was totally responsible for having used her. His obsession got the better of him. He'd had enough. Then, out of the blue, when he was on the verge of walking into the Commissioner's office, Mei suddenly turned up.'

'Where had she been?'

'Bangkok. Chien Mai. Tokyo. Amsterdam.'

'She'd been with a man who offered her protection against the friends of the pair she'd grassed up. He promised her security. She would work for him. He showed her the high life. In Europe. In South East Asia. You name it. They became lovers. She was besotted with him. Winston, naturally, questioned her about him. She chose to tell Winston where she'd been. She named the places and the times. She mentioned everything – except she wouldn't say who this man of hers was. She claimed it was all over with him. She promised to turn over a new leaf. She would start a new life. Study law at university. So Winston rented her the flat in Chung Hom Kok.'

'Where she lives now?'

'With two Siamese cats. Family life went back to normal. Normal, that is, except for one thing. One major exception. Winston harboured the obsession. Revenge. Revenge no matter what the cost. He had no idea who the guy was she'd been with. But he set about finding out with the determination we know about. He was going to nail him once and for all. Then Kitty fell ill. And I don't have to tell you how fast she deteriorated. Winston nursed her. He was even the one who administered her the drugs towards the end. Along with Diane when he was on duty. And there was a terrible two-day period when he was nowhere to be found. He vanished into thin air. For two days. When he came back it was the only time I really felt Diane lose her temper. She went for Winston. She attacked him because she believed Winston had found some other woman.'

'Winston?'

'Well, I was as surprised as you must be, Steve. The truth was that he hadn't. What he'd found out was the identity of Mei's lover. He was carrying out a routine investigation of a bent Malaysian captain. Just one of your ordinary drugs runners. This guy offered to trade the information for leniency of some sort. The man claimed to know Mei. He knew the identity of her protector-cum-lover, call the bastard what you want. He told Winston that the man was *still* seeing her and that he would kill anyone who took her from him. Who, Steve, who *is* he? That's what you need to ask.'

'Are you going to tell me, George?'

'Klaas-Pieter Terajima.'

'In the name of God –'

'Klaas-Pieter Terajima. We know he's getting closer, Steve. Mei is unfinished business. He wants her.'

'You mean he wants to kill her?'

'Who knows what he wants – aside from the sums of money from the Zhentungs you heard mentioned? I wonder if he himself really knows what he wants. One thing, though. If Terajima knows Rosslyn's aboard *Orient Angel*, I don't rate his chance of survival.

'Okay, George,' said Kwok. 'We'd better make our move.'

He called the Hotel Puduraya, only to be told that Rosslyn had checked out.

He put through a second call. This one to the headquarters of the police in Kuala Lumpur. He wanted his colleague to assist him with an urgent and covert matter.

The police officer should visit the Port Klang offices of Svenske-

Britannia immediately and take the most senior executive available into his strictest confidence. He should explain that this was a police matter. If the Svenske-Britannia executive proved unhelpful, then he should insist upon co-operation. If he still didn't get it, he should issue a warning.

What Kwok required his colleague to do was as follows. A short and very urgent message should be conveyed to a man called Alan Rosslyn who had a passage aboard the *Orient Angel*, leaving in the evening for Singapore.

The message must be handwritten. Secure in a sealed envelope. No copy would be kept. Along with the senior executive, he should supervise the secreting of the envelope in the Svenske-Britannia offices so that no one else could discover it. No safe or locked drawer was to be used. Kwok suggested that the envelope be taped to the underside of a table or desk.

Finally, Kwok dictated the message to the man in Kuala Lumpur, who took it down. The man in Kuala Lumpur read it back in confirmation, word for word:

> Attention Alan Rosslyn
> Unable to reach you at your hotel
> Do not , repeat NOT, board Orient Angel
> Call us
> Steve Kwok , George Tsang .

Before leaving the Hotel Puduraya, Rosslyn had left a message for Mei on her answering machine in Hong Kong with the details of his voyage aboard the *Orient Angel* and where she might contact him after his arrival in Singapore. It would be the final chance to contact him before he returned to London.

It was while he was settling his account at the reception desk that he received the telephone call from a man who said he was Jon Simpson.

Simpson claimed to be 'a personal friend' of Victor Michaelson's. Michaelson had given Simpson some information to pass on. Rather apologetically, Simpson asked if Rosslyn would be good enough to meet him within the hour at the Tasik Perdana or Lake Gardens.

Rosslyn agreed.

Simpson recommended that Rosslyn take a taxi from the hotel to the Jalan Perdana entrance. He said he would be waiting for him there alone. To make identification easier, Simpson said he would be wearing a Panama hat, striped club tie and an orchid in his button-hole.

Rosslyn said he was six feet three, white shirt, no tie, jeans, leather ankle boots.

And there he was. Jon Simpson. The middle-aged, overweight Englishman with round shoulders and chubby face, wearing the worn Panama hat, light green suit, dark glasses and Garrick Club tie frayed at the knot. There was a limp orchid in his buttonhole.

'Victor was frightfully insistent that I get hold of you,' Simpson said. 'There's been not a little interest at the embassy in your presence here.'

'You from the embassy?' Rosslyn asked him.

'Oh yes, didn't I explain? Consular and Visa Section.'

Rosslyn assumed that Simpson of the Consular and Visa Section was MI6. He imagined that news of his arrival must have travelled ahead of him – that Simpson's seniors in SIS headquarters at Vauxhall Cross were causing trouble. He didn't want some repetition of Henderson's efforts and decided to refrain from mentioning her name.

'I very much appreciate you taking the time to see me,' Simpson said. 'We can walk in the Bird Park hibiscus garden. I'll lead the way.' Lowering his voice, he added, 'For what it's worth – for Victor's benefit – the firm said that if I can open any doors for you, you only have to ask.'

'Thanks.'

'London is very cold, I gather. You must find KL a pleasant change from the miseries of Blighty. London's asked me to offer you a little advice. Strictly between ourselves, you follow? Thought you might like to see some Malaysian hornbills.' He gazed up at the enormous roof made of plastic net. 'Ornithology's been a passion of mine since I was up at Wadham with dear old Victor.'

'Let's have a look at the hornbills later,' said Rosslyn without interest.

They found a convenient place to talk alone. 'I gather from Victor that your task aboard *Orient Angel* is to vet the ship's security,' Simpson said. 'And the *bona fides* of her crew?'

'Correct,' said Rosslyn.

'Mostly Chinese, Malay, Korean or Indonesian, I suppose,' said Simpson. 'You do realise that they won't speak very much English.'

'I'm sure there'll be a ship's officer who can act as interpreter,' Rosslyn said.

'I can't imagine you'll want them in on the questioning, will you? Victor tells me that you're engaged on something, as it were, of a covert operation? Covertly as an insurance inspector. In reality, as an executive of Milo Associates, London. Private investigators?'

'Correct.'

'Small world,' said Simpson. 'I knew Duggie Milo's father. We were at Eton together. Good man. I got a letter from the Garrick the other day and see young Duggie's been made a member. Sunlight shining on a gloomy world. Do you have a London club?'

'No.'

'Then we must lunch next time I'm in London *à trois* at one of mine. Do remember me to Duggie. And you, Rosslyn, you were formerly with Customs, I gather. Undercover and so on? Now you're private. Good luck with that. For my sins, South East Asia secret intelligence is my small domain. Between you and me, one actually runs the show here from Hong Kong. Not from here in KL. KL runs Hong Kong. My idea. It sows a certain confusion amongst the Chinese. Sometimes, one's bound to say it even sows confusion at Vauxhall Cross.'

'Look, Mr Simpson, no disrespect, but I have to be at the Port Klang offices of Svenske-Britannia in a short time.'

'Of course you do,' said Simpson. 'This won't take long. Tell me, what do you imagine is the general level of security aboard *Orient Angel*?'

'I can't prejudge it,' said Rosslyn, unwilling to be drawn further. 'I haven't seen it yet. I have to keep an open mind.'

'As indeed do we all.'

The people at Ocean World Insurance had insisted Rosslyn keep the mission confidential. No matter that Simpson was Secret Service. It was a blanket veto.

'An open mind,' said Simpson. 'But the security arrangements in place aboard *Orient Angel* are doubtless, in most respects, not very different from those in the other ships we know about, whose inadequacies border on the negligent.'

'I've no way of knowing how good they are,' said Rosslyn. 'Not until I've seen them at first hand.'

'Quite. Actually, I think you'll find they're pretty good,' said Simpson, producing a pair of miniature binoculars. He removed his sunglasses and raised the binoculars to his eyes. 'How very beautiful. A rhinoceros hornbill. You want to look?'

'No, thanks. Let's talk about Victor.'

'Victor. Yes. It seems two friends have approached him. I gather they're acquaintances of yours. *Entre nous*, I'd tend to be guarded in what you tell them. They're very keen to make contact with you.'

'Who are we talking about, Mr Simpson?'

Simpson continued to peer into his binoculars. 'Burnal Graer and Birgit Swann want to be brought up to speed on what you may or may not find aboard *Orient Angel*.'

'I can't help them.'

'Very well,' said Simpson, looking at his wristwatch. 'Look, I don't want you to say yes or no to what I'm about to propose. Just consider being good enough to give me the benefit of your findings once you get to Singapore.'

'I'll have to get clearance first,' said Rosslyn.

'I'm sure no one will object,' said Simpson. Again he raised the binoculars to his eyes and Rosslyn could tell he was no longer searching for rare birds, but was looking at the other visitors. 'In so far as one reads the gospel according to Victor.'

'Which is what?'

'Do you find it hot in here?' Simpson asked. 'The humidity can sometimes be so oppressive. Personally, I've never *quite* learned how to love it. The frightfully sudden rain and so forth. But there we are. I'm sure you'll enjoy your trip to Singapore. Why don't we two get together when you get there? Dinner perhaps?'

'I'll bear it mind. If you'd excuse me, Mr Simpson. I have to go.'

'Do consider my offer, Rosslyn,' said Simpson. 'I can always have our travel people change your flight. You can stay on a few more days perhaps?'

'Thanks all the same,' said Rosslyn. 'I don't think that'll be possible.'

'Let me know if you change your mind.' Simpson said. 'Just make sure their security's up to standard. One final thing, given that merchant marine personnel are not subject to security vetting, I'd be grateful to you if you'd make no reference to what I've just told you.

You're the expert, old thing. You'll know what shipboard life is like. Talk is pretty free.'

'What's your point?' Rosslyn asked.

'It's very important that anyone who might conceivably have connections with organised crime is not alerted. Do you follow?'

'I imagine so,' said Rosslyn. Suddenly it struck him he might have walked straight into a trap. 'Mr Simpson – one question. What are we doing here?'

'Come, come, a man with your knowledge of intelligence. As a former Customs & Excise investigations man, I think you know precisely what I'm worrying about.'

'It isn't what you're worrying about. It's what the hell you and I are doing here that I want to know. I have to go now to see the people at Svenske-Britannia. Just tell me the information that Victor wants me to be told and let's not waste any more of each other's time, okay?'

Simpson looked at his watch again. He suddenly stared hard at Rosslyn. There was a smile on his lips but the bloodshot eyes looked dead. 'Here,' he said sharply. 'For God's sake use the glasses, man. If it interests you, Rosslyn, I don't give a croc's piss for ornithology. *Over there*. The woman in the skimpy white silk dress. Doesn't leave much to the imagination. All yours, old boy. Keep the bloody glasses. Happy landings.' With that, Simpson turned his back on Rosslyn and hurriedly walked away.

Rosslyn peered into the glasses and looked at the woman in the white silk dress.

She was Mei Lim.

72

Look your best in life as you wish to look in death.
CHINESE PROVERB

Terajima emerged from the Batu Pahat Rest House into the morning air. The sky seemed to have lowered and the humidity to have increased. He reckoned the weather couldn't be more perfect.

He looked slim and agile, and his glistening, sallow skin seemed to accentuate the depth of his eyes. The long, fine hair was newly gathered into a short ponytail.

Carrying a cheap black backpack, he had only a short distance to walk to the clandestine rendezvous with the American woman in thrall to Foster and Hastings Zhentung: the rendezvous they had given to him. The roundabout at the dusty junction of the roads to Ayer Hitam and Kukup. Terajima saw the taxi circle the roundabout twice and the white face glance at him from the rear window. He assumed correctly that this was the Zhentungs' woman: his fellow thief of secrets also travelling under an assumed identity. However, the battered taxi passed by and headed off towards the centre of town.

He only had to wait a few minutes for the other taxi to appear. It stopped by the side of the street, its engine still running. The woman opened the door and beckoned to him to get in beside her.

He noticed a backpack on the floor, identical to his own. The woman told the driver to head for the mosque.

Shifting across the seat, as if she disliked sitting too close to her fellow passenger, the woman shook Terajima by the hand and asked, 'How are you?'

He turned his doe eyes away from her. 'Bitten by leeches.'

'Where?'

'In the rainforest.'

'No, I mean where on your body?'

'Both legs.'

'Did you treat them?'

'I used salt and a lighted cigarette.'

Satisfied with the clandestine rigmarole of coded introduction, they continued their journey over the bumpy road in silence. It ended no more than a short walk from the mosque, the Art Deco building. The woman told the driver to stop. Without the driver seeing, she raised Terajima's backpack from beneath his boots. Identical in colour and make to hers, it contained a quantity of old newspapers to give it similar bulk. Terajima lifted her own backpack. It contained a substantial quantity of high denomination US dollar bills. The American woman told the driver to wait.

She was tall and blonde and reminded him of a tennis player he had seen on television. The shoulders were broad, the arms and long legs muscular. The woman could have been a man, he thought, and cursed the feelings of obligation he felt towards her. She said, 'Our friends are profoundly displeased with what you achieved in London. You had no orders to kill Anthony Zhentung.'

'Is he dead?'

'You must know he's dead. He died in the blast that destroyed his apartment. There were other casualties too.'

She showed him a Xerox of the Reuters report headlined:

>> CHINESE TYCOON ANTHONY ZHENTUNG DIES IN BOMB BLAST

'Tough titty,' said Terajima.

The woman put the Xerox back in the pocket of her jeans. 'The Zhentungs didn't intend his death,' she said. 'They only wanted to teach him a lesson.'

'Too bad he died, then. Clumsy-clumsy.'

'Along with his two small daughters? The British police are mounting a massive investigation. They will want to question Foster and Hastings Zhentung. You murdered kids.'

'That's their little problem. Nothing to do with me. Just a few more charred bodies among many others. That's the nature of what we do. You and me. You can't afford to be squeamish about the dead. It comes to all of us. One or two deaths in London won't interrupt my work. I have a team on stand-by. Ready to go. They're South East Asia's finest.'

'Where are they?' she asked.

'Staying in town.'

'Are they prepared?'

'Of course,' Terajima said.

'The money is in the backpack.'

'In US dollars?'

'In US dollars,' she said, adding, 'I have to tell you that there's been a minor change of plan.'

'Too late,' said Terajima. 'I can change nothing now.'

'Well, I guess it's not so much a change', she said, 'as an addition to the plan. You have the manifest of officers and crew?'

'Of course.'

'There will be two additional people aboard the target.'

'Will there just?'

Terajima noticed the beads of sweat on her forehead. 'Passengers,' she said. She seemed momentarily transfixed by a bug on the floor. Terajima trod on it. 'One male,' she added. 'One female.'

'It doesn't matter who's aboard the ship,' he said. 'There will be no prisoners. No survivors.'

'So long as that's understood.'

'You don't give me orders,' Terajima said.

'No survivors,' she said, ignoring his hostility. 'If not, we can't guarantee you'll be paid in Geneva or anywhere else.'

'Then you have a problem,' said Terajima, staring at the blue smoke rising from the makeshift chimneystack in the corrugated iron roof of the shack across the road.

'No,' she said. 'I have orders. *You* have a problem.'

'You know my fee,' Terajima said casually. 'You're talking additional disposals. Forty thousand bucks.'

'Our friends have honoured the agreement already,' the woman said. 'The sum's been agreed and paid. You know that.'

'Forty thousand or we abort.'

'Thirty.'

Terajima gave a hollow laugh. The woman had been taught to value agents, whether idealists or perverts.

'Okay,' she said at last. 'Our final offer. Forty thousand into your Luxembourg bank.'

Terajima nodded his agreement.

'You know where to reach me?' she said. 'If you need to re-establish contact.'

'I won't need to,' he said.

'It figures,' she said. 'I've been told to tell you are to contact someone else from now on in emergencies. Call the usual number and ask for Leech. You go through the same routine as this morning. And when you've finished you just say, "The treatment has been successful."'

'Okay,' he said. 'And you. What are you going to do?'

'Me? Little me is going home to Washington DC.'

'I don't trust you,' Terajima said. 'I don't believe that's true.'

She glared at him briefly. 'Wanna know something? I don't trust you either. I'm gone.'

'Wait,' he said. 'I do not have your full agreement.'

'For what?'

'Immunity from arrest and prosecution by either the British or United States government.'

'You have it, honey.'

'I want it in writing.'

'You want it *in writing*? There's nothing in *writing*. There never has been, honey. Never will be.'

Terajima put his face close to hers. 'You listen to me, pinko-vagina-face.' He touched her throat with his razor-sharp fingernails. 'If immunity isn't arranged, who will cut this pretty face?' She flinched. 'To slice you here. These tubes. We know who you are and where to find you. Your head will be delivered in an icebox to your children. So they can remember you. Sweet memories of Mother.'

'You revolt me.'

'As you do me. No immunity? Think of those little faces when they open the gift-wrap and find you looking kind of, well, detached and frozen. Can't you just picture their little faces? Oh, happy day.'

'You have your immunity. Our friends have long ago made arrangements. It's not your business to question details.'

'You'd better be right. If not, I take your head. Make sure you do your hair nicely these coming days.' He touched her blonde fringe. *'Look your best in life as you wish to look in death.'*

'Thanks for the advice, sicko,' she said, turning to head back to the taxi. 'Treat your victims on *Orient Angel* seriously. They'll sure as hell be armed.'

'Me too,' Terajima said.

'One more thing,' she said, pleased to be delivering the *coup de grâce*. 'The two passengers – they're lovers. One is a private investigator. A

Brit. His name is Rosslyn. Younger than you by far. His lover rice girl is Winston Lim's daughter Mei.'

'Say again?'

He remembered what Mei had said to him the night of her father's funeral. The night he had collected her from her apartment before long hours of lovemaking.

'SORRY TO HAVE KEPT YOU WAITING. I HAD A VISITOR. HE'S JUST SOME DUMB-FUCK BRITISH GUMSHOE.'

'Mei Lim,' the American was saying. 'Some pillow butterfly from your past, my friend, and now back again in your present. Without a future. Or with a present? All yours. Safe journey.'

73

Head down, eyes on the road, twisting the gold chains around his wrist, he walked back to the Batu Pahat Rest House for the penultimate briefing of his team of maritime terrorists. He didn't trust the American woman. Yet what she'd told him explained Mei's absences, her reluctance to answer her telephone. The distance she had explained away as grief.

JUST SOME DUMB-FUCK BRITISH GUMSHOE. NOW SOME DEAD MINUS COCK AND BALLS DUMB-FUCK BRITISH GUMSHOE.

They won't drift away on clouds of diamorphine like Lim.

He tried to focus his mind on the mission statement. It would be very clear. No change. *NO PRISONERS. NO SURVIVORS. TOTAL DESTRUCTION.* Restraining his gnawing rage, he would make some things very clear.

The master of the ship will be my business. There will be one male passenger aboard. He too will be my business. You are to understand that there will also be one female passenger aboard Orient Angel. *She will be my business.*

I WANT TO WATCH YOU DIE WITH EYES WIDE OPEN STARING INTO MINE STRANGLED WITH THESE GOLD CHAINS AND CHOKING ON YOUR STRANDS OF FINE DARK HAIR.

74

STATEMENT OF WITNESS

[Criminal Justice Act 1967, s.9]

Statement of: Alan Rosslyn
Age of Witness: Over 21
Occupation: Private Investigator
Address: Basement Flat,
                 195 Claverton Street,
                 London SW1

This statement consisting of 3 pages signed by me is true to the best of my knowledge and belief and I make it knowing that if it is tendered in evidence, I shall be liable to prosecution if I wilfully state anything which I know to be false.

'Please hold me?' Mei asked me. 'I'm so tired.'

I took her in my arms, wanting to tell her that I'd waited for this moment since last I'd seen her in Hong Kong. It seemed an inadequate expression of what I felt for her. Her white dress was stained. There was a small tear in the right sleeve. Her hair smelled of patchouli oil.

'I feel safe with you,' she said. She was distressed and seemed very frightened.

She told me that she had listened to my voice on the answering machine in her flat. Just the once.

'After that,' she said, 'it was too dangerous for me to stay on.'

I asked her if she was okay. It was obvious to me she wasn't.

'Tell me something, Alan —' I remember that this was the first occasion I'd heard her speak my name with real affection. 'Tell me', she said, 'that you've come back for me.'

I told her in a confused way that, well, yes,
amongst other things it was why I'd come back.

'It's not just to do with Dr Graer and his
American friend?'

I reassured her on that score and mentioned the
promise I had made to her father.

'Dad's gone,' she said. 'Nothing can bring him
back. I only have Botch and Chan now.'

I asked after the cats. She said Kasuko her
neighbour was looking after them.

I asked her about Steve and Catherine Kwok.
Surely they were people she could confide in?

'I don't trust either of them. They're tied up
with George Tsang. You remember George Tsang, the
blind journalist man? His wife Diane poisoned my
mother's mind against me. She made out that I'd
ruined my father. You don't know how much my
mother hated me. I was an intruder in her life
with Dad. She's passed the hatred on to Diane
Tsang. They just wanted me out. They wanted me
forgotten like some non-person. The Kwoks and the
Tsangs together have wrecked my chances of a
career with the police in Hong Kong. God knows,
what with Tsang being blind, with the Kwoks
unimaginably scarred for life, you'd think they'd
show at least a grain of feeling of compassion for
other victims. Alan — I don't want to go on. I'm
finished, right? You want to know something? I'm
the one who's responsible for Dad's death.'

I told her that she couldn't conceivably have
had anything to do with it.

'One day, if it's not too late, you'll find out,'
she said.

I asked what I could do to make matters better
for her.

'I need work,' she said. I explained that there
was very little time left to me before boarding
the ship for Singapore. I was leaving that night.
There really was little, if anything, I could do
to help her find work. It'd have to wait.

'I have to get away from here,' she said.
'Anywhere. Singapore. Indonesia. Philippines.' She
stared up at me with pleading eyes. 'You have to
help me, Alan. You promised Dad. You promised me.
I can tell what you feel for me. I heard it in

202

your voice when you left the message. Now I can see it in your face. We both want to stay together, don't we?'

For my part that was undeniable.

I wanted to ask her about Simpson and Victor's role in her reappearance. Simpson's remark, the one he made to me while he had been playing for time as we waited for Mei, sprung immediately to mind. What he'd said about the crew of <u>Orient Angel</u>: 'You do realise that they won't speak very much English. Mostly Chinese, Malay, Korean or Indonesian, I suppose?' and Mei said 'I can speak to them in their own languages. I can translate your questions more discreetly than any of the ship's officers. I have my passport, I'm coming with you.'

Signed: *Alan Rooslyn*

Signature witnessed by: Chief Superintendent Ronald Costley

Signed: *Ron Costley*

Signature witnessed by: WPC Michelle Seifert

Signed: *Michelle Seifert*

75

In the air-conditioned Port Klang offices of Svenske-Britannia, company executive Maureen Cheng offered no objection to Mei accompanying Rosslyn on the voyage to Singapore.

She introduced Rosslyn and Mei to the *Orient Angel*'s master Captain Brown, a dour Scot in his late fifties. His attitude suggested that the passengers were unwanted visitors from London. Insurance snoops.

'Sure,' Brown said. 'Happy for you to have permission to look at the excellent security arrangements aboard my ship.' Judging from his face, 'permission' might just as well have meant 'effrontery'.

Orient Angel was Brown's world. He was the master of it. *The* master. Thirty years a merchant mariner, he'd got by without advice on rules and regulations from the likes of this Rosslyn and his Chinese companion. He wasn't about to accept any warnings or new ideas from the London visitors, particularly from Rosslyn, whom the Svenske-Britannia executive had carelessly told him was a former Customs & Excise investigations officer. Even worse, Rosslyn was young enough to be his son.

'The first officer is Lars Kjellner, a Swede,' Maureen Cheng said. 'He'll show you the ropes. He'll show you around the ship. Shall we take a look at *Orient Angel*? She'll take your breath away.'

76

The eighty thousand tonne *Orient Angel* towered above Port Klang docks.

When Rosslyn and Mei boarded the ship, first officer Kjellner and company executive Cheng proved more accommodating than Captain Brown. Kjellner was full of facts: 'She's three hundred metres in length and forty-two metres wide. Her propeller weighs almost ninety-five tonnes. Her eighteen-megawatt power plant generates enough energy to supply a small city.'

Once on the bridge, the loquacious Swede explained the electronic navigation and radar system. 'The system uses satellite fixes to plot our position along the course line, automatically corrects the course if it discovers we are off the line. We also use radar and visual fixes of lights and navigation marks to monitor the electronic system.'

'Simplicity itself,' said Cheng.

Rosslyn and Mei listened patiently. Rosslyn wanted to consult Captain Brown's log and establish what sort of security assessments had been carried out on the ship and crew. And given that they would that night enter the Malacca Strait, the master should now be calling all hands to a presail meeting with a view to explaining the possibility of danger ahead. Kjellner seemed oblivious to Rosslyn's impatience.

'As for preventing an illegal boarding,' he said, 'radar is the best detection device.'

'How many radar systems have you got?'

'Three, one used for navigation, the others for collision avoidance.'

'And when you're deep sea,' said Rosslyn, 'what happens then?'

'GPS is used all the time. Wherever possible, we try to pass at least one nautical mile away from other ships. There are sets of traffic lanes for ships in certain parts of the world. Their purpose is to separate the traffic travelling in different directions. These lanes help ships to navigate a little more safely in areas such as the Dover or Malacca Strait.'

'Say a vessel tries to come alongside?' Rosslyn asked.

'We would take avoiding action.'

'In a ship this big?'

Again Cheng interrupted. 'It would be very unwise to attempt to board a ship this size. Remember that the Indonesian Navy has several high-speed patrol boats operating in the Strait. But when it comes to security, Mr Rosslyn, if you don't object I'd prefer that you talk to the master about it once you're under way.'

'Now if you'd follow me below,' Kjellner said. 'I'll show you to your cabins.'

Cheng shook hands with Rosslyn and Mei and wished them *bon voyage*.

77

Kjellner showed them to their cabins on the deck below. 'Adjoining cabins,' he announced.

In Rosslyn's cabin the telephone was ringing.

It was the master, Captain Brown. 'Once we're under way there'll be dinner for you in the officers' lounge. There's no alcohol in this ship. But the coffee's good.'

'We'd like to attend your presail meeting,' Rosslyn said.

'There isn't going to be one,' Brown said sharply.

'Why not?'

'Because we must get away on time. Time is money, Mr Rosslyn. I'll do my job. What you do with yours is your problem. You have your rice princess with you. I have my ship. I service my ship. She's my princess. You service yours, laddie.'

78

THE OPERATIONAL SEQUENCE

Defeating modern pirates depends on understanding their tactics and techniques, avoiding surprise, retaining mobility, and depriving the attacker of mobility.

The ambush process involves an operational sequence: Stalk. Site. Stop. Shock. Smother. Secure. Search. Snatch. Scram

MARITIME TERROR

J. GRAY, M. MONDAY, G. STUBBLEFIELD

Tropical mist blurred the sunset across the Malacca Strait. Everywhere there was the stench of swamp decay.

The five men finally emerged in single file from the near darkness of the swamps. Carrying guns, ammunition and high explosives, they had made slow progress from the riverine town of Batu Pahat to this point on the Malaysian coast facing the Strait and beyond, Sumatra. Their loose clothes, similar to those of local fishermen, were drenched in sweat, their boots covered with reddish mud.

Unobserved and led by Terajima, they reached their clandestine destination by the sea's edge.

Freed from the density of vines and creepers, Terajima looked out across the Strait. Whispering something in Korean to his deputy Kyung, who was close behind him, Terajima gestured – a Malay gesture: pointed fingernails held across his upturned wrist – towards the apparently abandoned wooden jetty.

Constructed of wooden boards and palm tree trunks, the jetty was a derelict structure. It stood in the grey and purple gloom at the end of a narrow inlet, beneath overhanging wet casuarina and banana trees. The two men made their way with caution across the sagging wooden boards. They moved warily, because the sodden boards were covered in lichen and slime. One or more might well be rotten and might collapse without warning beneath their weight. Fat rats slithered into the undergrowth.

Beside the jetty, a long craft floated motionless beneath plastic and canvas covers. It lay low in the fetid, slowly heaving water. Frayed ropes tethered it to the jetty. Creepers and palm fronds camouflaged it.

Once again, Terajima whispered in Korean to Kyung. In turn, Kyung motioned to the other men on the shore to join them at the end of the jetty.

Terajima took a long nail file from his shirt pocket. Filing his nails, he watched the men's progress.

They removed the camouflage and drew back the plastic and canvas covers to reveal the craft, a powerboat. Some thirty feet in length, it was streamlined and powerful, with a deep V-shape monohull. Its name had been excised from its bow and stern.

Replacing the long nail file in the chest pocket of his sodden shirt, Terajima ordered the men to carry the covers into the undergrowth and bury them.

The ghostly crowing of the birds in the falling darkness lessened. The row of the crickets faded.

Terajima switched on a pinpoint flashlight and set about his thorough inspection of the craft. Now he could hear the burbling of the powerful currents of the Strait: shifting water slapped tangled heaps of waterlogged plant matter against the supports of the jetty.

Ignoring the moths and flying insects attracted to the beam – white pinpricks dancing in the light – Terajima conducted a methodical inspection. It involved checks of the powerboat's twin engines. The ignition system. Fuel tanks and electrical circuits. Meanwhile, peering into the dark and mist, the others kept a three hundred and sixty degree watch.

No matter that this well-hidden place was mostly home to lizards, leeches, snakes and mosquitoes. Terajima was alert to more serious threats.

The possibility that some petty thief or passing fisherman might already have stumbled upon the craft and removed some of its parts to sell. Everything has its price in Batu Pahat. Moreover, there was always the nasty and real possibility that some unseen enemy – say, some prying and corrupt officer of the Malaysian coastguard service

– had stumbled upon the nameless powerboat and set up an armed ambush.

Indeed, some other gang of hustlers might very well have planted a clandestine remote control explosive device aboard. Armed, and bent upon extortion, they might at any moment appear out of the jungle to make demands.

Or an informant might have alerted the International Maritime Bureau's Piracy Centre. Terajima was familiar with the weekly status reports on world piracy that the Bureau posts on its website www.icc-ccs.org. The Bureau is a part of Commercial Crime Services, the division of the Paris-based International Chamber of Commerce. Terajima was wary of its success in finding hijacked ships. In the last twelve months the Piracy Centre had already helped to recover nine.

Thus, if Terajima's search revealed the slightest evidence of tampering, he would abort the mission and put Part One of Plan B into immediate operation.

Part One of Plan B meant that they would depart the way they had come, taking separate routes into the jungle darkness. They would meet up later at the low-rent bordello in Batu Pahat frequented by Singaporeans.

There, following Part Two of Plan B, Terajima would pay off the others in US dollars. If they blabbed, he would be the one who removed their eyes with sharp and pointed fingernails.

Fear bound them to him: fear of the clinical methods he used in the administration of extreme violence. For a pathological killer, Terajima displayed an unusual and almost military calm. They could see it in his stern and haunted doe eyes. Even when he was in disguise – whether, like tonight, as a fisherman, or more androgynous, say in one of the silk and cotton suits tailored for him by Burlington's of the Taj Hotel in Mumbai. Whether in Kuala Lumpur or in London or in Paris or in Mumbai, the stare was frightening. Only when he filed and polished his nails did the eyes seem to soften for a moment. The men had heard him boast to Kyung that his thumbnails were so beautifully polished he could use them as a mirror to see behind him. 'As if these are rear view mirrors. I have eyes in the back of my head.' The skill he had learned on Mother's knee.

Once he was satisfied that no unwanted visitor had tampered with the powerboat, Terajima issued the order to don black nylon face masks and pull on their one-piece black rubber wetsuits. He did likewise. All you could see were his mouth and the eyes with their long lashes.

He ordered the other men to remove their discarded clothes and backpacks and bury them in the undergrowth, as they had already buried the camouflage. Terajima now secured grappling hooks to the sides of the powerboat.

Without needing to be told, Kyung took his machete with him into the jungle to select four substantial lengths of bamboo. These he twined with rope. Once this had been done, he returned to the jetty and fastened them to the powerboat's sides next to the grappling hooks, readily accessible for the boarding of the target.

Moist with sweat, Terajima checked his wristwatch. In a little over two hours' time the assault on the target would be launched. Terajima's nine-point orders would be followed to the word.

The target was the eighty thousand tonne container ship *Orient Angel*. No prisoners would be taken.

79

The route of Terajima's target, the *Orient Angel*, was from north European ports to the Far East and back. She had loaded her full cargo of forty foot and twenty foot containers in Hamburg, Rotterdam, Southampton and Le Havre.

The ship's eight-day passage to the Suez Canal had been uneventful. Mostly blue skies all the way. She had loaded her full cargo of forty foot and twenty foot containers in Hamburg, Rotterdam, Southampton and Le Havre.

The business of the giant ship was the ferrying of cargo in containers between Europe and the South East Asian hub ports of Kuala Lumpur, Singapore, Hong Kong and Yokohama. One year into service, with many thousands of sea miles behind her, little romance attached to the routine tasks performed by the master, first officer and crew.

Stacked six high on deck and in the holds, the contents of the three thousand or more containers that *Orient Angel* varied from industrial equipment, household electrical goods, automobiles, to chemicals. Half the cargo was slotted into the holds. Those containers packed with hazardous or explosive cargo were secured in the deck stacks with a system of twistlocks and lashing bars.

Orient Angel had arrived off Port Said on a Friday evening and weighed anchor. At just after midnight it headed south through the canal. Next morning it had changed pilots at Ishmalia and headed for anchor in the Bitter Lakes.

It was while the ship waited at Ishmalia for the northbound convoy to clear the section of canal between the lakes and Suez at the southern end that the headquarters of Svenske-Britannia signalled its master with unexpected news.

Orient Angel would not be going any further east than Kuala Lumpur this voyage, fully discharging her cargo in the Malaysian port. Instead, one of her sister ships would make the run from Kuala

Lumpur to Japan and back. The sister ship would transfer the westbound cargo to *Orient Angel* in time to pick up her schedule homeward bound. The reason for the change to the schedule was a stop for modifications to be made to the main engine. The master and the twenty-three crew would have an unusually long wait in Kuala Lumpur, while the work was done, before heading for Singapore.

Across the Indian Ocean there had been south-westerly gale force monsoon winds and driving rain. The master had ordered a course north of the island of Socotra, and *Orient Angel* succeeded in avoiding the worst weather.

During the rainstorms off Dondra Head, the southernmost point of Sri Lanka, *Orient Angel* received a signal from the Southampton office that she was to take a passenger, Mr Alan Rosslyn, on board at Kuala Lumpur. This would be at the end of the ship's second week in dock, just before the journey through the Malacca Strait to Singapore.

Southampton signalled the master of *Orient Angel* somewhat cursorily and late in the day that passenger Rosslyn was an insurance inspector from the Southampton office of Ocean World Insurance who would be 'undertaking a routine review of security arrangements aboard merchant ships operating in the Far East'. No more than that. It was routine business. Nothing to get alarmed about.

Time to set sail. The sun was lowering over Kuala Lumpur's Port Klang when Svenske-Britannia's agent handed the port clearance certificate to the master. Once the pilot and master had reviewed the procedure for unberthing and the route of the outbound passage, the crew were called to stations. The lines were made fast to the tugs. *Orient Angel* was on its way. Mooring ropes were stowed below decks.

Clear of Port Klang and released from the tugs, the ship's engineers increased the main engine's revolutions, and the ship slowly worked up to her full speed of twenty-four knots.

Sitting in the master's quarters with Mei listening in silence, Rosslyn warned Brown that maritime terrorism was now a major threat to world shipping.

'The odds against attack are minimal,' Brown offered by way of immediate disagreement.

'What about *Manju Alpha*?' Rosslyn asked. 'The attack occurred shortly after she left Kuala Tanjung bound for Kobe.'

'We're always alert at that position,' said Brown. 'Someone blabbed that *Manju Alpha* was carrying a cargo of aluminium ingots worth twelve million dollars.'

'Twenty million,' corrected Rosslyn. 'Faced with a machete at his throat, *Manju Alpha*'s captain had no other alternative but to tell his crew to surrender. Bound hand and foot, gagged and blindfolded, they were dumped into inflatable rubber boats, weren't they? They drifted for two weeks before a Thai fishing vessel rescued them somewhere off Phuket.'

'You don't have to tell us, laddie,' said Brown.

'And you know what happened to the ship and cargo. Both made their way to mainland China.'

'Och,' Brown snapped, 'you don't know that for sure.'

'Where else, then?' asked Rosslyn. 'The network of minor ports combined with corrupt Chinese customs makes for the market in stolen cargoes. And a charge of smuggling drugs was brought against the master.'

'It was dropped,' said Brown. 'He was released.'

'And the raiders were repatriated to Indonesia.'

'What's new?' said Brown.

'Nothing much,' said Rosslyn. 'Except they're free to carry on with God knows how many others. And as if the attack wasn't bad enough, there are clear enough indications of a high degree of terrorist organisation. And the suspicion that the Chinese authorities colluded in the attack. The Chinese maintained they had insufficient evidence to prosecute the raiders. And that was bullshit.'

'Well, well,' Brown said. 'We are too big a ship for any pirate to consider hijacking.' He turned to first officer Kjellner. 'Wouldn't you agree? If any bastard tries it on us, well, we don't put up a struggle. We have orders not to risk people's lives by playing silly bugger heroics. But if it makes you two feel any happier, we have fire hoses at the ready to repel boarders. Otherwise, you must know that Svenske-Britannia doesn't permit officers and crew to carry weapons. Pity really. Now, if I had a shotgun . . . things would be very different, wouldn't they? Maybe you people should recommend that I be given one.'

'That's not the sort of protection you should be looking at,' said Rosslyn.

'It isn't, Mr Rosslyn?' said Brown. 'You tell me what is.'

'What about SHIPLOC?'

'What's that?'

'You don't use it?'

Brown looked conspiratorially at Kjellner. 'Never heard of it.'

'I'm going to tell you what it is. It's the International Maritime Bureau's anti-piracy tracking system. It has a website. Ship owners can log on to view the precise position of their vessels twenty-four hours a day. A small device shows the owners the position via a satellite network. www.shiploc.com allows owners to obtain data and charts online. They can make sure their ships are on course. If, say, one of their ships is hijacked, the Bureau can check the ship's exact position. That way, the nearest law enforcement agencies can take immediate action.'

'You won't catch Svenske-Britannia coughing up that sort of expense.'

'You think they can't run to a hundred and fifty quid?' said Rosslyn. 'That's what it costs. It's the size of a shoebox. Your crew doesn't need to know there's one on board. If your power supply is cut, then a back-up system allows the device to go on functioning.'

'Is that so, my friend?'

'That's what I'm telling you. And you are seriously telling me that you haven't got one installed?'

'No,' said Brown. 'And while I'm master of *Orient Angel*, we never will.'

'But you do receive the Bureau's weekly piracy report online?'

'What?'

'It's a daily satellite update issued by the Bureau's Piracy Reporting Centre in KL. It shows the location and precise description of assaults on shipping. So Svenske-Britannia could put you on alert when you're in waters where assaults have taken place.'

'Listen, Mr Rosslyn,' said Brown, 'I act on orders from the UK. I don't need all this high-falutin shite you're drivelling on about. See? Shite, that's what it is.'

That was the ill-tempered note upon which the meeting ended. Rosslyn said he'd take the air. He wanted to make a preliminary inspection of the security measures.

81

Later, alone on deck with Mei, Rosslyn told her he was appalled by what he had seen and heard. 'Maybe I should divide and rule or something,' he said. 'Persuade the first officer he must plant the idea of instituting change in the master's mind. I don't know how they get away with it.'

'Get away with what?'

'If you want to know what I'm talking about, Mei –'

She held his hand. 'Don't worry, I'm not my father's daughter for nothing. I learned it at his knee.'

'For a start, there wasn't even a presail briefing of the crew before we left harbour.'

'That may be because the master and first officer assumed the crew were aware of the itinerary. The ports of call and timings. They know about the risks to shipping.'

'You think they do?' said Rosslyn. 'What about confirming the watch procedures?'

'Everyone knows they're routine. They're second nature to them.'

'I wonder,' said Rosslyn. 'Do you realise there isn't a single night vision device aboard? And the only alert mechanism is that compressed air horn the first officer sounded.'

'You're sure?'

'I looked, Mei, I looked. And the majority of the access hatches and portals to the interior of the ship have no proper locks. The gangway ladders have no locks. Think how easy it'd be for raiders to just lower the gangways. It's an open welcome to them to board this ship. And the fact is that, once attackers gain access to the deck and the gangway to access points, they gain the advantage. They get control and there's nothing anyone can do.'

'I hope you're wrong.'

'Sorry,' Rosslyn said. 'I'm right, use your eyes. Have you looked at the ship's mast? Think of the radars the first officer was gassing on about. The radars ought to be capable of detecting any attacking craft's approach. You realise where the radar antenna's been mounted? On the forward section of the mast.'

'Be fair,' she said. 'It's the most effective position for the ship's navigation.'

'I'm being totally fair. There's a bloody great blind spot to its rear.'

'There's a three hundred and sixty degree night watchman on duty,' Mei persisted.

'There is not. You missed it. Believe me, there isn't. There's that blind area directly to the stern. It's all of a hundred and seventy or a hundred and eighty degrees.'

Mei looked at him in astonishment.

'Hasn't Winston's daughter noticed?' Rosslyn asked.

'That's your job,' Mei said. 'Mine's to speak to the crew with you in their own language tomorrow morning.'

'Breakfast at seven?'

'I'll be there,' Mei said. 'Walk me to my cabin.' She took his hand. 'Don't let this ship get to you.'

82

It already had.

Rosslyn lay awake listening to the low hiss of the air conditioning and the persistent rumble and vibration of *Orient Angel's* engines.

Unable to sleep, he decided to pay a visit to the bridge unannounced.

83

It was first officer Kjellner's duty watch on the bridge and Rosslyn was surprised to find Captain Brown there with him. 'If you have any more problems,' he said to Rosslyn, 'you'd better tell me about them. Get it over with now, don't you think?'

'They're not your problems,' Rosslyn said. 'They're Svenske-Britannia's. My people in Southampton will be in touch with them.'

Rosslyn followed the master's gaze into the darkness of the Malacca Strait ahead. The reinforced glass window of *Orient Angel*'s wheelhouse sloped away at an angle. Bound for Singapore, *Orient Angel* was now at the northern end of the Malacca Strait and would dock there in the morning.

Kjellner was staring at the computer screens of the integrated navigation display. The displays of information from the unmanned engine room's data points. The emergency fire alarm systems. The radar screens showing the coast of Malaysia and the blips of other ships in the waterway.

With fewer than twenty-five metres of ocean beneath her, *Orient Angel*'s powerful engine seemed be vibrating more than usual.

'I'm turning in,' the master announced. He wrote something in the orders book and then, in spite of what he had just said about turning in, lingered on the bridge a while.

'If some stupid bastard tries to board us,' said Kjellner, 'they won't get far, will they?' The remark was perhaps intended to prompt some further sharp remark from Brown. Kjellner seemed to derive satisfaction from the master's game of cat and mouse with 'the laddie from London and his rice princess'. And, as if to taunt Rosslyn even more, Kjellner touched a lever and *Orient Angel*'s klaxon gave a hoot of warning to any craft that might be in the vicinity.

Rosslyn glanced at the wheelhouse clock. It was just past four in the morning. Mei Lim was in her cabin. The crew, the Malays and

Indonesians, were in their quarters below deck. 'But if I were one of those bastards you've mentioned,' Rosslyn observed, 'this is about the time I'd choose. They're not as stupid as you think.'

'You might choose it,' said Brown, 'and you'd be bloody mad.'

Kjellner laughed.

'See you at daybreak,' Brown said. Then he rather sharply asked Kjellner to remember that someone should wake him before sunrise, in less than two hours' time.

Rosslyn followed Brown to the wheelhouse exit and out on deck.

The air was rank with the stink of the tropics: sour like rotting grass. It seemed strangely half-alive, like rotting grass. Kjellner had a point. Visibility was poor and the mist might offer attackers good cover.

'What is it you want now, then?' the Captain asked with the air of a man irritated by a curious child. He puffed out his barrel chest.

'Do me one favour,' Rosslyn asked. 'Just once. Tonight we're in the Malacca Strait. Would you mind locking your cabin door?'

'You don't need to tell me where we are or what to do, *laddie*.'

'You know the risks.'

'Listen here. I first sailed this route before you were born. Bandits, marauders, pirates, high seas terrorists, call the shites what you like. For thirty years, I've survived without them.' He sniffed the air and shook his head as if to reinforce the point. 'If you're worried about your own arse, you lock your bloody cabin door, young man. Mine stays unlocked. As it always has. That's the tradition. For thirty years. *Unlocked*.'

With that he headed off in the direction of his cabin on the deck below the wheelhouse, turning back only once to mutter, 'Trust me, *laddie*. Trust in God.'

Rosslyn left the bridge and headed below to his cabin.

Standing by the door, he hesitated. He could hear a movement inside. The handle turned. The door opened.

'Come in,' Mei said.

84

On the landing stage at the edge of the jungle, the waiting time was almost over.

Terajima and Kyung spoke in whispers.

'What was it you did in London?' Kyung asked.

'I was sort of a doctor.'

'*You* were a doctor?' said Kyung. 'I never knew. What sort of doctor. Doing what?'

'Appendectomies. Hernia repairs. Biopsies. You name it. Bowel and heart surgery. Anaesthetics. Good at stitching up. My mother taught me needle-point.'

'Good money?'

'Not enough.'

'You liked cutting people up, then?'

'It was a job like any other. I liked sewing them up. Skin is so pliable. Soft to the touch.'

'What did you like best about it?'

'The anaesthetics,' said Terajima. He withdrew a clutch of hypodermic needles and syringes from the belt around his wetsuit. 'I liked putting people to sleep,' he said. 'Sometimes I used this.' And he showed Kyung the long, fine nail file. Its tip was honed to the sharpness of a razor. 'There's a lot to be said for mercy killing.'

'You know what I overheard in Batu Pahat,' Kyung said. 'I heard that the Indonesian Navy has doubled the number of its patrol boats in the Strait.'

'Where did you hear that?'

'Kolekta Hotel in Batam. In the Rose Garden karaoke bar.'

'In Indonesia?'

'From a *cewek*.'

'From a hooker?'

'Right.'

'I don't trust men who need to buy sex. They're like the sad-sads who need to buy drugs to get dreams. The man who buys dreams is weak.'

'Well, the *cewek* has an Indonesian Navy officer for a regular client.'

'Does she?' said Terajima. 'What she didn't tell you is that our powerboat is double the speed of any crap boat the Indonesian Navy puts to sea.'

85

She slipped the latch on the inside of his cabin door.

Something of the Mei he saw that evening he visited her in her apartment had returned, and it seemed the fear had left her. She seemed almost amused by their predicament, by their being thrown together and now side by side on the bunk. 'I forgot,' she said. 'I need to use your toothbrush.'

'That can be arranged,' he said, starting to his feet. He noticed she was carrying a scrap of paper in her left hand.

She held his hand, suggesting that he stay seated next to her. 'You told me', she said, 'that – what was it? – you had "come back for me".'

'No,' he said, 'it was the other way round. You asked *me* to tell *you* that I had come back for you.'

'Then it wasn't just to do with that man Graer and the American woman?'

'No.'

'Or George Tsang, then?'

'Listen, Mei. I made a promise to your father.'

'And you seem to be keeping it.'

'That's what I intend.'

'Something I should tell you about Tsang. Sure, he's in with the police. But he has a hard living to make, and even he won't be averse to greasing up to the men from Beijing. He wants his day of glory. The big story.'

'You can't blame him for that,' he said. 'He's a journalist.'

'Who doesn't like me.'

'Why not?' he asked.

'Because I didn't live up to my father's expectations.' She laughed. 'I should've turned out more like you, Alan. Maybe, if I'd been born a boy, I might have done, and then I wouldn't have been responsible for Dad's death. See, he tried to keep me out of trouble. And, well, it's a long story, isn't it?'

'You want to tell it to me?'

'Some other time,' she said. 'What about you? Have you ever been married?'

'No.'

'What about women?'

'One or two. One I loved very much was shot dead virtually in front of my eyes. It took me a long time to get over her.'

'What was her name?'

'Mary Walker. She was a police officer.'

'You lived with her?'

'We worked together.'

'And who else has there been, like serious?'

'Cleo. She's Greek. That ended because we grew apart.'

'And now,' she said, 'you've come to me.'

'Yes, I've come back for you.'

'For me or for my father?'

'For you.'

'But I'm very selfish, Alan. I'm thinking what the hell is going to happen to me when this ship docks in Singapore? I'm going to be alone, aren't I?'

'No. I'm staying with you until my job's finished.'

'And after that?' she asked, and then suddenly placed her fingers over his lips. 'I have to tell you,' she said, 'I had this dream. True. In it you were making love to me. We were in bed in your place in London. I couldn't tell what it was like – your place, I mean. It was sort of sudden. I mean, we hadn't formed any relationship. No one else knew about us. The weird thing is we weren't strangers. For some reason I knew all about you. I asked you if I was the first Chinese girl you'd made love to. You wouldn't tell me. I asked how many women you'd slept with, and you said it was kind of sad for a man to keep count. I asked you if you took drugs and I said I was pleased that you had no need to buy dreams. Then I asked you about your other women. You said, "Who do you have in mind?" And I asked you their names. You said, "There's Mo and Elizabeth, Lindsey and Françoise."'

'*Four*?'

'Yes. You told me four. You said, "Let's see. Mo and Elizabeth and Françoise are married. They live in Canada. And Lindsey lives in Sri

Lanka. She's a teacher. Single. They're my sisters." And that was it.'

He watched her shaking her head, her wry smile.

'I wrote this for you,' she said, handing him the scrap of paper she had brought with her.

He read the lines aloud:

> The angels keep their ancient places;
> Turn but a stone, and start a wing!
> 'Tis ye, 'tis your estranged faces,
> That miss the many-splendoured thing.

'You wrote that?'

'Yes. For you. *The Many Splendoured Thing*.' He noticed her cheeks were slightly flushed. 'Listen,' she said, 'I can hear the engines.'

'We should take a walk on deck.'

'Not yet. Later. Because I've wanted you so much.'

He had heard the verse before. In London. At the Zhentungs' place.

86

Terajima gave the order to don matte black crash helmets with visors. The visors would shield their eyes against the wind and spray they would encounter in the Malacca Strait.

Each man strapped on a life jacket containing body armour encased in high tensile polymer fabric. Buoyant and water resistant, the life jackets were proof against attack by knives or bullets.

After Terajima had issued the crew with the AK-47 rifles, the ammunition and the portable canisters of Xeona nerve gas, he supervised the careful loading of the weapons: the lightweight rocket launchers and the high explosive devices. These were secured in the bows.

Giving the signal to the armed lookouts that the moment had come to depart, Terajima gestured to the crew to take up their positions aboard.

He told Kyung that he would check the landing stage to make sure nothing had been left behind. Once he was out of earshot he checked his wristwatch and made the shore to air call.

He spoke in Mandarin.

'I am leaving now. You should be above the target precisely on schedule.'

He looked up into the night sky. The pilot of the back-up helicopter would now be altering his flight path to head for the target area. This was one of two refinements that neither Kyung nor the rest of the crew knew anything about.

The crew were ready and in position. He gave them the thumbs up sign. Each crew member responded likewise. As they did so, he surreptitiously slipped a metallic container further beneath the pilot's seat. This was the second refinement only he knew about. The container was packed tight with high explosive.

The mooring ropes were loosened and stowed aboard.

Terajima inserted a fresh tab of snuff beneath his upper lip. He felt that familiar rush. He took his position as pilot on the starboard side and turned the key in the ignition. The twin five hundred horsepower engines came to life.

Gathering speed, the powerboat headed into the mist towards the open sea and the general direction of Singapore. Away from the shore, there was a cool sea breeze. The powerboat smacked into the waves and into slicks of oily, bouncing water plants tangled up with floating trash. Sea birds circled above its widening wake.

The moan of a ship's warning horn sounded in the distance. Somewhere in the mist, the raiders' prey cruised steadily southwards at full sea speed through the darkness near One Fathom Bank.

87

Kissing deeply, they pressed their bodies together, moving slowly to the edge of the narrow bunk. 'Let me undress you,' she said. 'Don't talk.'

He felt the coolness of her hands exploring him.

'Alan. Please. Touch me. Here.'

She was stroking her tongue against his. Then his ear. Her head was rocking from side to side. Coarse hairs were in his mouth. 'Look into my eyes. Don't stop. I can feel you. I love you. Do you love me? Tell me, Alan.'

'I love you, Mei –'

'Watch me.'

She gripped first one ankle and lifted her leg behind her neck. Then the other.

'I don't ever want you to forget me,' she said. 'Now, do it now. Right inside me. Deeper.'

88

Wind whipped the spray against Terajima's visor. He was familiar with the hazards in the Strait, the variable depth of the relatively shallow waters, the local tides and the sea swells. The currents can flow as strongly as six knots. Underwater wrecks and shifting shoal banks make navigation difficult. The unpredictable conditions concentrate the minds and skills of even the most experienced of navigators. Paradoxically, the conditions favoured Terajima. The powerboat was faster, lighter and far more mobile than any other craft in the Strait that night. Terajima knew the powerboat could easily outmanoeuvre his elephantine prey.

In the cockpit, his mind alert to every shift in the strength and direction of the waves, Terajima carefully adjusted the powerboat's stability. With his right hand he moved the small levers upwards to raise the bow or pressed down on them to lower it. Only the gentlest touch on the wheel was required to correct the powerboat's course.

89

Rosslyn and Mei joined Kjellner in the wheelhouse.

Kjellner offered them strong, sweet tea. Standing side by side, they stared in silence at the shifting sea ahead. Just south of One Fathom Bank, *Orient Angel* was making a steady twenty-four knots, when the uniformed Malay lookout man joined them. He smelled of stale garlic and cheap cologne. He perused the night orders Brown had written in the orders book.

'Phones dead?' the Malay asked.

'On the blink,' said the first officer. 'That's why you have to call the boss just before 0600 hours.' The lookout man began chewing on a wooden toothpick. He was very nervous.

'Why are the phones dead?' Rosslyn asked.

'Because some jerk in KL got the wiring wrong,' said Kjellner.

'And that's not all that's dead,' said Mei.

She was staring at the CCTV security monitors which should have been showing the illuminated stern area and the port and starboard companionways. None of them was working.

'When did they go down?' Rosslyn asked.

'A few minutes ago,' Kjellner said. 'I think.'

'You think? What do you mean – *you think*?'

'No need to worry, Mr Rosslyn.'

'Don't you recognise the signs?' said Rosslyn.

'What signs?'

'This ship is completely bloody vulnerable. Can't you see it?'

Kjellner was smiling. 'You're full of bullshit.'

The Malay lookout man was staring at Rosslyn transfixed with panic.

90

Occasionally, as if sensing danger, Terajima checked the rear view mirrors for signs of anyone in pursuit. To his left, Kyung as throttle man maintained the crucial rate of speed across the Strait. Speed, timing and surprise combined were as much the essence of the plan of attack as mobility.

Terajima was scrupulous in his observance of the rules of seamanship. The only exceptions he had made were those of safety. True, his men wore life jackets. But none of the powerboat's lights was illuminated – and no one had been informed of its departure or, as local regulations also stipulated, the time of its return.

To mask the approach of the powerboat among the buoys and sea clutter, Kyung reduced speed and Terajima began to steer a zigzag course, making it very hard for even the most alert of radar operators to plot the powerboat's course.

The spreading wake from the massive stern of *Orient Angel* was now in sight. There she was. Lights blurred by the dark green tropical darkness, unaware and vulnerable.

91

'Isolate the bridge, Kjellner,' Rosslyn yelled. 'Call the master. Lock the bloody doors. Lock them. *Isolate the bridge.*'

He grabbed two life jackets, one for himself and one for Mei.

Taking Mei by the hand, he threw open the wheelhouse door to the deck.

Slipping on the life jackets as they went, they hurried along the narrow gangways, passing the towering stacks of containers on the starboard side and on towards the stern.

Not quite halfway there, from somewhere in the mist above, he heard the thwacking sound of the rotors of an approaching helicopter.

'Could be a police patrol,' Rosslyn said.

'Looks to me more like a Chinese helicopter gunship,' Mei said.

Rosslyn was straining his eyes to see the approaching helicopter when the ship's lights went out. It was then that they heard the first muffled shouts.

Nearing the stern, they stopped in their tracks. Rosslyn saw the unmistakable wake of the powerboat in the ocean below. Somewhere in the darkness he heard some whispered threat in Chinese he didn't understand and shouts which seemed to be coming from below the starboard rail.

'What are they saying?'

'They're boarding ship.'

At the same moment, Rosslyn heard dull thuds behind him. Glancing back, he saw the masked figure scrambling over the deck rail. Then, in the sea, directly beneath the stern, he saw the powerboat itself. It seemed lodged at an angle. He could see another masked figure steadying a very long bamboo pole. He heard a metallic sound, its pitch distorted by the wind.

Fear rising in his chest, he turned, intending to run back to the bridge.

He saw hands and fingernails gripping Mei's throat: her head pushed forward and downward.

Rosslyn jumped at the attacker, driving his fist against the side of the man's masked head.

92

Terajima sensed the lessening of the engines' vibrations: *Orient Angel*'s speed had considerably decreased.

The pair whose task was to isolate the bridge had already done so. They would now be on stand-by awaiting the signal to return to the powerboat.

The third member of the raiding party would be below. Having secured the exits to the *Orient Angel*'s crew accommodation, he would be on armed stand-by in the event that any of the crew offered resistance.

The master of the ship will be my business. There will be one male passenger aboard. He too will be my business. You are to understand that there will also be one female passenger aboard Orient Angel. *She will also be my business.*

With one of the rocket launchers strapped to his back, two canisters of Xeona nerve gas clipped to his belt and carrying his loaded AK-47 rifle, Terajima headed for the stairs leading down to the master's cabin. With the ship's lighting system down, he needed his flashlight to find the way.

Reaching the deck below, he was disturbed to find some lights still on.

Perhaps some emergency back-up lighting circuit had been activated. But suddenly the lights went out and the ship returned to darkness.

He was further disturbed to find the door to the captain's cabin was unlocked and heard the Scots voice demanding, 'What do you want?'

The flashlight's beam swept around the cabin and illuminated Brown's terrified face. Standing in the centre of his cabin, Brown was blinking. He was barefoot and dressed only in a vest and boxer shorts.

'Open the safe.'

'You can have whatever you want,' Brown said.

'Open it,' Terajima insisted.

Brown crossed the cabin to the safe that stood beside his desk.

'Open it.'

'I heard you the first time.'

Kneeling on the carpet, Brown twisted the combination lock. He got slowly to his feet and stepped back.

He was saying 'Help yourself –' when the blow from the fist stopped him. It struck hard into Brown's mouth. Reeling backwards and sideways, Brown was unable to avoid the second blow, which felled him, and was unable to offer any resistance to Terajima's fingernails. He screwed his eyes up. *'Not my eyes. Not my eyes. please –'* He could offer no resistance to the sweeping of the nail file blade.

Terajima slit Brown's throat from ear to ear. Then he turned his attention to the contents of the safe. The gift of the unwitting US weapons industry to the People's Republic of China.

93

Rosslyn tore the face mask from Mei's attacker to find himself staring into the terrified eyes of the Malay lookout man.

'Master's orders,' the Malay yelled. 'Make sure you cause no trouble.'

Rosslyn struck him hard, knocking him sideways to the deck next to where Mei lay semi-conscious.

Blood was running from her neck.

Orient Angel was motionless. Stopped dead. Rosslyn could hear the deafening row of the helicopter in the darkness above. It must surely be engaged upon a rescue mission. The awful thought of Winston's fate flashed across his mind. There was no sign of the crew. Where were they?

Realising that in the open they were both ready prey for the attackers, he lifted Mei away from the side rails as gently as he could to where there was a narrow gap between the nearest of the container stacks. The thudding of the rotor blades grew still louder. Crouching over her, he pressed his right hand tight against Mei's wound to stem the flow of blood. Her blood seeped through his fingers. Blood gurgled in her throat.

Why isn't the helicopter using its searchlight beams to illuminate Orient Angel?

Whoever was up in the helicopter must now have realised the ship had been boarded by raiders. The thudding and the droning of the helicopter beat in his head like a knell and he saw that Mei had been right. It was a Chinese military gunship.

He looked out across the twilit ocean's slow swell below. Then up at the helicopter again.

Then he saw the figure. *Whoever he is, he's armed.*

He's looking for someone. For us. We're cornered. He could sense it in his gut. *He's looking for us.*

Slowly, taking Mei with him, he squeezed himself further into the recess between the containers.

The man was feet away from him. He glimpsed the jungle boots. The hands. Even in the half-light he could tell the hands were drenched in blood. The man was now so near that Rosslyn could see the glint of gold chains twined around the left wrist. He was hesitating. Searching. Mei moaned weakly and before she could cough he held his hand across her mouth. Her chest convulsed. He hated hurting her. He had to do it. His heart thudded. He held his breath.

He's got to see us.

Suddenly he was gone.

Rosslyn waited a few long minutes before moving.

The helicopter seemed to be descending. He thought he could make out the shape of a figure in the open doors. He couldn't be sure. The figure seemed to be unfurling a set of ropes and lifting gear.

The helicopter was descending still further. Lifting gear was being prepared. He saw ropes and a lifting cradle drop downward on to the top of a container stack. Now he saw two figures crouched on top of the container on which the lifting gear had settled.

He watched them attaching harnesses to the cradle. Feeling helpless and terribly alone, he felt sure Mei was dying. Drifting in and out of consciousness, she seemed to be staring up in horror at him. Her bloodied, swollen lips were parted.

Finally he moved out of the recess. He could see the shape of the cradle in the sky. First slowly, then faster, its load and two figures were winched upwards towards the helicopter's open doors.

'You'll be okay, Mei?' he whispered.

She managed to say, 'Leave me here. You go –'

'No,' he said.

'They're going to blow the ship up.'

Now the dazzling white light of the helicopter's searchlight came on.

His eyes cleared enough for him to see a masked figure, dressed in combat gear, hauled aboard the helicopter. It seemed bizarre. He was carrying an object something like a medium-sized suitcase. Rosslyn was convinced it was the man who had been looking for them.

Mei's moans were louder.

'Come with me,' Rosslyn told her. He lifted her in his arms and carried her to the side rail. 'Just do what I tell you,' he said.

'Leave me.'

'Do what I say.'

94

Terajima had set the rocket launcher on the floor of the helicopter beside the open door. *There is one female passenger still aboard* Orient Angel. *One male. They're my business.*

JUST SOME DUMB-FUCK BRITISH GUMSHOE. NOW SOME DEAD MINUS COCK AND BALLS DUMB-FUCK BRITISH GUMSHOE.

I WANT TO WATCH YOU DIE WITH EYES WIDE OPEN STARING INTO MINE STRANGLED WITH THESE GOLD CHAINS AND CHOKING ON YOUR STRANDS OF FINE DARK HAIR.

If you're dead, you're dead.

If not, you're still mine.

The searchlight beam illuminated the powerboat below. The rest of the crew were now aboard and the engines roared into life.

Bows raised, the powerboat charged into the waves and away from *Orient Angel.*

She had travelled a distance of half a mile when Terajima activated the remote control system. It detonated the explosives he had secured beneath the pilot's seat.

The wall of white light brought a moment's blazing daylight to the Malacca Strait, followed by a simultaneous blast of deafening thunder which raised a cloud of steam and purple smoke into the night sky.

Seconds later, white-hot fragments of the powerboat fell into the ocean and sizzled audibly. Then they seemed to evaporate in the darkness.

The helicopter pilot changed his flight path. Now the searchlight beam swivelled towards the bows of *Orient Angel.*

NO PRISONERS. NO SURVIVORS.

THIS MOMENT IS FOR ME.

THE DOOR HAS BEEN OPENED.

I AM CHOSEN.

MOTHER GAVE ME THE STRENGTH TO BE HERE WITH YOU TONIGHT.

ONLY YOU KNOW THE PEACE I FEEL.

95

Pushing his arms beneath her armpits and the life jacket, Rosslyn heaved Mei to her feet. He managed to lift her so that she was precariously seated on the deck rail.

'Leave me –'

Twice he rocked her backwards and forwards, and then put all his body weight behind the push.

Feet first, Mei dropped down into the ocean.

Rosslyn climbed the deck rail. Pushing hard against it with his feet, he propelled himself into a dive of some forty-five degrees.

Moments later, he surfaced close to Mei, who had lost consciousness, and held her head above the water. Swimming powerfully, he dragged her clear of the ship. Metre by metre, working his way steadily, heaving Mei after him. If and when *Orient Angel* was blown to kingdom come, he prayed they would be at a safe distance.

96

Aboard the helicopter, there was a conflict of opinion. The pilot's second-in-command was barking advice about the unleashing of the missile at the crucial angle to avoid the danger of back thrust from the launcher. Terajima was concentrating. Trying to get the right aim. Trying to steady himself.

The second-in-command resolved the conflict. He ordered the helicopter pilot to alter the direction of the flight. He ordered a crew member to fasten the harness. To lower the winch. The missile would be fired in relative safety from below the helicopter. It was a risk. But it had been achieved before during the rapid response training in Guangzhon.

97

The sight of the figure being winched downwards beneath the helicopter spurred Rosslyn on to greater efforts.

At the outer edge of the spreading searchlight beam, he saw the
man raise the weapon resembling a small tube or pipe. Then he saw
the red and green and yellow and white of the vivid electric flash. He
cupped his hand over Mei's mouth.

Dragging Mei with him beneath the surface of ocean, Rosslyn
prayed that he could avoid being sucked to death by the downward
pressure spreading from the sinking *Orient Angel*.

It ended in a few seconds of electric daylight across the Malacca
Strait.

98

Towers of steam and boiling water erupted from the disintegrating bows.

The greater part of the ship lifted and sank, as if dragged below the surface by submarine suction.

The explosion seemed to spread and strike backwards at the containers on deck. The heat melted the first of the steel containers' protective walls. Then the containers self-ignited. They spewed blue and red flames into the sky.

Multiple detonations released some enormous centrifugal force of burning chemicals. The force sent a towering spray of heated fluorescent fragments outwards and upwards. The screaming of splitting iron accompanied the illumination of the night sky, seen for many miles along the coasts of Sumatra and Malaysia.

It was this apocalyptic sight – violent colours, spray and white waves – that Rosslyn first saw when he resurfaced. Gasping for breath and retching, he was supporting Mei's head above the water.

Underwater explosions beyond the centre of the fire on the water sent eerie pulsations through his body. There was the hissing, the stench and the spread of the burning oil, most of which had mercifully been blown and blasted in the opposite direction.

Debris was still dropping into the frothing water. One chunk of red-hot steel fell into the water fewer than fifty metres from her. It hissed and screamed and then vanished in a cloud of white steam.

Eyes closed, spitting oil and water, Rosslyn kicked out hard. He succeeded in keeping Mei's head just above the surface.

The core of the explosion had by now subsided. Rolling clouds of smoke and steam merged into cloudbanks. Somewhere above them, across the Malacca Strait, appeared the first thin streak of natural dawn. Then, like some vulture searching for carrion, the helicopter gunship returned.

FOUR

Know the enemy's plans; calculate their strengths and weaknesses.
Provoke him, to know his patterns of movement.
Determine his position, to know the ground of death and of life.
Probe him, to know where he is strong and where he is weak.
The ultimate skill is to take up a position where you are formless.
If you are formless, the most penetrating spies will not be able to
discern you.

SUN TZU

99

Old hands of Jon Simpson's generation call the Shangri-La Hotel 'The Shang'. With its tropical gardens, waterfalls and *koi* ponds, The Shang is not far from the Consular and Visa Section of the British High Commission on Tanglin Road.

Here Simpson's veteran Singaporean informer, Yeo Heng, waited for his British friend to join him for a champagne breakfast at their usual table in the Lobby Court. Yeo Heng had bad news to tell.

A middle-ranking official in Singapore's Ministry of Defence, Heng had been Simpson's close ally since the Briton's arrival in Singapore a decade before. Like Simpson, Heng was a public servant nearing retirement.

After breakfast, they would follow a leisurely routine. Tennis on one of the hotel's courts. Sweating in the sauna to clear the pores, a long shower and a relaxing massage were followed by lunch at one or other of the outdoor restaurants between Orchard and Tanglin Roads. The anglophile Heng provided Simpson with secret intelligence. He was Simpson's most reliable source and highly valued by the South East Asia desk at SIS headquarters in London's Vauxhall Cross.

Since the return of Hong Kong to the Chinese, Singapore has been the stage on which the officers and agents of the several dozen major players in the international secrets trade, like Simpson, act out their roles.

Heng's speciality was Chinese political and military intelligence and the accelerating progress Beijing was making in modernising its military capabilities. Heng it was who had first handed Simpson the details of China's major coup: the theft of the research and blueprints, *in toto*, of the W-88, the US miniaturised thermonuclear warhead.

The results and timing of this gift of Heng to SIS placed Simpson's star firmly in the ascendant. SIS obtained the nugget at least eighteen months before the CIA eventually discovered that Beijing possessed the legacy codes containing the records of the US nuclear testings. The CIA was too late. China had successfully boosted the accuracy of its ballistic missiles. And the executives of the American corporations known as the Rope-Sellers continued blithely to sell China high-tech knowhow. This was the rope which the Chinese thought might hang the USA and its allies.

Strengthening control over its military destiny, China was well on the way to achieving domination of its own hemisphere. London, of course, had passed most of the detailed intelligence to Washington whilst keeping the source of it secret. The source was Heng. Simpson the conduit. London the reservoir. London paid Heng very substantial rewards for the work he carried out in secret for the security of the United Kingdom.

100

Heng was waiting for Simpson at the corner table by the window in the breakfast room.

'I thought perhaps you'd left town,' Heng said. He seemed relieved to see his companion. 'I've been calling your home number for the last three hours.'

'I overslept,' Simpson said. 'Stayed up too late glued to the TV for anything more on the Zhentung business. Not nice. Not nice.'

Simpson invited Heng to order his customary English breakfast, but Heng only wanted fresh mango juice and coffee. 'I expect you've heard the news?' he said.

'What other news, Yeo?' asked Simpson.

This was how they always began the exchanges of intelligence when they lunched. However, this was breakfast. For Heng to pitch straight in so early in the day was the exception. Heng would assume that Simpson already knew of some new development. This was their regular procedure. Simpson would ask the What. Not necessarily always in this order, there would follow the Why, the When, the Who and the How. It would be left to Simpson to interpret Heng's nuggets. London would compare and contrast Simpson's interpretation with whatever might be thought significant on the databases. Simpson would await additional instructions from London: for example, whether or not to probe Heng or any other of his less valuable sources for further information. Essentially, Simpson's role was that of the passive listener and conduit.

Heng looked Simpson straight in the eye. 'You heard about the ship that's been lost in the Malacca Strait? The eighty thousand tonne container ship belonging to Svenske-Britannia. The *Orient Angel*. Blown to smithereens.'

'What ship did you say?' Simpson asked, without betraying the slightest emotion.

'*Orient Angel.*'

'I believe she's one of the Zhentungs' ships. Tell me what happened, Yeo.'

'Blown up and sunk. She was carrying industrial chemicals, amongst other things. The cargo caught fire and exploded. Not all that surprising when you think that she was loaded with over five thousand tonnes of acetylene. Mix that with water and I hate to think of the result. The explosion must have been gigantic. More than twenty dead and missing. No known survivors.'

'You say *no* survivors – not a single one?'

'None. The duty officer at your High Commission's being kept in the picture. The High Commissioner's been informed. So has your Defence Adviser.'

'Then they'll have the formalities in hand, Yeo.'

Simpson thought of Rosslyn and Mei.

Heng was saying, 'There's an additional sensitivity you need to know about. The official line is that it was an accident. What happened was not an accident. It was a premeditated and highly organised act of maritime terrorism.'

Simpson already guessed as much. 'Is that so?' he said. 'How come?'

'It was the result of a highly planned raid. There's another complication. The ship's master was carrying some sensitive material in his safe. It will have been taken.'

'What material was he carrying, Yeo?'

'Key miniature components for new ICBMs. American components for the fifteen thousand kilometre range MV-54 and the twenty-five thousand kilometre range MV-65. Others for the submarine ballistic missile the BX-70, the naval version of the MV-54, with components of ground positioning systems. They were destined for Penang. The master and first officer were working for a Chinese diplomat in London by the name of Zhu Jianxing. Does the name mean anything to you?'

'Never heard of him,' said Simpson. 'Tell me, Yeo, how did you come by all of this quite so soon after the event?'

'I can only tell you that our people planned to detain the *Orient Angel* once it berthed here at the Tanjong Pagar terminal. The master and first officer had a rendezvous with Chinese security service agents in an apartment at the Mariners' Club on Cantonment Road.

All of which is now pretty much academic. The view is that the attackers lifted the material before the ship sank. A PLA rapid response unit Z-9W, a helicopter gunship, was seen in the area of the disaster. Presumably Beijing had some prior warning of what was going to happen here. They must have known our people had their agents under surveillance.'

'Who do we think is responsible for the attack?' said Simpson.

Without answering Simpson's question, Heng passed the first of two small plain folders across the table. 'Take a look at the photographs. Tell me if you recognise anyone.'

The folder contained several rather blurred photographs, which seemed to have been taken from a long distance and considerably enlarged. Six of the stolen shots showed a masked man. Wearing a wetsuit, the man was standing on a quayside with some Chinese in quasi-combat gear. Another four showed the same man seated at the controls of a streamlined powerboat, this time wearing a helmet and darkened windshield visor.

'You know him?' Heng asked.

'He doesn't mean anything to me,' said Simpson. 'Who are we looking at?'

Heng glanced at Simpson with a flicker of surprise. 'A man called Klaas-Pieter Terajima.'

'Doesn't ring any bells with me.'

'He's working for the Zhentungs, the owners of Svenske-Britannia,' said Heng. 'The company that owned the *Orient Angel*.'

'And he blew up *their* ship?'

'You must know about him.'

'I'm afraid I don't,' Simpson said.

'Then ask London,' said Heng.

'If you insist, Yeo. Of course I will. If you say so. But you must give me one damn good reason.'

'I've told you. The man Terajima was responsible for the attack on *Orient Angel*.'

'Then who exactly is he when he's at home?' Simpson asked.

'You mentioned the Zhentungs. Terajima works for the surviving Zhentung brothers, Hastings and Foster. They've assumed financial control of Svenske-Britannia. A high degree of secrecy attaches itself to Terajima's work for them, just as it does to his private and professional life. Highly mobile, he lives mostly on the wing. The clearest example we have seen of the entirely new breed of terrorist. Without ideals or passion. This man is quite different. A most exceptionally dangerous figure. If thwarted in his efforts, God alone knows what greater damage he might do.'

'What's the evidence he's responsible?' Simpson asked.

Here he paused to allow the waiter to refill his cup of black coffee. Once the waiter was out of earshot, Heng continued.

'One of my agents – for the sake of his protection let's call him Lee – came out from behind the moon. He telephoned me at the very first moment it was safe for him to do so. He told me that Klaas-Pieter Terajima was planning to launch an attack on a ship passing through the Malacca Strait.'

Simpson allowed Heng to continue with Lee's record of events uninterrupted. Heng described the crew. The use of the bamboo poles twined with rope to board the ship. The arms, the ammunition and rocket launchers they had loaded aboard, including the substantial quantity of high explosive.

'Lee didn't know the identity of the ship that was being targeted. It could have been any of several dozen heading through the Strait in the midnight hours. None of the terrorists was intended to know the ship's identity until they reached it. Once there, of course, they could read the name on the stern or bows. Not that the name would have meant very much to any of them. Finally, Lee was emphatic that there was no way he could communicate with me again.'

'Why on earth didn't you alert the authorities?'

'What was I to tell them? That there's the constant likelihood of attacks on shipping in the Strait. They know that. The whole world knows it.'

'I rather wonder whether that's the case outside South East Asia. But then – what happened?'

'According to Lee, the raiders reached *Orient Angel* some time about four o'clock this morning. They boarded her and overpowered the crew. Faced by armed raiders, the crew put up no resistance. Terajima went to the bridge, had the engines stopped and then shot dead the first officer and several others. He then went below to the master's quarters. He took what he wanted from the safe there and killed the master. Lee believes that Terajima even went so far as to gouge out the man's eyes. One of Terajima's hallmarks is to remove such organs, freeze them and later deliver them to his victim's families to extort still further sums of money. Mind you, he doesn't exactly need the money. Quite simply, he likes to study people's reactions to personal pain and family life. He's known in some quarters as the Scholar of Extortion.'

'The Scholar of Extortion?'

'Yes. On the west coast of Malaysia, in Indonesia, in Manila and among some of the nastier elements of organised crime in Japan.'

'What happened next, Yeo? How did this man Lee escape?'

'When he saw the PLA gunship overhead he got clear. He dived into the ocean. Minutes later the powerboat was blown up. He believes that a remote control explosive device must have been used. After a desperate struggle through the debris in the water, he was picked up by a local fishing vessel that took him to Batu Pahat. He called me from there. You should know that, in his view, there were two passengers on board. A British national and a Hong Kong Chinese woman.'

God help us. Rosslyn, Mei, thought Simpson.

'After that?' he asked impassively.

'Terajima was lifted aboard the helicopter gunship. A missile was fired. It blew *Orient Angel* to kingdom come. I should add that Lee says they were also carrying nerve gas canisters. They're of Japanese manufacture and nasty, very nasty. I guess Terajima intended to use them in the event that they were captured. Lee is certain that they weren't used.'

'Where is this man Lee now?'

'Still in hiding. Somewhere south of Batu Pahat. But I imagine he will have been wise to have moved on.'

'Will Terajima suspect he escaped?'

'Lee is certain that Terajima will not have seen him.'

'Is he one of the men in these pictures?'

'Yes,' said Heng. He identified Lee for Simpson's benefit. 'My man's safe. That's the good news.'

'And the bad?'

'The Prime Minister's office has ordered the Defence Minister to throw a very tight security blanket over the whole incident. It's to be treated as an accident. No mention will be made of any raid or Terajima's involvement.'

'Why on earth not?'

'Your guess is as good as mine.'

'You must know why not, Yeo.'

'I don't.'

'You can't stop the UK government coming clean,' Simpson said. 'I mean, after what you've just told me. For a start, I have my responsibilities to London.'

'I know that,' Heng said. 'But I can tell you this. Once you return to your office you'll find that your people are taking the same line. The strictest veto's been applied. I think you'd better speak to London pretty soon.'

Simpson considered what Heng had said.

It was highly improbable that, if London knew anything about the man Terajima, they would not have informed him of the attack already. Except of course for the fact that he had been temporarily *incommunicado*.

His first guess was either that Terajima was acting on his own initiative – it fitted the profile Yeo Heng had given him – or that a major international criminal syndicate had employed his services. There was also the little matter of the favour he'd done for Victor Michaelson. *I must get hold of Victor.* Perhaps he should have asked Victor more about Mei Lim and the man Rosslyn. *I could, I should, have made sure Rosslyn and Mei never got within spitting distance of the* Orient Angel. *But then I didn't know what they were about to walk into.* He felt sick inside.

'Yeo, I think we'd better postpone tennis and lunch,' Simpson said. 'I do apologise, old boy.'

'Me too,' said Heng.

'Oh dearie me,' said Simpson, calling the waiter to settle the bill. 'It seems I'll have a long day at the office instead.'

'One last matter,' said Heng. 'An important matter you may be able to help me with.' He passed the second folder across the table. 'Aside from Terajima, could you identify the person in these photographs?'

'Let me take a look,' said Simpson.

If Heng read anything into Simpson's expression as the perspiring diplomat examined the several photographs in that second folder, he never said.

Once or twice in Simpson's career it had proved necessary to rely on that natural instinct for deception that distinguishes the exponents of his craft and sullen art. He was possessed of the skill of feigning and of disguising surprise. Simpson, of course, already knew something of what his prized informer had revealed. Shock and fear, though, are more physical in their impact. The involuntary response is difficult to disguise.

It is hard to say what expression Heng must have read in Simpson's bloodshot eyes when he saw the photographs of Mei Lim.

Yes. Certainly I know the identity of Terajima's companion. Heng is one step ahead of me. And he seems to know perfectly well who is gazing into Terajima's eyes with the unmistakable look of love.

Perhaps it was when Simpson shook his head that Heng's limpid eyes and subtle smile showed him that he also knew. He couldn't tell.

Simpson returned the photographs to the folder. 'Who is she?' he asked, disguising his fear with a smile. 'A tart?'

'Jon,' said Heng, 'are you *absolutely sure* you don't know who she is?'

'No idea,' Simpson said. 'Are you going to tell me?'

Heng was silent.

'Tell me more then,' Simpson asked. 'Is she one of your people, Yeo? Do you want me to discover her identity for you? Shouldn't be too difficult. One owes you more than a few favours, Yeo.'

'No,' Heng said. 'I want to know whether she was one of yours?'

'Not one of ours,' Simpson said truthfully.

She's Victor's.

'You see,' Heng said. 'She was the other passenger on board *Orient Angel*. As to her name –' Heng paused and reached across the table to retrieve the photographs. 'We're pretty sure,' he said, 'as sure as dammit, that her name's Mei Lim. Daughter of Winston Lim, the Hong Kong Police officer who lost his life in that typhoon.'

'Sorry, Yeo,' said Simpson. 'Never heard of her. Can't help you with that one.' He settled the bill in silence. 'Let me know what you find out,' he said, disguising his inner turmoil.

Heng looked at Simpson with that subtle smile. Only the flicker in Simpson's watery eyes revealed his awareness that Heng knew he was lying in his teeth.

'One favour before you go, Yeo,' Simpson said. 'Could you spare the photos? London will be terribly grateful.'

Heng removed the photographs from the file and handed them to Simpson. 'Please return them to me next time we meet.'

'Delighted.'

Heng got to his feet. Turning on his heel, he walked slowly to the restaurant exit without another word.

101

Alone in his office at the Consulate, Simpson tried and failed to reach Victor Michaelson in London.

The outside world was told that the disaster had been the result of a massive chemical explosion, and the police forces of several nations in South East Asia were launching major investigations.

STATEMENT OF WITNESS

[Criminal Justice Act 1967, s.9]

Statement of:	Alan Rosslyn
Age of Witness:	Over 21
Occupation:	Private Investigator
Address:	Basement Flat,
	195 Claverton Street,
	London SW1

This statement consisting of 5 pages signed by me is true to
the best of my knowledge and belief and I make it knowing that
if it is tendered in evidence, I shall be liable to prosecution
if I wilfully state anything which I know to be false.

Blurred lights penetrated the murky dawn of the
Malacca Strait.

Lights from other ships in the immediate vicinity
of the mass of floating debris. I expected them to
be searching for survivors. On the contrary, they
were keeping their distance from the immediate
area of the sinking. Maybe they feared that there
would be still more explosions. Some of them fired
flares. I thought I saw several search and rescue
planes and helicopters.

Searchlights probed the gloom. Each time I saw
one I told myself our chance of survival was high.
The truth was that Mei was fast losing strength.
The time passed with a terrible slowness. I told
myself that when daylight came, the number of air
sea rescue planes would increase.

I can't say how long we'd been in the sea when
the helicopter located us.

It was the same helicopter gunship. I reckoned
she must by now be low on fuel. But I hadn't
reckoned with the AZ-9W. Later I was told it was
an attack helicopter with a maximum range of about
seven hundred kilometres and a flight ceiling of
four and a half thousand feet. Perhaps it was
operating from a helicopter support ship. This one
was armed with two ugly 23mm cannons for aerial
dogfights against other helicopters. Painted in
combat camouflage, it had a roof-mounted optical
sight for search and tracking, which it had
presumably put to effective use.

Time and again the helicopter circled over us.
Then it lowered to about sixty feet and the rescue
swimmer made his jump into the swell.

I shouted to him to take Mei first. He swam
towards us and when he reached out for her I
thought I saw again the gold chains around his
wrist and realised that this was the man who'd
been looking for us aboard Orient Angel. I didn't
want to believe it. They'd come back for us. For
what reason? Surely not to save our lives? Or
had there been a change of mind? He dragged Mei
close towards him. I followed close behind.
Then he yelled at me in English. 'KEEP AWAY.
ONE AT A TIME.'

Now I realised for sure that instead of rescuing
her his intention was to kill her.

He was screaming at her in Chinese. Twice he
struggled and failed to detach the chains from his
wrist, and when he failed at the second attempt he
seemed to give up on the idea altogether. Instead
he suddenly seized her by the throat.

I twisted in the water and succeeded in driving
my knee as hard as I could manage into his crotch.

Floundering, he swallowed seawater and choked. I
tried to secure the safety harness to Mei. Mei's
assailant was still choking when I waved at the
man gesturing frantically in the open sliding
doors to begin the lift.

Instead of doing so the man aboard the
helicopter cut the rope. For several minutes the
helicopter, its sliding doors still open,
continued to hover overhead. Then I distinctly saw

the figure of the man standing in the exit. He was aiming a rifle at us.

Immediately I pulled Mei beneath the surface.

I manoeuvred myself on to my back and surfaced for a second. Mei and I gulped air. I heard more rifle shots and submerged again. How many metres I swam drawing Mei after me I cannot recall. I just went on repeating the business until finally, beyond exhaustion, I surfaced and saw to my overwhelming relief that the helicopter was heading off.

As to the other man, I saw him swimming away from us. He had adopted much the same tactic for avoiding the rifle fire as I had. He was a very powerful swimmer. And in what seemed to me to be some mirage, I thought I saw a second swimmer in the water, and heard him shouting something in what could have been Korean. Mei whispered in confirmation, 'He's Korean.'

To my astonishment I saw that the gunman aboard the helicopter was training his fire on the man swimming for his life. By now, however, the man was either out of range or the movement of the helicopter made it impossible for the gunman to hit his target.

And there we stayed. Mei and I. Floating. I willed any nearby vessel to see us.

The other man disappeared from sight.

Eventually morning came and the daylight revealed a vast pall of greyish smoke stretched high above the Strait. Mei was breathing with difficulty. I told her to relax as best she could. Rescue was surely not far off.

It was some time later when I saw the plane emerge from the pall of smoke. It was heading in our direction. Then it made a steep left turn and was lost from sight.

When it next reappeared, the plane was flying lower over the quadrants of the ocean, searching section by section. Again it repeated the manoeuvre and was almost directly overhead. This time a helicopter accompanied it.

I can remember very little of the actual rescue. The helicopter seemed to be military. I could see a figure in the opening of its doors. It was about sixty or seventy feet above us when the figure was lowered down towards me.

The man asked me a question in Chinese. I told him I didn't understand what he was saying.

Then, in English, he asked me if we were okay. I told him Mei was badly injured and that I was totally exhausted. He put a sling around Mei and said he'd take her up to the helicopter with him.

Then he returned for me and repeated the same procedure.

The paramedics aboard the helicopter must have reckoned my chances of survival were fine. They confirmed what I already knew. I was suffering from severe exhaustion. Before one of them gave me an injection someone asked me my name and Mei's.

The next thing I knew we were making a very sudden landing and we were being transferred to separate ambulances.

Heavily sedated, I was just aware that I had been provided with an armed guard.

I couldn't tell whether it was day or night when we reached the final destination.

According to the doctor who examined me, I had sustained injuries that were more serious than had first been diagnosed. I heard the doctor say that trauma and the regime of drugs prescribed to ease my pain would mean my interrogation would have to be postponed. I very clearly remember that he said 'interrogation'.

I thought of Mei. Was she still alive? Where was she?

For the time being I was told nothing. God knows what they had injected into my bloodstream.

During intervals of consciousness, I noticed the nurses were armed with handguns in shoulder holsters and that during what must have been daytime the light from the tiny windows in the ceiling were suffused with green.

Where was I? Surely the man Simpson would raise the alarm? Or had I been given up for dead? And where was Mei?

Had the other man in the water been Terajima? If

so, why had the gunman been intent on killing him
and who was on whose side? Perhaps they had
returned afterwards to finish off the job of his
disposal, leaving his corpse to float with the rest
of the flotsam and jetsam in the Malacca Strait?

Signed: *Alan Rooslyn*

Signature witnessed by: Chief Superintendent Ronald Costley

Signed: *Ron Costley*

Signature witnessed by: WPC Michelle Seifert

Signed: *Michelle Seifert*

103

No news of Rosslyn. None of Mei. Simpson desperately wanted to learn the details of their fate.

He had begun to suspect, in a way that was hard for him to define, that day by day he was being marginalised. London told him that there were unspecified problems with the police in Hong Kong and in Kuala Lumpur. The scenario of enquiry was continually being changed. Not by him. By London. And Victor Michaelson had gone to ground.

In London there were signs of other intensifying conflicts of interest.

Along with his wife, the Prime Minister was being accused of accepting the Zhentungs' hospitality, and there was the thorny question of the Prince of Wales connection and the rumours about the offer of the peerage that had apparently been made to Anthony Zhentung. The Deputy Prime Minister had issued what amounted to a denial of his friendship with the Zhentung brothers.

Simpson wanted facts and failed to get them. He tried to contact Yeo Heng, only to be told that Heng was on indefinite leave in Tokyo.

Finally, London signalled an instruction that he should prepare a file for the South East Asia desk on the general background of *Orient Angel*. They gave him the name of Maureen Cheng, senior executive of Svenske-Britannia in Kuala Lumpur, who might prove helpful. He should go to see her in Kuala Lumpur.

Take Soundings.

Get the Feel of Things.

Best Keep Things in the Family.

Keep Things Ticking Over.

It was as vague as that, and Simpson was uneasy.

Filing information on merchant shipping and sea disasters was Simpson's usual business, but he agreed to fly to Kuala Lumpur to see Cheng. He wondered whether London or even Victor Michaelson might have already picked her brains about developments. There was the outside chance that she might tell him something of Rosslyn or Mei.

He even considered having a word with Dr Graer or Swann. Best Keep Things in the Family, though; and he thought better of involving either the Australian he had never liked or the American he considered too clever by half.

104

Before leaving for Kuala Lumpur he spent several hours writing a report in longhand on his recent encounter with Yeo Heng at The Shang. He described the meeting with Rosslyn and the subsequent encounter with Mei Lim in the Lake Gardens in Kuala Lumpur and included the details of the favour he had done for Victor Michaelson. He made a copy of his report with copies of the photographs and lodged them in the Consular and Visa Section office safe. He sealed the original in a slim envelope watermarked:

MAYFAIR WHITE

SMYTHSON

OF BOND STREET

That would put paid to his being marginalised. Furthermore, just in case of any awkwardness down the line, it would ensure that he received no black mark in his annual report from Personnel that might result in any reduction of the pension of two-thirds of his salary that he would receive on his retirement. He could ill afford the cut. He was relying on SOAF – Save Own Arse First – an art he had long since mastered, and he was determined that the skills he showed in his report on his involvement with Michaelson and his friends would have maximum effect.

105

Victor Michaelson had not so much gone to ground as taken to the air. He felt himself under considerable duress.

His flight paths had taken him from London to Stockholm, where with Anthony Zhentung's lawyers he had prepared the ground for secret negotiations about the future of Anthony Zhentung's massive financial holdings – a future in which he had good reason to believe he might have a substantial share. No sooner had the first round of discussions opened than Foster and Hastings Zhentung had reached the lawyers' offices. Asking Anthony Zhentung's Swedish lawyer, Ulf Jensen, to leave the room, the brothers told Michaelson that any discussion of the disposal of their brother's fortunes was to be postponed. They maintained they could offer Michaelson no reason to be particularly hopeful he might be a beneficiary.

'Anthony gave me his word,' Michaelson protested.

'His word was worth very little in his lifetime,' said Foster Zhentung. 'In death it's worth nothing.'

'I would like to see the papers.'

'Not possible,' said Hastings Zhentung.

By way of retaliation, Michaelson said coldly, 'I need to remind you of one or two things. I did exactly as you asked. Acting as Leech I received the call from your hired gun. I gave you the message. "The treatment has been successful." Don't for one minute think that I'm unaware of what that implied.'

'Are you making at attempt at extortion?' said Foster Zhentung.

'Oh, I wouldn't go so far as to say that. But it was suggested, was it not, that an arrangement be put in place for Mr Rosslyn and Miss Mei to be aboard *Orient Angel*. I successfully called in some old favours on your behalf. It was a potentially dangerous risk. Nonetheless, I did what I was asked. Now one has to draw one's own conclusions. Miss Lim most obviously represents some threat to you. You have to bear in mind I am not, how shall I put it, unaware of the nature of your dealings in South East Asia and China. One can only assume – I repeat, assume – that the threat Miss Lim may pose has more than a little to do with her connections to those engaged in the pursuit of maritime terrorism. Perhaps you would disabuse me?'

'What is it you want from us?' said Foster Zhentung.

'Only my entitlement.'

There was more than a flicker of anger in the eyes of both the brothers. Perhaps Michaelson interpreted the flickers as a response to the fear he hoped to instil in them. What he wanted was not only the great deal of money he had been promised by Anthony Zhentung for services rendered, but also a sense of complete certainty that no one would suspect he had dirty hands.

'I do, of course, exert some influence in the secret world,' he said. 'One only needs to lift the telephone.'

'You're attempting to blackmail us?' said Foster Zhentung.

Michaelson ignored the barb. 'On the contrary, I am attempting to protect you both. Suppose those who initiated the sinking of *Orient Angel* were traced by any of the authorities in one or more of the states bordering the Malacca Strait? Well, I scarcely like to imagine the consequences.'

'Suppose', said Foster Zhentung, 'we were to enlist your services more formally to protect our interests against any such accusation. Shall we say as a protector of our reputations? What would feel about it?'

'I would be delighted to help,' said Michaelson. 'If, on your part, you would be good enough to reconsider the matter of my entitlement.'

Foster Zhentung looked at his brother, who raised his hands in a gesture of what seemed to be both resignation and agreement.

'Very well,' said Foster Zhentung. 'In the first place, we would be grateful if you would agree to open some negotiations with a contact in Hong Kong. Might that be acceptable to you?'

'Certainly,' said Michaelson, without realising that he had signed his own death warrant.

106

Simpson proposed to Maureen Cheng that they meet in the Port Klang offices of Svenske-Britannia. She was a small and businesslike woman and Simpson wasn't quite sure but thought they might have met before. His memory was no longer what it had been, and he was very tired. So was Maureen Cheng, who had been weeping.

Cheng accepted his condolences for the loss of her colleagues and then tearfully described the background to *Orient Angel's* legitimate business.

The master and first officer were utterly trustworthy and experienced. Their deaths were a shocking and terrible tragedy.

She confirmed the nature of the cargo. The iron, industrial equipment, electrical household goods and chemicals, including the vast quantity of acetylene. She said six hundred or so containers had been packed into the lower decks. Any containers of inflammable or explosive cargo would have been on deck.

There would be the enormous losses to be met by the insurers. The damage to the families of those who had perished. There was also the matter of the inevitable inquiry into the loss being faced. It was anyone's guess how long the inquiry might take. It would almost certainly result in still more massive insurance settlements. Perhaps legal proceedings would be begun. Maureen Cheng looked utterly exhausted and downcast.

'Do you know how it happened?' Simpson asked her.

'It's too early to say,' she said with a look of pain. 'We will naturally co-operate with all those whose services will be enlisted to find out.' It looked unlikely, whatever she knew, that she'd allow herself to be drawn on this particular subject. She spoke as if she had committed her remarks to memory. From some statement prearranged by company lawyers, Simpson reckoned.

'Tell me about the lead-up to the disaster,' Simpson asked.

'Nothing unusual about the voyage until the Malacca Strait?'

'Only that she would not be making her Japan calls,' Cheng said. She opened a folder on the desk and described the ship's passage.

'The reason for the change of plan,' asked Simpson, 'what was it exactly?'

'A stop for modifications to be made to her main engine.'

'Could that have been the cause of the disaster?'

'No,' Cheng answered shortly.

'In the meantime,' asked Simpson, 'what happened?'

'In the meantime,' she said, 'her master and crew stayed two weeks here in KL.'

'And then at some point', Simpson said, 'she took on board two passengers. One was British, a Mr Alan Rosslyn, and Mei Lim, a young Chinese woman.'

'Yes. Mr Rosslyn had been asked to research the security of shipping in South East Asia. He arrived here accompanied by Mei Lim.'

'When exactly was that?' Simpson asked.

'During *Orient Angel*'s second week in dock.'

'Do you know why they boarded the ship?'

'We were informed that Mr Rosslyn was to inspect the security of the ship.'

'What precisely was Miss Lim's task?'

'She was his companion. They seemed fond. Actually, very fond. I thought they were lovers. They made a very attractive couple. I imagine she was going to act as Mr Rosslyn's interpreter. The crew were variously Chinese, Malay, Korean or Indonesian and spoke little English. We told the master to allow them a free run of his ship and he agreed – rather reluctantly, but he agreed.'

'Did you meet Mr Rosslyn and Miss Lim?'

'Yes, of course I did,' she said. 'I told you. I introduced them to the master and first officer, Lars Kjellner. I accompanied them to the ship, to the bridge and wished them *bon voyage*. That, sadly, was the last I saw of them.'

Simpson heard the evasion in her voice, the phrases chosen with too much deliberation. That's how he'd have played the interview. Careful to show that she had all the time in the world. With nothing to hide.

He wanted to discover whether the conversation was being taped. Taking a packet of aspirin from his coat pocket, he said, 'Forgive me,

I have a headache. Could you possibly get me a glass of water to take with a couple of aspirins?'

'Allow me,' Cheng said.

'You're too kind,' said Simpson. 'Most grateful.'

107

Once she was out of the room he moved fast to the other side of the desk. He riffled fast through the drawers and her handbag, and went through the few letters in the in-tray on her desk.
As he felt beneath the desktop for the telltale signs of a surveillance device, he found the open envelope addressed to Alan Rosslyn that had been forwarded to the Svenske-Britannia office. The letter it contained read:

> Attention Alan Rosslyn
> Unable to reach you at your hotel
> Do not, repeat NOT, board Orient Angel
> Call us
> Steve Kwok, George Tseng.

He returned the letter to its envelope. His fingers felt cold. At least he had found no sign of a hidden tape recorder. He doubted that Cheng herself was wired. The fabric of her dress was too thin to disguise the required technology of surveillance. In any case, what did she or her employers stand to gain from a recording of the interview? He doubted Svenske-Britannia would go in for such surveillance procedures. Still, you couldn't be sure, and Simpson wasn't about to have any of his next questions placed on record.

It was for this reason that when Cheng returned and Simpson had swallowed his aspirin, he suggested that they take a walk to where *Orient Angel* had last been berthed. The fresh air, even Port Klang's version of fresh air, would offer some relief.

Maureen Cheng apologised for her display of emotion. Simpson told her he quite understood and she readily agreed to his request.

108

Victor Michaelson took the first available flight from Heathrow to Hong Kong. Continuity was his watchword and – no change here – he was still acting for the Zhentungs. The office of Foster and Hastings Zhentung had arranged for him to be chauffeured from the airport to the Mandarin Oriental on Connaught Road where, as befits a lawyer of his distinction, he would be staying at their considerable expense.

He went straight to the Mandarin Suite, which had been reserved for him. He had only been there an hour when, following the instructions issued by the Zhentungs, he left the warning to Terajima.

Terajima called back from Kuala Lumpur and asked for Leech. The last time he had called, he'd said, 'The treatment has been successful.' In most respects, it was true. Now he went through the rigmarole of clandestine identification once more.

'How are you?'

'Bitten by leeches.'

'Where?'

'In the rainforest.'

'No, I mean where on your body?'

'Both legs.'

'Did you treat them?'

'I used salt and a lighted cigarette.'

'Very good,' said Michaelson. 'Where are you?'

'It doesn't matter.'

'Very well,' said Michaelson, 'I have to tell you it's imperative we meet as soon as possible.'

'Where?' said Terajima.

'Hong Kong.'

'Where?'

'The Mandarin Oriental. I'll meet you here.'

'No, you won't. You'll meet me tomorrow night at the Chungking Mansions on Nathan Road. I will leave the exact details of the RV point with reception at the Mandarin Oriental.'

'You do realise', said Michaelson, 'that the net's tightening? You should be extremely cautious. Things are none too healthy. Two friends have gone to ground.'

'Who are you talking about?'

'Marcel. Your boat supplier. And our American friend who saw you in Batu Pahat. People are on the lookout for you.'

'Like who?'

'One man in particular.' He gave Terajima details of Jon Simpson. 'He knows the score. The view in London is that you should remove him before KL's Svenske-Britannia executive talks to Simpson. The executive is a woman called Maureen Cheng. We can't risk them comparing notes. My instructions are that the damage must be limited.'

'I can be in Hong Kong tonight. I'll tell you where to wait for me.'

109

You could say that if Simpson had kept his eyes about him he might have noticed the hire car parked to one side of the exit from the Port Klang Svenske-Britannia compound. The car was a Fiat Punto and the driver Terajima.

Wearing a new tracksuit, trainers and dark glasses, Terajima was staring into the rear view mirror. The reflection in the mirror showed Simpson and Maureen approaching. To say the least, it proved unfortunate for Simpson that he was concentrating quite so intently upon his questioning of the emotional Maureen Cheng.

Terajima was poised to execute instructions.

Once out of the car, he withdrew the nail file from his tracksuit pocket and jogged towards them, then overtook them. 'University of Malaya' said the legend across the back of the tracksuit top. A crimson linen towel was tucked into the collar of it. With the nail file up his sleeve and with the look of someone who has forgotten something, he turned round and ran the short way back to them.

'Good morning,' Terajima said courteously. 'How are you?' He didn't wait for an answer.

Sun glinted on the nail file blade. Pointing its tip straight into Maureen Cheng's eyes, Terajima whispered, 'Watches, rings and cash.' Cheng's mouth fell open. 'Yours too,' Terajima told Simpson. '*Move it*.'

'Wait a minute,' said Simpson, with commendable *sang froid*. 'Don't I know you? What do you want my bloody wristwatch for?'

'You know Rosslyn?'

'Alan Rosslyn. Good man. Of course I do. Are you a friend of his as well?'

'And Mei Lim – *Mei Lim*?'

'Of course. Rosslyn's girl.'

'What did you say?'

'I said I know Mei and Alan,' said Simpson. 'Let's talk. Why don't we?'

Terajima turned to Cheng. 'And you – you know them too?'

'Yes,' said Maureen Cheng. Her lips were quivering.

'You allowed them to board *Orient Angel*?'

'Yes, I did.'

'Why don't we talk this over in Ms Cheng's office?' Simpson suggested.

Terajima stepped forward, at the same moment drawing the nail file's scalpel tip down the length of the right side of Cheng's face. Blood poured from the slash in a widening stream across her clothes.

'*Stop*,' screamed Simpson.

'*Wristwatch*,' Terajima snapped back. He waited a few seconds as Simpson removed his watch with shaking hands. 'Place it here,' said Terajima. 'Here. By my feet.'

Struggling to keep his balance, Simpson followed the instruction. 'It's an imitation,' he insisted. 'Worthless. You're welcome to it.'

As Simpson stooped, his hand a short distance from the surface of the road and Terajima's trainers, the nail file described a twisting arc. Snaking upwards, then sideways, it opened a second deep gash in Maureen Cheng's throat, centimetres below the larynx. As she collapsed, Terajima withdrew the blade with a jerk and directed it, shoulder high, at Simpson.

Terajima put his weight behind the cut into Simpson's neck. It penetrated a quarter of an inch deep into the neck just beneath Simpson's left ear and then continued downwards still deeper, severing arteries. Gurgling in his throat, Simpson toppled forward to the ground. The spurts of blood narrowly missed soaking Terajima's trainers.

Hands stained with blood, Terajima searched Simpson's pockets and removed the contents. Without hurrying, careful to avoid treading in the pools of blood spreading from the convulsing corpses, he returned to his hire car.

Once inside the car he opened the envelope he had taken from Simpson's pocket and first read the note:

Attention Alan Rosslyn
Unable to reach you at your hotel
Do not , repeat NOT, board Orient Angel
Call us
Steve Kwok , George Tsang .

Next, he turned his attention to the other envelope, which contained
Simpson's handwritten report and photographs.

He found himself staring at the images. Of himself with Mei Lim.

110

He drank deeply from a plastic bottle of mineral water. Time dragged by and produced a sort of paralysis of the mind.

For the first time in years, perhaps for the first time since childhood, he felt an unfamiliar spasm of fear. Mother had said he was like some child containing a whirlwind ready to break free. They were about the only words he could remember her saying that had been accompanied by a smile. She had always been inordinately proud of his displays of energy and willpower.

Stretching his arms ahead of him above the steering wheel, he felt the blood-red tips of his fingernails touch the windscreen. He dragged them downwards so that they made a screeching noise like metal against glass. It was the trick he'd used to good effect before, the trick that made listeners beg him to desist. The noise had never affected him like it affected others; similarly, he could bite on silver foil and the enamel of his teeth never caused him the pain it seemed to induce in other people. But now he was feeling some sort of new pain he found it hard to define. Pain that his reading of Simpson's account of things had caused him. *Speak to me, Mother.*

MOTHER:	Who taught naked Mei how to make love?
KLAAS-PIETER:	I did.
MOTHER:	Who showed naked Mei how to work her legs behind her neck?
KLAAS-PIETER:	I did.
MOTHER:	Who showed naked Mei the erotic contortions drawn by the master Shuncho and Utamaro?
KLAAS-PIETER:	I did. I did. I did. She's mine, she's mine.

Know your enemy; know yourself and you can fight one hundred battles without disaster. The words of Sun Tzu. He had lost count of the battles he had fought without disaster. Sun Tzu mentioned one hundred. *Was the next to be number one hundred and one?* He could find no answer.

He gazed ahead at the tower cranes silhouetted against the bright sky, which seemed to be moving slowly, almost as slowly as the minute hand of a clock. Another voice told him to continue calculating to achieve solutions. Solutions that would result in the death of his unfaithful Mei and her new-found lover.

He was breathing in fits and starts, almost to the point of hyperventilation. He jerked the rear view mirror at an angle so that he could assess the reactions in his face, and he hated what he saw. The veins on his forehead were bulging. He began to shake. *What the hell is happening to me?* Tears streamed down his cheeks. Again and again he saw Mei's wet lips, her shining teeth, her playful tongue and heard her whispering:

Come now. Come now. Inside me.

White foam dribbled from the corners of his lips. Opening a second bottle of mineral water, he looked through the car window and saw the stray dog that was sniffing at the corpses. The animal's tongue dangled from its reddened mouth. It flicked its ears and tail into the gathering clouds of excited flies.

I have been betrayed. The voice in his head was shaking. *Attack where they are not prepared, go to where they do not expect. Shoot heroin into Mei's veins.* He wanted to watch her drift into some nirvana of mindless pleasure and beg him to make love to her again and never stop.

Then he saw that two men in shirtsleeves were approaching the corpses lying in the road. The men were walking with strange and halting gaits. He could see that they were both wanting yet not wanting to stare the horror in its face.

Suddenly one of them pointed at his car. The other was fiddling with the mobile telephone.

I'm losing control of this.

Slouching in the car seat, sliding slightly and twisting, he tore off the tracksuit. Top and bottom. *Faster, faster.* He kicked off his trainers. *Easy, easy now.* He straightened out the lightweight trousers he was wearing underneath. *Stop shaking.* He made a hurried job of wiping the blood from his hands with the crimson towel.

He pulled on the matching jacket and, at the same time, slipped his stockinged feet into a pair of lightweight boots with elasticised sides. Even his feet felt cold and numb. Shoving the jogging gear into a brown paper shopping bag, he stuffed it beneath the passenger seat.

Then slowly he got out of the car, rubbed his eyes, stretched his arms above his head and yawned. He held the yawn at the point when his mouth was stretched open widest and then stared at the two men jittering around the bodies.

He walked towards them with the air of someone in control of events.

'What's happened?' he asked them in the local dialect.

'Don't look,' said the taller of the two men. His hands flayed around at the demented flies. The other man was making a noise like the whimper of a wounded animal.

'Call the police,' Terajima said. 'Use your phone. Call them now.'

'The battery's dead.' He kicked out at the stray dog and missed. 'The blood.'

'Then wait here. I'll get help. Don't move until the police come.'

The two men seemed relieved to be spoken to with such confidence and authority.

'Did you see who did this?' Terajima asked them.

'No.' The man fumbled with a pack of cigarettes. 'Did you?'

'No. I've been on night shift. Must have been asleep. Hey – don't smoke here, man. It's against Port Klang Multi Terminal regulations. This is so terrible.'

'You couldn't have seen it anyway,' the man said.

'Glad I didn't. What sort of person could do this?'

'Only an animal.'

Terajima looked at his car. With relief he saw that it was at an angle to the line of cars so that neither of the men could read the registration plate. He'd have to drive away very carefully, so very carefully, and cursed himself for not having left the area sooner. *Easy. Easy. There's plenty of time. No other cars moving in the area. Not yet. No faces at the office windows. Should've checked. Should've checked.*

'Stay cool,' said Terajima. 'So don't move from here until I call the cops. I'll be back in five minutes.'

He returned to the Fiat Punto. Sweat was pouring down his face.

He reversed out of the parking space, eyes ahead, eyes on the rear view mirror. The two men were stooping over the corpses. By now both had lit cigarettes.

Let the bastards blow the place to kingdom come.

Beyond the main exit to the docks he headed in the direction of Kuala Lumpur International Airport at Sepang.

111

On the freeway heading for Sepang he felt better. Always good to feel the rush of air from the open window.

Hold tight. I can do anything I want. I can give life. I can take it away. I am flying. Read their minds. Rosslyn and Mei.

> *Klaas-Pieter keeps his ancient places;*
> *Turn but a stone, and start a wing!*
> *'Tis ye, 'tis your estranged faces,*
> *That miss the many splendoured thing.*

Victory can be achieved. I know my enemy's plans. I know their strengths and weaknesses better than they do themselves. They do not know mine, do they? Speak to me. They don't. Now this Rosslyn and Mei. Together. Lovers? Does he know the terra incognita of her? The Many Splendoured Thing. Has he added to its wetness with his fluids? Provoke him to know his patterns of movement. Provoke him. Determine his position. I know the ground of death and of life. Probe him; probe him to know where he is strong and where he is weak. Probe him. Probe her.

> *Probe me with your love*
> *Kiss me your snake tounge*
> *Probe me with your love*
> *I don't care how long you take*

My ultimate skill is to take up a position where I am formless. If I am form-less, the most penetrating spies will not find me. The wisest counsels will not be able to do calculations against me. Kill Rosslyn. Kill Mei. Kill. Yea, in the night, my Soul, my Mei, cry, clinging Heaven by the hems. And lo, Klaas-Pieter walking on the water. Not of Gennesareth, but Thames.

He drove with a sense of relief so intense it acted on his mind like the snuff he craved. *Must get to Hong Kong. List. Must list things. Stalk Site*

Stop Shock Smother Secure Search Snatch Scram Bait the trap Set it Spring it Kill Rosslyn Kill Mei. Go through your plans in the temple and bring about the execution of those plans. Sun Tzu.

112

On board the flight to Hong Kong, two newspaper articles caught his eye:

South China Morning Post

DRAMATIC RESCUE IN MALACCA STRAIT
GFS HELICOPTER LIFTS 2 FROM SEA

Hong Kong Government Flying Service
helicopter rescued two persons from Malacca Straits
yesterday. Police Headquarters have withheld names
of a man thought to be in his early 30s and a Chinese
woman in her 20s. Police sources believe they were
survivors from super container ship *Orient Angel*.

Hongkong Daily

TWO SURVIVE ORIENT ANGEL SINKING

GFS rescue helicopter crew brought two persons
believed to be survivors from *Orient Angel* disaster to
Hong Kong yesterday. Police headquarters are withhold-
ing the identity of the survivors. One is thought to be a
British national, the other Chinese.

On arrival at Hong Kong airport, Terajima put through a call to London.

He had been thinking far ahead. The fail-safe if he was ever apprehended. Or faced trial. Or imprisonment. Beijing would cause him no
trouble. It would be the British who would be his most formidable
enemies. He needed contacts. Escape routes. A fellow hit man. When
the man's voice answered in Mandarin, the Pastor said, 'Snake.'

The other man said, 'Skin.'

'*Ni hao?*' ('How are you?')

'*Wo hen hao.*' ('I'm fine.)

'I have a red alert contingency.'

'Tell me what you need.'

'Stand-by motorcycles and London assistance. Safe telephone numbers.'

'For when?'

'On indefinite stand-by if and when I call you. Guarantee you will remain in the London area.'

'You have it, Pastor.'

'Your payment will be made in full.'

'*Xiexie.*' ('Thank you.')

'*Bukeqi.*' ('You're welcome.')

'We will need two Suzuki Freewind 650s,' Terajima said.

'Two Suzuki Freewind 650s,' the voice from London repeated.

'You will shadow me if I get to London.'

'How will I know when you've arrived?'

'If and when I do, you will read it in the papers. There will be mention of the Zhentungs. I hope it won't come to that. But if it does, if I am detained or even put on trial, you should be on twenty-four seven stand-by. The British will never dare convict me.'

'This is serious red?'

'Serious red.'

'I hope it won't come to this.'

'So do I. But we will not be unprepared.'

'I understand.'

'Just shadow me, right? Prisons. Police stations. Courts. Even the Old Bailey.'

'Serious.'

'Serious.'

'You have it.'

'*Xiexie.*' ('Thank you.')

'*Bukeqi.*' ('You're welcome.')

I have a rendezvous with destiny. I have destiny in my sights. I am many moves ahead of the British.

Terajima relished the rush of confidence he felt.

113

STATEMENT OF WITNESS

[Criminal Justice Act 1967, s.9]

Statement of: Alan Rosslyn
Age of Witness: over 21
Occupation: Private Investigator
Address: Basement Flat, 195 Claverton Street,
                    London SW1

This statement consisting of 1 page signed by me is true to the best of my knowledge and belief and I make it knowing that if it is tendered in evidence, I shall be liable to prosecution if I wilfully state anything which I know to be false.

It was more than forty-eight hours later when the plainclothes officer from B Branch of the Hong Kong Police told me I was being kept in solitary confinement in the interests of my personal safety.
   That's why I was being held in the compound being built opposite the Crime Wing at police headquarters. B Branch's VIP Protection Unit was now responsible for my security. Meetings were apparently taking place to discuss my future. I demanded to see a senior officer and was told it wasn't possible.
   I asked him how many other people had survived the sinking of <u>Orient Angel</u>.
   He told me he had no idea.

Signed: *Alan Rosslyn*

Signature witnessed by: Chief Superintendent Ronald Costley

Signed: *Ron Costley*

Signature witnessed by: WPC Michelle Seifert

Signed: *Michelle Seifert*

114

Go through your plans in the temple and bring about the execution of those plans. SUN TZU

The Commissioner closed the door to his office. 'I expect you know what this is about?' he said.

Steve Kwok manoeuvred his wheelchair so that it faced the Commissioner's desk.

He's going to issue me with a formal reprimand and warning for having kept my part in the investigation of Winston's murder to myself. It's a hell of a time to lay on the discipline. But he's done it before. I've seen him do it and it isn't nice. What the hell do I say to him?

He wrestled with the various kinds of apology he might make.

The Commissioner's eyes seemed even more hooded than usual. 'Let's not rehearse the past, Steve.'

'In all honesty, sir, I have to say that I've no regrets for pursuing Winston's killer in the way I have done. I admit that I should've followed the formal procedures.'

'Then why didn't you?'

Kwok shrugged. 'Because, regrettably, I've lost faith and trust in one or two of those involved.'

'I suspected as much,' the Commissioner said. 'It seems that Winston's paranoia remains infectious. But let me deal with your peers. They're still my responsibility. I want you to do what some of us around here used to call the decent thing.'

The decent thing? He's asking for my resignation.

'I've already told you that I'm going to retire.'

'I know.' The Commissioner lifted a file on to his table so Steve could see the wording on its cover: TOP SECRET.

'We have to establish order in the chaos. When I say "we" I mean you and me. I have Beijing on my back. Day by day control is slipping out of my hands. We have to act faster than our grey friends in the party can button up their nasty little suits. If we don't, then everything we stand for will collapse. Never forget that when we lost Winston we lost one of our finest officers. I don't have to explain that to you of all people, Steve. He was your greatest friend, wasn't he? I'm never going to be party to the abortion of the investigation into Winston's murder.'

'Tell me what it is you want of me,' Kwok said.

The Commissioner was toying with the TOP SECRET file. 'I won't take no for an answer, Steve. Don't even think of saying no. I want you to act as my second-in-command with this – to be my second pair of ears and eyes. That's what I want of you. I need someone I can completely trust.'

'Sir, look at me,' said Kwok. 'You have to believe me. I'm not up to it any longer.'

'What makes you think so?'

'Ask Catherine.'

'I already have.'

'You've spoken to her?'

'Sure. And she said – open quotes – *Yes, Steve's up to it* – close quotes.'

'What happens if I don't accept?'

'That's up to you. I suppose you'll go to New Zealand and those sheep you're going to breed. Except, Steve, I know you well enough to say you're one of the bravest officers I've ever worked with. Please don't disappoint me now.'

'I'll do my best. I'm very grateful.'

'I don't want gratitude. I want results. I want your total confidentiality. I want it now because we have senior colleagues to meet with in the conference room in thirty minutes. We're expecting two visitors to join us, senior criminal investigations officers from KL. And I want to talk to you about Alan Rosslyn and Mei Lim.'

'You know what happened to them?'

'Let me tell you.'

115

Rosslyn was woken by the man in the dark blue suit who showed himself into the cell and introduced himself as Li Juyi.

'I'm in charge of the Security Wing Operations Bureau,' Li Juyi said. He had a pronounced squint and had to raise his voice against the noise of the building work being carried out elsewhere in the compound. 'We handle security matters, VIP protection, counter-terrorism and security co-ordination.' He sat on the only chair at the bare table. 'I must apologise for the lack of comfort. It's cold in here. Something must be done about it. Even by Hong Kong police standards it's bad. But the renovations are taking far longer than we expected.' He spoke fluently with only the slightest traces of a Chinese accent.

'I regret you haven't been kept informed about the events of the past few days.' He looked around the cell, up at the small windows of green glass in the ceiling, at the rough brick walls. Outside, the noise of the builders' pneumatic drills started up once more.

'You from Beijing?' said Rosslyn.

Li Juyi blinked. 'You'll appreciate that, in the circumstances, there's been a great deal of diplomatic coming and going. How do you feel in yourself?'

'How do you imagine?'

'What can we do to make things more pleasant?'

'I could do with a shower and a proper meal.'

'It can be arranged without difficulty. Things are changing very fast.'

'Good,' said Rosslyn. 'Then I demand my right to speak to a lawyer and a senior officer from the British embassy. And I demand to be let out of this bloody place.'

'All in good time, Mr Rosslyn.'

'You realise I'm being kept here against my will?'

'Perhaps,' said Li Juyi vaguely, as if he were talking to himself. He got up from the chair and called out to one of the guards. 'Bring the English breakfast with coffee.' He turned to Rosslyn. 'Or tea perhaps?'

'Coffee will do.'

'Is there anything else you require to know?'

'Where's Mei Lim?'

'Here in Hong Kong.'

'Is she okay?'

'Yes.'

Rosslyn sank back on the bed, his head against the rubber pillow. He closed his eyes. 'Then tell me exactly where she is.'

'She's in good hands.'

'For God's sake, in *whose* hands?'

'Good hands. I'm dealing with her case. She asked after you with some tenderness. I explained to her that you're recovering from your injuries. So, incidentally, is she.'

'*Where is she?*'

Li Juyi squinted and stayed silent.

'When do I get out of here?' Rosslyn demanded.

'That depends on orders from Beijing.'

A guard whose face was new to Rosslyn brought the tray with the English breakfast. 'A cup for me too, if you wouldn't mind,' said Li Juyi. 'And another jug of coffee.'

Li Juyi watched Rosslyn devour the breakfast. 'Afterwards I will see you are taken to the shower. You have, I think, a long day ahead of you.'

'What the hell are you talking about?'

'You face serious charges from the People's Republic prosecutors.'

'Charges?'

'The former assistant defence attaché from the Chinese embassy in London has confessed to providing you with a false passport in the name of Li Kim. You of course know Zhu Jianxing. Zhu has given your name to his interrogators. He has also confessed to giving you a People's Republic diplomatic visa with your photograph in it. In addition, he gave you a large quantity of US and Hong Kong dollars and Chinese currency. It was most unwise of you, Mr Rosslyn, to have accepted it. Our security officers will present you with the details of the charges against you in their own good time.'

Rosslyn shrugged. 'You take sugar, Mr Li Juyi?'

'Three teaspoonfuls,' said Li Juyi. 'Your offence is punishable by death.'

'Thanks for telling me.'

'Meanwhile, your only contact will be with me. If you wish to explain things to me, you only have to ask the guards to let me know. You must get used to being here.'

'For how much longer?'

'How long is a bit of string?'

The guard was standing in the doorway. He was holding a towel and what looked like a safety razor and a bar of soap.

'You're welcome to take a shower,' said Li Juyi. 'We can talk again later.'

116

STATEMENT OF WITNESS

[Criminal Justice Act 1967, s.9]

Statement of:	Mei Lim
Age of Witness:	over 21
Occupation:	Nil
Address:	Apartment 2, Orchid House, Chung Hom Kok, Hong Kong, People's Republic of China

This statement consisting of 4 pages signed by me is true to
the best of my knowledge and belief and I make it knowing that
if it is tendered in evidence, I shall be liable to prosecution
if I wilfully state anything which I know to be false.

I always believed that it was impossible for
anyone to hide from Klaas-Pieter for long.
You know that phrase of Shakespeare's we were
taught:

> Why, then the world's mine oyster,
> Which I with sword will open.

Those are favourite lines of Klaas-Pieter's.
   If anything surprised me it was that I had
stayed free from him for quite so long. In the
end, he always got his way.
   So it came as no shock to me when the helicopter
tried to rescue me, that there he was, having
presumably masterminded the whole thing.
   I had come to accept my fate. My father's
enemies were mine and had been for far too long.
There had been no escape for my father from
Klaas-Pieter. Now there seemed no escape for me.

If the end came, well, I suppose that I hoped it would come soon.

I believed that the authorities in Beijing who controlled Klaas-Pieter must have done some deal with him. More than once in the past I heard HIM boast of what he called his 'arrangements and accommodations with Beijing'. His guanxi.

I thought that I had been put somewhere near the centre of it. What had he really intended to do with me?

It seemed to me that alive I was of no great use to him. Nor dead for that matter. What was it he now wanted from me? Not the same old obsessive love. He had already wounded Dad by taking me. Dad was dead. Perhaps Alan had taken on the role of most hated person.

The helicopter landed somewhere, presumably to refuel for the onward flight to Hong Kong. I remember being taken by ambulance to what I overheard someone saying was a secure unit. It was there that I was kept in behind locked doors. No one told me why I was being kept there. No one would tell me how long it might be before I was released.

I asked myself why the Englishman Simpson had arranged for me to meet up with Alan. I was so grateful to him at the time that I only asked how he had managed to find me. I recall that he said it had been a matter of asking a few of his old friends about me. Who they might have been I have no idea. He said something about acting on the instructions of some London lawyer. Someone who knew Alan's friends. I was to trust them. Alan would see I was okay. It never once occurred to me that by boarding the <u>Orient Angel</u> I had walked into a trap of Klaas-Pieter's making.

I really had no idea what they, whoever 'they' might be, had in mind for me.

The endless silence in the secure unit was oppressive. My only contact was with the women guards, who must have been under orders not to talk to me about anything. I heard them talking amongst themselves about 'the prisoner'. That was me.

I prayed that Klaas-Pieter had drowned out there

in the Malacca Strait. I was sort of full of
dread. I dreaded the return of Klaas-Pieter, who
might turn up again to kill me. I dreaded that
Alan might be told the truth of my relationship
with him.

Then one morning I received a visit from a man
called Li Juyi, who said he was from the Security
Wing Operations Bureau of the Hong Kong Police. Li
Juyi said that he had known my father. He didn't
need to explain it. I remembered that Dad had said
he was untrustworthy. Nowadays some party stooge.
He said he had very painful news. The authorities
would soon be prosecuting me for crimes against
the party. Li Juyi was under orders to obtain a
full statement from me about corruption in the
Hong Kong Police force and illegal dealings with a
British citizen, Alan Rosslyn. I might have
guessed something like this would happen. Anyhow,
it came as no great surprise.

How long all of this took, I cannot say. Now I
realise that these events were all taking place
during a much shorter period than I was imagining.
However you looked at it, there was a choice of
nightmares.

Then one morning the guard opened my cell door
and said I was free to go.

'Go?'

'Yes. Go.'

It was as simple as that.

So I left the police headquarters and returned
to Chung Hom Kok.

There is a Chinese saying Qian shi bu wang, hou
shi zhi shi ('Remembrance of past times is a fine
guide for the future').

I looked at things like this. I did not want to
remember my past. I wanted nothing more to do with
things. Nothing to do with Alan. The Kwoks. The
Hong Kong Police.

My neighbour in the apartment block, the
Japanese student called Kasuko who had been caring
for my cats Botch and Chan, said I could live with
her for as long as I wanted.

I told her that she should tell no one I was
staying with her and she agreed. She was
incredibly discreet. Everyone liked Kasuko.

So once I had decided what to do with Botch and Chan, I planned to disappear into thin air. The world was now my oyster and I had no need of any sword to open it.

Signed: *Mei Lim*

Signature witnessed by: Chief Superintendent Ronald Costley

Signed: *Ron Costley*

Signature witnessed by: WPC Michelle Seifert

Signed: *Michelle Seifert*

117

Rosslyn had no idea what time of day or night it was when he heard the voice outside the door ask, 'Is Mr Rosslyn in this one?'

'He is,' said Rosslyn, and Kwok wheeled himself into the cell. To his relief Rosslyn saw that he was unaccompanied.

'Would you leave, please?' Kwok told the guard, who was waving his hands around.

'I think he wants this,' said Rosslyn, handing back the towel.

Still the guard refused to leave.

'Soap and razor,' the guard demanded.

'I left them in what passes for the shower room. If I'm staying here any longer you might care to provide hot water.'

Kwok closed the door. 'I'm sorry to find you like this,' he said. 'Thank God you survived.'

'Where's Mei?' said Rosslyn.

'Somewhere here in Hong Kong.'

'Is she all right?'

'Yes, I think so. As good as can be expected.'

'What does that mean?'

'What it says.'

'You're sure?'

'As sure as I can be. I want to talk about you,' said Kwok. 'The chances don't look good. You know about the charges being levelled at you in Beijing?'

'I've already been told,' said Rosslyn. 'You'd think they wouldn't know what happened out there in the Strait.'

'They know,' said Kwok. 'You were lucky to get clear.' Kwok's face wore a hangdog look. 'Others have not been so lucky. Your friend Simpson. He's been murdered.'

'*Simpson?*'

'Someone stabbed Simpson to death at the Port Klang docks.'

293

'When did it happen?'

'A day or so ago,' said Kwok. 'Fortunately he left a report about you and Mei and Michaelson. It puts something of a new spin on the situation. Gives us new connections.'

'Such as?'

'Connections to the killing of Anthony Zhentung. It's up to the Malaysians to handle the investigation into Simpson's murder. There's a second murder victim. A woman called Maureen Cheng. One of Svenske-Britannia's people. She and Simpson were brutally attacked. Two office workers found the mutilated corpses. There was a man at the scene. The officer workers saw him. From the descriptions they've given it looks like the man was Terajima. He's still in business. A hire car was found abandoned at the airport. Fingerprints and bloodstained clothing all point to Terajima.'

'Where is he?'

'We don't know yet,' said Kwok.

'You have to get me out of here, Steve.'

'You've met the officer from the Security Wing Operations Bureau, Li Juyi. He wants you kept here under secure protection rules until Beijing's made arrangements for your transportation.'

'Then I'll get out of here, Steve.'

'That would be an unnecessary risk, Alan.'

'On the contrary, I think it'll be necessary.'

'You won't stand a chance in hell of getting out on your own accord,' said Kwok. 'Not from here. And even if you did, where would you go from there?'

'That's my problem.'

'Amongst others,' said Kwok. 'Now we've very little room left in which to manoeuvre, if any. Meanwhile, the Commissioner wants to talk to you.'

118

The atmosphere in the Commissioner's office was tense and hostile. Rosslyn felt the isolation of his predicament. Throughout the long hours of his solitary confinement he had been shut up, accused and denied his rights of access to a British diplomatic officer, a lawyer and any convincing news of Mei. Now he was facing deportation to the People's Republic of China. The destruction of *Orient Angel* might just as well not have happened.

The Commissioner told his assistant that they were to be left undisturbed. Rosslyn sat in an upright chair in front of the Commissioner's desk. Steve Kwok sat crouched in his wheelchair by the window. The Commissioner sat behind his desk in shirtsleeves. His uniform jacket was draped across the back of his chair.

He asked Rosslyn to rehearse the events surrounding the sinking of *Orient Angel*. Rosslyn outlined them in great detail.

Once Rosslyn had finished his account, the Commissioner said, 'The problem is we can't bring Terajima to trial here in Hong Kong. The Malacca Strait falls outside our jurisdiction. And the murders in Port Klang involve the Malaysians, not us.'

'What about Beijing's involvement?' said Rosslyn. 'That helicopter carried the markings of the PLA. People's Republic of China. The weird thing is that before they left the area they tried and failed to kill him.'

'He will have outlived his usefulness to Beijing,' the Commissioner said. 'It demonstrates their involvement, which leaves us very little room to manoeuvre. So what would you do if you were in the shoes of the people in Beijing? They will already have whatever it was you say you saw being lifted from the deck of *Orient Angel* before it was destroyed. They have their bounty. Terajima wanted to kill you and Mei for whatever perverse and personal reasons. So the support people in the helicopter left him to his business and then,

295

literally, cut the rescue rope. They will have reckoned on shooting him in the water.'

'They failed,' said Rosslyn.

'Sure, they failed,' said the Commissioner. 'Given the force of the currents in the Strait, they'll have doubted he'd make it to the shore.'

'Maybe he never made it,' said Rosslyn.

'More likely a fishing vessel picked him up,' said the Commissioner. 'Whatever the scenario, he survived and he murdered Simpson and Cheng. You see, he has to have found out about you and Mei. There's more than that to reckon with. He must have discovered a great deal from Simpson.'

'I met Simpson,' said Rosslyn. 'Whatever he might have known, I don't think he'd have blabbed.'

'Even with a knife at his throat?' said the Commissioner.

'Look,' said Rosslyn, 'Terajima must have thought he'd cover his tracks by making the attack look like it had been carried out by a mugger.'

'The only strange thing is that he left Simpson's wristwatch behind,' said Kwok.

'Maybe Maureen Cheng talked,' said the Commissioner.

'About what?' Rosslyn put in. 'I don't think so.'

'We can't afford to speculate,' said the Commissioner. 'Whichever way we look at it, your life still is on the line, Rosslyn. So is Mei's.'

'I want to get out there after him,' said Rosslyn. 'I told you. He was going to kill her.'

'I realise that,' the Commissioner said. 'But you can't carry out some kind of vigilante action. Meanwhile, I have to tell you there are people here in headquarters who don't feel the same way as we do about bringing Winston's killers to justice. They don't want the can of worms opened.'

'Why not?'

'If I were to tell you', said the Commissioner, 'about the inner workings of the party in Beijing, about their people we have here inside headquarters, about the Byzantine complexities of their network, we would still be sitting here this time next month. There are things I'll never know, things that you will never understand. No. To take out Terajima, we have to make a knight's move. You know the chess move – we have to move forwards and sideways.'

'And what can I do to help?'

'You can stay here in Hong Kong.'

'No, I'm sorry. My job was *Orient Angel*. I failed. It's all over. I should return to the UK. Call it a day.'

'That's impossible,' said the Commissioner. 'You aren't reckoning with an initiative from Beijing. Besides, you have a personal obligation to Mei.'

'I'll handle that in my own way.'

'Except that she'll never be safe from Terajima,' said Kwok. 'And you won't be safe while Terajima's out there on the loose. It just isn't in his nature to let things rest.'

'Even in his line of business,' said Rosslyn, 'he'll be facing up to his future. Securing some other big pay day. I know his kind. He'll go on with his professional life. He might even have decided to call it a day. Retire. Get out while he's still on top. Thinking about what happened, I reckon that's what I'd do. Has no one looked at his financial reserves? Haven't you followed the money?'

'We have,' said the Commissioner. 'There's a fortune in at least two banks in Luxembourg. Most of it's money that he's been paid by the Zhentungs.'

'How do you know that?'

'You remember George Tsang. *Maritime Confidential*?' said Kwok.

'I remember him.'

'He's working for us. He made tapes of business meetings between the two surviving Zhentung brothers and Terajima. We have the tapes. You can listen to them later. They condemn all three of them outright.'

The small red light on one of the Commissioner's desk telephones was flashing. He swung round on his swivel chair and listened briefly, 'Thanks,' he said. 'Put out two armed surveillance teams,' he added, and hung up.

'Here we go. We have what sound to be two more possible identifications of Terajima. One near Hung Hom Ferry Pier. The other in Chung Hom Kok.'

'Where Mei lives?' said Rosslyn.

'That's what we've been hoping for,' the Commissioner said. 'That he'd show up in Chung Hom Kok. What we need from you, Rosslyn, is to know you'll hang in with us a while longer.'

'For Winston's sake,' said Kwok. 'You know what Confucius said. "A broken promise is like a death."'

'Bluntly,' said the Commissioner, 'will you put your life on the line one more time?'

'What are we thinking?' said Rosslyn. 'Entrapment. Bait?'

'Double bait,' said Kwok.

'You and Mei too,' said the Commissioner. 'If you say yes, then I can get our friend Costley on the line, and have him and however many officers he needs to get here now. We have to get ahead of Beijing. We arrest Terajima. We extradite him. Costley takes him back to the UK and arrests him and the surviving Zhentungs for the murders of Anthony Zhentung and the others. There's no alternative. Beijing doesn't want this thing out in the open. They've got what they want. Terajima's seen to that. He will have done the deal to screw the Zhentungs. It's a question of the biters bit. Don't you see it? Now they all want total silence. Blanket blackout. Oh sure, I can call the meeting off. I can sit here. I can do nothing. I can let Beijing rejoice in silence – they can sit there grinning because I have lost one of my finest officers. One of my finest officers, who had traced the whole foul business via Terajima to London to Washington to Beijing. You have to realise Beijing's already tried to do other deals.'

'With whom?'

'Burnal Graer and the CIA woman Swann. She was the agent who paid out the Zhentungs' US dollars to Terajima in Batu Pahat. Graer and Swann are Beijing's stooges.'

'You have the proof?' asked Rosslyn.

'As much as we need,' the Commissioner said. 'They've played things every which way. Maybe I could arrange an alternative deal with Beijing on that basis. But I don't want to do that. It could rumble on for months and years, and we'd get nowhere.'

'And Mei,' said Rosslyn. 'What about her role in this?'

The Commissioner gently rolled and stretched his neck. 'We don't like to consider her future with Terajima on the loose.' His voice assumed a gentler tone. 'I have a personal question, Alan. You don't have to answer this if you don't want to. How much does the girl mean to you?'

'What do you think?'

'I think you want to answer me more positively,' the Commissioner said.

'Does she love you?' said Kwok.

'That's something you will have to ask her,' said Rosslyn.

'I've already asked her,' the Commissioner said. 'You're one lucky man. She answered yes. And she wants her father's killer brought to justice. Along with the man who put Steve in that wheelchair and destroyed Catherine's face. Are you up it? Double bait? You have to do it. You'll never forgive yourself otherwise. Terajima's out there somewhere and I can read his mind. He wants your head. Mei Lim's too.'

'Where is she?'

'You must believe me,' said the Commissioner. 'We don't know.'

'Have you been to her apartment?'

'Yes. She hasn't returned there. Maybe you know which friends she might turn to?'

'I don't know,' said Rosslyn.

'Is that true?'

'Yes. She made a point of telling me she had no friends.'

'Do you believe that?'

'Look,' said Rosslyn, 'what's the point of our sitting here discussing what I may or may not believe about Mei?'

'But I assume you were lovers?' said the Commissioner.

'*Were*? What do you mean, *were*?'

'We're relying on you.'

'Relying on me? When I'm going to be deported?'

'We will find a way to postpone it.'

'Let me tell you, Commissioner, I'm going to find a way to cancel it.'

'What do you have in mind?'

'That's my business.'

'Let's not quarrel, Mr Rosslyn. Please.'

'Let's call it family business,' said Kwok. '*Maritime Confidential.*'

'Whatever happens in this chaos,' the Commissioner said. 'Let's be clear of one thing. You have my trust, Mr Rosslyn.'

'I'd like to believe that,' said Rosslyn.

'I hope you will. I'm not sure I can say that about one of the people waiting out there right now for me in the conference room. Meanwhile, I have to meet the officers involved in the investigation. Before you give me your decision, I want you to take a look at three of those who want you and Mei Lim taken to Beijing. So you can see that I will do all that I can to secure your protection. I may succeed. I may not. Who can tell?'

The Commissioner switched on the small CCTV monitor on a side table. 'Watch the screen,' he told Rosslyn. He collected his files from his desk and opened the door for Steve Kwok to wheel himself into the conference room. 'I will conduct the meeting in English.'

'Some of our colleagues may not like it,' Kwok said.

'Too bad,' said the Commissioner.

Rosslyn looked at the CCTV monitor and saw what happened next.

119

Portrayed on the CCTV screen, Rosslyn saw the flickering images of the officers seated in order of seniority around the table. The Commissioner announced each officer's name, and told each in turn that he was sworn to secrecy. 'Gentlemen,' he said, 'the murder of Winston Lim. I am taking personal command of the investigation. Steve Kwok will be my deputy commander. I've personally selected this emergency seven-man investigation group.'

He formally expressed confidence in them and, having repeated what was essentially Rosslyn's version of the sinking of *Orient Angel* and the murders of Simpson and Maureen Cheng in Kuala Lumpur. Two senior criminal investigation officers from the Malaysian police would be investigating the killings. If they wished, members of the investigation group would have an opportunity to question the officers. He said he wanted the meeting to listen to some tapes and asked Steve Kwok to introduce them.

Rosslyn went to the window, which offered him an overall view of the police headquarters. He watched the teams of men who were finishing the day's work on the renovation of the Secure Unit.

He also took a close look around the Commissioner's office. It had three doors. One led to the outer area, where Rosslyn presumed the Commissioner's assistant had a desk. The other led into the committee room. He searched for signs of any hidden CCTV surveillance cameras and found none. Then he approached the third exit to the Commissioner's office. It was a door of reinforced glass.

He tried the steel bar and handle. It opened noiselessly. Outside a steel fire escape led to the temporary car park below. He could see several wagons parked there. Two of the wagons were being loaded with rubble. Another two looked like quasi-military wagons, so-called 'person carriers'.

A group of builders were changing out of their working gear. They were handing their hard hats to a man who seemed to be their foreman. Some of the men were washing their hands and faces in buckets of water. Others were lighting cigarettes and laughing. Others again were changing into clean trousers and linen or imitation leather jackets. By no means all of them were of Chinese or Asian origin. A number of them were Caucasian.

Rosslyn tried the fire escape door again and it opened easily. Then he returned to watch more of the meeting on the CCTV screen.

He reckoned that the fire escape offered him a reasonable chance of getting away.

After Kwok had played the tapes, he said that Terajima, multiple murderer, extortionist and maritime terrorist, had every good motive to kill Winston Lim. He also had the means and the opportunity.

'We must find him,' the Commissioner said. 'This is the moment the rubber hits the road.'

There was a protracted discussion about Terajima's likely where-abouts. It ended when Tao Kang spoke up. Tao Kang of the Criminal Intelligence Bureau was chief archivist of criminal records and the indices of suspected and convicted criminals and of Wanted and Missing Persons.

'Beijing feels', said Tao Kang,' that finding Terajima would be an easier task if Inspector Kwok had made the late Lim's files available.'

The look on the Commissioner's face suggested to Rosslyn that Tao Kang represented opposition.

'We're dealing with the present,' the Commissioner said.

'Winston kept many things to himself,' said Kwok, adding defiantly '– legitimately.'

'My point exactly,' said Tao Kang. 'He kept "many things to himself". The resulting damage has been considerable.'

'If you wouldn't mind,' said the Commissioner, 'gentlemen, we are not here to argue. We're considering Terajima's whereabouts. Winston was one of ours. We want Terajima brought to justice. We all want the same thing.'

The Commissioner was refraining from saying *where* he wanted Terajima brought to justice. Rosslyn reckoned that the Commissioner was going to angle for Terajima to face British justice for the London killings. Beijing had finished with Terajima. They had tried and failed to eliminate him. But with Terajima on the run outside China's borders, he represented a potent threat to the exposure of their covert operations.

The implications of this threat were now exposed, albeit somewhat indirectly, by Paul Zhengang, head of the Organised Crime and Triad Bureau (OCTB). Zhengang had a successful record of prosecuting organised crime syndicates, major triad groups and money laundering networks. Liaising with security agencies in Beijing and overseas law enforcement agencies, he was close to the Commissioner.

'We've traced Terajima's movements from London to Kuala Lumpur to Batu Pahat to Singapore,' Zhengang told the meeting.

'One of Terajima's associates is well known as a client of a *cewek* in Batam, Indonesia. He's a regular at a hotel, the Kolekta. The *cewek* also has an Indonesian Navy officer for a regular client. The woman said the man is paid large sums by a man with a foreign sounding name. She confirms that the name is most likely Klaas-Pieter Terajima. I personally have no doubt we are looking at Terajima.' He turned to Dr Han Zongyuan, head of the Forensic Firearms Examination Bureau.

Zongyuan said that his officers had traced the purchase of the powerboat to Terajima. 'It originated from a gemstone dealership in the Philippines. The same outfit brokers used cargo ships and motor yachts as well as powerboats. The purchase of the MV *Xiang Chuan* went through the firm's books. They have contacts and suppliers in Malaysia and Indonesia. The firm's most successful go-between is a suspected sex tourist. An Australian national who so far has stayed out of jail. We have a problem with him.'

Tao Kang interrupted: 'Which is – what?'

'We don't want to reveal the identity of the Australian national,' said Zongyuan. 'He goes under several names.'

'What's his name?' Tao Kang asked.

The Commissioner said, 'Dr Burnal Graer of the Australian High Commission. Here in Hong Kong. His friend and associate is Birgit Swann the American legal attaché, who is CIA.'

Tao Kang's brief smile suggested that he already knew.

Rosslyn turned away from the CCTV screen and searched the Commissioner's uniform jacket. It was dark blue with the gold badges of his rank on the epaulettes. The inside pocket contained his wallet. The wallet was leather and well worn. It contained about one thousand Hong Kong dollars or about ninety UK pounds. Not enough to pay for his survival on the run in Hong Kong.

There were also a number of credit cards. They would be too easy to trace if he used them. The rest of the wallet's contents proved disappointing. He glanced at the colour snapshot of a woman and two teenage boys; presumably the Commissioner's family. He was holding the wallet in both hands with his fingertips and as he pocketed the Hong Kong dollars and returned the wallet to the Commissioner's jacket, he felt something beneath the photograph. Slipping his fingers behind the photograph he withdrew two dark blue plastic cards. There was no lettering on them. But he recognised them as keys. Keys that would release a safe or locked cash box or desk drawer.

'Both the diplomats have disappeared,' Zongyuan was telling the meeting.

'How can you be sure of their identities?' Tao Kang asked.

The Commissioner turned to Xin Yeng, the Identification Bureau's leading expert in DNA, fingerprint identification and scene of crime photography.

'I have an extensive dossier on Graer,' Xin Yeng announced. 'The police in Indonesia are as anxious to press charges against him as we are.'

Johnson Zhi raised his hand to speak. Johnson Zhi ran the Operations Bureau dealing with counter-terrorism and internal security.

'With respect, Commissioner, I regret I have to call a halt to the proceedings,' Johnson Zhi said. 'There is sensitive background intelligence to this investigation involving policy in Beijing. We have to wait until we have more detailed instructions.'

Rosslyn tried each of the cards in turn in the drawers of the Commissioner's desk. The second card released the lock of the top drawer. Opening it, he saw a large white HSBC envelope. Inside it were some seventeen thousand Hong Kong dollars, the rough equivalent of some fifteen hundred UK pounds. He slipped the envelope inside his shirt.

It took him no more than a few minutes to find the small safe installed in the bookcase, and the second card released the safe lock. Inside the safe he found a handgun and holster and a small carton of rounds. He slipped the holster on beneath his shirt and put the carton of rounds next to the envelope containing the Hong Kong dollars.

Finally, he relocked the drawer and the safe and returned the cards to the wallet, replacing the latter in the Commissioner's jacket pocket.

Li Juyi, the man who had visited Rosslyn in his cell, was speaking in Zhi's support. 'Commissioner, you have quite rightly sworn this meeting to secrecy. Zhi, Kang and I are empowered to inform you that all matters concerning Klaas-Pieter Terajima will not be decided here. The investigation can only be continued under the control of a senior official not yet appointed.'

'You are telling me to call a halt?' the Commissioner said.

'Not me, Commissioner,' said Li Juyi. 'Beijing is telling you.'

'How does that affect Mr Rosslyn and Ms Lim?' said the Commissioner.

'They remain under our jurisdiction,' said Li Juyi. 'They face serious charges from the People's Republic prosecutors. The former assistant defence attaché from the Chinese embassy in London, Zhu Jianxing, has confessed to providing Rosslyn with a false passport in the name of Li Kim. Zhu Jianxing has given Rosslyn's name to his interrogators. He has also confessed to giving Rosslyn a People's Republic diplomatic visa with his photograph in it. The photograph was taken here, Commissioner, at police headquarters. You must understand there will be an inquiry into how Zhu Jianxing obtained it.'

Li Juyi was staring directly at Steve Kwok. 'I assume you, Kwok, will be able to enlighten the investigators?'

'I don't know what you're talking about,' Kwok replied with conviction.

Li Juyi was in pursuit: 'In addition, Zhu Jianxing gave Rosslyn US and Hong Kong dollars and Chinese currency. Beijing is wondering what contacts Zhu Jianxing had here in police headquarters. There is no alternative. Rosslyn and Mei Lim must be taken to Beijing. The prosecutors will seek the death penalty for anyone who is found to have been involved and rid us of the threat to freedom.'

* * *

That was how Rosslyn learned that his fate, along with Mei Lim's, had been sealed.

Now, moreover, not only had Beijing assumed control of the situation but the heads of Steve Kwok and the Commissioner were also on the block.

Rosslyn did not stay to watch the rest of the meeting. He opened the door to the fire escape and walked out on to the platform at the top of the steel steps.

120

Chungking Mansions is at the southern end of Nathan Road among the tourist honeypots of Tsim Sha Tsui. Terajima had sent word to Michaelson at the Mandarin Oriental that he was to be there on time. He said that a man called Kyung would meet him. Michaelson should avoid using the unreliable elevators. He was told to take the stairs instead to where Kyung would be waiting for him on the twelfth floor. Be there at exactly ten o'clock. More than five minutes late and the meeting would be aborted.

So Michaelson arrived thirty minutes early and he waited outside the Mansions, the labyrinthine seventeen-storey pile of more than nine hundred guesthouses and doss houses. Flashing neon signs shot livid, surrealistic patterns of light skywards. Neon strips of gold and blue shrieked P.a.n.a.s.o.n.i.c. The vast Steinway piano was delineated in maddening blues and yellows. A peacock's tail exploded with a burst. Vanished. Lit up again.

Here are tenements reaching for the sky. Some half a million residents crushed together in the square mile. Michaelson was a dot among them. The torrential rain and the continual and unwelcome solicitations of the hawkers, hustlers and guesthouse touts added to his nervous state. Peptic acid burned in his chest.

Drenched in rain and sweat, hands in his pockets, he was a lost soul among steaming Indian and Pakistani curry stalls and *dai pai dong*, and market stalls lit by naked light bulbs and fluorescent tubes that sold fried pig intestines, triple fried deer's penis and breast of monkey alongside others that offered Nina Ricci, Gap, Nicole Farhi and Armani repros. Satin panties, bras and stiletto shoes.

Sullen eyes stared at him out of gloomy doorways. A voice lisped, 'Hey, fucksta, visit Dildo Alley?' The man started to tug at his sleeve. 'No,' said Michaelson. Another voice cooed, 'You want boy or girl or ladyboy. Live fucky-fucky show. Jig-a-jig?' He'd last heard the phrase uttered decades before by a lubricious Maltese college scout at Oxford. Taking the hip flask from his pocket, he took deep gulps of brandy. He had already downed several miniatures from the mini bar in his hotel suite. The additional liquor did little to calm his increasing impatience and anxiety.

Unsteady on his feet and with fifteen minutes to spare, he entered Chungking Mansions. The staircase seemed to be hell's gateway. Negotiating a path through rain-soaked litter and open rubbish bags, he removed the white silk handkerchief from his shirt cuff and jammed it against his streaming nose to lessen the stench of stale urine and ammonia. Some Africans in tank tops, with shaven skulls and wearing dark glasses, elbowed their way past him. He jammed his hand inside the pocket of his sodden jacket, hoping to protect his passport and leather wallet. *Silly me. I should have left them in the hotel room safe.* If he were mugged, then he would offer the hip flask as booty and try to make a dash for it. Not that his inebriated condition would allow him to stagger far and the stairs were perilously slippery.

Between the sixth and seventh floors of Chungking Mansions, he was confronted suddenly by two skeletal Chinese girls. 'Wanna have fun-fun twosome?' they asked. One of them was scratching at raw blisters on her forearms; the other was toothless with a tattoo of a rat on her left cheek. Michaelson looked at them as if they were creatures from another planet. Breathless, shaking his head at them, he pushed on up the stairs to the sound of derisive girlish laughter below.

He reached the twelfth floor with a few minutes in hand. To his relief, he found it was deserted and took more swigs of brandy. He told himself that he should have chosen the rendezvous himself. Not let Terajima call the shots. *This is not a situation I can control. I'm the one who should be in charge of things.* He was returning the hip flask to his pocket when he heard the high-pitched voice behind him: 'Mister Michaelson?'

He shuddered at the mention of his name.

Leech was the code word and Leech had been ignored. He peered at the man emerging from the shadows. 'Who are you?'

The man wore a black leather jacket, no shirt, khaki denim trousers and a pair of soiled trainers. 'Kyung,' he said.

'Very well, Kyung. Good evening. Show me to our friend.'

'Were you followed, Mister Michaelson?'

'I've no idea. How the hell could I see anything in this bloody awful rain? For pity's sake, let's not waste time.'

'*We have all the time in the world*,' sang Kyung in imitation of Louis Armstrong. He led the way along a darkened corridor.

Michaelson steadied himself against the wall and followed Kyung until they stopped outside a dilapidated door reinforced with makeshift steel doors. Spray graffiti had obliterated the plastic sign above it. 'Been here before?' Kyung said.

Michaelson shook his head.

'Huh,' the man said, unlocking the door. 'Good place. Warm welcome.'

Michaelson stepped inside the darkened and windowless room.

Suddenly the lights came on. Temporarily blinded, he raised his hands across his face. Behind him the door slammed shut and he felt powerful hands grip his throat. His legs gave way.

Choking, he was pushed forwards violently to the collapsed low divan by the wall. He let out a strangled moan.

What few reserves of strength he had to resist deserted him. He couldn't keep his balance, couldn't control his bladder. His assailant punched him and pushed him downwards and head first on top of the three naked and bloodied corpses spreadeagled across the divan's rotten mattress.

A voice whispered something in Korean. Phrases Michaelson could not have heard in his blurred mind or understood, as the single blade essayed the long and sweeping cut, left to right, ear to ear.

121

Ron Costley, as was his practice on arriving in a foreign city in a professional capacity, bought two local newspapers from the news stand on the concourse of Hong Kong International Airport. He read the headlines with more than usual interest.

South China Morning Post

ZHENTUNG BROTHERS HONOURED
HONG KONG TYCOONS MADE PEERS
From our London Correspondent

Foster and Hastings Zhentung have today been created UK life peers by HM The Queen. The honours have been conferred in recognition of their substantial donations to UK arts, science and educational charities. Government ministers and leading knights and peers in the British arts and academic worlds have praised the Zhentungs with unanimity. 'The Zhentungs are examples of selfless generosity which is welcomed by leading cultural figures,' a senior government minister said today. 'The Zhentungs, major sponsors of theatrical, art and scientific organisations in the UK, are champions of the portrayal of real life,' said former film magnate Lord –

Costley flipped to the other front page.

ZHENTUNGS CREATED LORDS

Leading figures from the left and right in the UK have praised Hastings and Foster Zhentung, today made life peers. 'This great honour celebrates two UK role models. The honour is especially appropriate in the aftermath of the tragic death of their brother, philanthropist Anthony Zhentung,' a Zhentung Foundation spokesman told press and TV today. 'Premier establishment arts figures are proud to count the brothers as their equals.' According to the spokesman, the Zhentungs will take an active role in forming new, radical and visionary legislation in the House of Lords, where they will sit as independents. 'I know the Zhentungs' deep commitment to the highest standards of public life and radical architecture. They share my vision,' said Lord –

Ready to spit, Costley thrust the papers into the nearest rubbish bin.

122

On their arrival at Hong Kong International Airport not long before, Ron Costley and Elizabeth Henderson had gone their separate ways. More accurately, they had already gone their separate ways many hours previously at Heathrow. Henderson into First Class. Costley, *hoi polloi*, into Economy.

Before she was chauffeured to the High Commission, Henderson had given Costley the twenty-four hour emergency number on which she could be contacted. She insisted he report to her on progress in the investigation of Simpson's murder. Costley was left in the downpour to find a taxi to take him to police headquarters.

Costley sensed serious trouble. Back in London, Henderson had given him an outline of the circumstances surrounding Simpson's murder. Her people wanted Costley to leave for the Far East at once to discover exactly what had happened. Henderson told him that she had been given orders to find Simpson's agent, Yeo Heng. The official record would show that she never did succeed in doing so.

As for Costley, he would be liaising with officers from the Malaysian police. When Costley had first spoken on the telephone to Steve Kwok, he was offered few helpful leads. Instead he was given a brief, guarded and somewhat confused explanation of the internecine squabbles and bureaucratic obstinacy of the higher levels of the police headquarters hierarchy. To be sure, the investigation into the Simpson killing was under way. They had a suspect. Simpson's fate was one thing. Rosslyn's was the other.

Kwok's considered view was that Rosslyn's deportation to Beijing was inevitable. There was the business of the fake passport that had been issued by the Chinese defence attaché. God knows why the Chinese had confessed to supplying it. The passport had anyway been lost when *Orient Angel* went down in the Malacca Strait. Kwok told Costley that he seriously doubted whether permission would be given for him to visit Rosslyn. He told Costley – rather bluntly, he thought – that the Chinese prosecutors would demand the death penalty. As for Mei Lim, she had disappeared. 'We're looking for a needle in a haystack,' Kwok said. 'Given a population of over seven million, we're also looking for the haystack. No haystacks in Hong Kong.'

When Costley reached Steve Kwok's office at police headquarters, he found that matters had deteriorated.

Kwok skipped the pleasantries. 'Rosslyn's gone, the stupid bastard absconded from here this afternoon. Got out. Clean away.' Costley's instinctive reaction was to think the worst. Beijing had already snatched him. Kwok must have read his mind: 'Beijing could've lifted him.'

'What does the Commissioner think?' asked Costley.

'The Commissioner's in the wok. Been suspended. He's right out of it.'

'Suspended – for *what*?'

'Because he accepted full responsibility for Rosslyn's escape.'

'You say he's out of it – *where's he out of it*?'

'At home. Under house arrest.'

'Who's in charge here now, then?'

'New faces. Old faces,' said Kwok. 'Beijing's people. It's all over bar the shouting. If I were you, I'd get a good night's sleep, pack your bags and get yourself a reservation on the first plane out in the morning.'

'For God's sake, it's already morning,' Costley snapped. 'I'm not going anywhere. Understand? I'm staying put until I've found out who killed Simpson. Until we find Rosslyn and get a bloody hold on the man Terajima. Let me tell you why. I want the piece of shite to answer questions. I want him to answer to me, right? I want the bastard to tell me about the killing of Anthony Zhentung and very much more besides. I want you people to assist me. Then I'll assist you. And you can tell that to the Beijing buggers or whoever may or may not be in charge here.'

'It'll be dangerous,' said Kwok.

'I'll be the judge of that,' Costley said with fury. 'Bugger it.'

Kwok looked pained. 'I'm sorry. We reckoned we were near to striking a deal with Beijing to have them drop their charges against Rosslyn. We were too late.'

'It's *never* too late. You listen to me. I want Rosslyn out of this place. I haven't come here to hear you admit defeat. Or to have you tell me to pack my bags and piss off out. I haven't even unpacked my duty free. But before I do, I want three armed police officers with me, right? You understand me, old friend?'

Kwok was about to answer when the telephone cut him short.

Costley watched Kwok listening to whoever was on the line. 'Okay,' said Kwok. 'Have a six-seater waiting for me by the main gates.' He turned to Costley. 'You know a man called Victor Michaelson?'

'What if I do?'

Kwok was staring into space. 'His naked body's been found in Chungking Mansions. With two others. One Caucasian male. One Caucasian female who'd been sexually assaulted. Both naked. They were murdered.'

'*Michaelson?*'

'Victor Michaelson. That's what his passport says. They found it. Seems he'd been drinking. You can come with me and confirm the identification.'

'I want three armed officers with me.'

'That isn't possible.'

'You bloody make it possible. And I want a driver and a police vehicle.'

'You can have two officers and a driver.'

'He'd better be a bloody good driver.'

'He will be. You're looking at him. Even in my condition I can still drive.'

'Okay. You have a gun?'

Kwok opened his jacket and showed Costley his gun and holster. 'Welcome to Hong Kong, Mr Costley.'

'Thanks a lot,' said Costley. 'While we're about it, do you have the phone number and address of Mei Lim's place?'

'Sure,' said Kwok. 'I'll give you them to you on the way.'

123

Mei Lim's place in Chung Hom Kok overlooks the South China Sea. It's in the secluded residential area on the rocky peninsula between Repulse Bay and Stanley. Even in the torrential rain Stanley is no more than a ten-minute drive away. Twenty minutes or so and you're in Central and Causeway Bay. Fifty in Tsim Sha Tsui. One hour the airport. Rosslyn arrived in Chung Hom Kok by bus and walked through the rain to Mei's low apartment block. He had his hands deep in the pockets of the imitation Burberry mackintosh he'd bought earlier that night in Central. The holster and loaded gun were strapped across his shoulders beneath the jacket of his new suit.

There was no reply when he rang her bell. The window of her apartment was in darkness. He rang the bells of the other two apartments in the block and got no reply. Yet there was movement behind the blinds of the apartment above Mei's, the flat occupied by her blind Japanese friend Kasuko. He knew that being here was a terrible risk.

He wondered what reactions there had been to his escape from police headquarters. It wasn't hard to picture. It wouldn't be long before the police arrived with the warrant for his re-arrest.

He could imagine the Commissioner and Steve Kwok thinking that he'd been foolish to abscond, even though he felt, in a contrary sort of way, that he had done well to have kept his head and got clean away. True, the checkpoint at the gates had been disorganised, the workers' wagon overcrowded, overloaded too, the press of men unruly and disputatious and the guards had made the most cursory and rushed of head-counts. That was fine. He could have been far less fortunate. He had got away. But staying free, let alone getting out of Hong Kong, would be harder, if not impossible. The truth was that a sense of calm had begun to overtake him, a numbness; perhaps it was the inevitability of capture that numbed his nerves. The sound of the first police siren and it would all be over.

124

STATEMENT OF WITNESS

[Criminal Justice Act 1967, s.9]

Statement of:	Alan Rosslyn
Age of Witness:	Over 21
Occupation:	Private Investigator
Address:	Basement Flat, 195 Claverton Street, London SW1

This statement consisting of 1 page signed by me is true to the best of my knowledge and belief and I make it knowing that if it is tendered in evidence, I shall be liable to prosecution if I wilfully state anything which I know to be false.

Kasuko must have known where Mei was. It struck me as inconceivable that Mei would have left Hong Kong without calling her. There had to be a thousand reasons why she must have spoken to Kasuko. Kasuko was Mei's friend. It would be totally out of character, even in these circumstances, for her to have disappeared in silence. There was simply too much unfinished business. Even the cats. And I was also thinking of myself, with nothing left to lose.

I had to take the risk. I told myself that I had to get inside the apartment block.

Signed: *Alan Rosslyn*

Signature witnessed by: Chief Superintendent Ronald Costley

Signed: *Ron Costley*

Signature witnessed by: WPC Michelle Seifert

Signed: *Michelle Seifert*

Under the photographers' arc lights, overheating the stinking air of the room on the twelfth floor of Chungking Mansions, Ron Costley identified the corpse. It wasn't difficult. Michaelson's passport gave the proof. As to the other two corpses, identifying them was easy too. Swann and Graer's diplomatic passports were among the pile of bloodied clothing, blood-soaked but quite legible. He had no reason to remain at the murder scene and told Kwok to drive him to Chung Hom Kwok. The two armed police officers were waiting in an unmarked six-seat vehicle on Nathan Street.

Once outside, Costley used Kwok's mobile to call the emergency number Henderson had given him.

'Victor Michaelson's been found dead. Yes, Michaelson. In a room on the twelfth floor – some sort of whorehouse squat. Yes, I've seen it. It's an abattoir. I'm outside it now, in the bloody rain. It gets worse. Two other people are dead up there. An American. Thirty-eight years old. Birgit Swann. An Australian, Burnal Graer. Forty-two. Both accredited diplomats. *Who did it?* Don't ask me, dearie. The whole place is swarming with ghouls, pimps, loonies, scum and murder scene investigators. Forensic. Photographers. You name it. The works. It's chaos.'

'Where's Rosslyn?'

'How the hell would I know where he is?' said Costley. 'You stay by your phone.'

STATEMENT OF WITNESS

[Criminal Justice Act 1967, s.9]

Statement of: Alan Rosslyn
Age of Witness: Over 21
Occupation: Private Investigator
Address: Basement Flat,
                     195 Claverton Street,
                     London SW1

This statement consisting of 2 pages signed by me is true to the best of my knowledge and belief and I make it knowing that if it is tendered in evidence, I shall be liable to prosecution if I wilfully state anything which I know to be false.

One minor disadvantage — I didn't have a watch. So I had no idea what time it was when I saw the window in Kasuko's apartment being opened. It was impossible to see who had opened it. I could see not one but two figures there. I was ninety-nine per cent sure the two figures were male. Before I could call out, the window was sharply closed again. Now I could hear the sound of the cats howling in the darkness. Not one, but two. They kept on howling. Would Kasuko have turned them out and left them there? It seemed unlikely that she was the person who had dumped them on the very narrow ledge. No, I was certain I'd seen two men.

The noise of the cats lessened and then stopped altogether. It was some time later that I saw all the lights in the apartment block suddenly go off. It seemed to me either that the power had failed or, less likely, that it had been deliberately turned off.

318

Previously, when I had tried the bell, I could hear buzzing in the electrical system. When I tried it again, there was none. So I reckoned the power had failed. At least if I could break in, it would be under cover of darkness. The darkness might prove an ally. But what was I going to find?

I had no plan worked out. There was virtually no chance of entering the apartment unannounced. There seemed to be no approach to it other than through the front door or the windows of the ground floor apartment. I decided to take the latter route.

Signed: *Alan Rosslyn*

Signature witnessed by: Chief Superintendent Ronald Costley

Signed: *Ron Costley*

Signature witnessed by: WPC Michelle Seifert

Signed: *Michelle Seifert*

The police siren. Sweating, he was standing still. Trying to shake the glass splinters free from the open cuts burning in his raw knuckles. He'd just broken the window of the ground floor flat and had slowly worked it open. Had waited. Heard no sound.

The siren grew louder, and then cut off abruptly. He withdrew the handgun, inserted rounds and checked the safety catch. Now. Quietly. Across the rugs. The living room. Across a wooden floor. Nudged a low table. A chair. To the door. Eased it open. Left it ajar. Out into the hallway. Shoes touching the concrete floor. Stay quiet. Stay very quiet.

Very quiet. Then there was the sound. From outside the entrance. A scuffling on grit followed by a fist beating against the door.

He moved back inside the living room and stood still. Frozen.

'POLICE.'

The split beam of a flashlight shone at an angle from beneath the entrance door.

'POLICE.'

The thud of a steel hammer against the door. Two or three blows. The sounds of splitting wood and squealing metal. The frame had split. One more blow and the door gave way.

He saw three figures crash through the gap and sprint across the hallway, running for the stairs.

He stood his ground, listening: flinching when he heard the door to Mei's flat smashed open on the floor above.

128

Costley stayed several paces behind the two police officers in the shadows, a handgun at the ready. The officers were built like wrestlers, the size of their squat chests and shoulders exaggerated by bullet-proof vests, their heads in protective helmets. They were carrying guns and flashlights.

Inside the apartment, the first of the flashlight beams focused on the pale skin of a woman who lay prostrate on the floor. Her hands were behind her back, wrists fastened by black industrial adhesive tape. More industrial tape had been twined around her mouth.

The beam illuminated the figure of the second woman. She was naked and hanging suspended from the steel clothes rail by a single rope. Her legs had been twisted up behind her neck and fastened at the ankles with industrial tape. A pillowcase covered her head. The wreckage of potted plants lay on the floor beneath the window sill. Beneath the hanging woman was a tangled pale blue sheet, white clothes and a white silk dressing gown. Next to the door the large mirror had been smashed.

The officers had their guns trained on the figure of a man dressed in women's clothes. He was standing just behind the hanging woman holding a long sharp blade horizontally against her throat.

'DROP IT!'

The man shook his head. The flashlight beam glinted on the blade.

Costley moved out of the shadows and into the room and trained his gun on the man in woman's clothing. The beams from the officers' flashlights dazzled the figure with the blade. Costley was totally focused on the eyes of the figure in the woman's dress. His mind raced. *This has to be Terajima.* He'd given the orders not to shoot. He wanted Terajima out of here alive.

'You're Klaas-Pieter Terajima?' Costley said quietly. 'My name's Superintendent Costley, Metropolitan Police, London. I have a warrant for your arrest.'

'This is Hong Kong.'

'Thanks for the reminder.'

'Show me Rosslyn, asshole,' Terajima said.

'Let's release the girl,' said Costley.

'She's dead.'

Costley could see she wasn't dead. 'Okay. Then drop the blade. Move aside slowly. And let's leave here quietly. Let's talk.'

Costley's heart was thumping. His mouth was dry. Kwok was down there outside in the police vehicle. The firm agreement was that if Costley and the pair of armed officers didn't come out within ten minutes, Kwok would radio headquarters for support. That meant Costley would lose Terajima. There had to be a speedy resolution. If Terajima had silenced Michaelson and Swann and Graer, he knew that Beijing's people at police headquarters would get him clear and clean away. Maybe Terajima knew it too. He would be playing for time. In Terajima's shoes, Costley would have done the same.

'Okay, whitey. Let's talk,' Terajima said.

'Fine by me,' said Costley.

'Have these motherfuckers arrest me.'

Terajima knew the score. Arrest. Release. He knew the Beijing strategy. He had *guanxi*. This piece of pinko-grey British trash wouldn't even know what *guanxi* meant.

Costley might not have known the meaning of the word. But he knew the score. 'Let's just talk,' he said.

'You talk too much,' said Terajima.

One of the armed officers' short-wave radio crackled. He listened for a second. Then he turned and moved past Costley into the corridor.

The radio message had been clear. *There was someone coming and whoever was coming was armed.*

Costley moved towards the door. He wanted a very quick word with the officer in the corridor. They were running out of time.

129

The muscles in Rosslyn's chest tightened. He'd seen the figure in the stairwell. The man must have entered the building from the service entrance at the back where he'd crashed the electric power. He could make out a leather jacket and heard the sound of moist rubber soles squeaking on the concrete floor.

Rosslyn moved out of the living room. He could see the squat back of the man walking up the stairs. Slowly. Step by step. Now he saw Costley illuminated by the flashlight. The figure in the leather jacket paused. He raised his handgun, gripping it with both hands.

Rosslyn yelled, 'WATCH OUT!'

The beam swivelled, shining straight into the gunman's face. The armed police officer raised his weapon a split second too late. He took the first two shots in the left leg, just below the knee, and screamed with pain. The gunman turned sharply and fired a third shot at Rosslyn. Rosslyn didn't pause to think. Simultaneously, he fired straight at the man's chest. The man fell backwards, rolled over, reaching for the stair rail. The gun fell from his hand and clattered on to the concrete floor below.

Costley took the wounded police officer's flashlight. Rosslyn followed him into Mei's apartment. On the floor he saw the figure in the woman's dress driving the blade downward to the armed police officer's neck.

Costley yelled, 'Don't shoot!'

Barging past Costley, Rosslyn hurled himself forwards, both hands gripping Terajima's throat until he choked. Then Costley struck hard at Terajima's temples with the flashlight. The sharp, short blow drew no blood. The head just slumped. The open mouth pressed against the floor. The police officer was getting to his feet with difficulty. Costley told him to leave the building and tell the driver to stand by.

Rosslyn went to find a knife in the makeshift kitchen in the alcove. He found two. He and Costley began to lower the hanging figure. They removed the pillowcase. Cut away the industrial adhesive. She was breathing with difficulty, her face had been badly beaten. This was Mei.

Rosslyn checked her neck pulse. Beating. 'You're going to be okay,' he said.

The woman on the floor was Kasuko. Very gently, Rosslyn removed the adhesive tape bindings. He checked the pulse in her neck too. Still beating.

'I haven't come here for dead witnesses,' said Costley. He had his eyes fixed on Terajima, who was regaining consciousness. 'We have to get this pisser out of here straight to the Consulate. You too, Rosslyn.'

'On your feet,' Rosslyn told Terajima. Terajima was wearing one of Mei's dresses. Too small, it was unbuttoned down the front. Beneath, he wore green boxer shorts. The sight of Mei's dress made Rosslyn loathe him even more. 'Hands on your head. Thread the fingers. Now turn round.'

The police officer returned with handcuffs.

'Here – let me do it,' said Rosslyn. He snapped them on so tight behind Terajima's back that he reckoned he might cut off the blood flow to Terajima's hands. 'You make any sort of move and I'll kill you.' Terajima didn't flinch. Then Rosslyn pushed him towards the floor. 'Kneel. Don't move.'

He dressed Mei in her white dressing gown and wrapped Kasuko in the bed quilt.

Costley was on his mobile telephone to Henderson. He got the response he wanted. 'Let's go.' He told the police officer to stay with his colleagues until an ambulance arrived.

One by one, Rosslyn took Mei and Kasuko to the police vehicle waiting in the rain. He wanted to take Mei in his arms.

Costley brought Terajima down the stairwell. It was an awkward business. Terajima went limp.

'Who's your dead friend?' said Costley.

'Ask him,' said Terajima.

'You yellow fucker,' said Costley in Terajima's ear. He slipped his fingers through the chains round Terajima's neck and pulled. Terajima shook his head in protest.

'ID?' Costley whispered. 'We have ID, you cunt. All mine now.' He pulled so hard at the chains that their clasps snapped clean away. 'I don't like memories, see? I like souvenirs. And the bloody gold better not be counterfeit, or I'll have you for bloody forgery as well.'

Rosslyn helped Mei into the police vehicle.

'The cats?' she asked weakly.

Cats. All Rosslyn could do was smile. *I want to know what happened up there with Terajima. What he did to you. And I don't want to know.* He had no answer to her question about the cats.

Costley was on his mobile telephone to Henderson. He was talking fast about a 'shopping list'. Passports and tickets to London for Rosslyn and Mei Lim. Changes of clothing. Hotel rooms. Henderson was complaining about the expense. 'What do you mean, "there's only a limited amount the Consulate can offer"?' said Costley. 'Listen, I have two prime witnesses. You will give them what I say. They travel first class.'

Terajima was banking on Beijing. Beijing will show the British where to go.

If not, there is the contingency plan in place in London. The British will never dare to convict the Zhentungs. They are immune. And they can't convict me without the Zhentungs in the dock. This is war and it's going on and on and on.

He had once heard the Zhentungs mention that the British had a dubious preference for keeping records of the nation's dirtier secrets, and had heard the Zhentungs laughing with Michaelson in his cups about what he called the Damage Report and the pornography of politics.

'Believe me, the dirt is always on the record,' Michaelson had said. 'And it wouldn't be terribly difficult to obtain a copy if the shit ever hit the fan.'

Terajima had asked him to explain himself. And Michaelson, forever proud to be in the know and at the very heart of things, had told him precisely the significance of the Damage Report. He had never forgotten the details. It had been a discussion that appealed to Terajima's scholarship of extortion in all its forms.

131

A crowd of neighbours had gathered in the street. They stood in the rain watching the ambulances and police cars. Someone must have alerted the TV and radio stations. But by the time the media people turned up, the ambulance taking away the police officers had left.

More police officers had cordoned off the house. They ordered the TV and radio reporters to keep their distance. So the reporters interviewed the neighbours instead, and learned about the blind Japanese woman who lived in the top flat and about Mei, the daughter of Inspector Lim who had lost his life not so many weeks before. The ground floor flat had been empty for many months. In very recent times, a man had been making enquiries about renting it. Someone said she thought his name was Pastor Leung. Another said his name was Dr Hung and that she'd seen him arrive there earlier accompanied by another man, either Chinese or Korean. The only memorable shot obtained by the TV crews was of the child who brought a ladder and retrieved the two cats cowering on the window ledge.

British Consulate-General
Hong Kong

I Supreme Court Road, Hong Kong
Email: information@britishconsulate.org.hk
Tel: (852) 2901 3000 Fax: (852) 2901 3066
Open 8.30am to 5.15pm, Monday to Friday

SERVING THE PUBLIC

**A MESSAGE FROM THE BRITISH
CONSUL-GENERAL, HONG KONG**

We are committed to serving you with courtesy
and respect and ask that you treat our staff in the
same way. However, we reserve the right not to
serve visitors who behave aggressively or use
offensive language.

'Fuck you,' said Terajima in the secure room provided by the Consulate on Supreme Court Road.

In answer to his questions, Henderson told him, 'I can make no provision to supply you with money or pay bills or buy you a ticket, even if you've been the victim of theft.'

'This is a prison.'

'We have no powers to effect your release.'

'I insist on my right to have legal advice.'

'That's not a service the British government can provide.'

Rosslyn and Ron Costley watched her handle Terajima's protests with approval.

'I insist', Terajima said, 'that I be allowed to speak to police head-quarters.'

Ron Costley shook his head. 'You can insist on anything you want,' he said. 'You're under arrest. You're staying under arrest. So sit back and relax.'

'Remove the handcuffs.'

'I've lost the key. I'm sorry. I dropped it in the rain.'

'Then bring a locksmith.'

'I know a good one in London,' said Costley. 'He's presently in Belmarsh.'

'Where are you taking me?'

'Same place, cunt. Belmarsh.'

'Belmarsh?'

'It's a prison with a High Security Unit in south east London.'

Two security officers were preparing to stand guard over Terajima as Rosslyn and the others were leaving the Consulate.

Henderson had put in place the arrangements to take Terajima to London. Rosslyn wondered what deals had been struck to make it run so smoothly. Now, because Henderson was on a call to London, the departure was briefly delayed. 'Something else to celebrate,' she said with a satisfied smile. 'You'll be pleased to know that Foster and Hastings Zhentung were arrested an hour ago.'

133

Rosslyn was going home with Mei Lim. She held his hand when the British Airways 747 lifted from the runway at Hong Kong International Airport. 'Look down there,' she said. 'At the perimeter. That's where Dad took off on his last flight.' She was sucking on a boiled sweet. 'What happens when we get to London?'

'You can stay at my place until the trial.'

He hoped one day she would be able to forget the worst of the last few weeks. Meanwhile, Ron Costley would be taking witness statements from both of them. Right now didn't seem the time to discuss the future in much detail. Anyway, Mei fell into an exhausted sleep beside him.

They arrived in London on a perfect early spring day.

Costley had telephoned ahead for an unmarked police car to take them into London.

When Rosslyn opened the door to his Claverton Street flat, he could tell that others had been there in his absence.

On the table in his living room was a small bunch of roses. He read the handwriting on the card. *For Mei with thanks. From Ron and Elizabeth. PS Tell Alan there's something in the fridge for him.*

It was a bottle of champagne with a card tied round the neck. The message read: *Thanks. Tell Mei that the cats are doing fine. Kasuko.*

FIVE

The Spring

134

The clocks went forward and the arrest of the Zhentungs was news. From the newspaper photos and TV clips of them with royalty and establishment figures from so many walks of life, the faces of the Zhentungs became familiar than ever. There was talk of family rifts, of the Triads and even Mafia connections. Those numbered – mostly by themselves or their PR spokesmen – among The Great, The Wise and The Good, who had been so voluble in their praise of the brothers – well, they now fell silent. If the multitude of those who had accepted their charity and hospitality felt guilt by association, embarrassment even, then they weren't saying. No one had a good word to say about them. Grandees guilty by association could rely upon wonders lasting seven days. No one commented upon the foreign brothers being held in separate cells in Belmarsh prison's High Security Unit. With one exception. Paid five thousand pounds by a tabloid, the recently released prisoner from Belmarsh declared, 'Praise be. The brothers have found Allah.'

As for Klaas-Pieter Terajima, well, the assumption was that he was some stooge, sidekick, journeyman or ticket of leave man of the Zhentungs. The man was part Dutch, part Japanese. It was a racial mix the British found unusual and possibly, unpleasant in some ill-defined way. Terajima was being held as an A Category prisoner in Belmarsh. No one could find out anything terribly interesting about him.

As for Michaelson, the name wasn't exactly one to conjure with. The old story about the case involving arcane sexual practices with small, even miniature, dogs was, as it were, trotted out. The 'Canine Charmer' tag was resurrected in the obituaries, accompanied by the photograph of him at Battersea Dogs' Home surrounded by the unwanted poodles in fur collars. There were passing references to the Calvi business, but no mention of MI6 or MI5 or Milo Associates.

The man describing himself as a Doctor of Divinity at Oxford claimed to recall Michaelson 'sporting himself' on the banks of the Cherwell in a nudist club called Parsons' Pleasure. 'I don't recall his details,' the don offered, adding obscurely that Michaelson had 'cut something of a dash with a hip flask.'

The Foreign Secretary expressed dismay and outrage at the death of the diplomat Jon Simpson and said the thoughts of all decent people would be with Simpson's mother. The short obituary in the *Daily Telegraph* said simply that Simpson had been a selfless foreign servant. It ended: 'He never married' – the euphemism from which readers might deduce he was gay. The truth had been that he wasn't anything.

Later, it seemed that it was what *wasn't* said that was strange. There was, for example, scant mention of *Orient Angel*. But then few knew of Terajima's involvement in its destruction.

Others – for example, the Lord Chancellor, functionaries in the Prime Minister's private office, members of the Joint Intelligence Committee and the security services – were considering the darker implications of the trial. It had been brought forward as far as possible and was listed to take place at the Old Bailey before spring turned into summer.

Category A prisoner Terajima in Belmarsh was allowed no books, no radio, no TV. His only serious conversations were with lawyers provided for him under the auspices of legal aid. One of the clerks, an Anglo-Japanese, proved sympathetic to the case and agreed to make a telephone call to a priest on Terajima's behalf.

Two days later the clerk told Terajima that the priest had been friendly and that Terajima should be reassured that the contingency plans were in place. If Terajima were found guilty, why then the arrangements for an appeal would be made. If he were found not guilty, why then the priest would be waiting for him immediately the trial ended. The priest told the clerk to take comfort from the fact that he was offering daily prayers for his release. He said that he was looking forward to a holiday with Terajima. A motorcycling tour was planned and the priest had just bought a rather smart new Suzuki Freewind.

135

Rather to his relief, Rosslyn learned from Ron Costley that, in the interests of national security, the Old Bailey trial of Terajima and the Zhentungs would be held *in camera*. Officers from the security services would be present. Costley was unable to say for what precise reasons. Rosslyn's presence would not be required – indeed, would not be permitted. But he could, of course, sit in the public gallery when the verdict was given. Costley said he'd heard that issues concerning Sino-British relations meant the trial would take place in the near future. He took Rosslyn's witness statement, which Rosslyn and Costley signed at New Scotland Yard in the presence of a WPC, Michelle Seifert. The day after, Costley took Mei Lim's statement and she was told that she would be required to attend the trial as a witness for the prosecution. Costley also said that George Tsang would be present.

Costley, his nose closer to the ground than ever, told Rosslyn that the Lord Chancellor had made opaque arrangements to nominate a senior judge to hear the case. The judge was a veteran of hearing and defending applications for judicial review. Before leaving the bar he had spent five years as the Treasury Devil acting for a wide range of government departments. Well versed in issues of human rights, the judge had already received pre-trial applications from both the prosecution and the defence.

Terajima's solicitors had briefed as counsel the Old Etonian Julian Filster QC. Foster Zhentung's counsel was Patrick Hampton Hare QC, educated at Lancing and Jesus, Cambridge. Hastings Zhentung's was Caroline Herbert QC, St Felix Southwold and Brasenose. The prosecution was in the hands of Madeleine Burchfield QC, St Paul's and Trinity, Cambridge; Dominic Blenkert, Uppingham and St Catharine's, Cambridge; and Fiona Lloyd, Cheltenham Ladies' College and Girton.

'It's just a matter of waiting,' Costley told Rosslyn and Mei in his favourite pub, Roxy Beaujolais' Seven Stars in Carey Street off the Strand. Mei said she dreaded the whole business, Rosslyn promised to take her mind off things and Costley said, 'It helps to have something to look forward to, I find. Take her on the London Eye.'

Daffodils and crocuses flowered and withered in the London parks. Forsythia bloomed. So did the lilac, and the London plane trees came into leaf. They took the ride on the London Eye. A trip on the river to Greenwich. Spent days walking in Kew Gardens, in Richmond Park. He even showed her the offices of Milo Associates in Marylebone Passage. Mei showed no interest in them. Rosslyn took her to several Chinese restaurants, but she seemed to have lost her appetite. He would wake to find her weeping and drenched in sweat.

'What's going to happen?' she asked.

'They'll be sent back to prison for life and the judge will recommend that they never be released.'

'Why hasn't your prime minister had those peerage things taken from them? They're criminals.'

'Not until they're found guilty.'

'In China they'd be shot. Here you honour them and give them crowns.'

'It's complicated, Mei.'

'I'd say it was corrupt.'

It was hard to disagree with her.

On the day before the trial Rosslyn bought her a white gabardine suit at Nicole Farhi in Bond Street.

The weather forecast for the day of the trial in Court Number One at the Old Bailey was for heavy rain.

At the Old Bailey two security officers flanked Klaas-Pieter Terajima in the dock of Court Number One. Because the trial was being held *in camera* the benches usually occupied by the press were empty. Similarly, there was no one in the public gallery.

The jury was made up of seven men and five women between the ages of twenty-five and fifty. Of these, two were of Asian origin, two black and the remaining eight white. Looking tired and nervous, they took their seats on the benches, averting their eyes from the gaze of the judge and everyone else in the court.

The appearance of Terajima contrasted starkly with that of the Zhentung brothers, Foster and Hastings. Wearing a drab grey suit several sizes too large for him, Terajima cut an androgynous and vulnerable figure. The buttons had been torn from his stained white shirt, which was open at the neck. Looking younger than his years, he seemed shy and sensitive.

The Zhentungs wore dark suits, white shirts and sober silk ties. They had showed no sign of nervousness when the charges of murder and conspiracy to murder were read aloud. Similarly, Terajima had seemed uninterested when the same number of charges against him of murder and conspiracy to murder were read. To each one in turn, the Zhentungs and Terajima answered 'Not guilty.'

Opening the case for the prosecution, Madeleine Burchfield QC had a series of photographs passed to the judge and jury.

They showed the scenes of devastation in Hopton Street and images of the charred remnants of the corpses of those who had perished.

She summarised the events that had taken place on the night of the blast. Several times she referred to Terajima as Dr Terajima and the judge asked her to refrain from using the title 'Dr', which presumably he thought might in some way grant Terajima respect he did not deserve.

Madeleine Burchfield was careful to suggest to the members of the jury that the prosecution would not necessarily invite them to believe that any of the figures seen in Hopton Street had been identified as Terajima. She gave the impression that she had other rabbits up her sleeve and was ready to produce them later.

The first witness was the police photographer, who confirmed the veracity of the photographs.

The second witness was the check-in clerk from Heathrow who identified Terajima as Dr Hung, the man who had checked in for the flight to Amsterdam on the night of the blast and had boarded it the next morning. The clerk said he was one hundred per cent sure that his identification was correct.

Julian Filster, Terajima's defence counsel, cross-examined the Heathrow check-in clerk about the exact time he had first seen the man called Dr Hung.

Even assuming that Dr Hung was passenger Terajima – and the matter was in some doubt – it was surely most likely that the man, whoever he was, had been just one of many passengers who were of Asian origin.

Had not the man who faced him across the court arrived at the counter at least two hours early for the flight? At the time of check-in the delay to the flight had not been announced, let alone confirmed.

The clerk's answers were muddled and Filster had little difficulty in gently suggesting that he was confused, his memory indistinct. There was no written evidence or evidence stored in the airline's computer or on the CCTV tapes to support the clerk's supposition that Terajima had been Dr Hung.

The pathologist who followed the check-in clerk on to the witness stand described the condition of the various corpse fragments he had examined. The damage was consistent with death caused by bomb blast and burning. Each corpse had been identified by DNA samples and, in several cases, the victim's dental records. Filster had no questions to put to the pathologist.

Evidence was produced concerning the explosives employed in the making of the device that caused the inferno which killed Anthony Zhentung and the others. No specific connection was made to Terajima or Foster and Hastings Zhentungs.

The next witness for the prosecution was Mei Lim.

She was dressed demurely in the Nicole Farhi gabardine suit and white collarless shirt. A white ribbon gathered her hair into a ponytail. She spoke in a very quiet voice and without emotion, avoiding Terajima's blank stare.

138

Mei Lim, *Sworn*
From examination
by Counsel for the Prosecution
Madeleine Burchfield QC

Q   Where were you born?
A   In Hong Kong.
Q   And now – you live where?
A   I'm staying here in London.
Q   Where have you spent most of your life?
A   Hong Kong.
Q   When you lived in Hong Kong, who were the people you
    lived with?
A   My mother and father. Then later on at my apartment in
    Chung Hom Kok.
Q   Where is that?
A   Between Repulse Bay and Stanley. In Hong Kong.
Q   What profession did your father pursue?
A   He was a police officer.
Q   What rank?
A   Inspector.
Q   And he specialised in what?
A   Maritime terrorism and extortion rackets.
Q   And, sadly, he is no longer alive?
A   No. He died – he was killed on duty.
Q   In the South China Sea?
A   Yes. During an attempt he was making to detain maritime
    terrorist suspects.
Q   And you enjoyed a loving relationship with your father?
A   Yes, I did. We were very close.

Q Though I gather you were adopted, were you not?

A Yes, I was.

Q Perhaps that made you especially close?

A Yes, it did. I loved him very much.

Q And I gather he adored you.

A Thank you. Yes.

Q When did you first get to know Anthony Zhentung?

A Some years ago. I can't remember exactly when.

Q And for how long did you know him?

A I can't remember.

Q Would you say months, rather than days?

A Months.

Q And how would you describe the relationship you had with him?

A We were friends.

Q Could you describe the nature of your friendship?

A We were lovers.

Q You were lovers. That is to say lovers in what general sense?

A Physical. I loved him.

Q How would you describe it further?

A We made love together.

Q And where did your lovemaking take place?

A At his apartment.

Q Where was that?

A In Hopton Street. Overlooking the river.

Q Where did the lovemaking take place?

A In the apartment.

Q Yes. But where in the apartment?

A In his bed.

Q Anywhere else?

A Sometimes in the exercise area.

Q In the exercise area?

A Yes.

Q Would you tell the members of the jury the nature of what happened in the exercise area?

A Well, he liked me to put my legs behind my neck. Then he would sit and watch me. He would stroke me. Sometimes he would use a lubricant and then he liked to suspend me from the parallel bars so that I could lower myself on to him.

342

Q   Was this – procedure, was it one that he taught you?
A   No, someone else taught me to put my legs behind my neck.
Q   For purposes of sexual intercourse.
A   Yes.
Q   So you would lower yourself – on to what exactly?
A   His penis.
Q   His penis was, for want of a better word, erect?
A   Mostly. Not always.
Q   On what sort of routine basis did this exercise take place?
      How often, would you say?
A   Regularly.
Q   At his apartment?
A   Yes.
Q   Anywhere else?
A   In hotels.
Q   And where were these hotels, Miss Lim?
A   In London and in Hong Kong.
Q   Now, roughly speaking, when did this relationship end?
A   A month or two before his death.
Q   Could you give the court the name of anyone else you were
      seeing during the time you were Anthony Zhentung's lover –
      just a name, perhaps?
A   Klaas-Pieter Terajima.
Q   And this relationship with the man you were seeing,
      Mr Terajima – what was its general nature?
A   We were lovers.
Q   In what sense were you lovers?
A   In the physical sense. He was the person who taught me
      sex positions.
Q   He taught you sex positions?
A   Yes.
Q   Forgive me, Miss Lim, if my questions seem intrusive. But it
      will be helpful for the jury to understand the nature of the
      relationship we are discussing. Could you tell the jury about
      any other sexual practices you engaged in with Mr Terajima?
A   We practised anal sex.
Q   Of what description?
A   Anal sex. He penetrated me.
Q   With what did he penetrate you?

343

A His penis.

Q Anything else?

A Sometimes a vibrator.

Q Did he apply lubricants?

A His saliva.

Q Anything else?

A Mustard.

Q Mustard?

A Yes. He said he liked to see my vagina burning.

Q Would you please tell the jury what sort of protection Mr Terajima used?

A He didn't use any.

Q Never?

A Never.

Q Has it, may I suggest, occurred to you that what he taught you was of a somewhat unusual or perverse nature?

A No. It gave him pleasure.

Q And you – did it give you pleasure?

A I can't really say.

Q How else would you describe the basis of this relationship with Mr Terajima?

A Like I've said. It was physical.

Q Anything else perhaps? Emotional?

A Sexual mostly.

Q What was Mr Terajima's reaction to finding out about your relationship with Anthony Zhentung?

A He objected.

Q In what manner did he object?

A He was very violent to me.

Q In what manner was he violent towards you?

A He hit me. He beat me up.

Q He beat you up?

A Yes. He hit me with his fists. Cut me with a nail file.

Q How often did that occur?

A Regularly.

Q Did you mention this to anyone?

A Yes, I did. I told my mother.

Q Anyone else?

A She told her best friend, Catherine Kwok.

Q She did. You did not?

A She did.

Q And Mr Terajima. What did you feel he then felt towards you?

A He was very jealous.

Q And Mr Zhentung, how would you describe his feelings about this?

A I never told him about Klaas-Pieter.

Q But who else told him?

A I think one of his brothers must have.

Q His brothers – what were their names?

A Foster and Hastings Zhentung.

Q How did you first make the acquaintance of Mr Zhentung?

A Klaas-Pieter introduced me to him.

Q When was that?

A I can't remember.

Q You can't remember?

A He introduced me to him at the Savoy Hotel where I was staying with Klaas-Pieter. They had a long-standing business arrangement.

Q How did Mr Terajima react to the news of Anthony Zhentung's death?

A He was very pleased about it.

139

Mei Lim
From Cross-Examination
by Counsel for the Defence
Julian Filster QC

Q Miss Lim, Mr Terajima gave you sums of money, did he not?
A Yes.
Q I won't bother you with the exact sums. But he gave you some twenty thousand pounds. Something in that region?
A Yes.
Q Were they cash sums?
A Yes.
Q And that was when you were sexually involved with him?
A Yes.
Q I won't trouble you too greatly to recall exact details – but when he learned of your relationship with Mr Zhentung, you decided to end your relationship with Mr Terajima?
A Yes.
Q And when you learned that Mr Zhentung had been murdered, did you mention to anyone that you knew him?
A No.
Q Did you mention to anyone that Mr Terajima was responsible for the death of Anthony Zhentung?
A No.
Q If you knew both men intimately, surely you would have mentioned this to someone? Yet you say you did not. Is that what you're telling the court?
A Yes.
Q Miss Lim, did you ever discuss matters with Mr Terajima that he told you were secret – shall we say, matters that you

were not to repeat?

A Yes.

Q And were these matters to do with purchases that Mr Terajima had made?

A Yes.

Q Did you ever hear him mention the words 'high explosives'?

A Yes.

Q Did he ever say where these high explosives were to be employed or used, shall we say?

A Yes.

Q Did he say they were to be used in London?

A Yes.

Q I won't trouble you to recall the exact date, but would you say that it was some time prior to the death of Anthony Zhentung?

A Yes.

Q Would I be right in thinking, Miss Lim, that this was about the time you had a problem – a problem of a medical nature?

A Yes.

Q And was that problem directly related to drug addiction?

A Yes.

Q The drugs you took were heroin and amphetamines?

A Yes.

Q Did you seek treatment for this problem?

A Yes.

Q Was it Mr Terajima who introduced you to drug taking?

A Yes.

Q And your relationship with Mr Terajima was as both lover and receiver of drugs that fed your addiction?

A Yes.

Q You took very substantial quantities of these drugs, did you not, Miss Lim?

A Yes.

Q I suggest that you were also mixing in some very nasty circles in Hong Kong and generally throughout South East Asia?

A Yes.

Q Maritime people. Harbour low life throughout the region?

A Yes.

Q Was this the sort of life style you would associate with the daughter of a distinguished senior police officer?

A No.

Q Has it ever occurred to you that Mr Terajima might have been entirely deceiving you?

A No.

Q Did you ever tell him that you had been deceiving him?

A No.

140

Mei Lim
From re-examination by
Counsel for the Prosecution
Madeleine Burchfield QC

Q You have told the court the times and dates that you went
to a friend's house. Actually a friend of your late mother's.
How did you find her?

A She was very upset.

Q Why?

A I told her that I had arranged for the termination of my
pregnancy.

Q Someone close to you had found out. Who was that?

A My father.

Q How did he find out?

A I don't know. Somehow he found out. It really hurt him.
Maybe it was a physician who told him.

Q Why?

A I'd gynaecological damage and infection.

Q Then what did your father do?

A He raided some drugs squat on his own initiative to find me.

Q Then what did he do?

A He took me home forcibly.

Q And then?

A He had me checked into a clinic for treatment.

Q What was the result of the treatment?

A I mended and put the past behind me. In the intervening
period – we're talking years more than months – people I
had run up debts with made demands. Two or three
thousand here. Maybe more elsewhere. The circle of low

life has a way of closing in.

Q According to the interview record, you informed on two men. That is what the record of the Hong Kong Police tells us, isn't it? What happened?

A I grassed up two men.

Q Who were they?

A People from the merchant marine who sidelined in raids on shipping.

Q To start with, the men didn't, of course, know you'd grassed. What did your father tell you to do about it?

A To stay away from such people.

Q On what basis?

A He said they were evil.

Q And after that, what did you do?

A I left Hong Kong.

Q Your parents, what did they feel about that?

A They were beside themselves with worry and distress.

Q And then, as it were, you resurfaced?

A Yes. My father was on the verge of walking into the Commissioner's office when I went home.

Q Where had you been?

A Bangkok. Chiang Mai. Tokyo. Amsterdam.

Q Why was that?

A Because I'd been with a man who offered me protection against the friends of the men I'd informed on.

Q This man promised you what?

A Security and protection.

Q And in return you did what?

A I went with him.

Q What did he offer you in return?

A He showed me the high life.

Q Where did he show you the high life?

A In Europe. In South East Asia.

Q Then what happened between you?

A We became lovers.

Q What did you tell your father about that?

A Sorry?

Q What did you tell him?

A Where I'd been.

Q You mentioned the places and the times?

A I mentioned everything.

Q Except you simply wouldn't say who this man of yours was. Why not?

A Because it was all over with him. I promised Dad I would turn over a new leaf. To start a new life. To study law at university.

Q What was your father's reaction to this good news?

A He offered to rent me a flat in Chung Hom Kok.

Q And life went back to normal?

A Normal, that is, except for one thing.

Q What was that?

A My father harboured an obsession.

Q Which was what?

A Revenge.

Q Except that there was, as you have said, something missing. What was that?

A He had no idea who the man was I'd been with.

Q So what did he do?

A He set about finding out.

Q Then something tragic happened. What was that?

A My mother fell dangerously ill.

Q What was diagnosed?

A Cancer.

Q What happened then?

A She deteriorated. Dad nursed her. He even administered her the drugs towards the end.

Q And there was a two-day period when something else happened? Can you tell the jury about that?

A My father was nowhere to be found. He vanished into thin air.

Q For how long?

A For two days.

Q What happened when he was away?

A I administered the drugs to my mother.

Q What drugs?

A Basically morphine. Heroin.

Q Can you describe the temptation you now faced?

A I was tempted to take my mother's drugs.

Q How did you deal with the temptation?

A I resisted it.

Q To what degree – I mean to what extent did you resist?

A Completely.

Q What happened when your father came back?

A He'd found out the man's identity.

Q How?

A During a routine investigation of a Malaysian sea captain. Just one of your ordinary drug runners. This man offered to trade the information. He knew me. He knew the identity of my lover, or whatever you want to call him.

Q What did he tell you about him?

A He told me the man's name.

Q What was the man's name?

A Klaas-Pieter Terajima.

Q And what sort of contact were you having with Mr Terajima?

A I was still seeing him.

Q You were *still* seeing him. Would you, Miss Lim, please list, as far as you can recall in general, the quantity of drugs you have taken since you were, as it were, rehabilitated?

A I haven't taken any.

141

Counsel for the prosecution Madeleine Burchfield took George Tsang through his account of events. It was matter of fact.

Now it was the turn of Julian Filster for the defence.

Q Mr Tsang, forgive me, but for the benefit of the jury may I ask you, can you in so many words *see* me?
A I am sightless.
Q I appreciate that and profoundly sympathise with you in your disability. Nonetheless it is important that you please answer me with a yes or a no. Can you see me?
A No.
Q And have you ever seen Mr Terajima?
A No.
Q You are quite sure?
A Yes.
Q Can you see him now?
A No.
Q Can you see anyone in this court?
A No.
Q Have you ever spoken to Mr Terajima or he to you?
A No.
Q Could you, without using the words of others, describe him?
A No.
Q You have, of course, heard what others have told you is Mr Terajima's voice, haven't you?
A Yes.
Q Others told you it was his voice?
A Yes.
Q And, Mr Tsang, you are the editor and proprietor of a monthly private newsletter published in Hong Kong, are you not?

A Yes.

Q It goes by the name of *Maritime Confidential,* does it not?

A Yes.

Q You, as it were, obtain information on the inside track?

A Yes.

Q And you have long been in the habit of passing on such information to the Hong Kong Police?

A Yes.

Q Tittle-tattle, was it?

A No.

Q But perhaps, say, once or twice you have been proved wrong and your stories have been denied by shipping companies?

A It has happened.

Q Yes or no, please.

A Yes.

Q You have published apologies, have you not?

A Yes.

Q In so many words, you told lies?

A No.

Q But in the tradition of journalists the world over, you have not been averse to engaging in what we might call embroidery of the truth. At least you have been accused of doing that and have, in your apologies to the maligned, written as much, have you not?

A Yes.

Q On not one occasion but at least a dozen times?

A Yes.

Q Let us be clear. You did not tell the truth. Well, if we may return to the Hong Kong Police a moment. Have you received payment from any of their officers or representatives?

A No.

Q Hospitality in kind perhaps?

A I don't understand.

Q Allow me to put it very simply to you. We must be in no doubt. I would like to suggest that you have many times received hospitality from the Lim family in recognition of services provided. And from their friends. And the Kwok family and their friends. And that you have been the guest at the dinner tables and in restaurants of the Commissioner and countless senior police officers. Would any of these suggestions be incorrect?

A No.

Q And sometimes you were the beneficiary of off-the-record leaks, weren't you?

A Yes.

Q And would I be correct in saying that you have been in pursuit of Mr Terajima, let us say professionally, for your own gain, for some considerable time?

A Yes.

Q And though you have received complaints about your stories from international shipping interests, you have never once received a complaint from Mr Terajima. Not just once, perhaps?

A No.

Q Finally, may I put it to you that your evidence is the evidence of someone whom you heard and never saw?

A Yes.

Q And officers of the Hong Kong Police pointed you in the direction of that evidence?

A Yes.

142

After George Tsang had stepped down from the witness stand and left Number One Court, Burchfield spoke directly to the judge.

'M'lord, that is the end of the prosecution case.'

Julian Filster got slowly to his feet. 'I wonder if m'lord would be generous enough to allow – there is an application I wish to make in the absence of the jury.'

'Very well, Mr Filster. The jury will leave the court.'

'M'lord,' said Filster once the jury had left, 'it will perhaps come as no surprise to you that I wish to submit an application that there is no case to answer.'

'Is that your view?' the judge asked the other defence counsel.

'It is, m'lord.'

'Mr Filster?' said the judge.

'M'lord, our submission is that there is a demonstrable, indeed an overwhelming, lack of police evidence as to the identity of the defendant. We have, m'lord, the evidence of the booking clerk at Heathrow who saw many people of Asian origin at Heathrow on the date mentioned. Even had the identification been more accurate, had the witness been certain, his evidence cannot be said to connect the defendant decisively with the events in Hopton Street. Likewise, m'lord, the police evidence can in no conceivable way suggest that the defendant was present in Hopton Street at the time of the explosion, or indeed at any other time before or after it. Quite simply it doesn't exist. There is no evidence connecting the defendant Terajima to the purchase of explosive. Moreover, it is very clear that the man Tsang never saw Terajima. The transcript of the tapes and the tapes themselves are the work of a journalist proven to be unreliable who, to be brutal, is unable to see the difference between fact and fiction. I use the word *see* advisedly, m'lord. Indeed, though it may not be appropriate for me to say so, m'lord, neither is there any evidence whatsoever to link the defendants Zhentung to the defendant Terajima. I say that in the interests of saving your lordship's time.'

'Do you agree?' the judge asked the other defence counsel.

'We do, m'lord.'

'Very well.' The judge hesitated and then stared at Burchfield. 'Ms Burchfield, we are in agreement that this is a very serious case. You know as well as I do that if there really is no cogent evidence to suggest guilt other than what we have heard, then it is right for me to stop this trial.'

'I entirely appreciate the position, m'lord.'

'I gather, to my surprise, that the officers or interested parties from the security services will not be appearing.'

'That is correct, m'lord,' said Burchfield. 'It has rather taken me by surprise too. I gather that their evidence might have, as it were, underlined the determination of the Crown Prosecution Service to allow the case to come to trial in the first place.'

'That's as may be,' said the judge. 'The CPS can be somewhat, for want of a better word, peculiar. There we are. Nonetheless, so that there is no doubt whatsoever, you will realise that I am bound to put this question to you, Miss Burchfield. Is there any evidence that can be sent to the jury that will let them properly decide the question of guilt?'

Burchfield shook her head. 'No, m'lord, there isn't.'

'So be it,' said the judge. 'Ask the members of the jury to return.'

143

The public were now allowed into the gallery and with them Rosslyn.

Mei Lim glanced up at him from the bench reserved for witnesses. Ron Costley acknowledged his presence.

It was half past two in the afternoon when the jury filed back into court for the last time.

Also waiting for the outcome in the well of the court was the man in the grey suit from MI5, the Security Service. He had a slim briefcase handcuffed to his left wrist.

The judge's clerk spoke to counsel for the defence in a barely audible whisper. He invited them to join the judge in his room once matters were completed.

Terajima and the Zhentungs returned to the box.

'Ladies and gentlemen of the jury,' the judge said, 'this has been a very serious case. One, indeed, relating to national security that would have involved the presence of officers of the security services. Even though, in the event, their presence has not been required, that is why this trial has been conducted *in camera*. I am required to remind you of the importance of never discussing what you have heard in this court. I must once more make that very clear to you. As I told you at the start of this trial, the penalty for so doing is extreme. Have no misunderstanding. Be in no doubt of this – if my remarks to you are ignored, the penalty will be most vigorously applied.

'You will have heard that, before your short absence from the court, defence counsel asked that I receive an application. I have now heard it. Counsel for the prosecution has raised no objection to it. I am not required to explain its contents to you. I am only required to say here and now that the evidence submitted to this court shows that there remains no case to answer. Therefore I direct you to return verdicts of Not Guilty. Before you leave this court, I would like to thank you for the care and diligence with which you have listened to the evidence.' The judge paused and looked hard at Terajima and the Zhentungs. 'You are free to go.'

The court usher called, 'All stand.'

It was over.

Rosslyn looked at Mei, who had her eyes closed. She was lost in thought and did not bother watching Terajima hurry from the court.

It was left to the Zhentungs to embrace their lawyers and then shake the hands of the members of the jury in turn.

In the pouring rain, Terajima headed east from the Old Bailey to the rendezvous with Skin in Warwick Lane.

Skin was waiting in a doorway for him. The visor of the helmet obscured his face. He wore black leathers and heavy steel-tipped boots.

'*Ni hao?*' ('How are you?')

'*Wo hen hao.*' ('I'm fine.)

'I got fucking off.'

'I'm pleased.'

'Me too.'

'I have a red alert,' said Skin. 'We have to move fast now. We're looking at a black Ford Mondeo. I know the exit they'll be using. One driver. One MI5 officer, unarmed. The briefcase will be handcuffed to his wrist. We'll have to cut his hand off.'

'Easy,' said Terajima. He donned the leather jacket, trousers and helmet. The visor was dark.

Skin handed him a machete. 'We'll be going south to Millbank.'

Terajima slipped the machete inside the leather jacket and fastened the zip. 'Then to Heathrow. You have Rabbi Shemon bar Yochai's Hasidic case.'

'His case is in your bike storage box, Rabbi.'

'Your payment will be made in full in Hatton. We dispose of the bikes there.'

'Okay.'

'*Xiexie.*' ('Thank you.')

'*Bukeqi.*' ('You're welcome.') 'This is serious red.'

'Serious red,' said Terajima. 'We kill them.'

'My pleasure,' said Skin. 'The best place is at the junction of Coin and Stamford Streets.'

'You lead,' said Terajima.

In the judge's room, after introductions, the MI5 officer unfastened the briefcase that was secured to his wrist.

'You're from MI5?' said the judge.

'Correct, m'lord. Name of Burton.'

'Security Service?'

'Correct, m'lord.'

The MI5 officer Burton handed the contents of the briefcase – folders marked 'Top Secret' – first to the judge and then to the barristers, the counsel for the prosecution and defence.

'These are, m'lord,' Burton said, 'identical copies of the Damage Report.' For the benefit of the barristers, he added, 'I'm obliged, ladies and gentlemen, to remind you that the Security Service is required by statute to allow you sight of the report. This is in order that you may be satisfied as to the sources that were not offered in the court, in spite of the fact that the proceedings were held *in camera*. I'm sure you don't require me to explain that the contents of this report refer to secret operations which both security services require to be kept from all officers of the court other than yourselves.'

'I think we know that,' said the judge tersely. 'If you wouldn't mind, we have to proceed to various other matters.'

'I appreciate that, m'lord,' said Burton. 'I'm also obliged to remind you, m'lord, that other than your good selves, the only other people required by statute to read the Damage Report are the Prime Minister, the Director General of MI6 and the Director General of MI5.'

'Yes, yes,' said the judge, 'we know that.'

'Both directors have already read the contents of the report,' said Burton. 'The contents are top secret.'

'I would tend to be surprised', the judge said, 'if that were not the case. Please do let us proceed.'

The barristers and the judge skimmed their copies of the Damage Report. They read them with rapidity and with little apparent interest, as if they were telephone directories from some foreign city.

After less than ten minutes, the judge slammed his copy shut. 'There we are. It makes for pretty shabby reading, don't you feel?'

Counsel for the defence handed his copy back to Burton. 'I suppose one can be grateful, m'lord, that one isn't mentioned.'

'Yes,' said the judge. He in turn handed over the copy of the report he had just read to Burton. The other counsel for the defence and prosecution did likewise. Prosecution counsel looked defeated.

The judge looked at Burton. 'You may leave now.'

'Thank you, m'lord.'

Heading for the door, Burton heard the judge say, 'It's been something of a long day. How do you people like your Scotch – water, ice or unadulterated?'

146

While the news of the Old Bailey verdict was spreading to the news agencies and desks of the press, TV and radio, the driving rain and the evening rush hour had reduced the traffic crossing Blackfriars Bridge to a crawl.

The driver of the unmarked Ford Mondeo ferrying Burton to headquarters learned from the local news bulletin on the car radio that traffic in the Westminster area was at a standstill. He suggested to Burton that it would be for the best if they took a circuitous route south of the river. 'I can duck and dive, sir,' he proposed.

'Fair enough,' said Burton. 'Put your foot down. Let's just get back to Thames House as soon as possible.' He had the leather briefcase on his lap. Locked and handcuffed to his left wrist.

South of the river, as soon as the one-way system allowed, the driver turned right and headed west.

147

Ever since the Ford Mondeo had left the Old Bailey in the rain, Terajima, wearing black leathers, gloves and a helmet with a darkened visor, had been in short-wave radio communication with Skin.

One behind the other, they had kept the car in view. They followed it over Blackfriars Bridge, and on the south side of the river, when the Mondeo made its right turn, Skin overtook it. With his eye on the reflection of the car in his rear view mirror, he kept a safe distance ahead of the Mondeo until it reached the junction with Coin Street and Stamford Street. Deliberately and without warning, Skin slowed suddenly and made a controlled skid.

'Watch it,' Burton yelled to the driver. 'You'll hit him.'

Seemingly out of control, Skin's motorbike slewed across the road and Skin threw himself clear of his machine.

The driver of the Mondeo swerved violently. tyres squealed. The driver avoided colliding with the motorbike by inches. Skin rolled over twice and picked himself up. He remounted his motorbike.

'Don't stop,' Burton shouted. He was under orders to get back to MI5 headquarters no matter what. If there was an accidental mishap, too bad. It would have to be explained away some time later. The police would see to it that no action was taken that might attract the attentions of the press.

'Stupid bastard,' the driver snapped.

It was not far from the Stamford Road end of the York Road round-about when the lead motorcyclist overtook the MI5 car.

The driver saw the motorcyclist swerve in front of the car. This time he hit the brakes too hard. The car slewed, struck the kerbside at an angle, mounted the pavement and came to an abrupt halt. Both the motorcyclists were approaching. At first it seemed that they were about to remonstrate, to apportion blame for what could have been a nasty accident when Skin had fallen off his motorbike.

As to what happened next, the statements from witnesses varied. Those in passing vehicles said truthfully that, because of the rain, they saw nothing except what could have been a road rage incident. No one apparently witnessed what followed.

The blurred motorcyclists' helmets and visors were at the window. Glass shattered. There were sprays of water. Blunt steel hammered through the driver's side window. The front passenger window was split open with what seemed to be a machete. The driver tried to shield his face with one hand; with his other he reached for his mobile phone.

Terajima drove a heavy steel hammer through the driver's side window, unlocking and opening the door. Skin broke open the passenger window with a machete and dragged Burton out of the car.

With Burton staggering backwards into the road, Skin delivered two blows to the man's left wrist, amputating the hand. He retrieved the briefcase and tossed it to Terajima. The third and final sweep of the machete cut several inches through the nape of Burton's neck, killing him instantly.

Though winded, the driver tried and failed to make a grab for the nearest of the assailants. Then Skin's steel-tipped leather boot connected with the driver's groin and the machete cut into his throat.

A passing car swerved and clipped an oncoming white van. There was a screech of metal.

Leaving the two corpses in the road, Terajima slipped the briefcase inside his leather jacket

The pair of them then disappeared in the rain along York Road and Lambeth Palace Road in the direction of the Albert Embankment.

148

While radio and television stations interrupted their transmissions to report the Old Bailey verdicts, the Director General of MI5 waited in his Millbank office to receive the copies of the Damage Report. It was an unconscionable delay. He telephoned the transport pool, only to be told that Burton's car from the Old Bailey had not reached the underground garage in Thorney Street. Shortly after he had made the last of his searching calls, the Deputy Director General came into the office without even bothering to knock. 'The police have found Burton's car, sir.'

'Where?'

'Near Waterloo Station, near the Stamford Road end of the York Road roundabout. They've found two mutilated bodies. The driver and Burton.'

'And the Damage Reports?'

'They were in a briefcase secured to Burton's –'

'Yes, but where are they, man?'

'They've gone, sir.'

'All of them?'

'Yes, sir.'

'You do realise that the hard disk has been destroyed? We have no copies.'

'Yes, sir. Rules and regulations. No hard disks to be kept once the trial is over.'

'Has everyone else seen theirs?'

'Yes, sir, indeed they have.'

The Director General waved to his Deputy Director to close the office door. 'The Prime Minister must be told.' There was a silence. 'We have no idea who might have –'

'– have taken them, sir?'

'Yes. We have no idea?' said the Director General.

'No idea, sir.'

The Director General lifted the telephone on his desk. 'I want to speak to the Prime Minister. Now. Yes, it's a matter of urgency.'

While he waited for the Prime Minister to take his call, the Director General withdrew a file from the top drawer of his desk. Marked 'Top Secret' and entitled 'Damage Report. F. Zhentung/H. Zhentung/K-P Terajima', the file was empty.

Before he had time to open it, he heard the familiar voice.

'You want to speak to me?'

'Yes, I do, Prime Minister. It's very serious. I need to see you in person and alone.'

149

Rosslyn returned to Claverton Street with Mei.

She was downcast.

'There's something I have to tell you, Alan. I'm going home.'

'I understand.'

'No, I don't think you do. I've got an open ticket. I've got a seat. I'm going home tonight.'

'Tonight – why haven't you told me this before?'

'I didn't want to upset you.'

'When did you decide all this?'

'A day or two ago. Well, maybe earlier. When I made my witness statement. I've always believed that it's impossible for anyone to hide from Terajima for long. You know the lines from Shakespeare?

> Why, then the world's mine oyster,
> Which I with sword will open.

It isn't true. If anything's surprised me, it's that I've stayed quite so free from him for quite so long. In the end, he'll always get his way. Look what happened in the court. He must have masterminded the whole thing.'

'I doubt it, Mei.'

'I don't.'

'Look, Alan, I have to accept my fate. Dad's enemies are mine. They have been for years. There was no escape for my father from Terajima. Now there's no escape for me. If the end comes, well, I hope it'll come soon. Don't you think so?'

'I don't want you to go.'

'I know, Alan. You've been so wonderful to me. I feel so responsible for everything. So guilty. You don't need a woman in your life with the sort of baggage I've been trailing around for the last few years.'

'It's never crossed my mind.'

'What about my past?'

'I only know what you've told me.'

'You weren't in court.'

'What do you mean?'

'I want to make a new start. Those people in court – they made me sick. They dragged through my past like I was some sort of whore. And for what? So Terajima could walk free. I think that the authorities – his *guanxi* in Beijing – must have done a deal with him. You know? I've often asked myself why that man Simpson arranged for me to meet up with you. I was so grateful to him at the time that I only asked how he had managed to find me. I recall that he said it had been a matter of asking a few of his old friends about me. I guess that was true. Who they might have been I've no idea. He said something about acting on the instructions of some London lawyer. Someone who knew Alan's friends.'

'That was Michaelson. And he told you that I would see you were all right.'

'It never once occurred to me that by boarding the *Orient Angel* I'd walked into a trap of Terajima's making. I prayed that he'd drowned out there in the Malacca Strait. However you look at it now, there's only a choice of nightmares left.'

'Yes, but you taught me that Chinese saying: Remembrance of past times is a fine guide for the future.'

'Yes, maybe that's the difference between us. I don't want to remember my past. I want nothing more to do with it. Nothing to do with the Kwoks. The Hong Kong Police. Any of it. Once I've decided what to do with Botch and Chan, I'm disappearing into thin air. You're not to stop me, Alan.'

'I won't.'

The taxi pulled up outside Rosslyn's flat.

'You'll take me to Heathrow tonight?'

'Of course.'

'You're not angry with me?'

'No. Just sad. Very sad.'

369

150

He took her bags to the check-in desk.

'I have something to tell you too, Mei,' he said. 'Steve Kwok has invited me to stay with him in Hong Kong.'

'That's nice.'

'I think so too. He suggested that whatever happened we should mark the place where Winston died. If you don't mind me saying so, I think it would be nice if you were there.'

'He hasn't asked me.'

'I'm asking you, Mei.'

'All right. I'll be there. Just tell me when.'

'The day after tomorrow, Mei.'

'So soon?'

'Yes. There's something else I haven't told you. I'm flying to Hong Kong tonight. With you.'

151

By the time Rosslyn and Mei had reached Heathrow, Terajima had cut some ten minutes off his schedule on his way from the Hatton inferno to Heathrow.

There was no need to slide Skin's unwanted Suzuki into the murky waters of the River Crane. The fire had disposed of the motorbike along with Skin's corpse. He had left the passport in the name of Klaas-Pieter Terajima by the security gates. Diligent police officers would find it without difficulty. Now he had plenty of time in which to dress in the clothing neatly packed in Rabbi Shemon bar Yochai's Hasidic case.

He rode the Suzuki carefully, taking the familiar and circuitous route along Great South West Road to the junction with Bath Road while the inferno in the warehouse reached its zenith. He inserted a new tab of snuff beneath his upper lip and gums. The substance produced the familiar exhilarating rush.

He turned left beneath the Northern Perimeter Road into the tunnel, joining the slow-moving traffic to the Heathrow terminals.

Once in the BAA car park, he left the Suzuki in the ranks of the vehicles bearing the BAA logo.

The slim black case he took with him was, of course, Rabbi Shemon bar Yochai's. Inside the left-hand side pocket of his jacket he carried the US passport in the name of Rabbi Shemon bar Yochai. The rabbi's address was given as Lubavitch World Headquarters, 770 Eastern Parkway, Brooklyn, New York 11213, USA. The Hasidic case contained the rabbi's clothing, a yarmulke and a fedora in the style of the Lubavitchers' founder. A plastic box contained false hair and a battery razor. A side pocket contained the Lubavitch version of the prayer book by Rabbi Schneur-Zalman of Liady, the first Lubavitcher Rebbe, leader of the dynasty.

Terajima limped slowly past the BAA car park guard, who scarcely gave the disabled worker a second glance, and headed for the entrance to the terminal. Once inside the terminal, Terajima made his way to the nearest Toilet for the Disabled.

Locked inside the toilet, he stepped out of the motorcyclist's leathers and folded them into an unmarked white plastic bag. He rolled up his sleeves and wedged the bag hard into the toilet bowl. Then he squatted down and emptied his bowels. Without pulling the flush, he lowered the seat and washed his hands. He first washed and applied the full-grown beard.

You shall not round the corners of your heads, nor mar the edges of your beards (Leviticus 19:27).

For most Hasidic rabbis, curls – *payos* – and untrimmed beards are symbols of obedience to the laws of God. It is not necessarily the case that all Hasidic men cut their hair extremely short, though it makes for greater comfort when wearing the hat. Terajima was sufficiently well versed in Hasidic lore to know that except when they are young boys, before they've grown beards, Lubavitcher Hasidim do not wear *payos*.

He placed the yarmulke on his head. Slipped into his black shoes. Pulled on his coat. Then the fedora.

Without pulling the flush, he lowered the seat, washed his hands again, straightened his black coat and fedora, and let himself out of the toilet to join his fellow travellers.

The first class ticket he presented at the check-in desk showed Rabbi Shemon bar Yochai's name.

'Yes,' Rabbi Shemon bar Yochai told the check-in clerk. 'Yes.' He had indeed packed his own luggage and it contained no electrical equipment. The check-in clerk gave Rabbi Shemon bar Yochai a smile that suggested he too was a believer of some sort. The face of the rabbi seemed interesting. Rabbi Shemon bar Yochai thanked the clerk with courtesy and solicitude.

The X-ray security scanner arch sounded no alert when he walked slowly beneath the arch.

The security man asked the rabbi to step to one side, to raise his arms sideways so he could frisk him.

Then he asked the rabbi if he might see his small case. He asked him to open it. Rabbi Shemon bar Yochai did as he had been requested.

The security man examined the prayer book, the small toothbrush, the safety razor and the cardboard nail file.

'That's fine, rabbi,' he said. 'Have a good flight.'

'Why, thank you,' said Rabbi Shemon bar Yochai as the security man turned to face the next in line. Rabbi Shemon bar Yochai headed for the waiting area.

152

Rosslyn and Mei checked in, and the desk clerk explained that they probably hadn't heard that all flights from Heathrow might be subject to delays.

'What's it about?' asked Rosslyn.

'There's been a fire near Hatton Cross. Your passport, sir. Did you pack your luggage yourself?'

'I haven't got any luggage.'

The clerk turned his attentions to Mei. 'Did you pack your luggage yourself?'

'Yes.'

'Has anyone given you anything to take?'

'No.'

And so on through security.

The waiting area near the boarding gate was crowded with Chinese. Malay-sians. Singaporeans. The usual sort of Germans, barking orders into mobile telephones, and British businessmen and women crouching over laptops. Women with sleeping children. Many Hasidim.

Rosslyn and Mei helped themselves to cups of black coffee at the refreshment counter. All the seats in the lounge were occupied, so they found a free table to perch on. The Hasid standing opposite them was deep in prayer. Stroking his beard, he rocked back and forth to the inner rhythms of his prayers.

All my bones will say, Ha-Shem, who is like You?

Rosslyn and Mei passed the time watching Sky TV news. The news-reader said, 'A fire has destroyed a warehouse in the Heathrow area at Hatton. No casualties have been reported. Police say it was an accident.'

The flight departure was announced and Rosslyn and Mei boarded the plane together.

* * *

The Hasid paid no attention to his fellow passengers. He had much better things to relish during the flight to Hong Kong. *The files. The files.* He accepted the offer of a hot face towel from the steward, but courteously declined the offer of a glass of champagne. With a fixed smile, he ordered the most probably kosher vegetarian breakfast and then concentrated on the filing of the nails of his left hand. Once he had finished, he cleaned the file with care.

The vegetarian meal arrived and he savoured it as much as the prospect of the comfortable flight ahead. He deserved this luxury. The snatch had been a consummate success. A job well done – mission completed with military professionalism. He opened the briefcase, careful to hide the title pages of the three files. The scholar of extortion found much to entertain him in their contents.

He studied the file with the closest concentration. *I love files. Another's file satisfies me like no other can.* He was reminded of one of Mother's favourite songs, Carly Simon's 'Nobody Does it Better'.

Once he'd savoured the best bits of the meal, he adjusted his seat for comfort and arranged the blanket around his legs and body.

Declining the offer of breakfast, Rossyln wrapped himself in a blanket. Before closing his eyes, he unfastened the button of his shirt cuff and withdrew the ID tag that read 'Winston Lim'. Attached to the chain were the two small gold crucifixes and two silver hearts. One of the silver hearts engraved with 'Mei', the other 'Kitty'. He opened the fastener of the heart marked 'Mei'. Inside were threaded strands of her dark hair.

Cursing the British criminal justice system and all its ways, Ron Costley had given them to him outside the Old Bailey when they'd said their goodbyes.

153

Steve and Catherine Kwok were waiting for them at the airport with Kasuko and the two cats.

For Mei it was a tearful reunion. She ran to Kasuko and they fell into each other's arms. And she showered the cats with kisses. Rosslyn had never seen her look happier. Her smile was the smile he'd seen in his cabin aboard *Orient Angel*.

'Have you heard the news of Terajima?' Kwok said, 'His body's been found near Heathrow. It's been all over the press and TV. They identified him by his passport.'

'Can't say I'm too sad,' said Rosslyn. 'I'd have preferred to think that he'd spend the rest of his days in jail.'

'Better he's dead,' said Kwok. 'Burned alive without living trace. To put it mildly, I hope he rots in hell.'

'Let's change the subject,' said Mei.

'Let's go home,' said Catherine. 'Come on, lovebirds. You people need to rest.'

154

The Kwoks' house was warm and comfortable and she felt more secure than she had in days.

Rosslyn asked Steve Kwok about the arrangements he'd made to mark the place where Winston had died with the floral tribute.

'I've fixed up one or two surprises,' Kwok said. 'No more mourning. Winston would have hated that. It'll be a happy outing. The weather forecast for tomorrow morning is perfect.'

For once, the weather forecasters got it right.

No matter that Hong Kong police headquarters had not permitted any of their own helicopters to fly to the site where Winston had lost his life. Steve Kwok had called in favours owed to him by Kowloon Flying Services (KFS), a privately owned French-Chinese consortium, and KFS had provided not one helicopter but two. It had been Kwok's idea that two helicopters should fly in honour of Winston and respect for his memory. Kowloon Flying Services offered a pair of superb SA 330 Ba SAR Aérospatiale Pumas, formerly in service with the French Special Forces Helicopter Squadron (*Escadrille des Hélicoptères Spéciaux*) at Cazaux in southern France. Now they were in civilian use and flown by Kowloon Flying Services' experienced Hong Kong Chinese pilots.

Shortly before midday, the passengers assembled at the Hong Kong International Airport.

Rosslyn, Mei, Steve Kwok and the Deputy Commissioner. Rosslyn hadn't seen him since he'd visited him at Hong Kong police headquarters when he'd tried to engineer a place for Mei in the force. Still under suspension, the Commissioner was absent. Three junior officers, all of whom had served with Winston, represented the Commissioner.

At Mei's request, George Tsang had not been invited. She had, so she said, her reasons – reasons she kept to herself.

Three floral tributes would be dropped from the lead helicopter into the South China Sea. One a wreath of three dozen red roses from Mei. The second of white lilies from Rosslyn, Ron Costley and Elizabeth Henderson. The third was from Steve and Catherine Kwok and the officers of the Hong Kong Police, including the Commissioner.

The party gathered in the briefing room where the pilots and co-pilots were discussing the weather conditions and studying aero-nautical charts. Kowloon Flying Services had provided tea and cakes. Catherine said she would prefer to remain in the briefing room. She didn't feel up to flying. The passengers were requested to deposit their mobile telephones in a storage cupboard for safe-keeping.

Then the fourth wreath was brought into the briefing room.

A dapper and rather nervous young man in a dark blue suit carried it.

'The surprise,' said Steve Kwok.

He smiled warmly at the new arrival.

'Let me introduce everyone. This is Xiao Qingze of the Beijing Police.'

155

The white minibus ferried them the short distance to the area reserved for the Kowloon Flying Services' Pumas next to the Government Flying Service area at the perimeter of the airport.

Passengers and pilots boarded the helicopters. Rosslyn and Mei with Kwok and Xiao in the lead helicopter. The others in the second. They found their way to their seats. The doors and sliding doors on the port side were closed and fastened and the fastenings re-checked.

Seated next to Mei, Rosslyn listened to the co-pilot's voice over the intercom.

'Good morning, ladies and gentlemen. I'm your co-pilot Johnnie Lee. In the absence of Nick Tang, my new Kowloon Flying Services colleague Captain Shintara will be piloting this SA 330 Ba SAR Aérospatiale Puma. It's a great honour for us to have you aboard this special flight in memory of Inspector Winston Lim. Let us know if there's anything we can do to make your flight comfortable.

'You're all experienced flyers, but I'd appreciate it if you'd spare a moment to look over the safety instructions. International security regulations post-9/11 require us to keep the pilot's cabin locked throughout this flight. So I regret we can't allow you to pay us a visit up front. Let me tell you that our aircraft is fitted out with flotation gear. We carry first aid and air sea rescue equipment for all eventualities. And our new fuel capacities allow us to operate up to two hundred and twenty nautical miles from Hong Kong. We can spend up to thirty minutes over the position to which we're headed.

'We have clearance for take-off. The weather's great. So sit back and enjoy your flight. May I say again, on behalf of all of us at Kowloon Flying Services, that it's a great honour to have you aboard. Most of all, the very special Mei Lim. I'll be back to you during the flight. Thank you.'

* * *

The massive Puma lifted. Tilted. Rose. And rose again. Hong Kong was spread out below. It looked magnificent.

Exhilarated, Rosslyn squeezed Mei's hand. It was great to be with her. Last night they had slept naked in each other's arms. Mei was on the mend. She really did look more beautiful than ever. He turned to kiss her.

Instead he froze.

She was staring into his eyes.

He could read the fear. Beads of sweat had formed across her fore-head.

'No, Alan. No. We have to go back.'

'Mei – what's up, why?'

'You know who Shintara is? Henrick Shintara, Dr Hung, Pastor Leung – one and the same man.'

Rosslyn felt his body turn cold.

156

The proof, so far unseen, lay behind a locked door back at Hong Kong International Airport. It was behind the locked door of a cubicle in the men's room – not far from the entrance to the small offices used by Kowloon Flying Services.

It would have taken an inquisitive visitor to the men's room that morning to see the pools of blood seeping from the naked corpse of the late Captain Nick Tang. What was preventing the blood seeping out of the cubicle was the carefully placed pile of clothing discarded by Rabbi Shemon bar Yochai of Brooklyn.

157

'There has to be a way we can get into the cabin.'

And, of course, there wasn't.

Nothing more had been heard over the intercom from co-pilot Lee since take-off. And the Puma was lowering to the surface of the ocean.

Steve Kwok was still in his seat. Mei had taken the seat next to him.

'Reckon she's right about this Shintara?' Xiao shouted above the roar of the engines.

'I sure as hell hope she's very wrong.'

'I've been here before,' yelled Xiao.

'I know,' shouted Rosslyn. 'I didn't envy you the first time.'

'Let's not take any risks,' Xiao yelled. 'This man could have us all killed.'

'Is there no way we can speak with him?'

'No,' yelled Xiao, 'there isn't.'

'Then let's get into position by the doors,' yelled Rosslyn. 'If we're near the position –'

'– which we are.'

'We could still evacuate.'

Xiao looked out of the window. 'We're at eight, say, seven hundred feet and lowering. He doesn't seem to be ditching.'

Suddenly the intercom crackled into life.

The voice said, 'Up to you, Mister Rosslyn. I have the copies of the Damage Reports with me. You give me the sign and you get them. You bring Mei to the cabin door and you'll have the reports to take back to London.' There was a pause.

'Now shout, the system is on two-way reception.'

Rosslyn shouted, 'You go to hell.'

'As you wish.'

'WAIT!' Rosslyn shouted.

There was no reply.

A few moments later the first of the smoke poured into the passenger cabin.

The stench of the fumes was bitter in the nostrils. Choking, temporarily blinded, Kwok reached for the oxygen mask and placed it over Mei's mouth.

Rosslyn felt the helicopter dip and drop. Choking, he made his way to the exit doors.

Xiao knew the routine: *Level altitude at three hundred feet a minute descent. Where's the safety raft?*

Rosslyn and Xiao took deep inhalations of oxygen from the nearest available masks. Rosslyn held it in his lungs, then he and Xiao made their way to the doors. As he went for the exit, Rosslyn tugged hard at Mei's sleeve. Twice he pulled, urging her to follow.

He prayed that the back-up Puma had seen what was happening. Terajima was burning them all to death. He heard the failing strength of turbines. The hover became a drop. Its force drove the oxygen from his lungs.

He saw Xiao yank down the door release lever. Then Xiao lifted Kwok and drew him towards the exit.

Rosslyn didn't hesitate. He simply pushed Mei through the open door. Then he took a deep breath and jumped. Kwok followed. Then Xiao.

In mid-air, a deafening whistle filled his ears. His body gathered speed. He somersaulted. He found himself falling in a foetal position. Twisting himself, he managed to get his feet beneath him.

White spray clawed at his cheeks and eyes. Then the white turned black.

One by one, they plummeted into the ocean.

The South China Sea had never looked more beautiful. The calm ocean sparkled, turquoise and pale blue. It could scarcely have been more perfect. Only the Puma was smashing into it at a steep angle. Then it vanished in a cloudburst of white spray.

158

Between one and two in the afternoon, the police officers under the command of the Deputy Commissioner lifted them from the ocean.

The pilot of the back-up Puma radioed the first reports on the conditions of the survivors to the paramedic units at Hong Kong airport.

'Regret body of co-pilot Johnnie Lee lifted from ocean. No sign of Captain Shintara. Presumed dead. Suggest you send GFS search aircraft. Survivors – condition status as follows. Males. Xiao – Fractured ribs. Shock. Kwok – Suspected fracture of left arm. Minor lung damage. Shock. Rosslyn – Serious bruising left shoulder. Female. Mei Lim – Shock. No major physical injury. Will update. We're coming home. Out.'

Rosslyn cradled Mei in his bruised arms. He tried to ignore the searing pain. Mei's eyes were closed and she was breathing gently.

Very slowly, he tried to find the chains that Ron Costley had handed to him outside the Old Bailey. But, claimed presumably by the South China Sea, they weren't there.

Xiao sat beside Rosslyn.

'Twice in a lifetime,' he said with a wry and pained smile. 'It's enough.'

'Once will do for me,' said Rosslyn.

'You know what?' said Xiao. 'I hope I'm imagining this. But from where I surfaced in the water, you know what I saw? I saw this man swimming in the distance. Slowly. Surely. One hell of a swimmer. Believe me. I saw him. And he was still there when they lifted me in the shoulder harness. Swimming for his life. You know who I think it was?'

'Yes,' said Mei. 'I think I do.'

'Terajima.'